MICHAEL D. EVANS

To my very special friend
on the anniversary of
Corrie ten Boom's birth and death
" It's better to light a candle
than curse the darkness."

Mike Evans

APRIL 15, 2013

MIKE EVANS

The Locket

A NOVEL

TIMEWORTHY BOOKS

P.O. BOX 30000, PHOENIX, AZ 85046

Published by TimeWorthy Books
P. O. Box 30000
Phoenix, AZ 85046

The Locket

Design: Lookout Design, Inc.

USA:	978-0-935199-26-0
Canada:	978-0-935199-27-7
Hardcover:	978-0-935199-28-4

This book is dedicated to

General Yossi Peled,

One of Israel's most distinguished diplomats.

Yossi Peled was born in Poland. His nickname was "Little Joe." During World War II, his family fled to Belgium where Yossi and his sister were entrusted to a Catholic family for safekeeping.

All of his family members except his mother and sister died in Auschwitz during the Holocaust. After the war, his mother reclaimed him and his sister and made _aliyah_ to _Eretz Yisrael_. Yossi joined and served in the Israeli Defense Forces for thirty years and was a distinguished military leader during the 1967 and 1973 wars, and the first War with Lebanon.

General Peled joined the prime minister on his official visit to Germany, and according to Yossi, "Every day I remember my childhood, the eight years that I was forced to hide my identity. I grew up as a Christian boy that goes to church every Sunday and knows all the prayers by heart. I had a happy childhood thanks to my adopting family and in fact they saved me from the threat of the Nazis. But there were also moments of fear, which I understood only later in my life.

"Every day I think about my father, who was murdered in Auschwitz together with all his family, the father I never knew and which I don't have any memory of, and I hope that he looks at me from above. I think of my mother, who survived two terrible years the experiments of the notorious Dr. Josef Mengele. I think of them whenever I hear or read Holocaust denials around the world."

chapter 1

Autumn wind howled around the corner of our house and seeped through the cracks of the window frame. On the nightstand, the flame of the kerosene lamp flickered in response. From the street out front I heard the ice wagon go past, the clopping rhythm of a horse's hooves against the pavement, and the lonely whistle of a steam ship as it labored up the Danube. I paid them no attention and instead sat in the corner on a straight-backed chair, my eyes glued on Grandma as she lay in bed, struggling to breathe. Four years after the Great War, with all the changes it brought to our lives, and still no doctor in Linz could save her. I was only twelve years old but even now, when I close my eyes and think of it, I can feel the hard slats of the chair pressed against my thighs, the tingle in my legs as my feet dangled just above the floor, and I can hear the gurgling rattle that came from Grandma's chest with every breath.

Papa was huddled over Grandma, his ear close to her lips, his eyes focused on nothing as he once again strained to hear what she was saying. She'd been trying to speak all morning and each time her lips moved, Papa rose from his seat at her bedside and did his best to understand what she was saying. I felt sorry for him, hovering near her, his eyes squinted almost closed and his forehead wrinkled in a look of frustration, but he seemed to take comfort from his role as her interpreter. I suppose it took his mind off the inevitability of her demise.

Across the room my brother, David, leaned against the doorframe. Older and wiser, he seemed to take it all in stride. As if he'd seen it before and knew what to expect. But I knew the truth. I'd heard him two nights before when Grandma took a turn for the worse and Mama told us there was nothing anyone could do for her now. After she told us that, and we were all in bed and the house was dark and quiet, David cried himself to sleep.

Grandma was dressed in her favorite white gown made of plain cotton fabric with lace at the collar. Her hair was neatly combed in place and around her neck was a thin gold chain with a round locket resting on her chest just below the neckline of the gown. She wore the necklace every day but she never opened the locket. Once, when I asked her what was inside, I saw her eyes tear up and she had a faraway look, like she could see a day in the past as well as I can see this one now. For a moment I thought she was going to tell me about it, but then she cleared her throat and just smiled at me. I knew that what she remembered must have been more than I could ever imagine. I loved that locket. Not as much as I loved Grandma, but I loved it just the same.

My grandmother was born Hanna Assido and grew up in Hollabrunn, a town north of Vienna, in one of Austria's richest farming regions. The year she turned fourteen, she met Yoel Batsheva, the son of a local farmer and the man who would one day become my grandfather. Their courtship was something of a scandal—hers was a family of lawyers and merchants with a long history in the region; his ancestors had been wanderers, Ashkenazi Jews roaming over Eastern Europe in search of a place to call their own. She was fluent in at least four languages— Hebrew, German, French, and Spanish, along with the Yiddish phrases that would pepper her conversation throughout her life. He knew only Hebrew and the guttural German necessary to survive in a working-class environment. When Hanna was seventeen, she and Yoel married. From that day until the day he died, Yoel divided his time between the family farm and Temple Beth El, where he served as rabbi. They had three children. Moshe, my father, was the oldest.

From my place on the chair I watched and waited with a sense of sadness, knowing that this would be the end, yet confident that when the moment came, death would safely pass me by. Then Grandma drew a labored breath and tilted her head in my direction. Her eyes, clear and sharp, focused on me. A sinking feeling pressed against my chest and the sense of confidence and security I'd felt just moments before suddenly vanished.

Grandma's lips moved and Papa turned toward me. "Sarah, she wants to tell you something." Reluctantly, I slid from the chair, moved to the bed, and leaned over Grandma.

"Put your ear close to her lips," Papa directed. I did as he said and placed my left ear between her nose and chin. In the faintest whisper, she said, "The locket belongs to you."

A smile spread across my face. I tried to hold it in for fear Papa would be upset, but I couldn't and I'm sure Grandma didn't mind. I saw the corners of her mouth turn up ever so slightly. I looked up at Papa. "She said—"

Before I could finish, Grandma drew another heavy breath. Her chest heaved twice, then all the muscles in her body relaxed and she lay still. Papa leaned past me, nudging me aside, and once more leaned over her body. He listened for a moment with his ear near her nose, then he reached behind her head, removed the necklace and dropped it into the palm of his hand. "She is gone," he whispered. He looked over at Mama. "She is gone."

"Yes," Mama nodded. "She is gone."

Papa turned to me. "What did she say to you?"

"She said, 'The locket is yours.'"

"I thought so," he nodded.

David pushed away from the doorframe and stood up straight. "We must make arrangements."

Mama shot him a cold, hard glare. "The breath is barely from her body and already you are talking about arrangements?"

Papa gestured for quiet. "It is okay, Orna. David is right. We must think of the arrangements."

"What?" Mama gestured to the body lying on the bed. "Why do you talk like this in front of her?"

Papa did not reply but instead turned toward the door. "I will go see Rabbi Gavriel. He will know what to do."

"It is still the Sabbath," Mama protested.

"Death does not work by the calendar."

"You should see Alois," she offered once more. "He can help with these things."

"Orna, I have told you many times. Alois is a lawyer. We do not need the courts to help us. This is a matter for the rabbi."

Papa crossed the room to the dresser, put the locket and necklace in Grandma's jewelry box, and started toward the door. David followed him, and I listened to the sound of their footsteps as they walked through the house. Then I heard the front door bang closed.

When they were gone, I looked over at Mama. "Why is Papa so worried?"

"The authorities," she sighed.

"What about them?"

"We must bury your grandmother within twenty-four hours."

"So, we bury her," I shrugged. "The Sabbath will be over tomorrow."

"Already you are twelve, but you do not understand?" Mama shook her head. "Tomorrow is Sunday. They do not like to have Jewish funerals on Sunday."

"Who doesn't like it?"

"The priests and the bishops."

"The Christians?"

"Yes. The Christians. That is what I have been trying to tell you. The Christians do not like for us to have funerals on Sunday."

"But we are not Christian."

"But the chancellor is and so are all the important government officials. They do whatever the church tells them to do."

"Then why doesn't Papa want to see Uncle Alois? He could help with the authorities."

"Your father does not want to involve the authorities."

"But Uncle Alois has many friends. They can help. That's what he does."

"How do you know such things?"

"I have seen them when they come to his house."

"Uncle Alois has many friends, but your father wants to handle this himself. Come." Mama gestured with a nod toward Grandma's body. "We must cover her now."

"We can do that?"

"You see any men around her to do it?"

Mama turned toward the doorway to leave the room and I started after her, but she stopped and turned to me. "No, no, no," she shook her head. "You must stay." I didn't want to sit alone in the room with a dead body, even if it *was* Grandma's, but Mama wouldn't let me. "We cannot leave her alone," she said sharply. "I have a clean sheet in the closet. I will be just a minute. Then we will cover her and light some candles." She shooed me back toward the bedroom. "You stay with the body."

With halting steps, I backed my way into the room and took a seat on the chair in the corner. Mama was in the closet upstairs—I could hear her footsteps above me. I sat on the chair and stared again at Grandma, this time not watching her breathe but how still and motionless she'd become. As I watched her, my mind wandered to what Mama had said about Uncle Alois and I knew that if I were an adult and needed help, he would be the first person I contacted. Grandma never seemed to like him, but of all the people on Mama's side of the family, he was my favorite.

Just then, Mama returned to the room. "See? That didn't take long."

I came from the chair and moved near the bed, still thinking of Uncle Alois. "Mama," I began, "why didn't Grandma like Uncle Alois?"

"Who told you such a thing?"

"I could tell by the way she acted."

"It is nothing."

"It must be something."

"Where did you learn to talk to me like that?"

"Does Papa like Alois?"

"Yes," she replied in a matter-of-fact tone. "Alois is my brother. Your father is my husband. Of course he likes Alois."

"Then why didn't he want Alois to help just now?"

"Never mind all that." She spoke to me in the dismissive tone she used when I'd asked one too many questions.

"I like Uncle Alois," I offered, trying to turn the conversation in a new direction.

"I like him, too," she agreed quickly. "Now, hush. We have things to do besides talking about our relatives."

chapter 2

*L*ater that day, I left the house and wandered down the sidewalk. A chilly breeze blew my hair and sent a shudder through my shoulders. Around me life seemed to go on as usual. A delivery truck sputtered past and from down the street the bell rang as a trolley car rolled by the next corner, but in my mind I could only think of Grandma.

Near the middle of the block I came to the Eichmann house. Adolf, all of sixteen years old, was sitting on the front step, reading a pamphlet that he held in his hand. He looked up as I came near. "Why the long face?"

"My *bobeshi* died today."

"Your grandmother?"

"Yes."

"I heard she was sick."

"She has been very sick."

"So, tell me, where do Jews go when they die?"

"To the place of the dead," I shrugged, not really knowing what that meant.

"And that is it?"

"Rabbi Gavriel says they will rise again one day."

"Hmm. That's what they say at church, too."

"Do you believe it?"

"I don't know." He put aside the pamphlet. "I just go because my father says so."

By then I was curious about what he was reading and I pointed to it. "What is that in your hand?"

"A pamphlet about Argentina." He gave me a curious look. "You know where that is?"

"Of course I know where it is," I said with a hint of indignation. "It's in South America."

"Right." He seemed a little downcast, as if he'd wanted to tell me about it but I robbed him of that chance. "I forget you aren't a little girl anymore."

I ignored the last remark and gestured toward the pamphlet. "Where'd you get it?"

"Someone gave it to my father."

"What's it say?"

"It says with a little work people are making a go of it as farmers. Ranchers, actually. Raising cattle." He held it so I could see the picture on the front.

"They look like cowboys in America."

"Yes," he nodded. "They do, don't they?"

"So, you want to be a cowboy?"

"It looks like fun," he grinned. "And everyone has to do something. Lots of people are going from here to South America. Lots of Germans."

"But your father manages the electric works. Who would keep the lights on if you all left?"

"Oh, I don't mean all of us would go. Just me."

"Oh."

He had a questioning frown. "How do you know so much about my father?"

"I hear people talking about him." I thought my answer would show him I was old enough to be interesting. "I know a few things about you, too."

"Well," he grinned. "I know a few things about your family, as well."

"Like what?"

"Your father is a shopkeeper and your mother plays violin with the orchestra. And your brother plays piano but really wants to be a soldier."

"How do you know that about David?"

"I listen," he said with a look of satisfaction. "Was your grandmother a musician?"

"No," I said slowly. "She was…Grandma."

Just then I noticed Karl Eichmann, Adolf's father, standing on the porch behind us. "Music is a waste of time," he growled. "Might be nice entertainment for some who have nothing better to do with their time, but it contributes nothing to the good of German society."

"We are not in Germany." I meant no harm at all and was only trying to engage him in conversation.

"But we are Germans," he growled right back at me.

"My father is a shopkeeper," I said defensively. "That's a useful thing."

"Yes," he conceded, "he sells lace and cloth at exorbitant prices. Preying on women who don't know they're being robbed."

I bristled at his comment. "And what is the price of electricity?"

Karl's eyes flashed with anger. "You stupid Jew," he snarled and moved toward me. "I ought to—"

Adolf stood and looked down at me. "What he means is, your father is a nice man, but he produces nothing of value and only makes money for himself. That is all we are saying."

"Don't people need clothes to wear?"

"My mother has been to his shop many times. She says he sells his goods at very high prices."

Karl was standing near the door, watching and listening to the exchange between us. He was still angry but not so much as before and snarled, "Adolf, send your little Jew friend home. We need you inside."

The tone of his voice was more of disgust than disdain and the sound of it hurt my feelings almost as much as the words he said. A lump formed in my throat and tears filled my eyes, but I swallowed hard and forced myself not to cry. At the time, I thought of his remarks only as the words of a disgruntled middle-aged man. Later, as events unfolded, I realized this was the moment my life changed. This was the beginning of the atrocities that would mark the next twenty-five years of my life.

Adolf did as he was told and went inside. I wandered back up the street to our house. This time, however, as I came through the front room, the house seemed different and I looked at things in a different way. Papa and Mama were both well-educated with a cosmopolitan view of life. Papa's business relationships stretched all across Europe. Mama had studied music in Berlin and Paris and when they settled in Linz she earned a chair in the orchestra where she played violin. Musicians often visited our house for dinner, which naturally led to a lively discussion of the arts followed by impromptu concerts and demonstrations of the latest musical pieces. Many times David joined them on the piano. Our life was full and rich, all of which was reflected in the house where we lived and the furnishings that filled it. Original paintings hung on the walls in every room, many of them created by artists who were friends of my parents or grandparents. When we ate, we sat at a long dining table made of walnut with a burled top. The plates we used were of the finest china, complemented by sterling silver dinnerware. Furniture throughout our house was well made. Our house looked and felt like it was home to an educated, capable family. When I reached the kitchen, Mama was standing at the sink. I asked her, "Are the paintings on our walls worth anything?"

She glanced back at me over her shoulder. "Why do you ask such a thing?"

"Adolf and his father don't like artists and musicians."

"Adolf Eichmann comes from a difficult situation."

"What happened?"

"His mother died when he was just a boy. His father remarried to a nice woman, but he is never around much. Always down at the Electric Works. And always with those bombastic comments."

"They think Papa charges too much in his store."

"Papa charges what he must to make a living. I don't like you going down there."

"Adolf is my friend."

"Just the same, I don't like it. A twelve-year-old girl ought not to be hanging around with a sixteen-year-old boy. He's almost a man."

"He's nice to me."

"He's nice to everyone, but it doesn't mean he won't do you harm."

"He would never hurt me."

"I don't like it, Sarah. I think you should stay away and mind your own business."

chapter 3

Not long after I returned home, Uncle Alois arrived with his wife. Their sons, much older than I, lived in Italy. They could not make it in time for the funeral, but Alois was there and I was happy to sit and listen to him talk. A little while later, other relatives and friends began to arrive and soon the house was alive with the sound of voices, many I hadn't heard in a long time, others I'd never heard before. I helped in the kitchen and did my best to listen in on every conversation.

In spite of what Mama had said about waiting for the Christian Sabbath to pass, Rabbi Gavriel decided we should hold the funeral the following day, Sunday. All afternoon and all night, Grandma's body lay on her bed beneath the sheet we placed over her. Each of us took turns sitting with her. I wanted to hide in my room or play outside, but Mama would not allow it. Instead I had to sit downstairs with the others and take my turn. Late that afternoon, as twilight turned to dusk, I spent an hour seated on the chair in the corner, waiting with Grandma. I didn't mind so much that she was dead and only a few feet away, but as I sat there I kept thinking about what would happen to her after she was buried and the worms came to eat her flesh. Even now I still have those images in my mind.

That night, with the traditional Sabbath over, even more friends and family members gathered. So many of them came, I only had to sit with Grandma just that once. The rest of the evening I spent in my room and when it was late I went to sleep to the sound of visitors and the murmuring of their voices downstairs.

The next day, I awoke early and dressed on my own for the funeral. While everyone else was busy getting ready, I went downstairs and tiptoed through the kitchen to the doorway of Grandma's bedroom. Her body was gone. Women from the Chevra Kadisha—the burial society—had come before sunrise and took it away, still I felt like a criminal as I crept toward the dresser. When I reached it I found the jewelry box in its place below the mirror. I lifted the lid and there was the necklace neatly coiled in a circle with the locket resting in the middle. Carefully, I grasped the clasp with my fingertips and lifted it up, letting the necklace stretch out its full length, the locket dangling beneath. Then I unhooked it and put it around my neck. Just as the clasp closed, Mama appeared behind me. "What are you doing?" she scolded.

The sound of her voice made me jump. "It's mine," I snapped, recovering quickly. "It's mine and I want to wear it."

"You'll do no such thing." Her eyes flashed with anger as she reached over me and pointed toward the jewelry box. "Put it back." She jabbed the air with her finger for emphasis. "Put it back right now."

"But it's mine," I protested. "She gave it to me."

"This is a funeral," Mama said in a huff. "Not a celebration of your newfound favor. You shall have that necklace when your father says so and not a minute earlier."

While she was talking, Papa appeared in the doorway. I could see him behind me in the mirror. He said, "It looks nice on you," but I knew from the way his eyes scrunched up at the corners that I would not wear the necklace that day.

"Thank you," I said, doing my best to delay the inevitable. "Where did she get it?"

"It had belonged to her grandmother."

My eyes opened wide. "Her grandmother gave it to her, and now she gave it to me?"

"Yes."

Mama stood nearby with her hands on her hips, but she said nothing. I glanced at her, then back at Papa, hoping that if I kept talking he might change his mind. "Did you know her, my great-great grandmother?"

"No." He shook his head. "She was dead long before I was born."

"What happened to her?"

"She died in Russia when they—"

"Moshe," Mama spoke sharply, interrupting him. "You should get ready."

"I am ready."

"This is too much to talk about now." Mama shook her head. "We should discuss this some other time. We must get going."

"But Grandma said it was mine," I sighed, knowing better than to talk to Papa the way I talked to Mama.

"Yes," he nodded calmly. "And someday you will get to keep it in your own jewelry box on your own dresser. And then you can decide when to wear it. But for now, we'll keep it in here." Then he unhooked the clasp and removed the necklace from my neck.

"I wanted to wear it to school tomorrow, too," I pouted, on the verge of tears.

Without replying, he leaned over my shoulder, returned the necklace and locket to the jewelry box, and closed the lid. "Come." He placed his hands on my shoulders and guided me toward the door. When we were in the kitchen, he let go of me and took Mama by the hand. "We must go. The others are waiting."

From the house we rode to the synagogue in Papa's car, a 1905 Daimler Mercedes. Made before the Great War, it smoked and sputtered on its best days and spent more time in the garage than on the street, but it was a car just the same. Papa took it in settlement of Mr. Dassanowsky's account. Dassanowsky was a tailor for the royal family in the years when we were ruled by a monarchy. That position afforded him many privileges that were denied to ordinary people. Among them was the use of a royal retreat when it wasn't otherwise inhabited by the family. Mama said he stayed there more often than the emperor. Papa said he was royalty from his head to his toes, all except for his pocketbook. When he could no longer afford to carry Mr. Dassanowsky on his books, Mr. Dassanowsky offered Papa the car as settlement. Papa was glad to get it.

After a chilly but brief drive, we arrived outside the synagogue. We parked at the curb and stepped from the car but did not go inside the building. As we straightened our coats, the doors to the building opened and the men appeared with Grandma's casket. They walked with three men on each side; arms stretched across each other's backs, the wooden casket positioned between them on their shoulders. We waited until they were in front, then followed them in a procession to the cemetery that was located behind the building.

As we made our way past the building, the sound of angry voices drifted toward us. To the right I saw a group of men, women, and even young children gathered on the sidewalk. It was Sunday and they used it as an excuse to shout obscenities at us, to ridicule our manner of dress, and to accuse us of desecrating the Christian Sabbath with our gathering. I took Mama's hand, and David moved up beside us, positioning himself between us and those who were shouting. The commotion they created attracted others and by the time we reached the grave, the small group at the street had grown to a mob.

Mama seemed intent on ignoring them and held her chin at an imperious angle, her nose tilted up in a way that made it impossible for her to see the ground as she walked. She wasn't looking in that direction anyway but I was worried that if she didn't she might stumble into the grave. I tugged at her hand in an effort to move her to one side but she just shook her head and, without looking down at me, warned, "Stay beside me. Do not be afraid."

We followed Papa to the far end of the grave and took our places. Then the congregation that joined us formed a circle around us. I could still hear the people shouting at us and once or twice I could see them as their crowd continued to grow.

The casket sat on the opposite side of the grave from us and rested on the ground with ropes stretched out beneath it. I wondered what the ropes were for but there was no time to ask. Before I could get Mama's attention, Rabbi Gavriel took his place beside the casket and began with a prayer, which he chanted in Hebrew. As he spoke, I glanced to the right, past David, and saw that the angry crowd had moved even closer. Some of them were standing just a few meters from our group.

Then just as the prayer ended, a bottle flew past Uncle Alois' head, struck the corner of the casket, and shattered into pieces. Suddenly the air was filled angry voices and vile words no one should ever hear. Bottles, bricks, and rocks rained down on us, striking those around me on the shoulders and head. Being younger and shorter, most of the objects flew past me without effect, though a brick bounced off someone and struck me on the shin, and several people stepped on my feet as they moved to get out of the way.

Mama put her arm across my shoulder and bent over me, turning her back to the onslaught, shielding me with her body as we ran, away from the mob. David followed us and I could hear Papa's voice shouting first at the crowd then at our friends. Those standing near the back took the worst of it. Many were beaten bloody with fists and clubs. One had a broken arm. We made it to the alley on the far side of the building and were about to turn toward the street where our car was parked when a group of men appeared to block our way. Grinning at us they brandished clubs and rocks and shouted as they came toward us, "We got you now, Sheeny! You won't get away from us!"

As they were about to overwhelm us, the police arrived and began accusing members of our group of starting the trouble. Papa heard them arguing and turned back to join the dispute, but Mama grabbed him by the sleeve of his jacket. "No, Moshe." Her voice was firm but she was not angry. "The children," she urged. "We must think of the children."

He hesitated and glared at her. "But I can't just—" Mama caught his eyes and shook her head.

Reluctantly, Papa led us down the alley toward the street. The crowd that had blocked our way stepped aside to let us pass. They jeered at us as we moved by, but we made it to the car without being attacked again and started for home.

"What will we do about Grandma?" I asked from my place in the back seat. "We can't just leave her."

"We aren't just leaving her," Mama replied confidently. "Alois will take care of her."

"Rabbi Gavriel will take care of her," Papa added. "We must take care of you and your brother."

"And ourselves," Mama chimed in.

As we drove away, I stared out the car window and watched the crowd. They were laughing as they dispersed and regaling each other with details of what they had done. Then at the corner I caught sight of Karl Eichmann, Adolf's father, watching through the window from inside a café down the street from the synagogue. His eyes met mine and followed us as we slowed, turned the corner, and he disappeared from our sight.

chapter 4

The next morning was Monday. I awoke with a start and stared up at the ceiling, my eyes wide open, my body fully awake, and my mind focused only on Grandma's necklace. All I could think about was wearing it to school and what the girls at school would say when they saw it. None of my friends had anything like it, not even the *goyim* in our class who came to school by private car. Maybe if they saw it they would leave me alone and stop calling me names.

I listened awhile, hoping to hear the clock downstairs as it chimed the hour, but when it seemed a long time had passed and the clock still hadn't sounded, I glanced out the window to see the sky still was dark with the stars clearly visible, the moon bright and full. The sun wouldn't rise for hours.

Moving as quietly as possible, I eased back the covers, slid from my bed, and walked out to the hallway. At the bottom of the stairs, I made my way down the hall to the kitchen and across it to Grandma's bedroom. Moonlight glowed through the window, casting a glare across the room that lit the way to the dresser. I reached it with just a few quick steps and lifted the lid on the jewelry box.

The top tray held several pieces of costume jewelry—earrings with glass for stones in a setting made of pewter, a ring with an oyster shell stone made to look like pearl, and two bracelets made of gold-colored metal. The necklace lay in the corner. I took it from the box and held it in the light.

Just then a hand touched me on the shoulder. I gasped and turned to see David standing beside me. "Don't do that," I whispered. "The sound will wake them."

"You aren't supposed to be in here," he grinned.

"I just want to wear it."

"Father won't like it."

"He'll never find out."

"He always finds out."

"Not this time."

I dropped the locket and its chain into the palm of my left hand and clenched my fist tightly around it. Then I closed the lid of the jewelry box and looked David in the eye. "Not a word of this to anyone. You understand?"

"Okay," he shrugged. "It's your life."

"What does that mean?"

"It means the life you've known so far will come to an end when they find out what you've done."

"They will never know," I answered as I started toward the door.

A few hours later I was awakened by Mama as she stood near the bed and shook my foot. I dressed as usual and brushed my hair into place, then tucked the necklace and locket into my pocket. Downstairs, I ate breakfast with David and Mama. Papa had already gone to the store. David made no mention of what had transpired the night before, not even offering his usual knowing looks that gave everything away.

When I reached school I took the necklace from my pocket and placed it around my neck with the locket positioned in front, resting on the lace at the collar of my dress. As I moved it into place my friend, Sarit Haza, appeared beside me.

"I heard about your—" She stopped short and her mouth fell open. "What is that?" She pointed toward my neck.

A smile spread across my face. "What?" I asked casually. I knew exactly what she was pointing at but wanted to enjoy the moment.

"That!" She touched the locket with her finger.

"It was my grandmother's," I beamed with pride.

"She gave it to you?"

"Yes," I nodded. "Right before she died. Her grandmother gave it to her, and she gave it to me."

Sarit's eyes filled with tears. "She gave it to you as she was dying?"

"Yes," I nodded. "It was—"

Before I could finish, Senta Hollerer, one of the many goyim in our class, elbowed her way in front of me. "Look," she sneered, "the Yid has a new trinket."

Hedy Berger was behind me. "Let me try it." Her fingernails scraped against my neck as she clawed for the clasp of the necklace.

"No," I protested and jerked my head to one side, trying to avoid her hands.

"Hold still," she barked. "You'll break it."

Then she unhooked the clasp and held the necklace for everyone to see. She had a wide, fake grin at first, mocking me as she bounced the chain up and down on her finger. Then her eyes opened wide as she realized what it was. "Hey," she exclaimed. "This feels like gold."

A crowd had gathered around us and someone chided her. "How would you know what gold feels like?"

"Give me that," Senta demanded and snatched it away. She held it in her hand a moment, studying it. "Can you imagine? A Jewish schoolgirl with a gold necklace, and I don't even have one made of tin." She draped the chain over her finger and twirled it around, the locket whirling round and round in the air.

"Gold!" Hedy chanted. "The Yid has gold. Gold. The Yid has gold."

Suddenly the clasp came open and the locket flew through the air. It struck Hedy on the shoulder and dropped to the floor. I dropped to my knees and groped between them in a desperate attempt to find it.

Senta held on to the necklace and dangled it over me. "Looking for something? she teased. "You'll never find it."

Tears welled up in my eyes and a feeling of desperation overwhelmed me. Why did I take it? Why did I think this was a good idea? If only I had listened to Papa and left it in the box.

Then I heard a familiar voice growl, "Give it back." I looked up to see Stephan Rovina, a boy in our class, holding Senta by the wrist. "Give it back."

"Eww!" Hedy squealed. "A Jew touched you. She staggered about in mock distress, clutching her stomach and pretending to be sick, all the while laughing and giggling. Senta laughed, too, but Stephan still held her at the wrist and would not let go. "Give it to me!" he demanded and held out his hand.

Senta tossed the necklace across his shoulder and jerked her arm free. "Take it," she snapped. "And don't ever put your filthy hands on me again."

As she stepped back, I saw the locket on the floor where she'd been standing. She'd hid it beneath her foot all the time. I picked it up and checked to make certain it had not been damaged. Then I stood and turned to Stephan.

"Are you okay?"

"Yeah," I sniffed. "I think so." He handed me the chain. "Thanks."

"You're welcome." He held the end of the chain and threaded it through the opening at the top of the locket, then reached around me to put it on my neck. "Lift up your hair." I held it out of the way as he slid the necklace in place. His fingers were light against my skin and the touch of them sent a tingle down my spine.

When the locket was in place again I looked at him and smiled. "I suppose we should get to class."

He pointed to my neck. "Maybe you should tuck that inside your dress for the day. You don't want that to happen again."

"Good idea," I nodded, and I slipped it below my collar.

* * *

That afternoon while I was walking home from school I saw Adolf at the corner. I ran to catch up with him and met him at the corner. I looked up at him and his eyes seemed sad.

"What's the matter?"

"Nothing," he replied glumly.

"You look sad. Have a bad day?"

"Nothing you would know about."

"You mean in school?"

"Yeah."

"What happened?"

"Math."

"Oh."

"See. I told you you wouldn't know."

"Algebra," I nodded. "I bet it was algebra."

"Something like that."

"I could help you."

"I don't think so."

"Why not? I'm smart."

"It's a little more than your twelve-year-old mind could understand. Besides, you're a girl."

"What does that mean?"

"One day you will be a woman and you'll understand, women can't do this. Only men."

I wasn't sure what he meant but I didn't like it. Still, I liked him and I tagged along beside him. "I had a bad day, too," I offered.

"Oh? What happened to you?"

I took the necklace from beneath the collar of my dress and laid it on top for him to see. He stopped and stared at it. "That looks like gold."

"I think it is gold."

"Where'd you get it?"

"It was my grandmother's."

"And it's really gold?"

"Maybe."

"Should someone as young as you be wearing something made of gold?"

"I don't know. I suppose not, but I wanted my friends to see it."

"Are all you Jews that rich—so rich that even their children wear gold?"

"I don't know about everyone. I think Mr. Rothstein is rich. And Mr. Edelman. I don't know about any others."

"And you."

"I'm not rich."

"I think your father is rich. Getting rich off the high prices he charges in his store."

"He doesn't charge extra."

"All Jews charge extra. They're sucking the life out of the country. It's happening all over Europe."

We continued to talk and I took no notice of time or place. Then suddenly he came to a stop and I saw that we were at the walkway to his house. His father, Karl, was standing on the porch, glaring at us. Adolf stooped down and looked me in the eye. "I have to go inside now," he said in a low voice. "You must go home."

"But I can help you with your schoolwork," I argued.

Karl overheard us and burst out in jeering laughter. "You really are stupid. Both of you. A stupid Jew helping a stupid German," he scoffed. "That is the best joke I've heard in a long time."

Adolf turned toward his father. "She was only trying to help."

Karl's face turned red and his eyes narrowed. In an instant he charged from the porch, took three long strides to where we stood, and struck Adolf with a fist on the side of the head. "Get in the house!" he shouted. "That Jew has you under her spell and you're too much of an idiot to recognize it."

Adolf looked down at me once more and, with the kindest expression, said quietly, "You should go now."

I turned away and started up the sidewalk toward our house. As I did, I looked back over my shoulder and saw Karl holding Adolf by the collar, pushing him toward the porch. With every step, he slapped Adolf on the back of the head, barking at him like an angry dog. Moments later, the front door banged shut and I could hear shouting from inside their house. I returned home with the sound of those voices still in my head, the anger and intensity of it was almost more than I could comprehend. Why was Karl so angry?

chapter 5

At home I found Mama in the kitchen. David was with her, and as I came to the doorway he gave me a knowing look and made a gesture toward his neck. I touched my neck and felt the necklace. Before Mama noticed, I turned aside, removed the necklace, and placed it in the pocket of my dress. Then I came back to the doorway, crossed the room to where she stood at the sink, and kissed her on the cheek. She looked up at me. "So, how was school today?"

"It was fine."

"I heard there was trouble with one of the girls."

I shot a look at David but he just shrugged. "Not much." I did my best to avoid the subject.

"You must not antagonize them."

"I don't."

"If there is trouble," Mama continued, "you will be blamed for it."

"I know, but I don't like it. It's just not fair. They get to say whatever they want and if I reply, then I am the one who gets into trouble."

"That is the way it is." Mama set aside the dish she was holding and dried her hands on a towel. "You know that is how it is, so why struggle against it?" She pointed to a head of cabbage that sat on the counter. "Chop that cabbage for me."

I washed my hands at the sink and took a knife from the drawer. Outer leaves of the cabbage felt smooth and waxy against the palm of my hand as I steadied it against the countertop. Then, with careful aim, I pressed the blade of the knife against it and pushed down. The leaves made a crunching sound as the blade sliced it into chunks.

While I focused my eyes on the cabbage and the knife, my mind revisited the scene a few minutes earlier outside Adolf's house. Images from that moment filled my mind—the kindness in Adolf's eyes as he told me I should go home, the fear on his face when his father grabbed him, the pain and anger as his father's fist struck his head. "Mama?" I said finally, in as disarming a voice as I could muster.

"What is it now?" she sighed.

"Why is Karl Eichmann always mad?"

"You have been to their house again?" She was not pleased.

A sense of guilt swept over me. I had forgotten all about her earlier warning not to go there. "I walked home with Adolf." I was trying to diffuse the situation with my explanation.

"I told you to leave them alone. Those people are not good for us."

"We were going in the same direction. He is our neighbor. I couldn't ignore him."

"Just the same," she grumbled. "You should leave him alone."

From the tone of her voice I could tell she was not angry with me, so I pressed on for an answer to my question. "But why is his father always mad?"

"Karl Eichmann is trouble for us," she repeated.

Still, I would not give up. "He's not just mad at me. He gets mad at Adolf, too."

"Are you chopping the cabbage? All this talk is slowing us down."

"I saw you walking home with him," David added. "What were you talking about?"

"Math."

"Math?" David laughed. "You were talking to Adolf about math?"

"He's doing poorly in school and we were talking about it."

"That is what this is about?"

"Yes," I nodded. "His father overheard us and got mad."

Mama set a pot of potatoes on the stove and glanced in my direction. "That is all he was mad about?"

"I guess. I offered to help and he got mad."

"You offered to help?" David laughed even louder than before. "Adolf is far ahead of you in school. He's even ahead of me—studying algebra, geometry, and who knows what. What do you know about that?"

"Ahh," Mama nodded. "Now I see why he got mad. What did he say?"

I kept my eyes on the cabbage and lowered my voice. "I don't know." I was trying to avoid the question.

"Tell me," Mama insisted. "What did he say?"

"It wasn't anything," I shrugged. "Really. It's okay."

She stepped away from the stove. "Sarah, tell me what he said."

From the tone of her voice I knew there would be no peace until I answered so, reluctantly, I told her, "He said, 'A stupid Jew helping a stupid German, what a joke.' Or something like that."

"See. That's what I mean." Mama's voice was loud, her words emphatic. "He wasn't mad because of the math. He was mad because you are a Jew. And Karl Eichmann hates all Jews."

David spoke up again. "Adolf would do better in math if he studied more."

"It's not that," Mama dismissed the comment with a wag of her finger. "Some people have trouble with math. Alois was not so good at math when he was a boy." She came and stood beside me, then she spoke to me in a calm, even tone. "This was not about math or school or anything like that. This was about the fact that you are a Jew." I felt her hand on my shoulder. "But you already knew that, didn't you?"

"Yes, Mama."

"And it bothers you."

"Yes, Mama."

"But I want you to remember this day. Because this is the way life is for us. If you accept it and live within the limitations, you can have a good life. If you try to get beyond it, you will only have trouble."

When I finished chopping the cabbage, Mama put it in a pot to boil on the stove. Then she went to the front room for a rest. While she rested, I slipped away from the kitchen to Grandma's bedroom. Walking as quietly as possible, I made my way to the dresser and opened the jewelry box, being careful not to make a sound. I took the locket and necklace from my pocket, held it up for one last look, then lowered it into its place at the corner of the tray.

A feeling of satisfaction came over me as I closed the lid. In spite of all that had transpired that day, no one would ever know what had happened. Taking the locket from the box, wearing it to school, losing it on the floor and finding it again—all of that would be a secret I could keep to myself. In only a few seconds the sense of satisfaction turned to smug self-confidence. I was a clever girl.

As I turned to leave the room, feeling warm inside and sure of myself, I found Mama standing behind me. My heart sank as her eyes bore in on me.

"Your father told you to leave that necklace alone." When I didn't respond she pressed the issue. "Didn't he tell you to leave it in that jewelry box?"

"Yes. He did."

"And you disobeyed him."

"Yes, Mama."

"And that is what the trouble was about in school."

"How did you know?"

"People talk."

"David told you."

"No. Your brother did not tell me. He did not have to. I already knew before he got home."

An awful sense of guilt and shame came over me. Tears welled up in my eyes. "I'm sorry."

"Listen to me." I had expected to hear her fuss at me in an angry voice, but instead she spoke to me in a kind and tender way. "This is what I was telling you about in the kitchen just now. Life imposes limitations on us. I don't know why, but we must accept them as something God uses to teach us a lesson. You must learn to live within those limitations. If you do not, they will take more from you than your grandmother's necklace."

Tears streamed down my face as she spoke. I could only nod in reply. She put her arm around my shoulder and pulled me close. "But all is well for now. Things worked out. And this will be a matter between us. There is no need for anyone else to know." I wrapped my arms around her and held on to her with all my might.

* * *

Late that afternoon, not long before twilight, Mama sent me to the grocery store. It was located down the street about three blocks. I had to walk past the Eichmann's house to get there. Unlike earlier in the day, this time I remembered what she told me and stayed away from their house, walking on the opposite side of the street to avoid the possibility of any temptation to stop and talk. The trip didn't take long. Mama only needed three or four items. I've often wondered if she didn't send me there to give me a chance to practice what she'd said.

Walking past the Eichmanns' from the opposite side of the street seemed like more than merely avoiding trouble. It seemed like a statement, like I was shunning them and it made me uncomfortable to do it. So, on my way back home, I cut over to an alley that ran behind the houses on our block and came up that way, to avoid going past the front of their house where someone might see me and wonder why I was walking on the opposite side.

As I came behind the Eichmanns' house I heard Karl shouting again. The shades were partway up and I could see him standing in one of the back bedrooms. He was wearing his trousers and just an undershirt with the thin straps that go over the shoulders. Between the shouts I saw him raise his arm in the air and then come down with something in his hand. When he did it a second time I could see he was holding a leather belt. And I heard his voice. "You want to hang around young Jew girls? Is that it? You'd rather do that than schoolwork? Well, think about this!" And then he swung the belt again. From the things he said, I knew he was talking to Adolf, and from the way he stood and the angle of his head, I was certain Adolf was on the floor.

All thought of my conversation with Mama flew from my head. I crept up to the house and peeked through the window. Sure enough, Karl was standing over Adolf, berating him with his words and beating him with the belt. Large red welts showed on his arms and legs.

"How could anyone be so stupid?!" Karl shouted. "Haven't I taught you better?"

A door to the room opened and Maria, Adolf's stepmother, appeared. "What are you doing?" she demanded.

"This is between me and my son," Karl retorted.

"No, this is too much." She strode across the room and snatched the belt from his hand. "You cannot do this to him." She reached down and helped Adolf from the floor. "I will not allow it. Next you'll be beating me."

Frustrated and angry, Karl pushed his way past them and stormed from the room. I stood there at the window, mesmerized by what I'd just witnessed. Then I noticed Maria looking in my direction. She wagged her finger at me and waved with her hand in a shooing gesture. Moments later, the back door flew open and Karl appeared on the screened porch.

I backed away from the window, hoping he didn't see me and trying to be as inconspicuous as possible, but it was all to no avail. His voice boomed out loud and rough. "Stupid Jews!" he shouted. His face was red and the veins in his neck throbbed. "You've ruined our country and now you think you can ruin my family?"

I backed away quickly, but when he started toward door I broke into a run. "You better run!" he yelled. "And don't come around here again!"

A rock flew past my head and another struck the ground beside me, but I didn't look back. I kept my head down and ran as fast as my legs would carry me.

chapter 6

The following afternoon, I did not see Adolf as I walked home from school. The day after that, I stationed myself along the route home and waited for him a few blocks from our street. Still, he did not appear nor was he seen throughout the week. When he wasn't there on Friday, I was worried. Something was wrong.

Yes, Mama had told me not to go to the Eichmann residence and to leave him alone, and his father had warned me never to come back there again, but I had to find out what had happened to Adolf. I felt responsible and he was my friend. So, Friday afternoon, when he still wasn't there, I walked around to the café where I had seen Karl the day when we were coming from Grandma's funeral, and I checked to see if he was there. Sure enough, Karl was seated at a table near the window with five or six of his friends, laughing and having a good time. From the number of steins and empty glasses on the table it looked as though they'd consumed several beers already.

With Karl away, I ran back to our street and down to Adolf's house. I stepped quickly onto the porch and without hesitation knocked on the door. In a few moments, the door opened and Maria appeared. "What are you doing here?" She sounded startled and looked past me to glance up and down the street. Seeing no one to notice us, she looked down at me, trying to make her face seem stern and unyielding, but I knew she liked me. "You heard what my husband said. If he finds you here, you'll be in trouble. You and all of your family."

"I came to see about Adolf."

"Adolf?" A frown wrinkled her forehead. "What about him?"

"I haven't seen him on the way home from school this week. He's always walking this way when I come home and he hasn't been there at all this week. I wanted to know if he's all right."

"Yes, of course he's all right." She looked troubled, as if I had stumbled on to a secret she wanted no one to know. "Why wouldn't he be?"

"I wasn't sure," I began. "After what happened and—"

"What are you talking about? Nothing happened." Her countenance turned cold and she pushed me away. "I've heard quite enough from you. You must go now."

Just then Ilsa, Adolf's sister, appeared beside Maria. "What do you care what's happened to him?" She glared at me. "You think he's interested in you?"

"I was just wondering if he is okay."

"His condition is none of your business," Maria snapped. "You must leave."

She stepped back to close the door, but Ilsa didn't move. "First you kill your grandmother," Ilsa snarled, "and now you want to kill my brother? Is that it? You want to kill my brother like you killed your grandmother?"

"Ilsa," Maria sighed in a parental tone. "Is that really necessary?"

Ilsa's words cut me deeply, and I could feel tears welling up in my eyes but I was determined not to cry. "Why do you say such things to me? You know they aren't true."

"Stop coming around our house, you filthy swine. No one here wants to see you." Ilsa stepped aside, grasped the door with her right hand, and slammed it closed. Dazed by the sudden outburst, I turned away from the door and slowly made my way back to the sidewalk. Tears I'd kept in check so valiantly now rolled down my cheeks.

As I reached our house I thought of going inside, but if Mama saw I'd been crying she'd want to know why and she wouldn't give up until I told her. Then I'd be in trouble and Papa would learn about all that had transpired since Grandma's death. So I continued past the house and walked a few blocks farther to clear my mind and regain my composure. Then I saw Adolf coming down the street and I ran to meet him.

Instead of books and a notepad, he was carrying a lunch pail and was dressed in work clothes that were dirty and grimy. "Where have you been?" I asked.

"At work."

"Work? What about school?"

"I don't attend school anymore." He looked neither happy nor sad about it.

"Why not? Why aren't you in school? Is it math? I'll help you."

"Father said if I wasn't going to study, I might as well get a job. He found one for me at a machine shop across town."

"Math isn't always about how much you study."

"Where'd you hear that?"

"My mother. She says some people just have trouble with it. Her brother had trouble with math when he was in school, and he's a lawyer now."

"I don't want to be a lawyer."

"Well, I was worried about you. I didn't see you on the way home all week. And after what happened before, I wanted to know if you were all right."

"After what happened? What do you mean?"

"I saw you through the window in the back room of your house."

"Oh. That. You saw that?"

"Yes. I was on my way home from the store and I came up the alley. I saw through the window of your house."

"Well, everything's better now."

"No one would tell me where you were."

Suddenly he looked worried. "You've been to my house?"

"Yes."

He stopped and turned to me. Then he stooped over with both hands on his knees and his face inches from mine. "I want you to listen to me. You must never go there again. Do you understand?"

"But I was worried."

"Never mind about that." He spoke with the kindest voice I'd ever heard. "Did they hurt you?"

"Not really."

"Not really?" He looked alarmed. "What happened? What did they do?"

"Nothing."

"Sarah, tell me what they did."

My eyes darted away. "They just said mean things to me, but I don't mind." I looked him in the eye and smiled. "Especially now that I know you're okay."

"You must never go there again. Never!"

"But I can help you with school."

He raised himself up and began to walk again. "Why would you help me?"

"You're my friend," I insisted as I tagged along beside him. He reached over and tousled my hair. I can still feel the touch of his hand on my head.

In the middle of the block, Stephan Rovina joined us. Adolf seemed less than happy to see him, as if Stephan was intruding on our conversation. I didn't think much of it then but later I would wonder about it again.

The three of us walked together, me chattering on about nothing, Adolf nodding and laughing, and Stephan just being there. Two blocks from our street, Adolf stopped and turned to us. "I must go the rest of the way alone. If my father sees you with me, it will only make things worse." He gave me a knowing look and for the first time I felt the pleasure of secret knowledge that comes from a relationship. I knew what he meant, just from the way he looked at me. "You two wait here until I reach the next corner. Got it?"

"Okay," I nodded, eager to please him. "We'll wait." Then he stepped off the curb and started across the street.

Stephan and I stood together watching as Adolf made his way to the next corner. I was hoping he would look back with a wave or a smile, but his head never turned left or right. When he reached the next cross street, Stephan took my hand.

"Come on," he tugged. "We can go now."

chapter 7

On Monday, Papa was waiting for me when I came home from school. He was sitting at the table in the dining room as I came through the house and he called me aside. I took a seat across from him and when he looked me in the eye I knew things were serious.

"Sarah, have you been in your grandmother's jewelry box?"

Panic seized me and I struggled to find an answer. To be caught by Mama was one thing, but to be confronted by Papa, in such a formal manner, was quite different. I didn't want to tell him the truth and I didn't want to lie. "Why do you ask?" My eyes darted away, avoiding his gaze as I tried to avoid the question.

"Everyone is saying you wore it to school."

My face was warm with embarrassment and I was unable to speak. Then Mama came into the room. She glanced around, first at me, then at Papa. "Moshe, what is this about?"

Papa took a document from the inside pocket of his jacket and handed it to her. "The authorities want to know about Hanna's estate."

Mama had a troubled frown. "Why do they care about her estate?"

Papa looked back at me. "Karl Eichmann has filed a complaint with the Economic Rehabilitation Board. He says we did not pay the death tax when Grandma died. Now they want to conduct an investigation."

This was the first I had heard of such a thing and I wasn't sure whether he was talking to me or to Mama. When she didn't answer, I asked, "There is a death tax?"

"A tax on the property of all who die."

"That is ridiculous," Mama muttered.

I pursued the issue, seeing it as a way to avoid any further discussion of the necklace, and whether I had worn it to school. "All Austrians have to pay such a tax?"

Papa did not respond at first, but Mama spoke up quickly. "Erma Buresch did not pay such a tax when her father died. I was there. I helped her settle his affairs. There was no mention of a tax."

"Erma Buresch is not a Jew," Papa replied.

I gave him a confused look. "Only Jews must pay the tax?"

"Yes. Only Jews. And Karl Eichmann thinks we should have paid it." He focused his gaze on me even more intently than before. "Any idea why he would think such a thing as that?"

Finally I could stand it no more and I burst into tears. "I didn't do anything wrong," I protested. "Yes. I wore the necklace to school, but that is not wrong. I just wanted to wear it so my friends could see."

Papa was unmoved by my display of emotion. "And in addition to that, you've been going down there to the Eichmann house, stirring up trouble."

"I didn't stir up trouble." I wiped my eyes with my hands. "Karl Eichmann is the one causing trouble. He beats Adolf."

"That is none of your concern."

"Adolf has trouble with his grades," I continued. "They took him out of school because his grades are bad. I wanted to help him. He's my friend."

"I understand that he is your friend," Papa said patiently, "but you cannot go down there. It is too dangerous."

"Too dangerous for what?"

"Adolf's father is an influential member of the Workers Party. They do not like Jews. You must not provoke him."

"But what about him provoking me?"

Papa raised an eyebrow. "Did he touch you?"

"No." I looked down at the tabletop. "But he said mean things about me."

"Like what?"

"They said I was trying to kill Adolf just like I killed Grandma."

"Ah," Mama gasped. "Who would say such a thing to a child?"

"It does not matter," Papa slowly shook his head from side to side. "It does not matter what they said. Words do not matter. They cannot hurt you unless you allow them to. I want you to stay away from there." He looked up at Mama. "Perhaps we should sell the locket."

"No!" I shouted. "You cannot sell it." Tears streamed down my cheeks once more. "It is mine. Grandma gave it to me."

"It's okay," Mama put her hand on my shoulder. "No one is going to sell the locket." She looked over at Papa. "Your mother gave it to her on her deathbed. There must be a reason God put such an idea in her mind. I don't think that reason was so we would sell it." She gave me a hug. "We should help Sarah find that reason. Karl Eichmann can rule his own house, but we cannot let him rule ours, too."

Papa sat there staring at us for what seemed like a very long time. Then, finally, his shoulders relaxed and his countenance softened. "Okay," he sighed. "The locket is in the jewelry box and that is where we will leave it."

I wiped my eyes with my hands once more. "But what about the tax?"

"I will take care of that," Papa replied.

"Perhaps Uncle Alois can help," I suggested with a smile.

"Yes," Papa nodded, "perhaps he can."

* * *

Papa's warning not to go down to the Eichmanns' house scared me and in response I decided to simply stay inside when not in school. Two days after he confronted me, I came home as usual and went up to my room. Sometime later I became aware that darkness had fallen and evening was fully past. Yet Mama had not called me downstairs to help with supper. I was concerned and came from my room to see what was wrong.

As I reached the bottom of the stairs I heard Mama in the kitchen, nervously flittering about. "I am sorry," I apologized. "I did not realize it was so late. Where is Papa?"

"Today is the day he had to answer the complaint about the tax."

"So soon? He only got the papers a few days ago."

"I do not set the times for the Rehabilitation Board."

"Did Uncle Alois go with him?"

"Yes."

"Good," I smiled confidently. "Everything will turn out right."

Mama was puzzled. "Why do you say that?"

"I've seen the way people look when they come to his house for help. They arrive sad and they leave smiling. He makes things turn out right."

About an hour later, Papa finally arrived at home. I saw him coming from the front window and ran outside to greet him. He was tired but smiling. I hooked my arm in his. "What happened?"

"I told them the story."

"The story? What story?"

"That my mother died and she owned only the one necklace and locket, that my daughter took it from the jewelry box and wore it to school because she missed her grandmother. Others saw it and were mistaken about what it meant."

"And what did they say?"

"They said I should keep my children under better control, and then they dismissed the case."

"Was Adolf's father there?"

"No," Papa shook his head. "No one was there for the other side."

By then we were at the front door. Mama was waiting for us. She gave him a knowing look. "We dodged the trouble this time?"

"Yes," Papa nodded. "But I do not think we will be so lucky again." He kissed her on the cheek as he came inside.

Mama took his arm and walked with him through the house to the kitchen, where he washed his hands. Then we followed him to the table and took our seats. As we passed the bowls of food, Papa's face turned solemn. "We can be happy among ourselves for what has happened, but we must say nothing of this to others." He looked across the table at me. "Understand?"

"Yes, Papa," I replied.

"You must not brag about it to Adolf or that little boy you've been hanging around with." His expression softened ever so slightly. "Stephan? Is that his name?"

The sound of his voice made me giggle. "You know his name?"

"Of course he knows his name," Mama reassured. "He just doesn't want to admit that his daughter might have a friend who is a boy."

"He is my friend."

"That's what you said about Eichmann," David added.

"He is my friend, too," I continued. "But not his parents. And not his sister."

Papa looked up from his plate. "Why do you say that?"

"They said mean things to me."

"If you stay away from their house, you won't have to worry about that, will you?"

"No, Papa."

He gave Mama a worried look, then cut his eyes back at me. "See that you remember it."

"Yes, Papa."

chapter 8

One afternoon the following week, after I was home from school, Mama came up to my room and sat on the bed. I was at my desk, reading a history lesson. As she came in I put the book aside and turned toward her. She looked tired and her eyes were sad. Mama patted the bed. "We need to talk. Come and sit beside me."

I moved from the desk to the bed and took a seat next to her. "What's the matter?"

"Your father and I have been talking." She seemed nervous and awkward. "Things here are not as they seem."

"What do you mean?" My forehead wrinkled in a frown. "I don't understand."

"Life in Linz is changing. Austria is changing. It is not like it used to be. Your Aunt Haya in Spain has offered to let you live with her and attend school there."

I could hardly comprehend what she was saying. I had lived in Linz all my life. All my friends lived there and to now move away and leave them seemed unfathomable. "Spain? Why? What are you talking about? Why are you telling me this?"

"We think it would be better for you to go there."

"This makes no sense to me," I argued. "Has something happened? Has someone caused more trouble?"

"Not exactly," she sighed.

I lay back on the bed and shook my head. "I don't understand."

Mama turned in my direction and for the first time I noticed she was crying. "It would just be better if you went to school somewhere else. It's for your own good."

"What about David? Is he coming, too?"

"David is older. And," she shrugged, "he's a boy." She took a handkerchief from her pocket and dabbed the end of her nose.

I propped myself on my elbows. "Why is that different, just because he's a boy?"

"It shouldn't be that way, but it just is. He will be finished with school before long. But you … you must leave Austria for now."

Then suddenly I knew. "This is about Karl Eichmann, isn't it?" When she didn't respond I sat all the way up. "I knew it was something more than you were saying."

"We are concerned for you. Things here are not as they seem anymore. Others have left already. You should go, too."

"What did he say?" She turned away, shaking her head. I grabbed her by the arm and pulled her back toward me. "Tell me," I insisted. "What did he say?"

Mama reached out with her arm and pulled me close. Her lips were near my ear and I could hear the raspy sound of her breathing as she spoke. "Yesterday, when your father left the shop, Karl Eichmann asked about you."

"He asked about me?"

"Yes."

"That was nice of him to remember me, wasn't it?"

She shook her head. "He wasn't being nice. He wanted to know why we raised you to be so disrespectful of adults and why we hadn't taught you your place in life. And he said if we didn't put you in your place, he would."

I leaned away from her to look her in the eye. "Put me in my place?" I gave her a puzzled look. "What does that mean?"

"It means what I was telling you before, about living within the limitations life gives us."

"I don't understand. He thinks he can teach me how to act?"

"They want you to act like one of the Germans instead of who you really are."

"And who am I?"

Mama grabbed me against her and hugged me even closer. "You are beautiful and smart."

I loved it when she held me like that. "And funny?" I giggled, trying to break the tension of the moment.

"Yes," she smiled. "And funny." Then she leaned away and the serious expression returned. "But funny will get you into trouble." She gestured with her hand for emphasis. "Austria is no longer a place where young Jewish girls can afford to get into trouble of any kind." She stood and straightened her dress. "Now come with me to the kitchen. We have work to do before supper."

"When will I go?"

"I do not know yet." She moved toward the door. "We must make arrangements." By then she was in the hall. "Come. We must get busy."

After supper that evening, Papa and I sat in the front room. He asked if Mama talked to me about going to visit Aunt Haya.

"She talked about me going there to school."

"Yes," he nodded. "That's what I mean." It seemed difficult for him to talk about it. "For you to attend school."

"What about you and Mama and David?"

"What about us?"

"Will you be coming to Spain, too?" I already knew the answer but I wanted to hear him give it.

He looked away. "Perhaps we will join you later."

"Join me? You are certain?"

"Yes," he said, nodding his head vigorously. "Perhaps."

"And we will all be together again?"

"I should hope so." He had a tight, thin smile.

"You would do that?" I pressed. "You would move all the way to Spain?"

"Nothing has been set for certain, Sarah. I haven't even talked to Haya about that part, but I don't see why not." And I knew that was the truth.

"But I still don't understand why I am going."

"Things are changing here," he said, trying to explain. "It is no longer good for you."

"Is this really because of Adolf's father? Is that all that happened?"

"Your mother told you about that?"

"Yes."

"He is just part of the problem. The situation here is changing. Things have taken a turn. I can't explain it. It's just not good anymore."

"Aunt Haya knows of this? Of me coming?"

"Yes. Of course. That is what I've been telling you. Didn't your mother explain this to you?"

"Yes. You have heard from her directly?"

"No. Through a relative."

Just then Mama entered the room. "Perhaps we could have a party before you go," she smiled. I was certain she had been listening to our conversation from the other room.

"A party?" I grinned, trying not to be sad or dour. "That would be lovely. How soon am I leaving?"

"Soon," Papa replied. "Soon."

"If we had a party, I could say goodbye to my friends."

"No," Papa shook his head earnestly. "That would not be a good idea."

"But why not?"

"It would draw too much attention. You should simply go, with no more said about it than if you were walking to school. Just get on the train and go. No fanfare."

Fear struck in the pit of my stomach. "Will I travel alone?"

"We...are arranging someone to go with you."

His hesitancy made me nervous. "Who? Who is it? Is it someone I know?"

"A friend. Someone Uncle Alois knows."

I looked up at Mama. "Who is it?"

"We aren't sure yet."

* * *

Mama and I spent the next two weeks preparing for my trip—cleaning and sorting my clothes, gathering essential items, then packing everything into a large trunk. The night before I was to leave, Uncle Alois came to the house with an envelope. He handed it to Papa and smiled at me. "This is a great opportunity for you, Sarah. Haya is a wonderful host and you will do well under her care."

"I have never been on a train before."

"Then this will be an adventure for you." He rested his hand on my shoulder. "In fact, when Haya went to Spain with Carlos, it was her first train trip, too."

"How old was she?"

"I don't know," he shrugged. "Maybe nineteen or twenty."

"I am only twelve."

"Well," he patted me on the shoulder, "we will take care of everything. Don't you worry."

"Aunt Haya was glad to go to Spain?"

"She was happy to go," he smiled. "We all thought she was crazy, not so much for going to Spain but for marrying that Carlos Murillo. He was a character."

"What happened to him?"

"He was killed."

"How?"

"I don't remember the exact details." He took a watch from his pocket and checked the time. "Oh my. It's getting late. Orna," he glanced at Mama, "I have to be going now. You will have her at the station in the morning?"

"Yes," Mama nodded. "We'll be there."

The next morning, David and I said goodbye before he headed off to school, then Papa and Mama drove me to the train station. We arrived a little after seven. The train was scheduled to leave at eight for the first leg of our journey that would take us across the border into Switzerland. We stopped at the ticket window and Papa took an envelope from his pocket and handed a slip to the clerk. It was the same envelope Uncle Alois had given him the night before. The clerk issued tickets for the trip, stamped each of them, and handed them to Papa. A porter took my trunk and then we walked out to the boarding platform. The air was unusually cold that morning and I pulled the collar of my coat up around my neck.

Across from the main station, the train that I was to take sat idle on the tracks, but the doors to the cars were closed. Down the platform to the left I saw steam seeping from the locomotive, and through the morning glare I saw soldiers and policemen on patrol. Papa checked the tickets and led us to a car near the end of the train. We stood there, trying to think of things to say, alternately hoping the time would pass quickly and desperately clinging to every second.

Half an hour later, an older couple arrived. They were both smiling as they approached and acted as if they knew us. I had never seen them before. Mama was polite but reserved, especially with the woman. After exchanging a greeting, Papa introduced them to me as Ernst and Julia Deutsch. "They will ride with you to Cordova," he explained.

"We will look after you," Julia smiled, "and see that you get there safe and sound. Don't you worry."

Mama could see I was afraid and she hooked her arm in mine. "It's okay, Sarah," she spoke softly. "This will be good. You will see. Everything will work out."

I leaned my head against her shoulder and whispered, "I am afraid I will never see you again."

Tears rolled silently down her cheeks. "We must be brave. These are difficult times. Only God knows why He has sent them to us. So we must be brave and trust Him for His own purposes."

While we stood there waiting, an Austrian policeman approached us. He glanced at Ernst and Julia, then looked at Papa. "Your identification cards, please."

Papa took a card from his coat pocket and handed it to the officer. He glanced at it, then handed it back. "What about these two?" He gestured at Mama and me.

"Our daughter is taking the train," Papa explained. "Orna and I shall remain here."

"You have tickets?"

"Yes." Papa took the tickets from his pocket and showed them to the officer.

"The girl can't board without an identity card."

"Yes," Papa nodded. He returned the tickets to an outer pocket of his jacket and withdrew a second card.

The officer took it from him, studied it for a moment, then handed it back. "Very good. Everything seems to be in order." He turned to Julia and doffed his cap. "Have a pleasant journey."

When he was gone Papa handed the card to me. "Put this in your purse and do not lose it." Then he gave me the tickets. "Do not lose these."

I took them from him and placed them in my purse, then gestured with a nod toward Ernst and Julia. "Why did he not ask them for their cards?"

"Hush, now," Papa cautioned. "This is not the time for questions. Everything has been arranged. Just do as they tell you, and if anyone asks let Ernst answer first."

A few minutes later, the doors to the train car opened and a conductor appeared. He climbed from the car, opened a compartment beside the door, and took out a small step stool. When it was in place below the door, he turned to face us and in a low voice cried, "All aboard!"

"It is time." Papa tried his best to smile, but I could see he was struggling to keep from crying.

Ernst and Julia boarded the train and waited for me inside. I said one final goodbye to Mama, gave Papa a hug, and stepped aboard. Ernst led the way down the narrow corridor through the center of the car to our compartment. I was glad it was located on the platform side of the train. When I was settled into my seat, I leaned my head against the window and waved to Papa and Mama. Papa smiled bravely and waved. Mama wept. Soon the train car lurched forward and we began to roll from the station. I stared out the window, watching them standing there together on the platform, until the train rounded a curve and the station was out of sight.

chapter 9

For the remainder of the morning, I sat by the window and watched as the Austrian countryside moved past. In spite of my sadness at leaving my family behind, I was fascinated by the things I saw. This was not only my first time to travel by train, it was also my first time traveling west of Wels, a city not far from Linz. Papa went there once to attend a fabric market and took me with him. I was four years old and the world beyond our neighborhood seemed strange and wonderful. It was equally as strange and wonderful as we rode on the train, but I already missed home and especially Mama.

Around noon, we crossed the border into Switzerland. Julia and Ernst expected the train to stop to allow Swiss officials to check for visas and travel documents, but the train continued without even slowing. A little while later, when they were certain we really weren't going to stop, we walked to the restaurant car and ate lunch.

We arrived in Zurich around three that afternoon and got off to change trains. I wanted to go inside the station and look around but Ernst would not allow it. He said we should stay on the platform. Benches sat nearby and we rested on them, but after two hours I was sure we called more attention to ourselves just sitting there than we would have by wandering around inside the building. Still, Papa said I should not ask questions and do what they said, so I did my best to obey him, but it wasn't easy.

At five that afternoon we finally boarded a different train and traveled southwest to Geneva. It was a short trip and, because of the delay in Zurich, we had little time at the station to catch the next train. We ran to the platform and were the last passengers to board. I liked that we didn't have to sit and wait. By the time we reached our compartment the train was moving.

Sometime after midnight, the train slowed to a stop on a siding. Ernst thought we were not far from Lyon. Outside the window there was only darkness. Then I heard the heavy thud of boots as someone walked along the corridor, coming in our direction—walking, stopping, walking some more, but always growing closer and closer. And there were voices. Gruff and loud, they reverberated through the walls. I glanced around nervously. Julia caught my eye and smiled at me. "Just a short delay. Nothing to worry about."

In a moment, the door to our compartment opened and the conductor appeared. Beside him was a man wearing a dark suit and behind him was a soldier. "Identity cards and travel documents," the conductor growled in the same gruff, officious tone I'd heard through the walls.

I turned in the seat for my purse, but Julia gently touched the back of my hand. "I have them right here," she said calmly. She opened her travel bag and took out an envelope, which she handed to Ernst. He passed them to the conductor.

From my place on the seat I saw that he held three sets of papers in his hands and, as he turned the pages, I saw they all bore Christian names. The clerk examined them a moment, then handed them back to Ernst. "Very good," he said, then he closed the door and they all trouped to the next compartment.

Ernst returned the documents to the envelope and handed it to Julia. She placed it in the travel bag and latched it closed. As she slid them in place I leaned near her and asked, "What was that all about?"

"Nothing." She closed the clasp on the bag and looked over at me. "Nothing at all," and then she patted me on the thigh. "Try to sleep now."

Moments later she was sound asleep, and I turned again to stare out the window into the darkness.

Sometime in the night I fell asleep to the gentle rocking of the train coach and the clatter of the wheels against the rails. I awoke to find my head resting in Julia's lap. The glare of the morning sun streamed through the window. "Where are we?" I was barely awake.

"Southern France."

"Not far from Toulouse," Ernst added. "We'll have to change trains again."

"I'm hungry. Can we go to the restaurant car for breakfast?"

"Better to stay in here," Ernst warned. "We can try the restaurant after we've crossed into Spain."

Julia opened her travel bag and took out a brown paper sack. In it were three rolls wrapped in paper. She handed one to me and I took a bite. The food was dry and crumbly but I ate it without complaint. They had one too, and we all smiled as if we were on a picnic. All the while, I wondered why we were waiting until we reached Spain to go to the restaurant car.

* * *

At dusk the following day the train entered Cordova. I had expected to find it a sleepy town and was surprised to find it was a city. I stared out the window at the brown and tan buildings and was struck by how different it looked from what I was used to. Austria seemed farther away than ever.

In a few minutes we came to a stop at the station. I was tired of sitting and tired of being confined to our cramped compartment. Even sleeping didn't make me feel any better. As people began to file off the car, Julia turned to me. "Your Aunt Haya will be waiting on the platform. How long has it been since you've seen her?"

"I'm not sure," I shrugged. "It's been a while."

"Will you recognize her?"

"I think so. Won't you be there?"

She picked up her travel bag and stood. "We'll get off ahead of you."

Ernst reached past her, opened the compartment door, then leaned aside to let her go first. When I turned to follow, he held out his arm. "Come behind me," he smiled. "You get off last." I was puzzled by what he said and I think he must have known it because he patted me on the head and said, "It's okay. Don't worry."

I waited as they made their way into the aisle, then stepped from the compartment behind them. As I did, another couple moved ahead of me, separating me from Julia and Ernst. I could still see them just a few feet ahead and watched as they continued down the aisle to the steps at the end of the car. When they reached the platform, they turned to the right and moved out of sight. It seemed odd to me, what they had said before we left the compartment and the way they left the car, but I wasn't worried. I just wanted to get off the train.

As Julia had said, Aunt Haya was standing on the platform. I spotted her as I came down the steps and moved past the conductor. Although I had not seen her since I was three, her picture was in a frame on Mama's dresser. I recognized her immediately. While I was still a few feet away, she stepped toward me, wrapped her arms around my neck, and pulled me close. My face was buried in her chest. She smelled like roses with a hint of mineral water. The smell of it tickled my nose. I had to concentrate to keep from sneezing. When she finally let me go I turned to introduce Julia and Ernst, but they were gone.

"Never mind about that," Aunt Haya said. "I'm sure they know their way around." She took me by the hand and we started from the platform. "We should get you home. I think you could use a nice hot bath."

The thought of a bath made me smile, but then I remembered my luggage. "I have a trunk," I worried that it might get left behind. "We should find it first."

"Alberto will get it."

"Who is Alberto?"

"My driver," she answered over her shoulder as she led me toward the station.

Inside the building, we quickly crossed the lobby to the front door and stepped outside. A very large Packard automobile was parked at the curb. Behind it a tall, slender man was strapping my trunk onto a luggage rack above the rear bumper. Haya waited for him to finish, then he came around and opened the rear door. She climbed in back and gestured for me to follow. "Sit right here beside me." She patted the seat cushion with her hand just like Mama did when she wanted me next to her and I was struck by the similarity of their mannerisms.

Though older than Mama, Aunt Haya had a quick mind and sharp eyes, but she coughed most of the way from the station and we could hardly talk. Alberto pointed out some of the sights as we made our way through town. A few minutes later we crossed a river I later came to know was the Guadalquivir. Broad and peaceful, it meandered through the city at an almost imperceptible pace. All around me were buildings and houses with stucco exteriors, flat roofs, and all of them painted and finished in same earth tones I had noticed from the train as we entered the city. Back in Linz, the houses were made with clapboard siding and gabled roofs, most which were trimmed in white. The difference in appearance took a while to get used to.

Across the river we turned right, passed several shops, then drove up a low hill. At the top, Alberto slowed the car and turned into a short driveway that ended near the front steps of a large house. "This is home," he announced.

I leaned my head to one side to see out the window and looked up at it. Like most of the buildings I had seen that day, the house was the color of sand, with a stucco exterior and clay tile roof. The central portion was three stories high and around it the first floor spread out on all four sides in a rambling fashion. Sitting atop the hill as it did, the house seemed to tower above the neighboring structures. It looked to me like a mansion.

We stepped from the car and were greeted by the housekeeper, Maria Landa. She was tall and slender with smooth brown skin and black hair. I learned later that, as a teenager, she had been offered a job as a model but her father had made her turn it down. She smiled at me, and when she spoke her accent made the words sound like music.

While Alberto wrestled my trunk from the car, Maria escorted us up the steps and into the front parlor of the house, where we found a young woman waiting for us. Aunt Haya introduced her only as Alona. She spoke with an eastern accent and from the sound of it I thought she might be from one of the countries to the east of Austria, but I had never been beyond the Austrian border in any direction. She was about twenty and I liked her from the start.

After we exchanged greetings in the parlor, Maria led me upstairs to the second floor and showed me to a bedroom. Unlike the exterior, walls inside the house were painted white. The bedroom was no different. It had white walls and a white ceiling with white curtains hanging over a single window that stood opposite the doorway. A wardrobe stood along the wall and a dresser sat beyond the window. In between was the bed with a nightstand on one side and a washbasin on the other.

"This is your room," Maria gestured with a broad sweep of her arm. "You can put your things in the drawers and wardrobe. Use the basin if you like. The bathroom is at the end of the hall."

While Maria showed me the room, I saw Alona in the bedroom across the hall. Alberto came with the trunk and set it in the corner. It looked worn and dirty next to the stark white walls.

When Alberto and Maria were gone, I raised the lid on the trunk and caught the smell of home as it wafted up to my nose. I removed the top tray and set it aside on the floor. Beneath it, in the bottom of the trunk, were all my clothes. A dress lay on top, neatly folded and packed in place. I picked it up and held it to my face, breathing deeply the scent of home. All at once, I felt like crying.

"You had a pleasant trip?" a voice behind me interrupted the moment.

I turned to find Alona standing in the doorway. "Yes. It was as pleasant as it could be."

"Good." She entered the room and took a seat on the bed. "I have been here only a few days myself."

"Where did you come from?"

"The East." Her eyes darted away as she spoke, and I had the feeling she didn't want to tell me exactly where she'd come from. "But I did not travel by train," she continued. "At least not for most of the journey."

"How did you get here?"

"I left my home in the back of a truck, then I rode down the river on a boat. Later, they placed me in an automobile. I did not take the train until I reached the Spanish border." She rose from her place on the bed and leaned over the trunk. "You have some very pretty things."

"Thank you," I smiled. "Mama made most of them."

"She is a talented lady."

"Yes, she is."

"Haya is your aunt?"

"Yes," I nodded. "Mama's sister."

"Haya is older?"

"Yes."

"They are wonderful," she sighed, "Haya and all her family."

We continued to talk while I unloaded clothes from the trunk and placed them in the dresser drawers. Alona was easy to talk to and we rambled from topic to topic. Before I knew it, the trunk was empty and Maria was calling us to supper.

Over dinner I learned that Alona was from Poland and on her way to Palestine. "Hopefully," she added a glance in Haya's direction.

"You will get there," Haya reassured her.

"Papa went to Poland once," I offered. "A friend suggested glassware would make a nice addition to the merchandise in his shop. Papa traveled to Warsaw to meet with a manufacturer. It was a wonderful trip and he liked the things he saw, but Uncle Alois told him not to do business with the company. Papa wanted to do it anyway but Mama persuaded him to follow Uncle Alois' advice. It was a good thing, too. A few months later, the man who owned the company was arrested and the business was closed."

At the far end of the table, Haya cleared her throat and changed the subject, asking about David and Mama. Talking about them made them feel closer and while I was speaking I felt as though they were right there in the room. But as the conversation moved on to other things I realized again how far away they were and I missed them even more than before.

Alona disappeared after dinner and, while Maria cleared away the dishes, Haya led me to the front parlor. She took a seat in an upholstered chair near the fireplace. I took a seat on the sofa to her right.

"You are safe here in Cordova," she began, "but you must be careful. Openly practicing our religion is forbidden, but no one will harass you on the street so long as you avoid making your Jewishness an issue."

"That is a problem?"

"What?"

"That I am a Jew. It is a problem?"

"Yes." She had a troubled look and waited a moment before continuing. "You must keep your hair trimmed." She pointed to my curls. "Shorter than you have it now."

My fingers twirled around the curls that dangled just behind my ear. "I like my hair the way it is."

"It looks nice, but the curls have to go." She spoke in a matter-of-fact tone and continued without waiting for me to respond. "Dress with color. And above all, smile."

"I will do my best."

"I know you miss your family and it will take some time for you to get settled here, but it is in your best interest to adjust as quickly as possible."

Aunt Haya sat quietly for a moment and I was unsure if I should speak. Finally I asked, "How long have you known Alona?"

"Not too long."

"Why is she here with you?"

"As you heard, she is from Poland. Jews are in a very bad way there and I am simply trying to help her."

"That's hard to understand."

"What?" She turned in the chair to face me with an indignant look. "That I should help her?"

"No. That someone would be in a bad way because they are Jewish."

"Did your parents talk to you about why you were sent here?"

"Only that things were no longer good for me in Linz."

"Things are no longer good for anyone in all of Austria who is Jewish."

"What do you mean?"

"The trouble you had with your neighbor—"

"Karl Eichmann?"

"Yes. That was but a hint of the things to come. He and the National Socialist Workers Party want to remove us all from Europe."

"Why would anyone want to treat us that way?"

"They hate us. And they've been deceived. They believe lies told by people who only want to manipulate the public into supporting the political ambitions of tyrants. This will get much worse before it gets better."

"Well, whatever happened in Poland, Alona doesn't seem to want to talk about it."

"You may talk to her but do not discuss her with others."

"Is she in trouble?"

"She's not a fugitive. But we don't want any trouble, either. So, whatever you know about her, keep it to yourself when you go beyond the walls of this house."

"I will."

Conversation lagged again, then Aunt Haya picked up where she'd left off with details of my stay. "We will go to the Interior Ministry tomorrow. We must get you the proper identity papers."

"I have papers in my purse."

"Those are Austrian papers. They won't do you much good here. It's better to fit in as much as possible." Abruptly, she placed her hands on the armrest of the chair, pushed herself forward, and stood. "Maria should be done with the dishes by now. We need to get your hair trimmed." She motioned for me to follow and continued talking while she walked. "After we get the papers, we'll go to the school and register you for class."

"School?" I slid from the chair and followed after her. "So soon?"

"Yes." She glanced back at me. "Is that a problem?"

"I hadn't thought about going to school. I mean not so soon. Will they take me in the middle of the term?"

"I have made arrangements."

"I hope I can keep up."

"You have no choice but to try. The sisters will admit you now. In the fall, they may not be able to take you in."

"Sisters?"

"You'll be attending a Catholic school."

"Is that all right?"

"Yes. It is perfectly fine. And it will help you fit in here. Most of the country is Catholic."

When we reached the kitchen, Maria was waiting with a stool and towel. I took a seat and she draped the towel over my shoulders. She took a pair of scissors from a drawer beneath the counter and began cutting my hair. I watched as clumps of hair fell to the floor. Haya watched for a moment, then disappeared. I heard her coughing from down the hall.

Half an hour later, Maria was finished with my hair. She took a mirror from the drawer where the scissors had been and handed it to me. I held it up to see how I looked. The curls were gone and my hair no longer touched my shoulders. Mama would not like it but I thought it was cute. I smiled at Maria. "Good job."

"You like it?"

"It looks great."

"Good," she smiled. "Go show Mrs. Murillo."

I came from the kitchen and walked up the main hall to the front parlor. Aunt Haya was sitting in the chair near the fireplace. She looked up as I entered the room. A broad smile spread across her face. "Come here," she said, gesturing with her hand. "Let me have a look." I stood in front of her and slowly turned around. "That will do just fine," she said admiringly. "With it short like that, you don't look Jewish at all. You look…European, which is a good thing these days."

When she'd looked me over, she stood and started toward the stairs. I followed after her and we climbed up to the second floor. When we reached the upstairs hallway, she turned to me. "We go to the Interior Ministry early tomorrow. Maria will wake you." She placed her hands on my shoulders, drew me near, and kissed me on the cheek. "I am glad you are here. This will work out well for us both." Then she patted me on the back and started down the hall. "I must rest now. Tomorrow will be here soon."

I stood there a moment and watched as she tottered into her bedroom. When she closed the door, I turned and entered my own room. The door to Alona's room was closed and the house was suddenly dark and quiet. With nothing else to do, I changed into my pajamas and crawled into bed. It felt good to stretch out. I found it hard to believe that just a few hours earlier I had been on the train with Julia and Ernst.

chapter 10

As planned, Maria awakened me early the next morning. I washed my face at the basin in the room and went downstairs for breakfast. Afterward, Alberto drove us downtown to a building located not far from the train station. We climbed the stairs to the third floor and entered the office of the Interior Ministry. Inside the office, a counter ran across one end of the room. Aunt Haya stopped there. A few minutes later, a clerk appeared. "May I help you?" she smiled.

"I should like to see Juan Diego Berlanga," Aunt Haya instructed.

"And is he expecting you?"

"Yes."

"Very well." The clerk led us around the far end of the counter and escorted us through a doorway to an office. She rapped on the door and pushed it open to reveal a slender man with olive complexion and dark hair, seated at a desk. A table sat along the wall to the left and another to the right. Both were covered with stacks of files. The man at the desk looked up as we entered, then stood and gestured toward chairs that sat near the desk. "Mrs. Murillo," his eyes flitted from her to me and back to the desk. "Please. Have a seat."

While we took our seats, the clerk stepped outside and closed the door behind her, leaving us in the room alone with the man behind the desk, who I assumed was Berlanga. Aunt Haya didn't introduce him.

"This is your niece?" He avoided looking at me and instead focused on a file that lay open on the desk. "The one you told me about?"

"Yes," Aunt Haya nodded. "You are still able to help us?"

"Yes. Of course. It is my pleasure to assist you." He opened the top drawer of the desk and took out a form. "This is the application we discussed. I have taken the liberty of filling in most of the information." He glanced at it, then handed it across the desk. "You can look it over and make certain it is correct."

Aunt Haya took the form from him and scanned the information. I leaned to one side and read it while looking over her shoulder.

Berlanga continued to talk. "I used your address, and because you mentioned she would attend a Catholic School, I noted on the form that she is Catholic."

I was appalled but kept quiet. Haya smiled. "Good," she nodded. "Very good. I see you included Carlos' name."

He looked up at us. "Everyone likes families," he smiled.

"Right."

"And with his name, perhaps no one will ask questions."

"You have checked a box here that implies she is my daughter."

"As I told you before, this is the easiest way to obtain the necessary documents. No one will question this application. If I change it to note a more tenuous relationship, it could be months before the documents are issued, if at all."

Aunt Haya shook her head. "We don't want that."

"I did not think so."

Aunt Haya scooted the chair forward, laid the form on the desk, and reached for a pen that lay on the open file. Berlanga picked it up and offered it to her. She took it from him and handed it to me, then pointed to a line on the form. "Sign your name right there." I did as she instructed, then she signed below me and handed the form back to Berlanga.

While he blotted the ink from our signatures, Aunt Haya opened her purse and took out an envelope, which she laid on the desk. Berlanga set aside the blotter and picked up the envelope. "Very good," he smiled. He placed the envelope in the desk drawer and stood. "This will take only a few minutes. You can wait here." Then he came from behind the desk, crossed the room to the door, and was gone.

When we were alone, I turned to Aunt Haya to ask a question, but she held up her hand to stop me and shook her head. "Better to remain silent."

Before long, Berlanga returned and handed me an identity card and passport. "This will prove your identity and allow you to travel as a citizen of Spain." He offered me his hand, which I took. "Welcome to your new country."

I wasn't sure how to respond but after a moment managed to say, "Thank you." He nodded to me politely, then glanced at Aunt Haya. "Please send my greetings to your son."

From the time Mama first mentioned sending me to Spain, I had thought of many things—what it would be like to live far away from my immediate family, how different life in Spain might be from the life I had known, and I had wondered about the real reason they were sending me away. I had studied the picture of Haya on Mama's dresser and asked questions about their experiences growing up together. But in all of that, I never once asked about Haya's children. She had a daughter, Pilar, who lived with her husband in Malaga, on the Mediterranean, and a son, Oscar, who lived not far from Aunt Haya's house. Pilar was in her late teens when I was born. We never met. Oscar, on the other hand, was a little closer to my age. He came to our house once, when I was a young girl and he was about to graduate from high school. I remember the visit because in almost every conversation he mentioned something about his pending graduation, and after they returned home his comments became something of a joke between our parents.

On the ride back to the house I asked, "How does Berlanga know Oscar?"

"They met some years ago," Aunt Haya explained, "when Oscar was still in college. Juan Diego taught one of his classes."

"What does Oscar do now?"

"He works for the foreign office. You'll see him later." About that time we reached the house and she gestured out the window of the car. "I think he's here now."

Alberto turned the car into the driveway and I could see an automobile parked in front of the house, near the steps. We stopped behind it and I opened the door. Aunt Haya took my arm. "Wait, Alberto will get the door. That is his job. You mustn't take it from him."

I slid back in the seat and pulled the door closed. "I wasn't trying to take his job."

"I know." She patted me gently on the knee, just like Mama did when she'd spoken more strongly than she should. "I know you meant no harm."

Alberto opened the door for us and we started up the steps. Oscar came from the house and met us on the porch. "She's getting the last of her things now," he said, as if continuing a conversation already in progress.

"Good," Aunt Haya nodded. "She is anxious to go."

"I hope she isn't bringing too much."

"She only has the one piece of luggage."

"I was thinking of the weight."

Aunt Haya frowned at him. "They'll give her a stateroom, won't they?"

"Yes, but…I don't know," Oscar stammered. "This one makes me nervous."

"Relax." Aunt Haya patted him on the shoulder. "Everything will work out." She caught hold of his arm and gently turned him toward me. "Do you know who this is?"

"No," he had a puzzled look. "I can't say that I do." He smiled at me. "Have we met?"

"I am Sarah."

"Sarah?"

"This is your cousin, Orna's daughter."

The expression on his face stiffened.

"You'll be seeing more of her now. Perhaps you'll find the time to get better acquainted." Aunt Haya moved past Oscar and entered the house. Oscar followed her and I trailed behind. Alberto came last and nudged me at the door. I glanced up at him and he handed me an envelope.

"You left this on the seat." I recognized it immediately. It held the documents we'd just received from Juan Diego Berlanga at the Interior Ministry. "Better put them in a safe place," he smiled. I thanked him and hurried upstairs to my room to put them away.

When I returned downstairs I heard Aunt Haya's voice coming from the kitchen. She was louder than usual and so was Oscar. I tiptoed down the hall and stood near the door, listening.

"I can't take one more with me," Oscar said in an abrasive tone. "We are full for this trip."

"I'm not asking you to take her," Aunt Haya replied. "We couldn't send a child off like that anyway. Not at her age."

"Then what is the point of this?"

"She is staying here with me," Aunt Haya explained.

"No, Mother," Oscar argued. "She can't stay here."

"Why not?"

"It threatens everything. If the Nationalists find out, they'll use it against us. It'll become a scandal."

"Since when were you so worried about what the Nationalists have to say?"

"I'm not, but our ties to the monarchy are the only reason we are able to do this. If someone finds out that you used those connections to harbor her, they will use it to show that the monarchy is a government of special favors."

"Isn't it?"

"Yes. But that is not our problem. Our problem is getting Alona and people like her safely to Palestine. Or any other country that will take them."

"Relax," Aunt Haya lowered her voice. "This will all work out. You will see."

"No, it won't," Oscar argued angrily. "Not unless we make it work out. If this becomes a problem, they could force Interior officials to stop helping us. The entire operation will collapse. Lives will be lost."

"Sarah's life will be lost if I send her back."

"I know it's a difficult choice but—"

"No." Aunt Haya cut him off. "It's not difficult. She's my sister's daughter. I know what I must do."

"You must—"

"She stays and that's final. Now get on with your business and don't speak to me of this again."

Oscar stormed from the kitchen, brushed past me, and strode to the bottom of the staircase. "Alona!" he called in a loud voice. "We must be going."

Aunt Haya appeared at my side and we stood there together, watching as Alona came down from the second floor carrying a suitcase at her side. Oscar took it from her and started toward the front door. She turned toward us and we stepped forward to say goodbye. Before we were through, Oscar opened the door and called once more, "We really have to go." Alona turned away and walked to the door. As she stepped outside, she glanced back at us and waved.

I heard the car door close and the engine start, and then they were gone. Aunt Haya and I stood in the hall a moment longer, listening to the silence. Finally she spoke. "You heard our conversation in the kitchen?"

"Some of it." I looked up at her. "Would I really die if I had to go back to Austria?"

"Don't worry. I will never let that happen."

I knew she meant it, but already I had seen enough to know that forces were at work in our lives that neither of us could control. And the question occurred to me: If I would be in danger living in Austria, what about Mama, Papa, and David?

chapter 11

The following day, Aunt Haya enrolled me in school at the Cathedral of Cordova, a massive complex located across the river from our house. I was nervous and intimidated by the surroundings and by the language. I knew only a few words in Spanish. The school had no textbooks in German so they gave me books in French. Between the two—the smattering of Spanish I already knew and my anemic ability with French—I had a tough time keeping up.

At noon, we went outside to a courtyard to eat our lunch. We sat on the grass. Class members sat in groups of three or four. I sat down to eat alone. Before I could open my lunch, a girl sat down beside me and thrust her hand toward me. "I am Claudia Molla," she said in perfect German. "I am pleased to meet you."

As we talked I learned her family had recently returned from Germany, where her father worked at the Spanish Embassy in Berlin. While we were getting acquainted, a boy named Gabino Vega joined us. Gabino spoke only Spanish, so he and I communicated through Claudia.

* * *

Over the next few weeks, Claudia, Gabino, and I became good friends. Aunt Haya would not allow me to bring them to the house, but she did permit me to visit them in the park on Saturdays, and once or twice I accompanied them to church on Sunday. Each time, I was aware that policemen in blue uniform kept a watchful eye on us, usually from a respectful distance. And once or twice I noticed a man following us. He wore a dark suit and broad-brimmed hat and looked like something one might imagine from a Georges Simenon novel.

One Saturday, while the three of us were sitting on a bench in the park, one of the police officers who had been lurking about us all morning approached and began asking Gabino questions.

"I have noticed you in the park before—with your friends." He nodded to tip his hat in our direction. "But I never see your parents. Are you from around here?"

"Yes," Gabino replied.

"And what is your name?"

"Gabino Vega."

"I see. And do you have your identification card?"

"I am a student."

"Students are not exempt."

"He lives in the city," Claudia spoke up. "He isn't required to carry it. And besides, he's not old enough. Children are exempt."

"And who might you be?"

"I am Claudia Molla. My father works with the diplomatic office."

"I see." He turned his attention back to Gabino. "You realize if I take you into custody, your parents will have to appear in our office to obtain your release."

The tone of his voice irritated me. We had done nothing wrong. "Why would you do that?"

The officer cut his eyes at me. "You are not from Spain. Where are you from? Your accent. You are German?"

"Austrian."

"A Jew?"

"A girl. A schoolgirl who has done no wrong."

"Well, schoolgirl from Austria, do you have identity papers?"

"They are at the house."

"Did no one tell you that you are required to have them with you at all times?"

"I don't have mine, either," Claudia offered.

"Are you not a citizen of this country?"

"Yes. I am."

"Then you are not required, as long as you remain within the city." He looked at me. "But you, young lady, are supposed to have your identity card with you at all times."

"I won't forget it next time."

"See that you don't."

Claudia nudged me. "We should be going now anyway. Our parents will wonder where we are." She stood and turned to leave. The officer stepped aside to let her pass. I took Gabino by the hand and we followed her.

As we hurried down the walkway, he called after us, "Perhaps you should find somewhere else to play next time." We paid him no attention as we made our way from the park to the street.

At the corner, Gabino and Claudia boarded the bus. As she paid the fare, she glanced back at me. "Do not worry. He meant us no harm. My father would not allow it." I waved to her as she followed Gabino down the aisle to a seat.

In Linz I had been aware that some did not like me simply because I was a Jew. Karl Eichmann had made that painfully obvious, as had those who attacked us during Grandma's funeral. Living in Cordova, I found that most were accepting of me, but that day in the park I had a sense that other issues were at work, issues I did not fully understand or appreciate. When the officer approached us, I fully expected to be the focus of his attention, but I wasn't. Instead, he turned his attention to

Gabino, who, other than being a boy, bore no distinguishable outward difference from Claudia, and not much from me, either. I thought about this as the bus drove away from the park, turned at the next corner, and disappeared from sight.

Soon after the bus was gone, Alberto arrived to collect me. We returned home without further incident until I entered the house and discovered Oscar was waiting with Aunt Haya in the front parlor. Aunt Haya called me over to the sofa where she was seated. "Sit here with me. There's something we need to discuss."

Oscar, who stood near the fireplace, was less diplomatic. "What happened in the park just now?"

"How do you know about the park?"

"Never mind about that," he retorted. "Tell me what happened."

I told him about the policeman and how he questioned Gabino until first Claudia and then I intervened. My explanation did not allay Oscar's anger.

"Gabino Vegas' parents are Basques," he fumed. "They are part of a separatist organization—a group that wants to break away from the Spanish government. From the monarchy. The police are watching them. That is why he asked those questions."

"I am not Basque."

"He wasn't there to talk to you. He was just there to watch Gabino."

"We had done nothing wrong."

"It doesn't matter. You must have nothing more to do with this kid... this Gabino." He glanced over at Aunt Haya. "Actually, it would be better if she had nothing to do with either of them. Claudia's father works with the diplomatic staff." Aunt Haya raised an eyebrow and nodded her head.

"But they are my friends," I blurted out. "And they did nothing wrong."

Aunt Haya placed her hand on my knee. "Listen, Sarah," she began quietly. "What Oscar is telling you is important. I know it sounds harsh but you must trust me on this. You must have nothing more to do with them. Especially Gabino."

Tears filled my eyes. "This is worse than Austria. Gabino and Claudia are my friends."

"I know they are your friends, but we can't take the risk right now."

"But why?"

Aunt Haya turned sideways on the sofa to face me. "Sarah, political groups in this country are arguing over control of the government. The Basques are part of that disagreement. They want to break away and form their own territory with their own government. Others want to dissolve the monarchy entirely. We are caught in the middle."

"But how does that affect Gabino and Claudia?"

"Gabino's parents are active in one of those groups."

Oscar was frustrated. "She can't possibly understand," he sighed angrily.

"Can't understand what?" I retorted. "That you bring strangers to Haya's house but don't want *me* here? I understand very well what you mean. You don't mind associating with Jews, or protecting Jews, so long as no one knows you're a Jew, too."

"It's not like that."

"It is, too. If they find out I'm Jewish, they'll figure out you are, too. And you don't want them to know."

"Now, now. Let us not say things we will regret later. One day this will all work out, but we must be cautious. We are involved in a struggle as well and we must take care not to call attention to ourselves."

"We? I'm not involved in any struggle."

Aunt Haya gave me a knowing look. "Sarah, you above all people know the struggle we face. That is what brought you here. Oscar and I are doing our part, as is Alois. I know you are young, but it is time you face up to your responsibility as well. We are all in this together and we must all do our part."

"What does Uncle Alois have to do with anything?"

"He arranged for you to come here, for your safety after your conduct called attention to yourself."

"That was Karl Eichmann."

"Yes. But you disregarded the advice of your parents and ignored their warnings. Your imprudent behavior gave Karl Eichmann an opportunity to exploit the situation. He is a dangerous man and part of a dangerous group." She looked me in the eye. "These are dangerous times and we must each do our part if any of us is to survive."

"You know him? You know Karl Eichmann?"

"I remember him from when I was a little girl. He was older, a handsome teenage boy, and I was infatuated until my friends helped me see what he was really like and helped me understand the struggle we face." She looked away and coughed. "You must do as we say and avoid Gabino from now on."

"How will I do that without being rude? I see him every day in school."

"He will understand," Aunt Haya reassured. She started coughing again and I tried to comfort her but she waved me off. "It is nothing," she said as she dabbed the end of her nose with a handkerchief. "Now run along upstairs and wash. We will eat before long."

I stood and turned toward the doorway, but Oscar stopped me. "There is one more thing." He drew an envelope from the pocket of his jacket. "This came for you today." From the writing on the outside I could see the envelope contained a letter from Mama. I reached for it, but he moved it away. "I will give it to you, but I must tell you, I have asked them not to write. And you must not write to them."

Anger flared inside me. "Why not?"

"It is better if no one knows you are here."

"But I have papers from the government. Official papers that say I am here legally."

"And they will help you when you travel, but most people in the neighborhood already know who you are. We don't want to answer questions." He handed me the envelope and I rushed upstairs to read it. Loneliness swept over me, and the thought that I should be prevented from writing to Mama and Papa seemed absurd. No one could stop me from communicating with them.

* * *

The next morning I came downstairs for breakfast, still angry about the things Oscar and Aunt Haya had said to me the day before. As I entered the kitchen I found a stack of books on the table, all of them written in German. Aunt Haya stood near the counter, sipping a cup of coffee. I looked over at her. "What are these?"

"Your schoolbooks."

"They will let me use books in German?"

"You aren't going back to school," she said flatly.

"I'm not?" My lack of proficiency in Spanish made school difficult but I was doing better. That she suddenly would take me out seemed odd, especially after she'd made such a point of registering me. "Why am I not going back? I thought it was important."

"Education is important, but there are too many things about Cordova you do not yet understand." She gave me a thin smile. "It's not your fault. It's just the way things are. Enrolling you in school now was a hasty move on my part. That was my mistake. You will study here at home for the remainder of the year, and then we will see about school in the fall."

"I thought you said they might not take me in the fall."

"That may be a problem. But right now we have bigger issues to worry about. You can learn at home. I will help you and if that proves unworkable, we will hire a tutor." Maria set a plate of eggs on the table before me as Aunt Haya continued to talk. "You will follow a schedule. Class in the morning, and then you can help me in the afternoon." She gestured toward the plate. "Eat your breakfast before it gets cold."

After I finished eating, I took the books to a room off the parlor and sat at a table with a view of the garden.

* * *

At first I didn't like studying at home. School was always fun, even when classes were hard, and I enjoyed seeing my friends. Studying at home didn't feel like *real* school. After a few days, however, life settled into a rhythm. As Aunt Haya had instructed, I rose early and spent the morning studying downstairs. After lunch we worked together. She had an office on the third floor and some days we sorted through files up there. Other days we weeded the garden and worked outside as the weather allowed.

About three weeks after I left school, I was in the garden when a voice called to me in a coarse whisper, "Sarah. Sarah."

I turned to look behind me and there was Claudia, peeking out from behind a tree. She smiled at me and stepped out in the open. "Where have you been?"

"Right here."

"Why haven't you been in school? What's the matter?"

I looked away. "I can't talk about it."

"This is me," Claudia came near to press the issue. "You have to tell me what happened."

"It's because of Gabino—his parents, actually."

"What about them?"

"That day, in the park, with the policeman. That's why he was asking Gabino all those questions. He was only interested in me because I was with Gabino and I spoke up."

"I spoke up, too."

"Yes, but your father works for the diplomatic staff and I'm sure he knew it already. Besides, he wasn't really interested in you. He was following Gabino."

"And your aunt is afraid he will come for you, too."

"Yes," I nodded. "And they are worried about what might happen to me if I must return home."

Claudia looked puzzled. "I thought this was your home?"

Suddenly I realized I had said too much. "You should go now. I can't talk." I turned away and started toward the house. It was an abrupt departure and a few steps down the garden path I realized it must have struck her as rude, but when I glanced over my shoulder, Claudia was gone and I decided to leave it at that. It was best for us both.

As I came in the side door to the kitchen, I expected to find Maria standing near the sink or bent over a pot on the stove. Instead, the room was quiet, the stove was cold, and she was gone. I crossed the room to the hall and walked toward the stairs. As I turned to go up, I glanced into the parlor. Aunt Haya was seated in the chair by the fireplace. A man and woman sat on the sofa with a little girl next to them. They all turned to look in my direction as I came by. From the looks on their faces I was certain I had interrupted a conversation. To break the moment I caught Aunt Haya's eye and gestured over my shoulder. "Where's Maria?"

"I sent her to the store." She stood and came from the room to the hall where I was standing. When she was in front of me she lowered her voice. "Help me get them downstairs." She gestured with a roll of her eyes toward the people in the parlor.

All of this puzzled me. "But the bedrooms are upstairs."

"We don't need a bedroom." Her voice held a hint of frustration. "Help me get them downstairs. Quickly. Before Maria returns." I could feel my forehead wrinkle in a puzzled frown, but I nodded, "Okay."

Aunt Haya motioned for them to come and then she led the way down the hall to a door near the kitchen. She opened it to reveal a staircase that went down to the basement. We followed her down the steps and made our way past the furnace and coal bin. Beyond them we came to a wall lined with shelves. On the shelves were rows of jars filled with canned vegetables that had been harvested from the garden. Aunt Haya moved to the corner and grasped the end of a shelf. She glanced back at me and nodded. "Help me."

I stepped quickly to her side. "What are we doing?"

"Pull this away from the wall."

I grasped a lower shelf and pulled with her. Slowly all the shelves moved toward us and I could see the wall they were attached to was really a large door. Behind it was a finished room with four chairs, a table, and two small cots. A single light bulb dangled from the ceiling.

Haya turned to the man. "Wait in here, and do not be afraid."

"Yes," he nodded. "We will wait."

They stepped inside and then we closed the door. Aunt Haya checked to make sure all the jars were in their correct place, then we trouped back up the stairs. As we came to the first floor and closed the basement door, Maria entered through the side door carrying an armload of packages from the store. I helped her put them away while Aunt Haya took a seat at the kitchen table. When we finished with the packages, I helped Maria prepare supper. Aunt Haya watched. As I peeled a potato I glanced over at her. "Will the others be joining us?"

My question seemed to catch Aunt Haya off guard, but she quickly recovered and gave me a blank look. "What others?"

"The ones in the—" Haya cut me off with a look. I suddenly realized she didn't want Maria to know. My mind raced as I searched for a way to get off the topic. "I...thought...you said someone was joining us."

"They left already."

My attempt to cover for the mistake only made things worse. Maria had a quizzical expression. "Someone was here?"

"They stopped by while you were gone," Aunt Haya explained. "Nothing important. Just saying hello."

That night after dinner, I found a note on my bed. Written in Aunt Haya's hand it said simply, "Come to my room." I tucked the note into my pocket and walked down the hall to her bedroom. She was lying in bed, propped on pillows, reading a book as I stepped through the doorway. She gestured with her left hand and said in a coarse whisper, "Close the door." I pulled it shut behind me and stepped to her bedside. She patted the mattress with her hand in a gesture for me to sit, which I did. "I wanted to talk to you about what happened earlier in the kitchen, when you and Maria were preparing supper."

"Yes," I nodded. "I said too much."

"We must not talk about the things that happen here in front of Maria," she continued, still in a whisper.

I nodded once more. "But why not? Is she not helping us?"

"I'm not sure about her. Oscar said he heard some rumors about her and until we find out the truth, we'll have to be careful."

"Does she know about the room in the basement?"

"No." Aunt Haya gave her head a shake. "It was there before she came to work for me and I haven't told her." She pointed at me. "And don't you tell her, either." We talked a little longer, then I went to my room.

Late in the night, I was awakened by someone banging on the front door. For a moment I thought of all those things Oscar and Aunt Haya had said to me about the policeman in the park. Images flooded my mind with all the things that might happen to me. Then I heard Maria's voice as she answered the door. Moments later the sound of footsteps came from the hallway, followed by Haya's voice from downstairs. "There's no one here. No one at all."

A male voice responded in a gruff and demanding tone. "We have received evidence that you are harboring illegals. Recently arrived to the country. A man and woman with a young girl." I threw back the covers, came from the bedroom, and appeared at the top of the stairs. From there I had a clear view of the entryway at the front door and I could see the man was a policeman dressed in a blue uniform. He was not the officer who confronted us in the park and from that I gained great comfort. In my young mind I thought that if there were to be trouble over that incident, the officer we saw would be the one who caused it. That a different officer appeared at our door must mean trouble of a different sort.

When he saw me on the stairs he pointed up at me and called out in a loud voice, "You there! Who are you?"

"I am Sarah," I replied as politely as I could, not at all afraid anymore.

Haya looked alarmed. "She's my niece." I could hear the worry in her voice.

The officer's eyes were still fixed on me. "Let me see your papers," he demanded.

"They are in my room."

"Get them."

I hurried to the bedroom and opened the trunk. The envelope we received from the Interior Ministry was in a compartment on the top tray. I found it and took out the identification card, then rushed downstairs and handed it to the officer. While he looked at the card, I did my best to engage him in conversation. "What's your name?"

"Mendez," he answered without looking up.

"Is that all of it?"

He glanced at me. "Fernando Mendez."

"And where do you come from?"

"Barcelona."

"Do you have papers?"

He stopped reading and looked me in the eye. "I don't need papers, young lady. I am a soldier and a police officer."

"But how do we know that?"

"I have a uniform," he said with a tug of his shirt for emphasis.

"That's a nice uniform," I said with a smile. "But any good tailor can make a uniform."

"Yes," he grinned. "I suppose so."

I pointed to a medal on his chest. "You are wearing army medals on your policeman's uniform?"

"It is allowed. Now, about this—"

To his consternation I cut him off and continued to talk. "Any good silversmith could make those medals. What are they?"

He placed his finger on the first one. "This one is from a battle in France."

"You were in the war?"

"Yes."

"In school they told us Spain was neutral."

"That is true," he said with pride, "but I joined a separate unit. We defended the honor of the German people."

"And whose side are you on now?"

"The king, of course."

"And does the king—"

He saw my point and held up his hand for me to stop. "I have heard enough." He handed me the identity card and nodded to Aunt Haya. "Sorry to bother you. I am sure it was all just a mistake."

When they were gone, Aunt Haya glared at me. "That was very dangerous."

"It worked."

"Yes." She stepped toward me. "It was brilliant, but it was also very dangerous." Suddenly she grabbed me and hugged me close. "And very brave." She held me tight a moment, then let me go and pointed up the stairs. "Now back to bed."

chapter 12

The next morning, I was in the study reading and doing school-work, as had become my regular routine, when Aunt Haya entered the room. "I need your help. Come quickly."

I rose from my chair with a worried look. "Is something wrong?"

"We have to get the people from the basement." She was already at the doorway to the parlor. "Come quickly."

"But what about Maria?" I asked in a stage whisper. "What do we do about her?"

"I sent her to the meat market." She crossed the parlor to the hall with me following behind. "We'll have to hurry," she huffed. "Oscar will be here any moment."

She led the way down the basement steps and I helped her move the shelf aside. The man and woman were seated in the chairs. The little girl was asleep on one of the cots. When we entered, he stood to face us. "It's okay," Aunt Haya smiled. "It is time to go." They seemed not to understand at first but then the man smiled and nodded. He picked up the girl from the cot, and the woman, still looking a little confused, followed. We pushed the door closed with the shelves back in place and then started upstairs.

As we came up the hall toward the front door, Oscar arrived. I could see his car through the window. Just then, I heard the side door open and there was the sound of footsteps in the kitchen. Panic seized me. Aunt Haya turned to look over her shoulder in my direction. From the look in her eye I knew she was scared too, but in an instant I knew what to do.

I gestured for them to go ahead and while they continued toward the door, I stepped in the opposite direction and entered the kitchen. Maria stood at the icebox with several packages of meat. They were wrapped in white paper from the butcher and stacked in her arms like firewood, which made it difficult for her to move. I stepped toward her. "Here, let me help you." I reached around her in an awkward manner and clumsily opened the icebox door, making sure to do so carelessly. As I did, the door banged into the packages in her arms, knocking them to the floor.

"Oh no!" I exclaimed. "I am so sorry."

"It is no problem," she replied with a strained smile. "You were only trying to help."

We stooped to pick them up and I made sure to drop them again. It became comedic and I started giggling. Then Maria began to laugh and by the time we finally got the packages in the icebox, we were out of breath. As we closed the door, Aunt Haya entered the room. "Did you get everything?" she asked with a smile.

"Yes," Maria nodded. "I purchased everything you asked."

"Great," she beamed. "We will have an excellent dinner tonight." Then with a stern expression she pointed at me. "And you, young lady, need to get back to your studies." The tone of her voice was gruff, but I could see the twinkle in her eye and knew she was pleased with the way I handled the situation.

* * *

The next day, Maria asked if I could accompany her to the central market, a rambling collection of shops and kiosks that covered a city block near the middle of town. Aunt Haya was opposed to me going but Maria persisted and, reluctantly, Aunt Haya agreed. Alberto drove us there in the car. After we were finished shopping, we were supposed to take the bus back as far as the river, and Alberto would collect us there.

At midmorning we left for the market. Alberto dropped us on the corner near the fish merchants. I walked with Maria as she moved slowly and deliberately from vendor to vendor. She spent a lot of time looking at the items each merchant offered for sale, but I noticed her shopping basket had little in it.

An hour or so into our venture, I stood near a bin filled with apples, wondering about the price for just one, to eat right then. I turned to ask Maria but she was nowhere in sight. Just then Gabino stepped out from behind a stack of wooden crates. The sight of him startled me and for an instant I smiled at him, then I remembered the warning from Oscar. I turned away and moved down the aisle, my head down and my eyes focused on nothing but avoiding Gabino's gaze.

He came alongside me, as I knew he would. "Please, don't ignore me," he implored. I glanced at him. "I need your help," he pleaded. He had an earnest look on his face, but his eyes showed no fear or worry.

"With what?" I tried not to sound interested.

"My parents were killed and I have nowhere to go."

"And you think I can help?"

"I have heard your aunt gives safe passage to those in need and I was hoping you would convince her to help me." His face softened as he spoke to me and his words sounded stilted and awkward. Still, he was my friend and I felt obligated to help. I was about to agree to speak to Aunt Haya when I caught a glimpse of Maria, watching from the corner of a vendor's booth not far away. Then I remembered Aunt Haya's suspicions about her.

"I'm sorry," I said, shaking my head. "You are mistaken." Then I turned away and walked in the opposite direction from where Maria stood.

Gabino followed after me. "But everyone says she can help," he said, sounding more angry than desperate.

"I am sorry you have believed those rumors." I spoke without looking at him and walked quickly toward an exit. "There is nothing she can do."

Behind me I heard Maria speaking to someone, but she spoke too rapidly for me to understand. Then I heard Gabino respond and my heart sank. I was certain it had been a trap designed to trick me into betraying Aunt Haya, a trap that I narrowly escaped. I quickened my pace to avoid being stopped by Maria and reached the exit before she could grab me.

Outside, I crossed the street to the bus stop and climbed aboard the first bus that came by. Thankfully, it took me all the way to the river and I walked home from there. Aunt Haya was surprised to see me back so soon. "You are home early," she smiled. "Where is Maria?"

"Still at the market, I suppose." Then I told about the incident with Gabino and how I was certain Maria had set it up.

Aunt Haya nodded thoughtfully. "You do not think Gabino's parents really were killed?"

"I think it was a trap."

"Why?"

"The way Maria acted, leaving me there like that and then watching. The way Gabino talked to me. I did not like it."

"You may be right. I will contact Oscar and see what he can find out."

For the remainder of the day I stayed in my room, reading and listening for Maria. I was anxious to find out what might happen when she returned, but by noon she had not come home and I began to wonder if she ever would. Then, a little before four, I heard her in the kitchen. Aunt Haya was down there and they were talking but I could not hear what they said, only the rumbling sound of voices as their conversation drifted through the house.

We had supper as usual. Maria served us in the dining room. She said nothing to me about our trip to the market and Aunt Haya made no mention of the day's events. Later that evening, Oscar came to the house. Aunt Haya called me into the parlor and I told them again what happened at the market.

Oscar was frustrated by my lack of discretion earlier, when we were preparing supper a few nights before and I mentioned the people in the basement room. He was certain that what I said made Maria suspicious and might have compromised their effort. But, having aired his sentiment completely on that matter, he conceded with a smile, "At least you had the presence of mind to keep quiet in the market and to come to us."

There was now no reason to avoid the questions that had been on my mind, so I took a deep breath and asked, "Why were the people hiding in the basement?"

Oscar stood near the fireplace. Aunt Haya sat on the sofa. He glanced over at her and she responded with a nod. Then his shoulders sagged, as if letting down his guard. "They were Jews escaping Germany, on their way to Palestine."

"Escaping Germany? Something has happened in Germany?"

"With the rise of the National Socialist Workers Party, things have gone from bad to worse for our people. They have not been very successful yet in elections but their campaigns have stirred the people against us. It does not look good. As many as are able are getting out."

"Alona was going to Palestine," I countered, "but she stayed upstairs in a bedroom."

"Alona was from Poland," Aunt Haya explained. "And she had proper documentation from the Polish government."

"And the others had no papers?"

"No," Oscar shook his head. "They had no papers and very little else except for the clothes on their backs."

"They were poor?"

"They were forced into it."

"But how?" It seemed incredible to me that one could be forced to live in poverty.

"Look," Oscar sighed. "I'm not sure how much of this you can understand or even need to know." He paused, as if considering whether to continue. "But," he said finally, "I suppose if you're going to live here you might as well know something of what we face." He placed his hands in his pockets. "The German process for emigration is unpredictable at best. Whether they issue proper documents to Jews depends very much on the clerk involved and the person making the request. The people you saw here at the house were certain they would never get official permission to travel. So they decided to leave everything behind and simply get out."

"They just walked away from everything they owned?" The thought of it left me feeling lonely and hollow inside.

Oscar turned away, a distant look in his eye. "If our sources inside the German government are accurate, they made a wise decision."

"They came to us," Aunt Haya continued, "because the British government controls Palestine and puts strict limitations on the number of Jews who can move there to live. We are able to get around those limitations by using our contacts in the Spanish government who issue the appropriate documents, as if the person were a Spanish citizen."

"A non-Jewish Spanish citizen," Oscar added. "There are no immigration limitations on them."

"Only, not everyone in Spain agrees with us," Aunt Haya interjected.

"As we mentioned to you earlier," Oscar went on, "we are caught in the middle, between those who oppose the king and those who are loyal, between those who hate Jews and those who don't, between those who want to return to Palestine and those who think it's a bad idea." He sighed, "And now our entire operation is in the hands of a ten-year-old."

"Twelve," I corrected.

"Okay," he shrugged. "A twelve-year-old."

"What about Maria? What will happen to her?"

"I'm not sure," Oscar replied. "Has she said anything to you about it?"

"No, not a word."

"Then don't say anything to her about it. Act like nothing has happened, at least until we find out what Alois says."

* * *

A few days later, I was studying in the room off the parlor when Oscar's car turned into the driveway. It came to a stop in front of the house and the passenger door opened. My heart leaped when I saw Uncle Alois climb from the front seat. I ran from the room, threw open the front door, and raced down the steps to him. He was startled when I wrapped my arms around his neck.

"They didn't tell me you were coming!" I exclaimed.

"I thought it would be best that way."

"I'm just glad you're here."

Oscar came from the driver's side of the car and took Uncle Alois' suitcase from the back seat. Then we all climbed the steps to the porch, where Aunt Haya was waiting. They greeted each other with a hug and a kiss on the cheek, then she took him by the arm and led him inside. Oscar carried the luggage upstairs and gestured for me to follow. When we reached the second floor he turned to me. "Let's give them a few minutes to visit alone. She hasn't seen him in over a year." I was disappointed not to spend every minute with Uncle Alois, but I understood their need to catch up on each other's lives. Instead of bounding downstairs, I retreated to my room.

A little while later, Aunt Haya called for me. I came to the hallway and leaned over the banister. She stood at the bottom of the stairs. "Come down here, please. You need to visit with your uncle."

When I reached the first floor I found Uncle Alois waiting in the hallway. Aunt Haya gestured to him and took me by the hand. "Let's take a walk outside. We can visit while we stroll."

We walked out to the front porch, then made our way slowly around the house to the garden. Aunt Haya suggested I tell him what happened at the market and I recounted the incident for him. When I finished, he had a thoughtful look. "You are certain Maria arranged this?"

"Yes," I nodded. "That was the way it seemed."

"And why do you think she did that?"

"I don't know, but she was suspicious when the others were here."

"Yes," he nodded. "You almost said too much."

"I know." I looked away and dropped my chin. "I should have been more careful."

"It was a mistake," Uncle Alois smiled. "But you learned from it."

"I felt certain Gabino was trying to trick me into showing him the basement room."

"More likely," Uncle Alois observed, "he wanted you to admit it was there and that Haya was involved in hiding people."

"That would have been worse," Aunt Haya added.

"In this business, our mistakes not only endanger us, they endanger many others as well."

I turned to Aunt Haya. "That's when I remembered what you said about not telling anyone about the room. So I just walked away from him."

"I am glad you did," she smiled.

The three of us continued to talk as we made our way through the garden and around to the front porch again. When we reached the steps, Uncle Alois suggested I might like a treat—ice cream or a soft drink. Aunt Haya agreed, though she declined to accompany us.

Uncle Alois and I took Oscar's car and drove across the river to a café on the south side of town. He had coffee and I had an orange-flavored soda. We sat at a table near the wall and talked of the latest news from home: Papa and the increasing difficulty he encountered running the shop, Mama and her role playing violin with the orchestra, and David still in school. Hearing about them made me happy, even if it reminded me that they were far away.

When we had finished our drinks we returned to the car. Uncle Alois drove slowly through town, looping past the railway station on what I was sure was the longest way back to the house. While we rode through the streets of Cordova, we talked about what was happening.

"Aunt Haya and Oscar are really helping people get to Palestine?"

"Yes," he grinned. "They really are. And you are helping them."

"They say you are helping."

"We are doing this together."

"Isn't that illegal?"

"Somewhat," he laughed. "For the British, at least."

"But not for us?"

"Not for the Spanish. They don't mind how many people go to Palestine."

"What about in Austria?"

"The Austrian government has tried for years to get rid of the Jews. They would be glad if we all moved there."

"So if you help Jews leave Austria, you are helping the Austrian government, too?"

"Yes," he chuckled. "I suppose I am. I'm helping the governments of Austria, Spain, and the settlers in Palestine." His eyes opened wider. "And Germany and France as well." We both laughed together and for a moment it seemed like nothing had changed between us, but we both knew nothing would ever be the same again.

An hour later, we crossed the river and turned onto the street that led to Aunt Haya's house. As we neared the driveway, I saw three police cars parked at the curb. Another was parked on the driveway near the front steps to the house. Two officers stood on the porch with Maria between them. As we slowly drove past the house, the officers escorted her down the steps.

Uncle Alois steered us around the patrol cars and we continued up the street. "Do not be afraid," he said reassuringly. "It is for the best."

"I'm not afraid. I was expecting something like this."

"You are a very perceptive young lady."

"Mama says I'm nosy."

"Not nosey," he waggled his finger. "Curious."

"Curious?"

"You have a natural curiosity about things. I noticed if from you when you were just a little girl. When you see things, you want to know why, or how. You don't even have to make yourself do it. Those questions naturally spring to your mind." As he talked, a wide grin spread across my face. He was right and we both knew it. "Don't worry," he nudged me playfully on the shoulder. "That's one of the traits that makes for a great lawyer."

Thirty minutes later we were back at the house and the police were gone. Oscar and Aunt Haya were waiting for us on the porch.

Uncle Alois stood with his thumbs hooked casually in the waistband of his trousers. "I see you confirmed what we already suspected."

"Yes," Oscar nodded. "They already had her under surveillance."

Their conversation puzzled me. "What are you talking about?"

"The police arrested Maria," Oscar replied. "She was working to destroy the monarchy."

"But why?"

"It doesn't matter."

"I think we're beyond that," Uncle Alois suggested. Then he turned to me. "Maria was part of an organization known as The Popular Front, a group working to overthrow the monarchy."

"Were they after me?"

"No," Oscar answered. "You were never their primary concern."

"In fact," Uncle Alois grinned, "your information about what happened in the market was the tip they needed. You connected Maria to Gabino's parents. Once they made that connection, they arrested her."

"And Gabino's parents were arrested?"

"That part of what Gabino told you was true," Uncle Alois nodded. "His parents were arrested last week. But the rest of it was a lie. He's been staying with Maria's cousin."

"So it really was a trap."

"A serious one."

"But we still have one serious issue remaining," Aunt Haya said grimly.

"What?" Oscar frowned.

"With Maria gone, who's going to cook dinner?"

"It will take some time to find a new housekeeper," Oscar observed. "Until then, you and Sarah will have to do your own chores."

"We can do that," I agreed.

"Cooking, cleaning, gardening, market." Oscar ticked them off on his fingers.

"We will manage," Aunt Haya insisted. Then she looked over at me. "But we will have to work together."

"We could find you another place," Oscar suggested. "Something more manageable."

"Nonsense," Aunt Haya scoffed. "I've been in this house since I married Carlos. I'm not about to move." She took Uncle Alois by the arm and leaned against him. "Come inside. We still have things to talk about."

cḩapter 13

*L*ife without a housekeeper was a little more difficult than I first imagined, but it soon settled into a rhythm—study in the morning, lunch, a trip to the market, followed by cleaning, gardening, more study at night, and sleep. Oscar and Aunt Haya continued to harbor people at the house, but with Maria no longer there, the guests were free to move about the upper floors, using the basement room only to hide when someone else came by.

As the years passed and I grew older, I paid more attention to the news and to events around me. I developed a greater awareness of just how vulnerable Jews were in Europe and of the sentiment gathering against us—discontentment in Germany over the way the Armistice was handled following the Great War; pervasive blame of the Jews as the real source of trouble; and deep divisions in Spain pitting Nationalists against the monarchy, workers and laborers against land owners and capitalists.

Nationalist groups continued to operate in the countryside but were largely ineffective until Francisco Franco defected from the army to join them. Very quickly he became the leader of the Popular Front, the same group to which Gabino's parents and Maria had belonged. The unrest they created put serious pressure on the Spanish government, first in the form of general strikes and later through military action, several times threatening to bring the government to an end. Oscar worked hard to stay on top of the latest developments, hoping to maintain his relationship with the existing government while developing new ones with the Nationalists. The chaos that often enveloped Cordova actually worked to our benefit. With so many people coming and going, no one paid any attention to visitors at the house.

At the same time, Haya's health continued to deteriorate, first confining her to the house, then to the second floor, and finally to her bed. As she became incapacitated, I gradually took over the task of running the household. My cooking wasn't that great at first but Aunt Haya never complained and I learned to make it better. Refugees who stayed with us pitched in to assist but even with that, cleaning and washing occupied most of my day. Many days, studying was limited to an hour or two in the morning and a few minutes at night before I fell asleep. Aunt Haya did her best to keep my mind active by engaging me in lively discussions of Jewish traditions and Spanish history. Most of those conversations were held in the evening while she lay in bed.

In the spring when I turned seventeen, Oscar arrived with news of rumors that the Nationalists would soon attack Cordova in an all-out push to gain control of the entire district. They had been fighting to the south and east but now Franco's troops also were amassing to the west.

"If they attack," Oscar worried, "the city will not fall easily. This could be a prolonged battle. Living conditions will become quite dangerous and miserable."

"What should we do?"

"You and Mother should go to the mountains," he suggested. "I know of a cabin that will be available. It will be much easier for you there. Here, the house is simply too large."

"You mean go to the hills above Cordova? That hardly seems worth the trouble."

"No, the mountains east of Granada."

"Out of the question," I objected. "Haya is not well enough. She can't travel like that. The trip alone would kill her."

"I'm not leaving," Haya announced from her bed. "If I must die, I want to die in my own home. I gave birth to my children here, I raised my family here—this is where I want to be, regardless of the consequences." Oscar tried to convince her to leave, but she insisted on staying and I would not abandon her.

* * *

A few months later, the Nationalists still had not attacked, though there were continual reports about forces gathering around the city and food was sometimes in short supply. Perhaps I was young and naive, but in those days I never gave much thought to what the fighting might mean to us. My primary concern was Aunt Haya. As time went by, breathing became more difficult for her and she coughed constantly, often spitting up bloody clumps of mucus. Most days she suffered from persistent fever, followed at night by profuse sweating, which meant her bedclothes had to be changed and washed daily. All the while her weight continued to drop. Many times I wanted to call a doctor but she refused to allow it. Near the end of his life, Haya's husband, Carlos, developed the same symptoms. A doctor prescribed medication for him but Aunt Haya was convinced it only made him worse.

One afternoon, late in the summer, I went up to Aunt Haya's bedroom with tea and a few small cakes arranged on a tray. We were in the habit of making it our supper, which we consumed together—her propped in bed, me sitting at her bedside in one of the straight-backed chairs. That evening as I came through the doorway, I saw her lying there, eyes closed, head slumped to one side. Her mouth gaped open and her tongue lay to one side. I knew she was no longer alive.

I set the tray on a bedside table and leaned over her, putting my ear near her nose. When I heard no sound of her breathing, I pressed my ear to her chest. There was no sound from her heart and her chest did not move. Tears filled my eyes.

Through the window to the west I saw the last rays of sunlight receding below the horizon. Darkness was close behind. I sat beside her on the bed and watched as shadows in the room faded into the blackness of night. After a while, I switched on the lamp by her bed. I thought of covering her body as Mama and I had covered Grandma years before, but she was already in bed with the covers to her chin, so I pulled the sheet a little higher and draped it over her face. Then I went downstairs to the phone in the hall and called Oscar.

Later that night, women from the burial society came to the house and prepared Aunt Haya for burial. A rabbi arrived at midmorning the next day and conducted a private funeral. Shortly after noon, I rode with Oscar to a cemetery on the north side of town and placed her in a grave. There were no friends or family present, just the two of us with men from the burial society who filled in the grave.

From the cemetery, we drove through town in silence. Then, as we passed the central market, Oscar cleared his throat and glanced over at me. "Sarah." His voice was tense. "I think it is time for you to return to Austria."

His words caught me off guard and I looked at him for a moment, unable to respond. Then finally I managed to ask, "But…why?" Since arriving in Cordova everyone told me that Austria was no longer a safe place for me to live and that I could never return there. I had not believed them at first, but now, after almost six years, I was convinced they were right. Returning to Linz would be a step back and the thought of doing so made me ill.

"Cordova is no longer a good place for you." Oscar used words he'd said many times before, only now as a reason I should leave. "Nationalists control most of the surrounding region. All but the city is in their hands. Soon there will be full-scale war."

I found his arguments disingenuous. He had said the same thing many times before and yet war had not come. I wanted to argue with him about that but I resisted the impulse and focused on the matter at hand. "Can't I go on to Palestine?"

"You have no money, and right now I am not in a position to facilitate such a trip."

"Then what should I do?" I was frustrated and on the verge of tears, but I willed myself not to cry, not in front of him.

"I am going to Granada," he said with a hint of cheer in his voice. "You must return to Austria."

"Is returning to Austria any better than remaining here?"

"I do not think it is as bad as they say. At any rate, you cannot stay here now. Perhaps in a year or two you may return."

"A year or two?"

"Look." His voice was sharp and his face even more serious than before. "There's a train leaving in the morning, probably one of the last to leave the city. I'll pick you up around eight and see you to the station. I can pay for your way back to Linz, but that's all I can do."

"Just like that?" I threw my hands in the air in a gesture of frustration. "After all these years, that's it?"

"I'm sorry." He turned away and looked out the side window. "It must be this way."

When we arrived back at the house, workmen were moving the furniture from the house and loading it onto a truck. I came from the car, mouth agape at the awful sight. "What are they doing?"

Oscar placed his hand on my shoulder. "I had hoped they would be finished by now and at least spare you the pain of seeing this."

"What are they doing?" I tried to move toward them but he stopped me.

A man dressed in an army uniform came from the house and approached us. He glanced at me but quickly turned his attention to Oscar. "The paperwork is waiting for you on the dining table." He gestured with his thumb over his shoulder. "See that you sign it in the places noted."

"I'll take care of it now," Oscar replied.

"I'll be back to get it in an hour," the officer continued. "The workmen should be finished by then." He nodded to me, stepped around Oscar, and disappeared behind the truck.

I followed Oscar inside. "Paperwork? What paperwork? What's he talking about? What are you doing?"

"The government is taking the house," Oscar explained in an officious tone.

"Taking it?" I shouted. "Just like that? They can't just take it."

"They're paying me for it. Not what I could have gotten for it a few years ago, but at least it's something. Enough to get me started again in Granada."

"This is why you're sending me home?"

"This is why you can't stay here any longer." He turned to face me and looked me in the eye. "Sarah, whether you choose to return to Austria or not is your business, but as you can see, staying here is no longer an option."

"But I have nowhere else to go."

"Then I suggest you be ready in the morning at eight. I've arranged for them to leave your room untouched until then."

chapter 14

In the morning, Oscar drove me to the train station and purchased a ticket for Austria. He handed it to me and walked with me to the platform. "I'm sorry it has come to this, Sarah. I really am. But I see no other way." He looked at me as if waiting for me to respond, but I had nothing else to say. The conductor alighted from the coach and called us aboard. I turned to leave and Oscar took my hand to help me to the steps. "I'll do my best to get word to your family of your pending arrival." As I stepped into the car I glanced back at him. "That would be good."

A few days later, I arrived at the railway station in Linz. Papa was waiting for me on the platform. He looked older and thinner and his face was lined with wrinkles. I departed the coach and gave him a hug. He embraced me but not at all in a friendly way. I ignored the stoic look on his face and started chattering about Mama and David. All the while, Papa kept glancing around nervously and finally insisted we leave at once.

At the opposite end of the train, workmen unloaded luggage from the baggage car. Some pieces they carefully stacked on carts and wheeled into the station. Others they carelessly tossed into a pile on the platform. My trunk was in that pile. "What are they doing with those cases?"

"Shh," Papa said sharply. "Don't talk like that."

"But why are they throwing those cases out like that? And why are we down here?"

"Don't you have a trunk?"

"Yes, but shouldn't we retrieve it from inside?"

"We'll get it here."

He moved gingerly through the crowd and I followed him to the pile of discarded baggage. There in the heap, I saw my trunk. "What is this?" I looked up at the men in the baggage car. "Why is my trunk thrown over here and not on a cart?"

A policeman moved toward me but Papa intervened. "I am sorry, officer." He removed his cap and bowed. "She is just visiting with us and does not understand our customs. I assure you she meant no offense."

He glared at Papa, then looked past him, his eyes roving over me. "See to it that you keep her under control."

"Yes, sir," Papa bowed once more.

He turned away from the officer, replaced his hat atop his head, and started toward the pile of luggage. As he passed me he said tersely, "Keep your mouth shut."

Papa pulled my trunk from the pile, hoisted it onto his shoulder, and carried it from the platform toward the station building. As we approached the doors, he turned and walked along the edge of the building to the corner. A cart sat there and he put the trunk on it, then walked around to the front and picked up the forks where a horse would have been harnessed. With slow, plodding steps, he started forward and we walked up the street away from the station.

I could not believe what I was seeing. "First, they insult us by tossing my trunk aside. Then an officer confronts us and you bow to him. And now we are walking?"

"The exercise will do you good."

"But why?"

"Because we have no car."

"What happened to it?" I walked beside him, flailing my arms and talking loudly. He remained expressionless, his head down, putting one foot in front of the other.

"Someone in the Ministry of Finance office wanted it."

"You sold it?"

"They took it."

"Took it?" I felt as if I had fallen into a nightmare. "They just took it? Without paying for it? Papa, that isn't right."

"They raised the taxes on it and when I couldn't pay, they seized it."

"Well, then why don't we get a taxi?"

"You ask too many questions. You always ask too many questions."

"But I thought you'd—"

"You should never have come back here."

"I had no choice. Haya died."

"I know she died, but you should have stayed there. Made a life for yourself."

"Oscar told me to leave."

"Oscar is an idiot. You never should have come back here."

A man banged into the cart. He shouted and yelled at us and kicked Papa in the shin. Papa doffed his hat and moved on. I was wide-eyed as I watched the scene unfold before me. "What has happened?" I scanned the streets and tried to make sense of it. Around us, the city seemed drab and grimy. The faces of the people we passed were blank and emotionless.

"Too many questions," Papa continued. "You ask too many questions."

"I want to know," I insisted. "I want to know what happened."

He brought the cart to a stop and turned to me. "Look around you, Sarah. Things have changed. This is not the Linz you once knew."

"But why?"

"The Republic is over. Fascists are in control. And they hate us."

"Hate us? Hate Austrians?"

"No, they hate Jews."

An hour later we arrived at home. Mama saw us coming and raced down the sidewalk to greet us. Like Papa, she looked older than I had imagined but when she threw open her arms and hugged me close, things seemed almost normal.

That evening, after supper, Stephan Rovina came for a visit. I had thought of him often while living in Spain, but until that night I did not realize how much I had missed him. He had the kindest eyes and when he looked at me everything else disappeared and it was as though we were alone, even on a crowded street. We walked outside to the front porch and sat on the edge at the top of the steps.

"Mama and Papa do not seem happy to see me," I complained.

"Things are different now."

"Everyone says that. They said that when I left for Spain. They said it when they wanted me to leave Spain and come back here. Now I get back, and everyone is saying it again. Okay. Things have changed. But I'm still their daughter. I am glad to see them. Why can't they be glad to see me?"

"I'm sure they are, but when they see you here, they don't think of how beautiful you are, or how smart you are, or what a great future you have. They think only of what could happen to you and it makes them sad."

I smiled at him. "Did you just tell me I'm beautiful?"

"Yes," he grinned, and he leaned over to kiss me on the cheek. But before he could reach me, I turned toward him and met his lips with mine. His eyes opened wide and we giggled. Then he kissed me again and I enjoyed it.

"I am glad to see you," he whispered, "but even I wish you had never come back."

My forehead wrinkled in a frown. "I don't understand."

"In Spain, you were far from me and I thought of you every day. But I knew you were safe and nothing would happen to you there. At least that way we had hope for the future."

"You don't think there is hope for the future now?"

"When the Republic died, Austria died with it. Now all the anger and bitterness that lay beneath the surface has come out in the open. They hate us. And I don't think that will change for a very long time."

chapter 15

*L*ater that week, I enrolled for my final year of secondary classes. Unlike before, the school was divided into classes for Jews and non-Jews. Only Jewish teachers were allowed to interact with us, and each grade was limited to a single classroom. Often there were not enough desks or chairs for everyone. Many of the boys stood for the entire day, as no one was permitted to sit on the floor.

We were not allowed to loiter outside on campus either, even at noon, which meant we ate lunch inside, regardless of the weather. When we passed non-Jewish students in the hallway, we were forced to stand aside and let them go by unhindered. And when they went by, we were required to bow our heads and look down, never making eye contact with them. As you might expect from that, we were often subjected to hazing, harassment, and physical abuse.

Stephan and I had been friends all our lives and during that year our relationship became much more. I was fond of Stephan, and if I had been honest with myself I would have admitted that I loved him. Still, I was unable to shake the memory of Adolf and I wondered what happened to him. He was my first crush, a childhood infatuation, but I could not put him from my mind. Once or twice each week, as I came home from school or walked to the store for Mama, I found a reason to walk past the house where his parents lived. Each time, I studied the windows hoping to catch a glimpse of him.

Finally, one winter afternoon, I saw his sister, Ilsa, on the sidewalk near their house. I hurried to catch up with her and when I was along-side her I greeted her with a smile. She was startled to see me and before I could speak she hissed at me, "What are you doing here?"

"I was wondering about Adolf."

"What about him?"

"Where is he? I haven't seen him since I came back."

"He's not here," Ilsa growled. "Why do you ask so many questions?"

"I just wanted to know what—"

"You don't know anything."

"I was just—"

"I see you every day—coming by our house. Looking in from the alley. You think no one notices, but I do and I've got one thing to say to you." She leaned closer, her face just inches from mine, and shouted, "Stay away from our house!"

Her intensity startled me, but I refused to let her intimidate me. Instead I kept smiling. "I was just wondering about Adolf."

"Well, you should not be so curious."

"Why not?"

She turned away and continued up the sidewalk. "Because you are a filthy Jewish pig. And a stupid whore."

"Adolf is my friend," I continued, unwilling to give up.

"No Jew would ever be the friend of an Eichmann."

"Why not?"

"Because we wouldn't allow it!" she shouted. "That's why."

"Well, he's my friend."

"Don't talk to me," Ilsa shouted. "Leave me alone. Stay away from me. Stay away from us. We don't want you passing by our house." She spit on me and shoved me from the sidewalk to the street. "Walk on the other side!" she shouted and shoved me again. "Walk on the other side of the street."

By then others had stopped to see what was happening and they began to chant, "Other side of the street, Jew! Other side of the street!" When I didn't move fast enough, they stepped toward me shouting the phrase over and over as they drew closer and closer.

Just when I thought they would overtake me, Stephan appeared at my side and took me by the hand. "Let's go," he led me away. They followed us into the street, shouting and cursing. Someone threw a bottle at us. Several more threw rocks and others began shouting insults. "Get away from us! Stupid pigs! Haven't you got sense enough to know we don't want your kind around here?"

When we were safely away from them, Stephan turned to me with a desperate look. "What were you doing?"

"I was trying to talk to Ilsa."

"What?" He was beside himself. "Why were you talking to her?"

"I know her. She's our neighbor." Only moments before perfectly calm, even while the crowd yelled at me, but now my hands shook and my voice quivered. Yet inside I was determined to do as I pleased. "I only wanted to talk to her."

"Not anymore," he said grimly.

"What do you mean?"

"I don't know what it was like in Spain, but here in Linz it's forbidden for Jews to talk to them, unless they approach us first."

My mouth dropped open and my eyes were wide. "Forbidden?"

"I told you, things have changed. From now on, you don't know anyone who isn't a Jew."

"That's crazy."

"Yes, it is, but it's safe." Stephan quickened his pace. "We have to get you home."

"I would never live like that. Not talking to someone just because they are different from me is a ridiculous way to live."

"Yes, but it's a safe way to live. And you'll live that way," he insisted.

"I most certainly will not." I was angry. "No one can make me live that way."

"Yes, they can."

"Why? Why would anyone live that way?"

He came to an abrupt halt and took me by the arm. "Because you don't want to go to the camps."

"What camps?" I was puzzled. "What are you talking about?"

"The Nazis have camps. Concentration camps. That's where they send political enemies. That's where they send people who cause trouble. That's where they send people like us."

"We are not in Germany."

"Not yet." He let go of my arm. "But it's coming."

We started walking again and I could see our house in the next block. "I do not believe that. I do not believe we will be reunited with Germany. The Austrian people would never permit the Nazis to rule here."

Just then a man and woman passed by. The man bumped against Stephan's shoulder. He turned with an apologetic look and reached up to doff his hat, then he realized we were Jewish. The friendly expression on his face quickly turned dark. Instead of offering an apology, he cursed at Stephan and spat on him. A glob of spittle landed on the lapel of Stephan's coat. At the same time, the woman spat toward me, showering my face with her spray.

Stephan glanced over at me. "You think they do not want to be Germans? They already *are* Germans."

* * *

One evening, a few weeks later, I attended a concert with Papa and David. Mama was playing the violin with the orchestra and we went to watch her perform. Normally we sat down front, near the center of the audience, but that night we were directed to the balcony. The seats were cramped and the air was hot and stuffy.

Afterward, members of the orchestra were invited to attend a reception for orchestra patrons. Every year prior to that we had attended as Mama's guest, but that night when we appeared at the door, attendants shoved us aside. One of the maids working the reception told us we would probably find Mama waiting at the rear entrance. We went around there and found her standing outside in the cold. Papa wanted to speak to someone and find out why she was being treated that way, but Mama insisted that he not.

"Moshe, it will do no good. I enjoy playing and that is enough. Now let's go home." They turned to leave and David did also, but I just stood there and watched. When they realized I wasn't with them, they turned to face me. "Come, Sarah," Papa insisted. "You can't stand out here all night."

"Can't we get a taxi?"

David came back to me and took me by the hand. "Taxis do not stop for Jews now," he said softly. "We must walk."

When we reached the next corner, a car came to a stop alongside us. The window rolled down and I could see Walter Proch, the orchestra conductor, seated inside on the back seat. Next to him was a young man only a little older than I. At first I thought he'd stopped to give us a ride, but my hopes were quickly dashed.

"Orna," Proch said through the open window. "I wanted to tell you that we no longer need your services."

Mama frowned at him. "What do you mean?"

"Your services with the orchestra are no longer needed," he repeated.

She stepped toward the car, a look of disbelief still on her face. "You are firing me?"

"You are dismissed."

"For what reason?"

"I am terribly sorry."

"For what reason are you firing me?"

"We have received complaints."

"Complaints? Complaints about what?"

"There are some who object to a Jew having a chair."

Mama's eyes lit up. "You mean a Jew having a chair at the expense of an Austrian."

"You understand the times," he shrugged. "There is nothing I can do."

"I understand I am as much an Austrian as anyone." She pointed at him. "Perhaps even more than you."

"Well, not in the eyes of some."

The young man seated beside him spoke up. "Father," he scowled. "It's cold. Roll up the window."

"So sorry," Proch said. Then he rolled up the window and the car sped away.

Papa took hold of Mama's arm and in the glare of the streetlight I saw tears streaming down her face. "Now, now. You can play the violin for us at home. David will accompany you on the piano."

Mama jerked her arm free of his grasp and shouted, "How much more will they take? Tell me, Moshe. How much more will they take? First they drive our daughter away, then they take the car. Now they've taken my music. How much more do they want?"

"All of it," David grumbled. "They want all of it."

Papa once more took Mama by the arm and we trudged through the empty streets toward home. The air was cold and when we reached the opposite side of town there were no streetlights. All of them had been extinguished in our neighborhood, officially to save on the expense of gas, but many of us felt it was to provide cover for the gangs that roamed the night. Walking in the dark I felt certain we would be accosted by a mob but none came out to confront us and I was left only with the thought of Mama's question and David's answer. I was certain he was correct. They wanted everything we had, even our lives.

chapter 16

In the spring I finished secondary school. Jewish students were not permitted to attend the official graduation ceremony. We were to receive our graduation certificates on the last day of class. But Mr. Zweig, our instructor, convinced school administrators to allow us to hold our own graduation ceremony at which he would confer our certificates. It was supposed to be a discreet affair but it soon became a very big event for the families involved. The ceremony was to be held in the synagogue on Michaelsbergstrasse and afterward a reception was planned for the basement. Mothers and other relatives organized committees for decorations and refreshments and even though no one had very much to contribute, they each agreed to bring what little they had to make it a festive occasion.

That same spring, the Ministry of Finance issued an order requiring all Jews to file a written declaration of their assets. Supposedly, this was to enable the accurate payment of taxes. Forms were available for making the required statement but there were no instructions as to how to fill them out, and confusion over the matter quickly became overwhelming. From the day the order was issued until the last week for filing, almost every conversation in the neighborhood turned to the matter of how to fill out the forms. Many thought government officials had simply overlooked the instructions and that they must be available at the Ministry office. Others thought the officials were imbeciles and took great joy in saying so. Mama thought they left off the instructions on purpose, so they could pick and choose which forms to accept and which to reject. I thought she was right.

Papa had the forms, and on several occasions he sat down at the dining table to fill them out, but each time fear of doing it wrong held him back. Finally the last day for filing arrived and he had no choice but to fill out the form as best he could and take it in person to the Ministry office. The only problem was, that day was the day of my graduation. He was in such a state over it, I offered to go with him to find the correct office, but he refused. "You must graduate."

"I will graduate," I replied. "In fact, I already have. The ceremony is just a ceremony. Mr. Zweig will give me my certificate whether I'm there or not. Several of my class won't be there anyway."

"Why not?"

"They're too scared to attend. Their parents think something bad will happen and they don't want to risk being attacked." I took his hand. "I'll be glad to go with you."

"No," he said once more. "You must attend the ceremony. You've earned it."

"Can Uncle Alois help?"

Papa looked away. "Not now." His voice had a hint of sadness.

"Why not?"

"He isn't allowed to practice law anymore."

"Not allowed?" I couldn't believe it. Uncle Alois had been a lawyer for as long as I had been alive. Practicing law and helping people was his life. "Why can't he practice?"

"Because he is a Jew." Papa looked up at me. "They hate us, Sarah. They will never let us be more than their slaves and servants."

"Then why didn't you bring Mama and David and come to Spain?"

"I wanted to, but your mother was against it. She was born here. She didn't want to live anywhere else. And she didn't like the idea of running from trouble. Neither did I, but I was ready to run just the same."

All day long I waited by the window in the front room, hoping Papa would file the declaration and get back in time for the ceremony. But when it grew late and he still wasn't there, Mama insisted we go on without him. She and David walked with me to the synagogue.

In spite of our worry, the event went off without trouble. A few hecklers gathered on the sidewalk across the street, but they only shouted at us for a short while and when they got no response they just watched us coming and going. No one attacked us. After the ceremony we all went downstairs to the basement for punch and pastries.

When the event was over, I walked home with David and Mama. Stephan and his mother joined us. David was worried the five of us would attract too much attention, but we walked together anyway. When we arrived back at the house, Papa was sitting at the dining room table. Mama was worried. "Did you file the papers?"

"Yes," he nodded. "I filed them."

"What happened?"

"Nothing," he said blankly.

"Nothing?"

"Nothing at all."

"They must have said something. What did they say?"

"It was nothing. There was nothing to it."

I was suspicious and sat down beside him. "For nothing, it sure took a long time."

"I had to wait in line. There was a long line."

Stephan and his mother were at the house and in spite of the punch and pastries we ate at the ceremony, everyone was hungry. So Mama went into the kitchen to prepare something for us to eat. I joined her with Stephan's mother.

"What does he mean, there was nothing to it?"

"I don't know," Mama shrugged. "But it's his business."

"It can't be *nothing*."

"Leave it alone, Sarah."

"Mama," I pleaded. "It has to be something. Something happened. What was it?"

She turned from the counter to face me. "I said, leave it alone, and I meant it. This is your father's business. When he's ready to talk about it, he'll talk about it."

I was about to say more but Stephan entered the kitchen and took my hand. "Come on," he smiled. "Let's sit outside." I wanted to stay in the house and pressure Papa to tell me what happened, but Stephan insisted we sit outside. So I walked with him to the front porch.

We sat on the steps and I stared up at the night sky. "I don't understand why Papa won't tell me what happened."

"It's humiliating for him."

"It's the government. Everyone has to comply with their orders."

"Think of it," Stephan countered. "He's a Jewish man, and here he has to make such a declaration, and he can't figure out how to fill out the form. Goyim don't have to do it. And it's yet one more reminder of how fragile life is and how vulnerable we are."

Neither of us said much for a while, then I looked over at him. "Do you think we will be sent to the camps?"

"I think the Germans want to rule all of Europe and we are next on their way to doing that."

"You mean there will be war?"

"Not here," he scoffed. "Everyone in Austria except the Jews wants the Nazis to come."

"I don't."

"Neither do I, but I think it is inevitable."

"That is a big word."

"Yes," he laughed. "It is a big word. And I feel the need for it now that we are graduates."

* * *

A week or two after graduation, three long black cars drove down our street. David and I watched from the window as they went by, then we walked outside to see where they went. The cars came to a stop at the curb in the next block, in front of Hyman Rothstein's house. We walked in that direction for a closer look.

While we watched, the car doors opened and six men stepped out. Dressed in black suits and wearing black broad-brimmed hats, they looked ominous and threatening even from a distance. Moving in a deliberate manner, they made their way to the Rothsteins' front door. One of the men banged on it with his fist. In a moment, the door opened and I could see Rothstein standing just inside. Moments later, the men filed through the doorway and closed the door behind them.

Within the hour, news of their arrival spread up and down the street. Before long, everyone knew the men visiting Hyman Rothstein were officials from the Finance Ministry's Office of Economic Rehabilitation, along with agents from the Ministry of Public Security. David and I slowly moved closer and finally stood on the sidewalk one house away from where the cars were parked. Gradually, people from all over the neighborhood gathered with us, and a crowd formed. Mama came outside where we were standing. "This is what your father feared."

"What?" I asked. "Papa was afraid?"

"This is why he was upset the night he came back from filing the papers."

"This?"

"Yes," she nodded. "They have come to verify that the information on Rothstein's form is correct. Your father was worried they would use the forms against us. If we lie and don't put down everything, they will come and find it and punish us for withholding. If we put the truth, they will use it as a shopping list and take whatever they want."

In a little while, Rothstein's door opened and once again the men appeared on the porch. This time, Rothstein followed after them, shouting, "There is no discrepancy! I declared everything!"

One of the men held up a box he was carrying. "Then why is this silver service not on the list?"

"It is on the list!" Rothstein protested. "I put it on the list!"

The man who appeared to be in charge held up a paper. "Not this one," he dangled the paper in a teasing manner.

"I filled it out. I put it on the form." Rothstein's eyes opened wide in a look of realization. "That's not my form," he pointed to the document. "That's not my signature."

A cold look came over the man with the form. "You are accusing the Ministry of lying?"

"That's not my form," Rothstein continued to insist.

Now the man with the form was angry. His face was red and his jaw clinched. "You would dare to—" Suddenly one of the men with him drew a pistol from beneath his jacket. He placed the muzzle against Rothstein's head. Time seemed to slow and I saw Rothstein's eyes were wide with fright. His legs shook violently and he urinated on himself. Without a word, the man holding the pistol squeezed the trigger. The gun fired and a bullet exploded through Rothstein's head. A window in the front door turned red with fine mist of blood that sprayed from the wound. Rothstein's body crumpled to the floor.

At the sound of the gunshot, the door jerked open and Rothstein's wife appeared in the doorway. For a moment she stared at Rothstein's body, her mouth open in a look of terror and disbelief. Then she wailed, "No! Why did you do that? Why did you kill my husband?"

"Because he attempted to hide assets from the Ministry and then tried to cover his error by accusing the Ministry of fraud."

She leaned over the body. "Hyman would never do such a thing."

"Are you accusing me of lying?"

The man with the pistol pointed it toward her and a second shot rang out. She fell backward against the door and slid to a sitting position. He stepped closer, pointed the pistol at her once more, and shot her again. A red dot appeared in the center of her forehead and blood trickled down her face.

The man in charge turned in our direction and faced the crowd that had gathered outside the house. In a loud voice he said to us, "We will not argue with you. If you falsify your declaration, you will suffer the consequences." Everyone stood and listened, as if in a trance, their eyes fixed and unmoving. When he finished speaking, he stepped from the porch and started toward the car. The men who were with him followed closely behind. They made their way to the cars, got inside, and drove away. When they were gone, the murmuring began.

"Those weren't Austrians," someone said. "They were Nazis."

"Nazi isn't a race of people," another countered. "It's a political party."

"No," a woman added. "It's a cult."

"They are forbidden in this country. Chancellor Dollfuss issued the decree."

"Dollfuss was one of them."

"Well, whatever they were," the first one insisted, "the men who came here today were Nazis. I saw the SS on the collars of their shirts."

chapter 17

Tension continued to rise in Austria as more and more anti-Semitic laws and regulations were enacted. With each new measure, people on the street became more emboldened to take things into their own hands. The chancellor of the Republic, Engelbert Dollfuss, had been murdered shortly before I returned to Linz. His successor, Kurt von Schuschnigg, proved a weak defender of Austrian independence. Faced with mounting pressure from Adolf Hitler, he deferred all but outright rule of Austria to the Nazi authorities. That worked for a while and we hoped that conciliation would bring peace and maintain our independence. Then the Nazis increased their demands. With each new concession, German troops moved closer and closer to our borders. Talk of war filled neighborhood conversations.

In spite of those developments, I still wanted to apply to the University. Living with Aunt Haya, helping her harbor those trying to escape to Palestine and listening to the things she talked about, awakened in me an interest in history, politics, and the extent of governmental authority. I wanted to know why things were the way they were, and whether government of any kind could do anything to move history off the cycle of war. In an effort to find answers to those questions, I decided to enroll at the University of Linz.

Mama didn't think I could get admitted. While we were discussing it, Mira Sokalow, a neighbor, stopped by to visit Mama. As I explained what I wanted to do, Mira just shook her head. "Austrian schools are no longer admitting Jews," she lamented. "They have expelled all Jewish professors, too."

"That is not possible."

"Yes." Mira nodded her head. "I read it today in the newspaper. No more Jewish teachers of any kind."

"It is true," Papa agreed. "They have issued an order expelling all Jewish intellectuals."

"What about musicians?"

"They already fired me," Mama chuckled. "What more can they do?"

"Next they will turn on the shopkeepers."

"They haven't threatened us yet," Papa laughed nervously.

After Mira left, I showed Papa the papers I received in Spain when Aunt Haya and I went to the Interior Ministry office. He studied them a moment and then said, "What are you proposing?"

"That I register as a citizen of Spain."

"I don't know," he shrugged. "It might work."

"But you have to apply in person," Mama warned.

"I will go with you," Papa offered. "We will go there together."

I reached over and hugged him. "Thank you, Papa."

"It is my pleasure," he smiled.

"You both are crazy," Mama groused.

"Crazy?" Papa responded. "My daughter wants to go to university. I am walking there with her to enroll. What's so crazy about that?"

"Applying in person," Mama groaned. "That's what's so crazy about it."

I looked at Papa. "Is it too risky?"

"Perhaps," he answered slowly, "the greater risk is in doing nothing except what they tell us to do. We cannot stop living merely because of the threat of violence." Then he pointed his finger at me. "But when we are there, you must keep quiet. And don't act like a Jew."

"Aunt Haya told me the same thing. I still don't know what that means, but that's what she told me."

"I don't know either," Papa replied with a smile. "But don't act like a Jew."

The next day, Papa walked with me to the University. We arrived there without trouble and made our way to the registrar's office. A counter sat along the wall opposite the door and behind it was a clerk seated on a stool. She wore a dark blue dress and her blonde hair was bobbed off just below her ears. Reading glasses rested on her nose. She glanced up as we came through the doorway and shouted for us to leave. When we didn't, she threatened to have us arrested. Then I showed her my Spanish papers. "Oh," she suddenly lowered her voice. "You are from Spain?"

"I arrived here last year."

She peered at me over the top of her reading glasses. "You don't look Spanish."

"It's a very lovely country," I said, avoiding her question. "You have been there?"

"No." She had a puzzled look, but she took a form from a bin on the wall behind her and handed it to me. "Fill this out. We'll get the process started." Filing the correct forms took longer than I expected, but when we left the school that day, I was enrolled for my first year. The term began in September.

On the way home, Papa warned me again to keep quiet. "You ask too many questions, Sarah. That was cute when you were a little girl, but now it is not good."

"I can't help it. Questions come to me without even trying and before I know what I am doing, I ask them."

"Then you must work harder to let some of them go unanswered."

"I'll try." I looked over at him with a grin. "But I don't think I will be successful."

"You must," he insisted, unwilling to engage me in lighthearted banter. "You cannot afford to cause trouble."

"Grandma used to say a little trouble was a good thing."

"Your grandmother was old. She had the liberty of saying things for which she would never bear the consequences."

* * *

That fall, I entered the university and began work toward a degree in history. I continued to live at home and when I wasn't in class I helped Papa and David at the shop. Most evenings, Stephan came for a visit. He sat beside me at the dining table while I studied. Then one morning he arrived to walk me to class. The weather was crisp that day and he wore a gray sweater. On it was a yellow patch of cloth cut in the shape of a star and stitched just above his heart. In the center of the star was the word *Jude* written by hand in ink.

"What is that?"

He looked embarrassed. "They are making us wear it."

"They? What do you mean?"

Stephan gestured with a nod toward the street. Dressed in brown from head to toe, officers from the Ministry of Public Security went from house to house, knocking on doors, passing out leaflets. While we stood there talking, they arrived at our house and asked for Papa. He came to the porch and one of the men looked up at him from the steps. "Moshe Batsheva?"

"Yes."

The official handed Papa one of the leaflets. "You are required by law and the regulation of the Ministry of Security to wear the star on your outer clothing." He pointed to the one on Stephan's sweater. "It must look like that and you must wear it at all times."

"Or what?"

"Or you will be sent away."

Papa looked at the man thoughtfully. "And where do we get this star?"

"You must make it yourself," he snarled. He turned to leave and we stepped aside to let him pass. When he was gone, Stephan looked up at Papa. "They were at our house last night when I returned home."

Papa glanced at the paper the official left. "I do not understand this." He gave Mama a pained look. "They see me on the street each day. They spit on me and call me names. At night they paint graffiti on the windows of my store and tell me I'm a Jewish pig. But they want me to wear a yellow star on my jacket so they know for certain I am a Jew? It makes no sense."

"I don't think that's what it's for," Stephan explained.

"Then why would they do this?"

"To make you identify yourself."

"What are you talking about?" Papa sighed. "I just said I am already identified as a Jew."

"Wearing the star isn't the same as saying I'm a Jew."

"Look at the one you're wearing." Papa pointed at him. "It says 'Jude' right there on it."

"Yes," Stephan nodded. "And if you asked me who I am I would say I am a Jew. But if you asked me what that meant, I would say I am a follower of the Most High God, who is pleased to have me as His own. But that isn't what this is." He tapped the star on his chest with his finger. "This star is a statement I am forced to wear on my chest that says, 'I am a stupid Jewish pig.'" He looked Papa in the eye. "That is what they want me to say about myself. To accept that I am less than they are. And that is why they want us to wear it."

Papa looked at me. "I told you, you should have never come back."

"Some are trying to leave now," Stephan added.

"But they are required to pay a tax to leave," Papa groaned. "A tax that equals one hundred percent of their net worth." He looked at Stephan. "It would cost us everything to leave."

"Better to get out alive with nothing," Stephan shrugged, "than to stay too long and die where we stand."

"I don't know." Papa heaved a heavy sigh. "I think it will be okay."

But it wasn't okay.

* * *

In the ensuing months, German troops continued their slow advance toward the Austrian border. They stopped short of crossing but more and more units joined them, amassing men, tanks, artillery, and heavy equipment. At the same time, non-Jewish citizens in Linz took advantage of the obvious move toward unification. Roving mobs patrolled the streets day and night, harassing anyone who looked like they might be Jewish. Then one day in the spring, a woman burst into the shop, her eyes alive with excitement. "Have you heard the news?"

"What news?"

"The Nazis are coming!" She wasn't Jewish and was obviously glad they were finally on their way.

"What do you mean?"

"I heard it on the radio." She glanced around the room. "They are coming. The German Army crossed the Inn River at Passau and Pocking yesterday. They will be here by tomorrow. This is a great day for Austria. Finally we will be united with the Fatherland." Then she stopped and her face turned serious. "You better get home."

"Why?"

"Because," she gestured with a broad sweep of her arms, "this place will be burned to the ground for sure." Then she pushed open the door, stepped out to the street, and was gone.

Papa locked the door, went out the back, and walked up the alley to a café on the corner. He wasn't permitted to eat there, but one of the cooks was his friend and often gave him lunch from the rear door. When Papa returned he told me it was true. The German Army had crossed the river at multiple sites. Troops were advancing from Salzburg toward Vienna and from Passau straight toward Linz.

"We should close the shop," Papa suggested.

"But it's not even noon yet."

"There will be trouble."

"Trouble?" For some inexplicable reason the thought of closing early seemed wrong. "The army won't be here for at least another day. And besides, no one will resist, will they?"

"It does not matter." He slipped on his coat and I knew we were leaving. "There will be trouble." He turned out the light and gestured for me to follow him toward the back door. "We must go home." We closed the shop and walked home, taking the long route down the alley. Papa thought it was safer that way.

When we arrived, Mama was sitting in the front room, listening to the wireless. She looked up as we entered. "You heard?"

"Yes," Papa nodded. "We heard."

"Schuschnigg has resigned. They're handing the government over to a group appointed by German authorities."

"I heard the German Army has crossed the border and is moving toward Vienna."

"And meeting no resistance," Mama added. "In fact, people are lining the roads and streets everywhere to greet them."

Papa listened a few minutes longer, then switched off the radio. Mama looked over at him with concern. "What does this mean, Moshe?"

"I don't know," he shook his head. "But it's not good." He put on his coat and headed toward the door.

Mama called after him, "Where are you going?"

"To check on the shop."

"But we just got here," I protested.

"Stay here," he answered as he closed the door.

David grabbed his coat and ran after him. Through the window I saw him when he caught up with Papa. They walked together up the street. "I should go with them," I lamented.

"No," Mama replied. "Stay here. That is why he came home."

"To bring me here?"

"Yes."

"He should not worry so much."

"No, Sarah," she said flatly. "Now is the time to worry."

I took a seat near Mama and we sat there in silence for about twenty minutes. Then she stood and put on her jacket. "I can't stand this."

"Stand what?"

"Waiting," she grumbled. "And not knowing."

"Where are you going?"

"To the shop. Get your coat."

We walked uptown together, but this time our trip was a little more difficult than usual. A group of boys was gathered on the corner near our house. They threw eggs at us as we approached. One of them struck Mama on the shoulder. Another landed near my feet and splattered my legs. To avoid them, we walked between two houses to the alley and came the long way around.

When we reached the shop we found a mob gathered in front of a store across the street from Papa's shop. Men, women, and children were screaming and yelling anti-Semitic slogans. We hid at the corner, ducking out every few minutes to see.

For a while there was only the sound of angry voices, then someone threw a brick through the window of a shop across the street. The sound of shattering glass made them laugh, so more followed and soon all the windows in the store were gone. About that time, someone arrived with a can filled with kerosene and before long smoke poured from the building.

Mama took my hand. "Come. We must go home now. We should never have come up here."

"But what about Papa and David?"

"They will be fine for now, if no one sees us."

"But the mob…"

"Those idiots don't know what they are doing. The store they attacked belongs to Hans Abetz, a Catholic. They attacked it because he sells kosher food. The people in that crowd don't even realize Abetz isn't Jewish. Come on." She pulled me after her. "We must go before they see us and figure it out."

chapter 18

For once, much to our disappointment, news from the radio proved accurate. German troops arrived in Linz the following day. Ahead of their advance, riots broke out uptown as bands of lawless thugs finished what the earlier mobs did not. The synagogue was burned to the ground and most of the Jewish shops were ransacked. By the following Monday, even the Nazis were appalled by the lack of order and put troops in the streets to stop the random attacks.

On Wednesday, I decided to go to the university. I knew Mama and Papa would not allow it, so I awoke early that morning and dressed quietly in my room. Then I slipped downstairs and made my way across town. I hadn't gone far when I realized how foolish I'd been for even trying. All across the city, every block was marred by the smoldering ruins of shops that had been set on fire or buildings with windows missing and the contents looted. Still, I wanted to attend classes, if any were being held, and I pressed on.

At the campus, students were gathered near the main building, a four-story brick structure with slate roof. In unison they shouted anti-Semitic slogans and when they grew tired of that they sang anti-Semitic songs. I watched from a distance for a short while, then returned home as quickly as possible. I arrived to find David and Papa seated at the kitchen table. Blood trickled from a gash above Papa's eye and dripped from David's nose. Mama stood between them, dabbing first one, then the other. They seemed hardly to notice that I had been out of the house.

"You must report this at once," Mama railed.

"I can't report it," Papa replied.

"Why not?" she shouted. "They destroyed the shop and stole your merchandise. You must report it."

My mouth fell open. "They destroyed the shop?"

"Yes," Papa nodded. "I'm afraid so."

"How badly is it damaged?"

"The glass was broken and the fixtures destroyed. But that isn't the worst of it."

"What could be worse?"

"They forced Papa to sign papers conveying it to a new owner."

"Who?"

"A German," Papa growled. "I don't remember his name."

"See," Mama looked at me. "This is what I'm saying. We must report this to the authorities."

"And I'm telling you, we can't," Papa retorted.

"And why not?" Mama demanded.

"If I report it," Papa struggled to maintain his patience, "they will know we are Jewish."

"As if they don't already."

"But a report will draw the attention of the authorities to us. If they find out Sarah is our daughter, she will be dismissed from school. She might even be arrested for being a Jew and attending classes."

"Those who work in the registrar's office will be arrested for admitting her," David added.

"It doesn't matter now." I was on the verge of tears. "There isn't much in the way of classwork there now anyway. They are all out in the streets, rallying against us and cheering the Germans."

Mama looked at me, her eyes once again opened wide. "You have been there? To the university?"

"Yes," I nodded.

"Just now?" She had a look of disbelief. "This morning?"

"I wanted to see if we were having class."

Mama was livid. "Are you crazy?! Your father and brother were beaten senseless by a mob. The store is lost. We have no way to make a living. And you go off by yourself to see if the goyim are having classes?"

"I wasn't in any danger."

"I don't care," she shouted. "You should never have gone. The world is going crazy. My family is going crazy." Then she turned on Papa. "Moshe, we must get out of this place. It is no longer safe."

"We don't have the correct papers."

"You will get the papers," she shouted. "We will make the move."

Papa shook his head. "The emigration tax will take everything we own."

"Haven't you seen what's happening on the street? Everyone is crazy. And now it's even affecting the mind of your own daughter." The longer she talked, the louder her voice became. "The Germans are here, Moshe! They are here! They're going to take it all anyway." She paused to take a breath and lowered her voice. "You'll take care of this, Moshe," she insisted, gesturing with the cloth she'd used to dab their injuries. "You'll do whatever it takes, but you'll get us out of here."

* * *

Three weeks later, things were back to a normal routine for most people, but not for us. Papa's shop was destroyed and we were forced to trade works of art from the house for food, but I still wanted to attend class. I had questions for which I wanted answers—how did things come to be as they were between Germany and the other countries of Europe, what political forces conspired to prevent Jews from participating in the normal activities of Austrian society, and why everyone hated us. Answers to those questions could be found in classes at the university. But more than that, in the depths of my heart, I harbored a dream that one day I would become a lawyer like Uncle Alois. If the mob on the streets or the German soldiers prevented me from attending class, they would rob me of that dream. I wasn't ready to give them my future. In fact, quite the opposite was true. I was prepared to risk my life for it.

At noon a few days later, Stephan came by for a visit. I told him of my desire to try one more time to attend classes at the university. He argued against it but when he couldn't dissuade me, he asked to accompany me. I did not want him to go.

"They will see you and become suspicious," I argued. "They won't notice me. They'll notice you."

"But it's too dangerous for any girl, Jewish or otherwise, to be out on the street alone," he countered. "I can walk with you part of the way, then drop back out of sight when you get near the school."

"But then you would have to walk home by yourself."

"I'll find somewhere to wait and walk back with you when you return. You really don't need to be out there by yourself."

Reluctantly, I agreed and we set out the next morning for the university. Halfway there, we passed a coffee shop. Through the front window I saw Adolf Eichmann seated at a table inside. He was older now and his hair was thinning. But dressed in a German Army uniform, he still cut a handsome figure. I said nothing to Stephan about him, and made no move to talk to him, but I was certain from the look in his eyes that Adolf saw me, too.

As promised, Stephan stopped about six blocks from the school and let me walk the remainder of the way by myself. To my surprise, the campus was quiet and I was able to attend two of my classes. On the way home, Stephan joined me. He'd been hiding in a burned-out building and smelled like smoke, but I was glad to see him and thankful he was around to accompany me.

Later that evening, Adolf came to our house, still dressed in his German Army uniform. Mama and Papa were nervous to have him in their home. David stayed upstairs in his room and never came down. Neighbors watched from the safety of their homes. We talked awhile and then he asked, "What ever happened to that boy who used to hang around when you were a little girl? What was his name?"

"Stephan."

"Ah yes," he nodded. "Stephan. How is he?"

I didn't like the way he talked about Stephan. The words were benign but the look in his eye was cold. Yet finding no way to avoid his question, I answered him. "Until your soldiers arrived, and the thugs went on a rampage, he worked at a tannery on the edge of town. It was burned down a few nights ago."

"Things are changing in Austria," Adolf shrugged. I had heard that so many times, I wanted to scream.

Papa pointed to the yellow star stitched on the front of his shirt. "Is this one of those changes?"

"Some of the changes are painful, I'm sure," Adolf nodded.

"Tell that to the ones your thugs beat to death in the street," Papa complained. "That so-called chancellor you installed didn't do a thing about it."

"Careful," Adolf cautioned. "People are being shot in Vienna for such talk."

"I am Austrian," Papa responded. "I can say whatever I want."

"Once, you could," Adolf shook his finger. "But not anymore."

"Then this isn't Austria anymore, is it?"

"Not the Austria you knew," Adolf agreed. "Have you thought about leaving?"

"This is our home," Papa countered. "And besides, we have no money for the papers and nothing for the trip."

"What if the government paid for it?"

"The government?" Papa scoffed.

"Yes."

"They would move me to a new country?"

"They would transport you and your entire family."

"What of our belongings?"

"What you could not carry with you in one small suitcase would become the property of the state."

"They would seize everything?" Papa gestured with a wave of his hand. "The house and all its contents?"

"Exchange it," Adolf had a twinkle in his eye. "Your things, for safe passage to a new destination. Palestine, England, the United States."

"That is preposterous."

"You would be alive."

"They would never do it."

"Perhaps you should look into it. But don't wait. Things are changing daily."

Papa should have followed Adolf's lead and inquired about the possibility of relocating to another country. Instead, he did nothing.

* * *

Not long after Adolf's visit, government officials issued a decree. All Jews living in rural areas were to leave the countryside and move to the cities. The first wave of displaced people arrived in Linz a week later. Many were housed in tenement buildings located in a poor section on the city's west side. The buildings, three and four stories tall, were once home to a thriving Gypsy community, but they were cleared out the year before and the residents sent off on the trains.

Left empty for almost a year, the buildings were in disrepair with broken windows, leaking roofs, and missing fixtures. The area around them was overgrown with weeds and littered with trash. The Germans constructed a fence ten feet high all the way around the property with strands of razor-sharp barbed wire along the top. Jews sent there to live were confined to the fenced-in space. A pass was required for anyone who wanted out to work or search for food. David and I walked there one day and we were appalled by the living conditions, but we consoled ourselves that the trouble was on the far side of town and would leave us unscathed.

Three or four days later, trouble came to our own neighborhood when a relocation officer knocked on our door. He was tall, with a thick chest and broad shoulders. He wore a gray uniform, neatly tailored and buttoned in place. Around his waist was a black leather belt with a holster that held an automatic pistol.

A family accompanied the officer—a man and woman with two children. When Mama opened the door, the officer rudely pushed his way past her and started upstairs. The family hesitated at the threshold, then reluctantly followed him inside. At the top of the steps he turned and opened the first door he came to. It led into David's room.

The officer walked inside the room and glanced around quickly. "This will do for you," he announced to the family, now standing beside him.

They leaned through the doorway with a bewildered look. "But there is only one bed," the man observed.

"It is enough," the officer replied.

"But there are four of us."

The officer placed his hand on his pistol belt. "You would like for us to give it to someone else?"

"No," the man answered timidly. "We will take it."

Papa came from the kitchen and shouted up from the bottom of the steps, "What is the meaning of this?"

The officer appeared at the banister and glared down at him. "You have too many rooms for one Jewish family. You must make space for others."

"But this is our home," Papa protested.

Once again, the officer placed his hand on his pistol belt. "We must all make our contribution for the good of the Reich. Are you refusing to make yours?"

Papa's shoulders sagged and his countenance fell with a look of resignation. He slowly shook his head and turned away. The officer came down the steps and walked out the front door.

With nothing to do but get along, we invited the family downstairs. Mama prepared hot tea and we sat at the dining table. They were the Murmelsteins, Benjamin and Andrea with their two children—I used to know their names but I can no longer remember them. I liked Andrea and so did Mama. Papa got on with Benjamin. Their children were well behaved and the house ran smoothly. They came with only a single suitcase each, but Benjamin made certain his was filled with the family silver and jewelry. Over the next few weeks, they were happy to use it to buy food, which we all ate.

A month later, the relocation officer returned with another family, which he crowded into my room. David and I slept on the floor downstairs. Not long after that, another family took over the attic and then another was added to the front room. Others occupied Grandma's room and the dining room. David and I were forced to sleep on the floor in Mama and Papa's bedroom.

Our house was comfortable for the four of us, and even when Grandma was alive we had plenty of room. Thirty, however, was more than the place could handle. The single bathroom was always filthy and constantly overflowing, which meant the backyard doubled as a latrine.

Flies swarmed everywhere and the odor was unbearable. Chaos overtook us, and with less and less food available we were hungry all the time. Any hope I had of attending classes at the university was lost.

Finally, one hot summer day, water stopped running from the kitchen faucet. Mama could take it no more and she shouted at Papa, "I told you we should leave!"

"Yes, you've said that before."

"Then why are we still here?" Her voice was loud and abrasive.

"When we could have gone," Papa said dryly, "you didn't want to go. Then when we couldn't, you finally decided you did, but by then it was too late."

"But look where we are now. They bring strangers into our house. Tell us we have to accommodate them. Is it our house anymore? No! It's their house. The Germans. The Nazis. They own this house now and they took it from us without the slightest nod to the legal system." She lowered her voice. "Alois was right. He saw it coming and you ignored him."

"I don't need Alois to tell me what to do with my own family."

The lone bright spot for me came with Stephan's visits. He continued to come by each evening and we sat together on the front steps. As more people were placed in the house, we resorted to walks at night in the neighborhood for a few moments of privacy. Those walks brought us relief from conditions at home but all around us we saw the scene repeated at houses up and down the street.

"How did it come to this?" I sighed.

"Greed," Stephan offered.

"That's it? This was all because of greed?"

"Yes," he nodded. "Greed and hatred."

"You may be right," I conceded. "They blame us for everything they think is wrong. Losing the war, losing the monarchy, snow in the winter, hunger. They blame all of it on us."

"When we are rich," he echoed, "they say we control the markets. When we are poor, they say we only want welfare."

"Where will it end?"

He grimaced. "Not in a good place, I'm afraid."

"What do you mean?"

"Word is, the Nazis are building camps here in Austria, just as they have in Germany."

"Camps? For what?"

"For Jews."

I still could not believe it. "They could do that? In Austria?"

"They're building one right now. Between Mauthausen and Gusen."

"That is not possible."

"I am afraid it is."

chapter 19

As summer gave way to autumn, officials from the Interior Ministry, along with German soldiers, came through our neighborhood. They tacked notices on the doors of each home and affixed them to streetlight poles and handed them out to anyone who passed by. The notice informed us that all Jews were now required to enroll with the Central Office for Jewish Emigration. Mama tore the notice from our door and brought it inside to Papa. He was seated at the kitchen table, which had become his place of refuge from the many who filled our house.

"We already filed forms with the Office of Economic Rehabilitation," she complained. "Isn't that enough?"

"This is different." Papa studied the notice. "That form was about the tax. This one is about something else."

"What else?"

"Emigration."

"Immigration? We are already here."

"*Em*-igration," he said, stressing the pronunciation of the first syllable. "They want us to leave."

"I do not want to go anywhere," Mama retorted. "This is Austria. This is my home."

"Just a few days ago, you said you wanted to go."

"I was mad then," she said, almost laughing. "They can't make me do anything I don't want to."

"I wouldn't be so sure."

Benjamin Murmelstein heard them talking and came to the kitchen. Papa handed him the notice. "Now they want us to register again."

Murmelstein read the notice and laid it on the table. "Some of the people upstairs do not want to submit to the authorities. They don't trust them."

"Who?"

"The man in the attic. I don't know his name."

"Ehud Averbuch," Mama added.

"Yes," Murmelstein nodded. "That's the one. And his wife, too. They are from a rural area. Somewhere west of here."

"A little village near Steyr," Mama offered.

Murmelstein seemed amused. "You know this much about them all?"

"I know most of their names," she smiled. "It would be rude not to know the names of your houseguests."

"They are hardly your guests."

"Ahh," she waved her hand. "They are in my house. They are my guests."

"Well, Averbuch does not want to file the form."

Just then Averbuch appeared at the kitchen doorway. "What is it I do not want to do?"

"We were discussing the form," Papa told him. He pointed at the notice that lay on the table. Averbuch picked it up, glanced at it briefly, then tossed it aside. "I do not trust them. Whatever they know about me, they will use against me. Why should I give them the ammunition for the gun they point at me?"

"I think you should comply. After all, they are the government."

"They are not *my* government." Averbuch placed his hand on his chest. "I still swear allegiance to Charles I."

"It doesn't matter to whom you swear allegiance," Papa explained. "We must deal with the Nazis now and I think it would be better if we complied."

"Better?"

"Everything they want to know is public knowledge—your education, training, and occupation."

"They will never get the form from me," Averbuch said defiantly.

Murmelstein did not like it. "You may endanger us all if you do not."

The following day, I walked with Papa, Mama, and David to the Central Office for Jewish Emigration. A clerk at the office reviewed our forms and accepted them without delay. Five hours later, we departed the building with identification cards, complete with our photographs, as proof of registration.

Early one morning the following month, agents from the Ministry of Public Security arrived on our block. I watched from the porch as they went from house to house on the opposite side of the street. Slowly at first, people came from the houses in ones and twos, each of them carrying a small suitcase. They seemed reluctant to go and the soldiers hurried them along.

As I watched through the front window I noticed no one had come from the Jelineks' house, directly opposite ours. A soldier stepped onto their porch and tried the door but it appeared to be locked. He turned toward the street, shouting and waving his arms, then three more soldiers joined him. To the right of the door I saw furniture in front of the window. Moments later, one of the Public Security officials came up the street and turned onto the walkway leading toward their house. Suddenly a window flew open upstairs and a chair sailed out. It landed on the sidewalk and smashed to pieces, followed by another that landed in the grass. Instinctively, the officer ducked with his hands over his head and backed out of the way.

Within minutes, an armored tank arrived, belching smoke and fumes. It turned from the street, bounced over the curb, and plowed through the front porch, smashing down the door. Soldiers stormed the house and we heard gunfire. A little while later, they led three men from the front door to the street and lined them up at the curb. An army officer, who supervised the attack, stepped to the end of the line, drew his pistol, and shot them in the head one by one. After that, most people moved a little more quickly to do as they were told.

All along that side of the street, people filed from their houses. Each of them clutched a single suitcase and a few held on to an extra box or bag. One or two pushed small carts or wagons. Soldiers wandered among them and every now and then knocked the extra bags from their hands so that everyone who left the block only carried one item. Seeing it made me angry and twice I wanted to run to the street to stop them, but each time David held me back—once before I reached the door and the last time only stopping me at the porch. Standing there at the top of the steps of our home I saw the look on the faces of those who were leaving and it made me gasp. They walked as if in a trance, methodically placing one foot in front of the next, eyes focused ahead in a blank, emotionless stare. No one talked, no one shouted, no one said a word. They just came from their homes and walked down the street to our left.

Then trucks arrived and parked in a line along the curb. Soldiers who had been patrolling the block entered the houses and began hauling out furniture, paintings, china, and other belongings. Most of it was stacked on the waiting trucks. What they found unfit for use they piled in a heap outside the Wallach residence three houses to our right. In a matter of hours, the houses were emptied and the trucks drove away. Shortly before noon, they set fire to the pile near the Wallachs' house, then they started down our side of the street.

About one o'clock, a Public Security officer came from the street and started up our walkway. I saw him coming and moved away from the window to stand beside the piano. I heard his heavy footsteps as he reached the porch, then the door rattled as he banged on it with his fist. The sound of it made me jump. Mama came from the dining room and opened it. The officer nudged her aside as he pushed his way into the house.

"We have received reports about your house," he glanced around in an imperious manner, as if offended by what he saw and afraid to come too far inside.

"Reports?" A frown creased Mama's forehead. "What kind of reports?"

"You have too many people living here. Conditions in this house are no longer sanitary." His face wrinkled in a scowl. "What is that awful smell?"

"The toilet," I explained. "It overflows almost every day."

"A pigsty," he grimaced. "Full of filthy pigs."

Papa came from the kitchen. "Your men brought them all here. If it's unsanitary in here, it's your own doing."

"That no longer matters," the officer replied dismissively. "All of you must relocate to other accommodations."

"Other accommodations?" Papa came closer. "We don't have any other accommodations. You've taken everything we had. Burned the shops. Looted the contents. Most of what's valuable has been sold or traded just to survive. We have nothing except this house and the few scraps you see here." Papa gestured toward the room with a sweep of his arm.

"I see you still have a piano," the officer smirked.

"Take it," Mama snapped. "Just leave us alone."

"I'm afraid we are well past that now," the officer answered, his voice betraying a hint of growing frustration. "You are to be relocated to alternative accommodations. You must pack at once. Bring warm clothing and food, if you have it. You are each permitted one small suitcase. No trunks." He looked around once more. "If you have a cart, you can haul your luggage on that."

"And just where are we going?" Papa asked.

"You will be shown where to go."

"And how long will we be away?"

The officer looked away. "You have ten minutes to pack," he barked. Then he turned on his heel and walked out.

For a moment we just stood and stared at each other. Then Papa clapped his hands. "Do as he says."

I ran to the bedroom and took my identity documents from the top drawer of Mama's dresser. A small leather wallet lay next to them and I put the papers in it. Mama came behind me and took a suitcase from the closet. Papa picked up Grandma's jewelry box.

"Not the box," Mama cautioned as she stuffed clothing into the luggage. "It is too heavy and takes up too much room."

"I'm the one carrying it," he replied. "I'll decide if it's too heavy."

Mama handed me a suitcase and I put my clothes inside. David took some food from a shelf in the kitchen and wrapped it in a towel with a few tins of crackers. He found a suitcase under the bed and used it. While we packed our belongings, others in the house did the same. I heard them scurrying around upstairs.

In spite of the way we felt about leaving, there wasn't much left to pack. Three paintings hung in the bedroom and a fourth was on the wall in the dining room, but they were too large to carry. All that was left was a few pieces of jewelry and the essential things we needed for daily life. We were ready in less than ten minutes and made our way to the front door. When we reached it, Mama hesitated. "Perhaps we should wait until that man comes back."

Papa reached past her and opened the door, then he took her by the arm and ushered her out to the porch. "If we must go, we might as well choose the time rather than waiting for them to drag us out." It was one of the few choices left for us to make.

As we came from the house, officials from the Ministry of Public Security met us at the street and checked our documents. I showed them my Austrian papers and handed them the card we received from the Central Office for Jewish Emigration. They checked the name on my card against a list, then stamped the card and returned it to me along with my papers. A soldier gestured for us to move down the street to the left and we started in that direction.

A few paces behind us Averbuch stood with his wife and their three children. They had refused to register with the emigration office and had only the usual identification papers. When the ministry officials checked their list, the Averbuchs were not on it. One of the officials struck Averbuch on the head and shouted. Averbuch became upset and started going on about Charles I and where his loyalty really lay. Before he'd gotten very far with it, soldiers grabbed him and threw him into the street. His wife rushed after him, crying and cursing the soldiers. Their children stood a few meters away with a look of terror on their faces. I wanted to grab them and hold them tight but before I could muster the courage to act, I heard the sound of a gunshot and saw Averbuch's body crumpled in the street. Blood flowed from a gaping wound to his head. An army officer stood over him with a pistol still in his hand.

Without a word, the officer pointed the pistol toward Averbuch's wife and shot her in the head. She fell atop her husband's body. I saw blood run from her nose onto Averbuch's white shirt. With the smell of gunpowder still in the air, other soldiers picked up the children and dropped them near their parents. Without hesitation or remorse, the officer with the pistol shot them, too.

Tears poured down my cheeks as I stood there gasping for breath. Words could hardly describe my despair as I thought of those children, helpless, unable to defend themselves, their lives cut short by such an outrageous act. Suddenly sorrow melted away, replaced by rage. How dare they treat us this way? I balled my fist and started toward the officer, but Papa's arm came around my waist. He lifted me off the pavement, swung me around in the opposite direction, and carried me up the street.

When we'd gone a few paces he set me down and, still holding me close, pressed his lips near my ear. "You must keep quiet. All of our lives depend on it." I turned to look back but he shielded my eyes. "No, Sarah. You cannot look back." He eased his grip on my waist but held on to my arm and hustled me forward. "Start walking."

Slowly I forced one foot in front of the other and began moving down the street. I imagined that I looked like all those I had seen earlier in the day, with their hollow eyes and blank, emotionless stare, only now I knew why.

A few minutes later, Stephan came to my side. His mother, Yardina, and Yosef, his brother, were close by. I looked over at him, still unable to form words to describe what I'd just witnessed and what I still felt. "I know," he nodded. "I saw them." He took my hand and together we followed the others from our street.

Soldiers directed us at each corner and about an hour later we arrived at the railway freight yard on the south side of the city. Long lines of rail cars sat on the tracks. They appeared to be cattle cars with slats for walls that allowed air to freely circulate. Bits of hay protruded from openings near the floor. We were herded toward them like animals. In the crush of so many people being forced together, families were separated from each other. I very quickly lost track of Papa, Mama, and David. Then a few minutes later Stephan's hand slipped from mine and he disappeared in a sea of faces. All alone, I clutched my suitcase in front of me, gripping it tightly with both hands as the surge of people pushed me toward a train car.

Unable to turn to the left or right, I followed the person in front of me up a concrete ramp, pushed forward by the press of people behind me, until I reached the door to the car. I stepped inside and moments later soldiers shoved it closed and latched it from the outside. By then, the afternoon sun was fading and the temperature was turning cold. I stood there, clutching my suitcase, thinking about all that had happened that day and wondering if I would ever see a familiar face again. Then I heard Mama and Papa talking and wedged my way to them. David stood nearby. Mama kissed me on the cheek. We lost everything that day and yet when I found them again in that rail car, and we were together once more, I felt as rich as ever.

chapter 20

The railcar had recently been used to haul livestock. Hay on the floor still bore droppings from the last load. The pungent aroma of manure stung my nose. We stood shoulder to shoulder, packed into the car so tightly I could hardly breathe. In spite of the openings along the walls, air inside the car quickly became stuffy and hot. Sweat ran down my neck and my hair was damp. Several older women fainted but, crammed together the way we were, their bodies never hit the floor. And there was no toilet. Before long, the pungent smell of manure was overpowered by the odor of our own urine and feces.

An hour after the doors closed, the train lurched forward and began to roll from the freight yard. Murmuring filled the car as we wondered aloud where we were going. Some thought they were taking us to Germany. Others thought we would be taken as far as France or Poland and dumped at the border. No one knew for sure what would happen and after a while, when all the obvious possibilities were exhausted, talk died away leaving only the rhythmic *click-clack* of the rails to fill the silence.

Probably four hours later the trained slowed. Someone looked out through a crack in the wall. "I see lights," she said. "It looks like a city."

"Vienna," Papa said quietly.

"Are you sure?" Mama asked.

"I think we have been traveling east," he replied. "About four hours have passed since we left Linz. That would put us in Vienna."

A few minutes later, the train rattled to a stop and shortly after that the door to our car slid open. German soldiers stood outside. "Get out!" they shouted. "Get out of the car! Bring your luggage and get out of the car!"

The floor of our car was three feet above the ground, but there was no ramp or steps. Those standing closest to the opening were hesitant to jump. The soldiers quickly became frustrated with our seeming refusal to move. Impatient and angry, they reached into the car, caught hold of those nearest the door, and pulled them through the opening. "Get out of the car!" they shouted louder and rougher than before.

People near the door tumbled to the ground. Those farther back saw what happened and moved quickly through the opening, jumping on their own rather than waiting to be pulled. I moved forward with Mama, Papa, and David, then we all jumped from the car at once so we could stay together.

As the cars emptied, the soldiers moved us into a line, then began marching us from the freight yard. The ground was rough and uneven and we stumbled along in the dark. Each time someone fell, soldiers rushed to kick and hit them and screamed for them to get up. Mama and I held on to Papa and David in an effort to keep our balance.

"This is Vienna," Papa announced quietly.

"How can you be certain?" Mama asked.

He pointed to the left across the rows and rows of tracks. "That is the Nordbahnhof station."

Mama shook her head. "It doesn't look the same. Nothing looks the same."

"What other city could be this big, and only four hours from Linz?"

They would have continued arguing but as they were talking a soldier pushed his way through the crowd around us and struck Papa in the back with the end of his rifle. "Be quiet!" he ordered. "Shut up and keep walking!" After that, no one said a word.

In a little while we came to a paved street that led through rows and rows of tenement buildings. The Danube River flowed by on the north side, separating us from the remainder of the city. For added security, a fence ran along the riverbank. At least twelve feet high, it had barbed wire along the top like the one David and I had seen in Linz. Every hundred meters or so there was a tower with armed guards and search-lights that cast a stark glare over the buildings.

We continued several blocks until we arrived at a broad intersection. A German Army officer stood in the center of the intersection, hands behind his back, his feet shoulder width apart. Beyond him were rows and rows of German soldiers, standing straight and stiff, hands by their sides, rifles slung over their shoulders.

As we came to a stop, the officer shouted a command and the sol-diers moved forward. My heart raced at the sight of them coming toward us. I was certain we were all going to die. Instead, they spread out before us and began to shout at us to get in line. They shoved us with their hands and beat us with the rifles until we formed into two rows that ran as far in either direction as I could see. Everyone was scared and con-fused but families who had been separated on the train used the chaos to find each other and stood more or less together in the rows.

Then the officer spoke again, this time to us. "Welcome to your new home. I am sure you will find Vienna to your liking. Soon you will be taken to your new quarters. You must keep them neat, clean, and in order. We will not allow anyone to remain here who does not follow the rules. Tomorrow at sunup you will assemble in front of your building for inspection. At that time, you will be given new identity cards and work assignments."

One by one, soldiers escorted families from the ranks. I watched as they disappeared into the shadows. Every now and then I heard the sound of a gunshot and was afraid to think about what had happened to those who were led away. Sometime past midnight, soldiers came for us. We followed them down the street and around the corner to a brick building six floors tall.

They pushed open the outside door and through it I saw nothing but pitch-darkness. One soldier switched on a torch he held in his hand, and a beam of light fell on a flight of bare wooden stairs. No one said a word as we followed them up the steps. Only the scuffling sound of footsteps broke the silence.

When we reached the fourth floor, they turned and led us down the hall. My legs ached with pain. The building smelled like the train car we'd just come from—a mixture of sweat, urine, and feces—but I didn't care anymore. I just wanted a place to lie down and sleep.

A little way down the hall, one of the soldiers opened a door and gestured for us to enter. "This is your apartment," he announced. "You must be on the street and assembled in formation by sunrise." Then he turned away and started toward the staircase. The soldiers who came with him dutifully fell in line and followed him downstairs. We stepped inside and closed the door behind us.

A single light bulb dangled from the ceiling in the front room. Papa located the cord for it and switched it on. The dim yellow light it produced revealed a dusty, bare apartment. We glanced around a moment. Then Mama shook her head. "We have no furniture," she lamented.

"We will find some," Papa replied.

"And how will we pay for it?" Mama grumbled. "We have no money."

"There's always furniture around for free," Papa answered.

To the left of the door, a stove and sink occupied a corner with a counter that ran along the wall. Mama checked the tap and water flowed from it. "It works," she had a look of surprise. "The water works."

David stepped to the sink and rinsed his hands. "Tomorrow," he offered, "I will find soap." He wiped them dry on the legs of his trousers. "Maybe I'll find a towel, too," he grinned.

At the end of the counter was a door that led to a bathroom with a shelf for a basin and a toilet in the corner. The apartment's only bedroom was next to it. A canvas tick filled with straw lay on the floor. Papa wandered into the room and set his suitcase on the floor, then dropped to his knees. I thought something was wrong and rushed to his side. "Are you okay?"

"I am fine," he said as he felt along the floor with his fingers.

I knelt beside him. "What are you doing?"

"Looking."

"For what?"

A smile spread across his face. "This." He tapped one of the floor-boards with his finger.

"What are you talking about?" I was more puzzled than ever.

"Watch, and I will show you." He reached into his jacket, took out a pocketknife, and opened it. Then he slid the blade into the space between the boards. Working it carefully, he pried loose the board he had shown me. With that one out of the way, he removed two more very easily. Then I saw there was a space between our floor and the ceiling of the apartment below us.

Papa opened his suitcase and took out Grandma's jewelry box. He gently lowered it inside the space and checked the height to make sure it fit. "Perfect," he reassured us. "This will do just fine."

I lifted the lid of the box and found several papers lying on the top tray. I pushed them aside and in the corner saw the locket with its necklace. Sadly, I whispered, "I never opened it."

Papa had sold many things from the house to buy food and heating oil, but the locket was one thing he kept. Seeing it brought to mind memories of my grandmother and put a smile on my face.

"One day," Papa said, "when this is all over, it will be yours. Perhaps then there will be time to open it and inspect its contents." He pushed the papers back in place and closed the lid. "But for now we will leave it here, where it will be safe."

The floorboards were held in place by two nails at each end. Papa removed one nail from each pair, making it easier to take up the boards next time. While he did that, I took out the leather wallet and removed the documents I had obtained in Spain. When I reached to open the jewelry box again, Papa stopped me.

"Those are your papers. You must have them with you, ready to show at a moment's notice."

"These are the ones I got with Aunt Haya in Spain. I do not want to use them now. No one will pay any attention to them and they will be lost."

"Perhaps you are right," he nodded. "Put them in the box."

I lifted the lid of the jewelry box and placed them inside, then closed it tightly and said a prayer. Papa slid the floorboards in place over the hole and pressed the nails back in their holes with the end of his knife. Then he stood and gently pressed down with his heel on each board to ensure they fit tightly and did not move, but one of them did.

Papa looked at me and shrugged. "It is the best we can do."

"Will they notice the loose one?"

"Let us hope not."

Our hands were grimy with dirt from the floor but I felt better knowing the jewelry box was safely out of sight. I dusted my palms together but it did no good, and when I glanced down at my fingernails I saw there was dirt beneath them. The front of my dress was smudged from the train trip and I was sure my hair looked oily and unkempt. No sooner had I noticed it than images of the Averbuch children flashed through my mind. I could see them once again, lying atop their parents, the life slowly oozing from their gunshot wounds. At least we were alive,

I told myself. That became the key for me—staying alive just one more day.

"Come," Papa insisted. "We can rinse our hands at the sink." I followed him into the front room and he turned on the tap. The water felt cool on my hands and after I rinsed them as clean as I could, I splashed some water on my face.

That night we slept together on the mattress tick. It was a tight fit but I lay next to Mama, and David was beside Papa. With no blankets for cover, we snuggled close to each other. It wasn't very comfortable, but we were together and finally able to relax. No one asked the obvious questions like, Why were we there? Would we ever get home again? Would we have anything to eat? Instead, we just lay there quiet and still. After a few minutes, I was fast asleep.

The next morning we rose before dawn and were outside our building as the sun came over the horizon. Hungry, tired, and filthy dirty, we stood in line with other residents from our unit and waited. About ten o'clock, four black cars turned onto the street and drove toward us. They came to a stop near our building and we could see soldiers seated inside. They got out and set up small desks at each building, then began the process of verifying our identity and the apartment in which we lived. After checking our papers against their lists, they issued us work cards, which we would use to obtain employment and our daily food ration.

Employment was really a misnomer, as we were not allowed to find work on our own but were assigned tasks on what appeared to be a random basis. Most of the work consisted of maintenance inside the ghetto, though occasionally work teams were taken outside the compound, usually to perform menial tasks non-Jews thought too demeaning to do themselves. We received no pay for the work, it being considered an exchange for the food the army made available to us.

Daily food rations consisted of a few slices of moldy bread, several potatoes, and a little jam. Sometimes they gave us a cup of dried beans, and once in a while a few beets or some cabbage leaves. Each month we received an allocation of sugar that amounted to maybe 250 grams, but there was no flour and no dairy products of any kind. Mama did her best to prepare edible meals for us, but we never had enough to eat and were always hungry.

Later that first afternoon, after we were dismissed from formation, I left the apartment and went to find Stephan. As I wandered the streets of the ghetto, I saw squalor worse than our own and the reality of what had happened to us began to sink in. Many of the buildings had no windows, only bare openings in the wall where the glass once had been. Side streets were unpaved and had become a muddy mess. Children played in them, sometimes miring up to their knees in gooey, stinking ooze. Seeing them made me once again remember the Averbuch children. Loneliness swept over me like a dark cloud and tears filled my eyes. I wiped them with the back of my hand and kept moving, desperate now to find Stephan.

At the far side of the compound the sewer pipes were broken, and grown men and women, emaciated and gaunt, waded in the runoff hoping to find bits of something to eat. The sight of our people being forced to live like that only deepened my sadness. The stench of it made me sick and I realized then the reason no one had asked why we were there or when we would be returning home. We were never going home. Most of us would be lucky to get out of there alive.

After a while I found Stephan on the corner not far from our building. He was standing with some friends we'd known in Linz. I was relieved to find him but felt angry when I wondered why he had not come looking for me. As I approached, Stephan stepped away from the group and took me by the hand. They all laughed when he kissed me on the lips. He blushed and led me down the street. "Where have you been?" he asked.

"Where have *I* been?" I retorted. "Where have *you* been?"

"Looking for you."

"On the street corner?"

"I searched for you all morning but couldn't find you. Where were you?"

"In the apartment."

"Well, then, how could I find you if I didn't know where that was?"

I knew he was right, and that wasn't really why I was upset anyway. Tears filled my eyes. He saw them and pulled me close. "What's the matter?"

"What's the matter?" I bellowed. "You can look at where we are and ask, 'What's the matter?'" I wrapped my arms around his neck and rested my head on his shoulder. "I can still see them," I sobbed.

"The family from your house?"

"Those children did nothing to deserve that." I pointed down the street to a group playing in the mud. "They don't deserve to live like this. None of us deserve this."

"I know." He placed his hand gently on the back of my head. "I know."

"These men are animals."

"They think *we* are the animals."

"What will we do?"

"I don't know. But some of us are thinking of resisting."

"Is that what you were talking about on the corner?"

"Yes," he nodded.

I looked up at him, still a little angry. "And that is what you were doing instead of looking for me."

"No," he insisted. "Not all the time. I went all the way around the ghetto twice looking for you." His face brightened. "I found Benjamin Murmelstein. When you see him you can ask him for yourself."

"Are you serious about resisting?"

"Yes."

"You will be killed." I wiped my eyes. "You know that, don't you?"

"Better to die free than to live a slave."

"And what will I do if you are gone?"

"Sarah," he said in earnest, gesturing to the scene around them. "I cannot live like this."

"At least we are alive."

"Look around you," he pointed for emphasis. "We are living here in the ghetto. Almost no one is allowed beyond the fence. The soldiers tell us where to go. And whatever we eat comes from their hands. We are not living. We are already slaves. The only question is whether we die as slaves."

"Or whether we live," I countered.

"I do not think living is an option." Stephan's eyes turned dark. "I do not think this will end before we are all dead."

chapter 21

everal days later, there was a knock on the door. Mama opened it and found Uncle Alois standing in the hall with Rabbi Gavriel. She shouted and laughed and hugged him with both arms. David and I came to see what the commotion was about and when I saw Uncle Alois I hugged him, too.

Just the day before, Papa found a chair in the basement and brought it upstairs. Mama placed it in the front room and we used it as the seat of honor for guests. That day, we placed Rabbi Gavriel on it and continued to fawn over Uncle Alois. We peppered Uncle Alois with questions until he told us where he'd been and why we hadn't seen him for so long.

"After they refused to let me practice law," he began, "I stayed at home and read."

Mama found that amusing and laughed out loud. "You read?"

"Yes," Uncle Alois nodded. "I had a house full of books, many of which I had never even opened, so I took the time to read some of them. Eventually I had to sell them in order for us to eat, but by then I had read a good many of them."

"When you didn't come around, I was worried." The expression on Mama's face turned serious. "I was afraid something had happened."

"And I was worried about you, too. But with the roving mobs on the streets, travel was out of the question. Then when they moved all the people in from the countryside, I was busy in my neighborhood trying to keep everyone alive."

"Keep them alive?"

"New people, new disputes. Everyone who'd lived there knew I was an attorney, so they came to me to resolve their disputes." He grinned. "I became the neighborhood judge."

We talked awhile longer, then Papa came from the bedroom. Uncle Alois looked over at him with a smile. "Just the man I was wanting to see."

"Alois," Papa nodded. "Good to see you, and to see you alive and well."

"And I you also."

Papa shook hands with Rabbi Gavriel. "I am honored to have you in our home. May I get you a drink of water?"

"No," Rabbi Gavriel replied. "I am fine. I've been enjoying the conversation. But I was wondering if we could find a place to talk."

Papa folded his arms across his chest. "Whatever you have to say, you can say here." He acknowledged us with a nod. "We are all family. Everyone is an adult now. Speak what is on your heart."

"Well," Rabbi Gavriel cleared his throat. "The Nazis require us to form a council to govern our people here."

Papa had a disapproving look. "A Community Council?"

"Yes," Rabbi Gavriel nodded. "The *Judenrat*."

Papa shrugged his shoulders in a dismissive manner. "What is there for this council to do? Don't the soldiers control everything?"

"They will permit us to keep order and they would like us to handle food distribution. Perhaps take care of other things as well."

"Are you asking me if we should do this?"

"No," Rabbi Gavriel responded. "We want you to serve on the council."

"I don't know." Papa moved his arms from his chest and ran a hand through his hair. "I don't like it."

"We would be in control of our own destiny," Uncle Alois added. "At least to some degree."

Papa shot a look in his direction. "And when one of our own breaks a German rule, what then?"

"We will administer discipline," Uncle Alois replied.

"We?" Papa's eyes opened wide. "They will let us administer justice for a Jew who breaks a German law? I do not think so. If a rule is broken by one of our people, the Nazis will make us find that person and give that person up. They will use us to enforce their will on our people by making us their policemen. We will be worse than our ancestors who collaborated with the Romans."

"I agree it is a difficult position," Rabbi Gavriel nodded. "But we have no choice. The council must be formed. If you do not serve, then someone else will take your place. Do you want someone else deciding the issues that affect us?" He glanced around the room. "Do you want someone else deciding issues that relate to the well-being of your own family?"

"We have many demanding to be included on the council," Uncle Alois added. "Some of them you know and respect. Some of them are… of dubious character. We are doing our best to see that only men of honor are included. That is why we came to you."

"The position includes an extra ration of food," Rabbi Gavriel offered.

There was a long silence. Then finally Papa spoke. "I will serve," he sighed. "But only if I may give my extra ration to someone else."

"Very well," Rabbi Gavriel nodded. "As you wish." He stood and shook Papa's hand. Uncle Alois hugged Mama and me, then opened the door and they both stepped out to the hall.

When they were gone, Mama turned to Papa. "You would give away an extra ration of food?"

"There are many here who are in much worse shape than we."

"We are not in such great shape as to be that generous."

"We are not in such great shape that we can afford *not* to be generous," Papa countered.

* * *

That evening, I left the apartment and went down to the corner. Stephan met me there and we went for a walk. As we picked our way along one of the paved streets, he took a small package from beneath his jacket. It was wrapped in paper and when he unfolded it I saw he had a piece of cake. For a moment I just stared at it, unable to believe it was really there. Then my eyes opened wide with excitement. "Where did you get it?" I asked finally.

"From the bakery," he grinned.

"What bakery?" I frowned.

"There's one a few blocks from here."

"Beyond the fence?"

"Yes."

"How did you get them to sell it to you?"

"Took off my jacket to hide the star, and folded it over my arm. Went to the back door. They sold it to me without question."

"Where did you get the money?"

"You ask too many questions," he laughed.

"How did you get out?"

"There's a way."

"What way?"

"I can't tell you." His eyes darted to the side. "You can't go anyway."

"Why not?"

"It is too dangerous and too dirty."

"What is it?" I insisted. "How did you get out? Tell me."

"You ask too many questions," he laughed. "Let's eat the cake before someone sees it and takes it away from us."

I pinched off a piece with my fingers and placed it in my mouth. It was sweet and creamy and more delicious than anything I'd ever tasted. Stephan had a bite and then gave me another. In only a couple of minutes it was gone and my head felt light from the sudden rush of sugar. My stomach rumbled from it, too.

When the last crumbs of the cake were gone, he gave me a boyish grin. "Okay, I'll tell you how we did it." Then he leaned near my ear and whispered, "We crawled out through the sewer."

My mouth dropped open. "The sewer?"

Startled by my sudden outburst, he clamped his hand over my mouth and glanced around with a worried look. When it seemed no one heard, he put his face closed to mine and said, "Don't repeat that. You hear?" I nodded my head and he moved his hand from my mouth.

"They guard everything but they leave open the sewer?"

"So far," he replied. "But you must keep quiet about it. You can't tell anyone. Not David. Not your mother. And certainly not your father."

I didn't like the way he referred to Papa. "Why did you say it that way? *Certainly not your father?*"

"He's...you know...one of them."

"One of whom?"

"The Judenrat. The council."

"You say that like there's something wrong with it."

"They are a detestable group."

Now I was angry. "What do you mean? My father is not detestable."

"I like your father," he said defensively, "but he made a terrible mistake joining the Nazis and their council."

"He didn't join the Nazis," I fumed. "He's a member of the council. The Jewish council. And they're doing a thankless task for our benefit."

"It is thankless," he conceded, "but it is not for our benefit."

"How can you be so mean?" I fumed. "Is this you talking, or some of your so-called friends you hang out with on the corner?"

"When the Nazis come for us," he argued, "the Judenrat will hand us over. When the Nazis choose who will live and who will die, the Judenrat will give them the list. When the Nazis have food for us to eat, the Judenrat will decide who is full and who goes hungry."

"My father is an honorable man," I argued. "He will do the right thing."

"Your father is honorable," Stephan nodded. "But he is a man."

"How can you say that? You act as if you don't even know him."

"We are all in a tough position, but members of the Judenrat give themselves special privileges. Your father will take those privileges just like all the others."

"What kind of privileges?"

"Extra rations of food. Better apartments. First pick of any clothing and furniture that comes available."

"We live in the same apartment we were assigned when we came here. As far as I know there have been no clothes available for anyone. We have one mattress that was there when we arrived and one chair Papa found in the basement. And as to the food, he was offered an extra ration, but he gives it to a family in the next building that has three small children."

Stephan looked at me a moment. "Perhaps he's an exception. But the others are just in it for themselves."

I turned away and continued walking. "I don't believe it." A few steps later, I wheeled around to face him. "My Uncle Alois is on that council, too. He would never agree to the things you suggest."

He looked at me and I saw sadness in his eyes. Then he said quietly, "I hope you're right."

* * *

One afternoon not long after my meeting with Stephan, I returned to our apartment and found Mama alone, seated on the chair in the front room. She was repairing a shirt using a sewing needle she'd fashioned from a piece of wire and thread she'd made by weaving strands of her own hair. The apartment was empty and the bedroom door was closed. "Where's David?"

"Out," she answered.

"And Papa?"

"In there." She cut her eyes toward the bedroom door.

"The council?"

"Yes," Mama nodded.

"Uncle Alois is with them?"

"Yes," she sighed in an exasperated manner. "Of course he's with them. Why wouldn't he be?" Her voice was tense and her tone was sharp.

"Is something the matter?"

"What do you mean?" Now she really sounded aggravated. "Why would you think something is the matter?"

"You sound upset."

She looked at me for a moment, then lowered her voice to a whisper. "Adolf Eichmann is with them."

My eyes opened wide. "He is in there now?"

"Yes," her voice was no longer a whisper. "Why do you think I just told you that?"

"How long have they been in there?"

"They just started."

I eased closer to the door and listened. The first voice I heard was that of Rabbi Gavriel. He was speaking softly and I thought perhaps he was praying. Then Adolf spoke up. "Moshe Batsheva, it was good of you to allow us the use of your room for this meeting."

"Accept it with my gratitude," Papa replied. "It was the least I could do." He sounded unusually conciliatory.

"As you all know," Eichmann continued, "I am head of the Office for Jewish Emigration. We control the ghetto, but to do that effectively we need your help, which is why I asked you to organize this council."

"We will be glad to assist in the administration of our people," someone offered. I felt my heart sink. Perhaps Stephan was right after all. Then the voice continued, "But we must have your assurance that we will have true authority over the matters entrusted to us."

"True authority?" There was a hint of sarcasm in Adolf's voice.

"If we are to have any legitimacy with the people, we cannot merely be your puppet. No one would listen to us."

"Yes," Adolf nodded, "I see your point. So let me make very clear how the system works, so there will be no confusion later should an issue arise. The people account to you. You account to me. I account to the Gestapo. If you work with me, I will work with you. But my word is the last word. Understood?" Several of them murmured and grumbled, but from the tone of the meeting I assumed they all agreed.

Adolf continued. "Our chief goal is for you to emigrate from Austria. You cannot live here any longer."

"But Austria is our home," someone protested. "We have always lived here."

"It is now part of the German state and it is Reich policy for you to leave." Adolf spoke with an authoritative tone. "We can assist you in moving your families to Palestine, but you must leave."

"Not all of our people are interested in Palestine," Uncle Alois offered.

"Perhaps some of you can go to the U.S. or Great Brittan," Adolf responded. "I don't care where you go, but you cannot remain here. You must get everyone to understand this. You must convince them."

"We can tell them," someone explained, "but the primary problem we face is the visa taxes you impose on us and the need for so many documents and approvals."

"We have nothing left," another added. "You have taken it all. We have no shops, no houses, no lands, no investments. It is all gone. Left behind when you sent us here."

"We are holding all of your assets in a closed account," Adolf explained. "You cannot access it, but we can. Those who can demonstrate their ability to survive in Palestine, or anywhere else they wish to go, will be supplied with the funds for the taxes."

"You would do this?"

"The Führer has agreed. He doesn't want you here and he is willing to help you leave. But your people must show some evidence of a trade, an occupation, a transferrable profession."

"And how shall we do that?"

"You can begin by taking a census of the entire ghetto, which will ascertain everyone's occupation. Those with sustainable trades and occupations will be given the assistance they need."

"And what about the others?" Uncle Alois asked.

"We will address them later."

"How do we take such a census?"

"Line them up and make them tell you." Adolf's voice was loud and abrasive. "Must I tell you even the simplest procedures? Line them up and make them give you the information."

"What if they do not comply?"

"Turn them over to me," Adolf roared.

"To you?"

"Give me the names of every person who refuses to comply and we shall deal with them."

"That is simple enough," Papa said, trying to lighten the mood. "We can take a census."

"There is one other thing," Adolf continued. "Already some of your people have exhibited an inclination not to comply with any of our requirements. They only want to make trouble, and that trouble will come back to all of you. We must work together to find them. They must be rooted out from among you."

"You want us to give them up?" Rabbi Gavriel questioned.

"If you do not," Adolf added sternly, "the army will move in to eliminate them. That will bring death and destruction on many more than just the troublemakers. Perhaps resulting in the liquidation of the entire ghetto. If you want to emigrate, or give your people that option, you must root out these troublemakers, and you must act quickly."

"We know of no one who is making trouble," Rabbi Gavriel replied.

"Or even planning trouble," someone added.

"That is because you have not been doing your job," Adolf shouted. "If you had been doing your job, you would already know all of the leaders in the resistance movement. Their accomplices, the names of their members, and where they live."

"What resistance movement? Where?"

"Here!" Adolf shouted. "Among your people. Are you blind? Have you chosen not to see? This is your job. To keep tabs on this sort of thing. You must develop connections, contacts, informants."

"Informants?"

"Yes." Adolf was still shouting. "Informants. How else will you know what is happening?"

"If you know of the existence of this person, give us his name?"

There was the sound of shuffling papers, then Adolf barked, "There. That is his name! Written down in black and white. Do I need to read it to you?"

Suddenly Mama took me by the shoulders. "You have heard too much," she whispered. I was about to protest but thought better of it and she steered me away from the door. "It is not good for you to know these things."

"What things? What is it not good for me to know?"

"You should let them do their own business." She pushed me toward the door, then reached around me and opened it. "Go downstairs. And do not come back until you see them leave."

On the street, I found Stephan and told him what I heard while listening at the door. He looked worried. "You are certain it was Eichmann in the room?"

"Yes," I answered. "Didn't you see him when he arrived?"

"No."

"Were you watching?"

"Yes. We watched the door the entire time and he didn't go in or out."

"How could that be?"

His face was clouded in thought. "This is a problem," he mumbled.

"Why?"

"If he entered the building without being seen, that means he knows about the tunnels."

"What tunnels?" I frowned. "The sewer?"

"No." Stephan shook his head. "The tunnel to the basement of the building."

"I don't understand. There's a tunnel?"

"Yes." He nodded. "Most of the buildings are connected by tunnels. They were designed that way for the steam pipes."

Now my eyes flashed with anger when I realized what he was saying. "You mean you could come to my apartment at night without being seen?"

"Yes."

"But you don't."

"This is why," he gestured.

"What is why?"

"The Judenrat."

"The council prevents you from coming to see me?"

His eyes blazed. "I can't go to the apartment of a man who is head of such council."

"He is not the head," I countered.

"They meet in his apartment, don't they?"

"They did tonight."

"Then he is in charge," Stephan insisted.

I was angry again that he would say things about Papa but still curious about the tunnels. "So how could Adolf get into the tunnel without being seen?"

"I don't know," Stephan replied, "but I feel certain he did." He stepped away as if leaving, then glanced back at me. "Don't say anything to anyone about it."

"I must tell my father."

"No," he snapped. "You can't tell him without also telling him how you know about them."

"I don't have to tell him about you."

"Just keep quiet," he insisted. "Just keep quiet." Then he turned away and started up the street.

chapter 22

As the months passed, life in the ghetto became even more restricted. A curfew was imposed and for the first time soldiers patrolled the streets at night. That meant no one could come or go from the buildings after dark without using the tunnels. At the same time, food became more scarce than ever before. Most people got by with only one meal each day.

We heard rumors that those living on a street five blocks over from us were being moved out. No one said where they were going, but for several days trucks moved in and out of that section. When I walked over there to see for myself, the streets were even more crowded than before. Stephan said it was because more people were being brought in to replace the ones who were removed. That didn't seem right to me, but I didn't question him.

Then late one night I was awakened to the sound of gunshots coming from the backside of the ghetto. I went to the window to look out, but Mama called me back for fear I would be seen by the soldiers and cause trouble.

The next morning, I walked a few streets over from ours to have a look. As I came around the corner, I saw three bodies lying in the street, all of them men. Dark blotches of blood stained their clothes, and flies buzzed around them. They had been dead for some time. No one on the street went near the bodies except for a woman who was on her knees beside one of them, weeping. As I approached she looked up. "They shot him," she cried. "He left the apartment last night and they shot him."

"Who did this?"

"The soldiers," she sobbed. "They patrol the streets at night just waiting for someone to come out. He was only going to find something for us to eat. And they shot him." She leaned over, her head resting on his chest. "We have nothing to eat since all the people came."

"What people?"

"More people from the countryside. They moved them into our apartment. Everyone has extra people now. We are living sixteen and twenty to a unit." She looked back at the bodies lying in the street. "They were only out here looking for something to eat."

When I returned to the apartment I told Papa what I had seen—the bodies lying in the street and the many people now living in each apartment.

"Yes," he nodded. "It is not good."

"They are moving in more people almost every day."

"Yes," he sighed. "They are moving people in as fast as possible."

"And where are they putting them?"

"They began in back." He gestured with his hand toward the window in the front room. "But they are working their way in our direction. Filling every available space. They even have people sleeping in the closets and in the halls."

"Who decided to do this?"

"The Nazis."

"Adolf Eichmann?"

He nodded his head slowly. "We certainly didn't ask for them."

Stephan was right again, I thought. The Judenrat put these people as far from their own apartments as possible. I was angry and frustrated. "But you told them where to begin." I said it as an accusation.

"Yes," he nodded. "They asked us where to begin and I said to begin in the front, where we live. But they wanted to begin in the back. So that is what they did."

I felt deflated and ashamed for what I had thought just moments before, so I changed the subject. "And the soldiers patrol the streets at night, shooting anyone who comes out. Even if they are only searching for food."

"I know," he nodded with a look of sadness. "I hear the shots every night."

"They killed three men last night."

"I know that, too," he lamented.

"Yet the council will do nothing."

"There is nothing we can do. The Nazis make the rules. Imposing the curfew was their idea. They told us to enforce it, but we said we had no way to enforce it. So they sent the soldiers to patrol at night."

"You must make them stop shooting."

He looked at me with tired, hopeless eyes. "Sarah, you have seen how we live. We are unable to make them do anything."

Later that day Papa left the apartment and went downstairs. He'd looked so forlorn when we talked that I was worried about him. When he walked out I waited until I heard his footsteps on the stairs and then I followed after him. He went down to the first floor, but instead of stepping out to the street, he doubled back to the hallway that ran past the staircase. At the end of the hall he opened a door on the right and disappeared. I hurried to keep up.

When I reached the door, I found it led to a stairway down into the basement. It was dark on the stairs so I left the door open to allow in enough light to see my way, but as I reached the bottom of the steps the door banged closed and I was in total darkness. Panic seized me, and my heart raced, but I told myself all I had to do to escape was to feel my way back up the stairs to the door. Gradually, my heart rate slowed and I got hold of myself.

After a minute or two my eyes adjusted to the darkness and I could see light coming into the basement from a coal chute in the center of the wall to the left. On the wall to the right there was a narrow window at street level with another a little way down from it.

As I stood there getting my bearings, I heard voices coming from behind the staircase. I crept around to where I could see and in the distance the soft glow of a candle illuminated an opening on the back wall. The closer I came to it the larger the opening became and I realized I was staring into one of the tunnels Stephan had told me about. Then I heard Papa talking and I knew the sounds I'd heard came from the Judenrat. They were gathered in the tunnel. At once I was comforted by the knowledge that my father was there and I was not alone, then I was terrified at the realization that Adolf knew exactly where they were and what they were doing. The council might have thought they were meeting in secrecy, but in fact they were more exposed than ever.

I moved closer and listened more intently, but the light behind me from the windows and the chute meant I couldn't get close enough to hear what they were saying without revealing my presence. Instead of trying, I backed away and stood near one of the narrow windows. They were dirty and grimy so I rubbed a spot clean with my finger and looked out. The windows faced the street in front of the building, and from my position I could see all the way to the corner. I stood watch there, hoping to catch sight of any soldiers in the area before they arrived to cause trouble.

After what seemed like only a few minutes I felt a hand on my shoulder. I turned to see Papa standing behind me and jumped at the sight of him. "Why are you down here?" he asked, paying no attention to the fright he gave me.

"No reason," I shrugged, trying to regain my composure. "Just needed a few minutes alone."

"You followed me."

"No," I shook my head. "I didn't."

"I heard you when you came from the apartment," he smiled, "and I saw you when I reached the first floor. Why are you following me?"

A lump formed in my throat and my eyes become moist. "Adolf Eichmann knows about the tunnel," I whispered.

Papa looked stricken. "How do you know this?"

"The other day, when he came to the apartment, I listened through the door."

"I thought so," he nodded. "I saw the shadow of your feet in the light from the space beneath the door."

"Did he know I was there?"

"I don't think so. He was standing with his back to the door. Go on, you were listening at the door..."

"Eventually Mama made me stop and she sent me out. While I was on the street I saw Stephan and told him Adolf was there. He was surprised to know that Adolf had reached the apartment without them noticing."

Papa frowned. "Stephan and his friends were watching the building?"

"They were only trying to help."

Papa had a solemn look. "You must stop seeing him." I could tell he wasn't angry, but he said it with resolve.

"But I love him," I replied in an unemotional tone.

"I know," he sighed. "But things are happening that I cannot discuss. Serious things, which make it necessary for you to stop seeing him."

"I can't break it off."

"You don't have to. Simply remain inside the apartment. That's all."
He stood there beside me and for a moment said nothing, but I could
see from the look in his eyes that he was deep in thought. Then he took
a deep breath and began again. "So, they did not see Eichmann enter the
building?"

"No."

"Very well. We shall meet somewhere else. The tunnels are no
longer safe." He placed his hand on my shoulder. "Come, we should get
upstairs." Then he guided me from the window to the stairway and we
started up toward the first-floor hall.

*　*　*

Just before sunset I was on the street near the corner with Stephan
and several of his friends. It was almost time for the curfew and we were
about to go inside when a truck turned onto our block. It rolled toward
us and came to a stop a few meters away. A squad of German soldiers
stood in back, dressed in gray uniforms and armed with rifles. Adolf sat
on the passenger side of the cab and when the truck stopped he was
directly opposite me. The coincidence of his presence made me certain
he'd been in the tunnel when the Judenrat met.

Adolf leaned through the open window of the cab. "Sarah," he said
in a syrupy tone, "I haven't seen you since you arrived."

"Adolf," I said, acknowledging him in a polite manner but with as
little affect as possible.

He glanced in Stephan's direction. "This is your friend? The one I
used to see when you were both so much younger?"

"Yes," I nodded. "This is Stephan."

In his eyes I saw the same look I'd seen months before when I ran
into him at the coffee shop. Not exactly hatred, but a look as if Stephan
was intruding. It was the same look Stephan gave when one of his friends

said something nice to me, only now, seeing it from Adolf made my skin crawl. The last thing I wanted was for him to be interested in me. We talked a moment longer, then he said something to the driver and the truck moved away.

When he was gone, Stephan looked over at me. "He likes you."

"How could he? I am just a Jew."

"Yes," Stephan nodded, "you are a Jew and he knows it, but he can't get past his attraction to you." His eyes met mine. "And you like him, too."

I glanced away. "Not like that."

"But you like him," he persisted.

"I liked him when I was twelve and he was a teenager," I tried to defuse the situation. "It made me feel grown up when he talked to me. But now he is a soldier in the German Army, and we are here because of him."

"But you still see him as a friend."

Stephan's needling was becoming obnoxious, but I did my best not to react. "My mind tells me he is no friend at all."

"But your heart won't let go of the past."

Finally I could stand it no more and I hit Stephan on the shoulder. "Stop it," I snapped. "You're making something out of nothing but a childhood memory."

"Just see that *you* don't make something of it," he warned.

chapter 23

$\mathcal{A}$ little after noon the next day, Papa arrived at the apartment looking worried and nervous. Hands in his pockets, he paced back and forth. I glanced at Mama but she seemed not to pay him any attention, then I looked back at Papa. "What is wrong?"

"It is nothing," he dismissed me with a wave of his hand.

"You don't act like it's nothing."

"Leave him alone," Mama said in a monotone voice. She stood at the sink, her head down, breaking the day's cabbage leaves into small pieces. "He will tell you if he wants you to know."

The door opened and David came in. "Hey, Sarah," he grinned. "I heard Adolf Eichmann stopped to say hello to you last night."

"What are you talking about?" His sudden appearance and jovial attitude caught me off guard, and I was worried about the mention of Adolf's name.

David seemed oblivious. "Everyone is talking about how he was in the truck with the soldiers and had them stop just so he could speak to you."

As I suspected, Papa was irate. "Haven't you learned yet?" he shouted at me. "You cannot have anything to do with that man. All your life you've pestered and hounded him, and each time it has only brought trouble." He looked at me, his eyes wide open, the veins in his neck pulsing. "Stop seeing that man!"

"I wasn't seeing him," I argued, taken aback by the ferocity of his tirade. "I was talking to Stephan and the truck came by. They stopped. What was I to do?"

"And what did I tell you about Stephan?" he continued.

Mama turned from the sink to face him. "Moshe," she said in a calm and even voice. "Why don't you have a seat?"

"I don't want to sit," he barked.

"You need to calm down."

"She can't stand around on the corner, Orna. It's an open invitation to trouble, which now has found her. And I specifically told her not to be out there with Stephan."

"Why not?" David asked, coming to my defense.

"This is why!" Papa shouted. "This right here. This thing we are talking about. Adolf Eichmann and a truck full of soldiers. That would have never happened if she had done what I told her to do."

David didn't back down. "But they were just talking. They didn't know Eichmann was coming."

"And that is precisely my point." Papa moved closer to David and continued to shout. "She didn't know. But she could have avoided it if she had been doing what I told her to do."

"But I love him," I said in a plaintive voice.

"I know you love him. I've recognized that before. That has nothing to do with this."

"Then what is it?"

Papa looked deflated by the question. He turned away and sighed, "I can't tell you."

That made me even angrier. "Why not?" I insisted. "Why can't you tell me?"

Before he could answer, there was a knock at the door. Members of the council arrived and as they filed through the door, Papa led them to the bedroom. Uncle Alois passed me without saying a word. When they were all in the room, Papa closed the door and Mama sent us out.

David and I went downstairs to the street and wandered up to the corner. As usual, Stephan was there with his friends. This time, however, they cut their eyes at me with looks of suspicion. Stephen took my arm and led me aside.

"You must not be here now." He spoke in hushed tones and his face was serious.

I didn't like it. "Why not? I can go wherever I want."

"Things are too dangerous," he insisted.

"What do you mean?"

"People have been asking too many questions."

"About what?"

"About you and Eichmann. About your father and the council."

"What people?" I demanded. "Tell me who they are."

"Everyone." He sounded exasperated. "Our people, their people. It's just not safe." He held me by the arm and led me back toward the apartment building. Before we reached it, he let go of me and turned back. I watched as he reached the group at the corner and felt my heart sink.

With nothing else to do but wait, I wandered back to the apartment building and sat on the curb. Half an hour later, Uncle Alois came out. I stood to talk to him but he shook his head and waved me off. "I have to go," he said softly. Before he was out of sight, the other members of the council came from the building. They passed me without saying a word as they went in separate directions.

Curious now about what had transpired in their meeting, I ran up the steps to the apartment. When I reached the door I heard Mama's voice. "No," she pleaded. "You can't."

"There is no other way." Papa's voice was angry and intense.

"You must find a way."

"I can't," he said, his voice calmer but still resolute. "This is how it must be done."

When the apartment grew quiet, I opened the door and went inside. Mama was standing at the counter. Papa stood near the stove. I glanced at them with a questioning look. "What's the matter?"

Papa did not reply but brushed past me, opened the door, and disappeared into the hall. I turned to Mama and now I could see she was crying. "Mama," I implored, "what is the matter?"

She took my face in both hands and drew me close. "We must be brave," she said softly. "We must be very brave."

* * *

The next morning, before the sun was an hour above the horizon, Stephan's brother, Yosef, came to our apartment. He appeared anxious and worried. "Stephan is missing," he blurted out. "Have you seen him?"

"Not since yesterday," I answered. "He was on the corner with all the others. He didn't come home?"

"No. When I left he was with Tomer Levy. They were still talking. I walked home alone."

Papa entered the room. He saw the look on Yosef's face. "What's the matter?"

"We can't find Stephan," Yosef explained. "He has disappeared."

"Perhaps," I suggested, "the soldiers took him last night by mistake."

"That is what worries us most." Yosef crossed the room and stood near Papa. "You are a member of the Judenrat. You can intercede with the authorities. At least find out what has happened to him."

"No," Papa replied dryly. "I do not think so."

Yosef looked hurt and confused. "Why not?"

"This is a matter for the Nazis," Papa explained. "It is not the kind of thing we do."

"Not the kind of thing . . ." Yosef stammered in frustration. "Then what do you do?"

"We distribute jobs, food, and sometimes assistance in other matters. We take up issues about apartments and living conditions and we—"

"Living conditions?" Yosef interrupted. "You call *this* living conditions?" His voice was loud and I saw his sense of frustration turning to anger. "Why won't you help us find Stephan?"

Papa looked over at Mama. They exchanged a knowing look, then he turned away and started toward the bedroom. "I am sorry. I can't help you."

Yosef rushed from the apartment with tears streaming down his face. I followed after him but he would not stop and I soon lost sight of him in the crowd that wandered the sidewalks. On the next corner, I found Tomer Levy standing in his usual place with the regular group of friends. As I approached, the others moved away, leaving Tomer to face me alone. "What happened to Stephan?" I asked.

"Why do you ask me? Why not ask your father?"

"You were the last one to see him before dark. What happened to him?"

He gave me an angry look as if he had more to say, then his shoulders sagged and he leaned closer. "Rumor is he was picked up by the SS."

"You saw them take him?"

"I saw them coming. We split up. When I glanced back, they were closing in on him."

"Why did they take him?"

An angry scowl returned to his face. "The Judenrat turned him in."

"No," I replied. "That is not possible."

"Yes. It is possible. Ask your father."

"No. If he is gone, I will find him."

"Don't be ridiculous," Tomer scoffed. "Just ask your father."

"I'm not being ridiculous," I hissed. "Show me the secret way out."

He gave me a look of mock confusion. "What secret way out?"

"I know about the sewer and the trips outside. Stephan brought me cake from the bakery. Now show me where it is."

"I can't." He turned away with a self-conscious look.

"Fine," I snapped. "I'll find the way out by myself." Then I started up the street toward the backside of the ghetto.

A moment later, Tomer appeared at my side. "Okay. I'll show you. But you must keep quiet about it."

We walked to a side street near the back corner of the ghetto, then turned down a narrow alley that led behind the buildings. Unlike the front side of the complex, where the fence and river separated us from the rest of Vienna, the backside was partitioned by a brick wall that stood ten feet tall. In between the building and the wall we came to an iron manhole cover. Tomer lifted it off and laid it aside. A pungent odor rose from the hole. My nose wrinkled and my eyes watered.

He looked over at me. "Are you sure you want to do this?"

"Yes. I must."

Then he knelt by the open hole and pointed to small indentations in the concrete walls of the shaft that led down into the darkness below. "These are places for your hands and feet. Grip the edges of the hole, lower yourself down, and put your feet in them. Then work your way to the bottom."

"How far is it?"

"About six feet."

"Does it smell like this all the time?"

"It's not so bad once you get inside. Go on," he urged. "I'll be right behind you but we must move quickly before the guards see us."

"There are guards?"

"They patrol along the walls with the dogs. Hurry up."

I did as he said and worked my way down the access shaft. When I was a few feet below the surface, he started down after me. Before I reached the bottom, he slid the cover over the manhole and plunged us into darkness. "Keep going," he urged. "There's light when you get to the bottom." My arms shook from fatigue as I struggled to keep from falling, but I forced myself to continue, carefully placing my feet in the holes beneath me as I gripped tightly with both hands.

In a moment I dropped from the access shaft into a pipe about five feet tall. About fifty meters away, the pipe opened into a canal. Light from the opening streamed into the pipe and I could see water draining down the center of it in a continuous stream. Then something touched my foot. "Oh!" I squealed and stumbled backward.

Tomer dropped from the ladder beside me. "Be quiet! The soldiers can hear you."

"I felt something on my ankle."

"Rats," he said flatly.

"Rats?"

He pointed to the opposite side of the pipe. "Look over there."

I focused my eyes on the water line against the pipe and in the reflection from the surface I saw them—rats twice as big as my hand— working like a swarm of insects. A shudder ran over my body. "I didn't know we had rats."

"We don't have rats in the buildings," he replied. "Just here."

"Why aren't there any in the buildings?" He turned to me and even in the poor light of the sewer pipe I saw the knowing look in his eye. Then the answer came to me. "We eat them?" I asked timidly.

"As often as we can find them."

Thankfully, most of the rats were on the other side and there was room along our side to walk without getting our feet wet. When we emerged at the canal, Tomer lifted me up to dry ground, then led the way as we moved along the bank. We walked quickly, doing our best to hurry without making any noise. The wall along the back of the ghetto had no towers, but guards patrolled it regularly on foot. It seemed odd to be out there in such an open location and I wondered how we would ever get across the canal without being seen.

A few minutes later I glanced up to see that he was leading me toward a bridge about twenty meters away. We reached it without being discovered and inched around the base of the buttress to a steel ladder that was bolted into place. "What are we doing?" I asked, unable to contain myself any longer.

"We're going across," he insisted.

"Across where?"

"Across the bridge."

"We're walking across the bridge?"

"Not on top of it." He pointed over his head. "Beneath it."

"How?"

"I'll show you," Tomer started up the ladder.

Overhead were steel girders that supported the bridge. Bolted together with cross pieces, they formed an angular structure that stretched across the canal to the opposite side. I didn't like the idea of crossing that way but I had no choice. We were outside the ghetto and if we were caught, we would be shot.

When Tomer reached the top of the ladder, he climbed onto the bridge structure and gestured impatiently for me to follow. I took a deep breath and began working my way up, gripping the cold metal rungs tightly and hoping I didn't fall. At the top, he helped me up from the last rung to the ledge and we stood on one of the beams. Then with careful steps, we made our way over to the opposite side.

Unlike the section of the city where we were forced to live, this area was clean and neat. People stared at us but I ignored them and pressed on, determined to find Adolf and learn what I could about what happened to Stephan.

Finally we reached a corner not far from the river. We paused there and Tomer pointed to a building down the street to the left. "That is the German headquarters."

"It looks like a hotel."

"It was until the German Army arrived." Three guards stood near the front entrance and I could see soldiers moving in and out of the building. Tomer glanced at me. "Are you sure you want to try this?"

"Wait here," I said.

Tomer grabbed my arm to stop me. "You can't just walk up to the front door."

I pulled my arm free of his grasp. "Well, I'll just have to figure it out as I go." Without waiting for a response I walked up the street toward the hotel.

As I neared the main entrance, all three guards turned in my direction. Two of them took halting steps toward me. I realized Tomer was right. It was highly unlikely I could get past them. But just as the plan seemed to fall apart even before it really began, I caught sight of an alley that led off to the right. I turned into it and soon came around to a service entrance in back of the building. The delivery door was open and I walked inside, doing my best to act as if I belonged there.

The doorway led to a wide hall, the far end of which opened into an area near the front lobby. As I came from the hallway, a group of soldiers passed by. In the midst of them was Adolf Eichmann. He was talking and laughing until his eyes met mine, then he came to an abrupt halt. My knees shook and my heart raced as the others in his group continued on while he turned aside and came toward me. He had a look of surprise. "Sarah?" He glanced around as if checking to see whether anyone else noticed me. "How did you get in here?"

I refused to be drawn into his conversation. "Where is Stephan?" I asked flatly.

"Stephan?" For an instant, something flickered in his eyes—the same look I'd seen before when he saw me with Stephan at the coffee shop and a few nights earlier when he saw us together on the street. I knew he had taken Stephan—my only worry was what he did with him. Adolf quickly pushed aside his initial reaction and appeared puzzled. "I don't think I know anyone with..." Then his eyes lit up. "Oh. Your friend." He took me by the arm. "I don't think I've seen anything about him. Why do you ask?"

"He's missing."

Adolf ushered me toward an elevator. "Let's go up to my office and see what we can find." I was fearful of what might happen if I went with him, but I had no choice. We rode to the fifth floor in silence and when the elevator door opened Adolf ushered me down the hall to the left. A few paces from the elevator we came to a door that opened into a hotel suite he had converted into an office. A desk sat opposite the door in front of a window along the far wall. It was cluttered with papers and files. Three men stood nearby, all of them dressed in the gray uniform of German soldiers. They looked startled to see me but said nothing.

Adolf made his way behind the desk and gestured to a chair that sat to the side of it. "Have a seat." Then he looked over at one of the men in the room. "Bring us some cheese and cakes with some wine." The man disappeared while Adolf shuffled through the papers on his desk.

In a few minutes, the soldier returned carrying a tray of cheese, meats, and small cakes with one hand. With the other he held a bottle of wine and two glasses. He set them on the corner of the desk in front of me and then retreated to the opposite side of the room. The bottle was open already and Adolf poured wine into the glasses. Then he raised a glass and smiled. "Have a drink, Sarah. I'm sure it will do you good."

I knew the honorable thing to do. My father would refuse to eat or drink even the slightest amount. Stephan would, too. But my stomach ached from hunger. I resisted the urge to eat, but only for a moment.

Reluctantly at first, I picked up a piece of cheese and placed it in my mouth. It tasted sharp against my tongue and I almost choked on the richness of its flavor. Adolf laughed at me and lifted his glass once more. "Have a drink," he grinned. "You don't want to die on a piece of cheese." I took a sip from the glass and had another bite of cheese. A napkin lay on the tray and I placed it on my lap.

After a while, when the cheese and meat were gone, Adolf took a seat in the chair behind his desk. "I am sorry," he sighed and gestured with both hands toward the papers on his desk. "But I don't see anything here about your friend Stephan. Are you certain he is missing?"

"We have looked everywhere for him."

"I am sure he is fine. He will turn up." He scooted his chair closer to the desk. "And in the meantime, we will continue searching for him. Are there any places you would like for us to look?"

The question was a trap, a chance to acknowledge the tunnels and all the other hiding places our people used. "None that we haven't already tried."

"You informed your father of your friend's disappearance?"

"I talked to him about it."

"And what did he say?"

"Nothing."

"Nothing?"

"He refused to talk about it."

"Interesting," he mused. He stared at me a moment, then a kind smile spread over his face. "You are a very brave woman, coming here like this. I could have you shot for being here. You know that, don't you?"

"I suppose."

"I could shoot you now and no one would do anything to stop me. While they hauled your body out, one of my men would pat me on the back and congratulate me for a job well done."

"Is that what you plan to do?"

"No," he shook his head. He leaned back in his chair. "I would prefer to keep you here with me, or at the least, drive you back to your apartment, but I am afraid neither of those things is possible right now. You will have to get back the same way you came, whatever that is." He propped his elbows on the armrest of the chair and laced his fingers together. "You understand that, don't you?"

"Yes," I nodded. "Thank you for seeing me."

"It was my pleasure." He stood and came from behind the desk. I stood as well and he took me by the arm to guide me toward the door. "One of my men will see you out."

"That won't be necessary," I said, anxious to leave. "I can find my way."

One of the soldiers opened the door and I stepped out to the hall. I hurried toward the elevator, then thought better of it and took the stairs. On the first floor I stepped from the stairwell into the hallway that led to the service area in back of the hotel. From there I walked out to the alley and made my way back to the front of the building. As I came past the corner, Tomer joined me.

"So, what did he say?"

"He said he will check."

"Yeah," Tomer commented sarcastically. "Like that's ever going to happen. We risked our lives for nothing."

"Not really."

"Then what?"

I reached inside the pocket of my dress, took out a small napkin, and handed it to him. Tomer opened it to find six pieces of cheese and three small squares of meat. His eyes were wide. "You stole this?"

"They gave it to me to eat." A guilty look made me blush. "I was too hungry to resist."

"Forget it." He stuffed several pieces of cheese into his mouth. "No one could resist such a thing."

We walked as Tomer continued to eat the cheese and meat. When he finished, he wiped his hands on the napkin and shoved it into his pocket. "Come on, we'll have to hurry. The sun will set before long and it will be difficult to see in the pipe."

Tomer set a quick pace and I had to work to keep up with him. We crossed the bridge without incident and worked our way up the canal to the pipe. As I turned to enter it he caught my hand and looked at me. "Listen, Sarah," he began. "I know Stephan had a harsh view of your father and the council. But they are only trying to do what they think is right. I do not agree with them, but I do not think they are bad men. Especially your father and your uncle."

"You know my uncle?"

"Yes," he nodded. "Alois is my father's friend. He has helped us many times."

His words did little to change my mind. "I used to share your opinion of them. But not anymore. I am almost certain the council betrayed Stephan."

"What makes you so sure?"

"The way Adolf talked. The things he asked about. The way he looked at me when I mentioned Stephan. I don't know. I just know." Sunlight was fading fast and I didn't want to talk anymore. I turned away and headed into the pipe.

chapter 24

All that night I thought of Stephan, the things that Yosef and Tomer had said, what I had heard from Adolf, and the conversations I had heard in the apartment. By dawn I was convinced Stephan had been taken by the soldiers and that they did it with the council's cooperation.

When sunlight hit the bedroom window, Papa rolled from the mattress, dressed, and left the apartment. Not long after that, Mama and David rose, too. I waited until they were out of the room, then I took my suitcase from the corner of the room and began gathering my things. I placed my clothes and put the leather wallet with my papers on top. Mama came into the room as I closed the latches on the case.

"What are you doing?"

"They turned him over to the soldiers, Mama."

"Who?" She looked puzzled. "What are you talking about?"

"Stephan. The Judenrat gave him up to the Nazis."

Papa entered the room. I didn't know that he had returned to the apartment. "It could not be avoided. The Nazis were threatening to kill everyone until they found him."

"Why?"

"He and his friends were plotting to revolt."

"We should revolt."

"We should stay alive."

"You call this living? We are merely waiting to die."

"A rebellion against the German Army cannot succeed. Any attempt to do so would only result in the death of our people. Perhaps all of our people."

"We are dying now already. What could be worse? The rest of the city does not live like this. Stephan is right. We are slaves." I grabbed my suitcase by the handle and started toward the door.

"Where are you going?" Papa called.

I turned back to look him in the eye. "Somewhere away from you. I will not live with a man who is a traitor to his own people." Then I opened the door and stepped into the hall. Sadness swept over me and tears filled my eyes as I hurried down the steps, but I felt I had no choice. Behind me I heard the sound of Mama wailing and shouting.

On the street, I walked up to the corner and over one block to the building where Stephan lived. I made my way to their apartment and knocked on the door. Yardina, his mother, opened it. I could see from the smears on her cheeks and the dampness of her eyes that she had been crying. She gestured toward the suitcase. "You have left home?"

I forced a smile. "Can I stay with you?" She nodded her approval and stepped back to let me inside.

The next day, I was on the street with Tomer and his friends, determined to help them in whatever rebellion they had planned. While we stood there talking, Papa came from his building and started toward us. He was on the opposite side of the street, but still our eyes met. When he looked at me, I turned away, ignoring him.

Someone nudged me. "There's your father."

"He's not my father," I snarled.

"Why would you say such a thing? Of course he's your father."

"He is a member of the Judenrat. All he had to do was stand up to the Nazis. They are not so powerful when someone opposes them. If he had done that, Stephan might still be with us."

Amos Lurie, an older man who was with us, looked over at me. "You think they are not so tough?"

"They are humans like the rest of us."

"You have no idea who you're dealing with or the awkward position they've put your father in."

I didn't want to hear what Amos had to say. To me, Tomer was the leader I looked up to. Amos was irrelevant, but when he seemed to suggest I was wrong about Papa, I became angry. "Look, I asked him to tell me what happened to Stephan. He refused. He knew what happened to him, but he refused to tell me. Why else would he refuse, unless he knew he had betrayed Stephan? It was an act of treason and treachery."

Amos seemed unmoved by my tantrum. "Maybe it is for your own good you don't know the whole story," he said quietly. "Perhaps it is for everyone's good."

"Why do you say that?" I smirked.

"What you don't know, you cannot be forced to tell."

"They wouldn't force me. I am a woman. They might try to make you speak, but not me."

"Do you know how naïve you sound?"

"Perhaps I am naïve, but I am not a coward."

"I am not saying your father and the others did the right thing," Amos continued. "But it is not so simple an issue as one might suppose." Amos glanced in Tomer's direction. "Perhaps you should show her the soldiers we deal with every day, then she will understand why she should respect her father."

"Respect him?" I shouted. "You ask me to respect him?" The others backed away, as if I had crossed a line I did not know existed, but I was too angry to heed the warning implicit in their reaction. "I can never respect him again."

"We are all on the same side," Amos continued in that same calm voice, like a teacher instructing a student. And then I remembered— Amos was a rabbi. "They do not agree with our tactics," he shrugged. "And we do not agree with theirs. But never forget, we are all on the same side." He glanced once more in Tomer's direction and said simply, "Show her."

With a heavy sigh, Tomer took me by the hand. "Come, you must see for yourself."

We walked two blocks farther into the ghetto, then Tomer led me down a narrow alley not far from where we'd entered the sewer the day before. Buildings rose above us on each side, and from the windows above I heard people talking. I wondered where Tomer was taking me and what he wanted me to see, but I kept quiet, hoping no one would notice us.

The alley ended at a cross street and when we reached it, Tomer stopped and pulled me next to the building on the right. It was strange the way he held me and I thought for a moment he was going to kiss me. Instead, he said, "You don't have to do this. I will cover for you with Amos."

"What are you saying?"

"He told me to show you. But you don't have to see it. I will take care of it with Amos."

"Amos is the real leader."

"Yes," Tomer nodded.

"And you all let the Nazis think it was Stephan."

"They had his name." Tomer had a sheepish look. "They were asking about him and about you. We let them think what they wanted to think."

"And the council?"

"They dealt only with them. We never had any contact with them."

For a moment I felt guilty for the things I'd said about Papa, then I remembered the look in his eye when I asked about Stephan. The council might not have given him over to the Nazis, but they knew what was going to happen to him and did nothing to stop it. "They are still traitors," I arrogantly dismissed his explanation. "What is it Amos wants me to see?"

"You don't have to see it."

"No," I said with a toss of my head. "Amos thinks I can't take it. Show me what there is to see and I'll prove to him how tough I am."

"Okay," Tomer sighed. "But it's not pretty." Then he slid along the wall to the corner of the building and peered out. After a moment he leaned back from the corner and nodded to me. "Okay." He gestured with a nod. "Have a look." I moved around him and poked my head out from the corner of the building.

Down the street to the right about two blocks away was a brick wall, part of the same wall that separated that side of the ghetto from the remainder of the city. In front of it, a dozen women stood in a line, their backs to the wall, facing a group of German soldiers. The soldiers milled about laughing and drinking, and every few moments one of them reached over to one of the women and stripped off an article of clothing. They found great humor in seeing it torn away and as more flesh was revealed, the soldiers' laugher became louder and more animated. Finally, after ten minutes or so, all the women were completely naked. I turned back to Tomer and whispered, "What are they doing with them?"

"Just watch."

I turned back to watch and saw a soldier draw a pistol from a holster on his hip. He brought his arm level with his shoulder and squeezed the trigger. There was the sound of a gunshot and one of the women collapsed to the ground. A second solider stepped forward and repeated the same thing. One by one each of the soldiers took their turn shooting until all the women lay on the ground. Then one of the soldiers tossed an empty bottle in the air and another shot it. Broken glass flew in every direction, and the others, apparently surprised the shot hit it, burst into laughter.

It seemed they were through with what I was supposed to see so I turned away, shaken from the sight of it but not at all surprised by their actions. "That's not all." Tomer turned me back to the corner. "They aren't through with their daily ritual."

"Daily ritual?"

"They do this every day at the exact same time."

With my head once more sticking out from the corner, I saw three babies lying on the ground near the soldiers' feet. They'd been there all along, but I hadn't noticed. One of the soldiers picked up a baby by the arm and plopped it atop the wall. Another solider came with two more, dragging one with each hand, and hoisted them onto the wall beside the others. The babies were too young to sit upright and kept falling over. When nothing seemed to keep them straight, they put them all on the ground again, leaning them against the body of one of the women. Then a soldier picked up a baby, set it on the wall, and held it in place with his hand gripping the baby's shoulder. He ducked to one side and shouted with a loud voice, "See if you can hit it without hitting me."

I gasped and tried to look away, but Tomer pressed his hand against my back and held me in place. "You wanted to see what we face. This is it."

A soldier standing a few meters away drew his pistol and fired. Instantly the baby's head exploded, covering the soldier who'd been holding it with bright red blood. They all burst into laughter, several of them bent double as they made fun of the one who was covered in blood.

While they were still laughing, another soldier arrived on a motorcycle. He dismounted and reached into a bag. From it he took three bottles and passed them around. Several of the men, already staggering, tipped them up for another drink.

When they'd emptied the bottles, two soldiers gathered the remaining babies and ran with them into a nearby building. Moments later, they appeared at an open window on the third floor. "See if you can hit this," one of them shouted.

Without warning, he leaned back and with a swinging motion threw the baby into the air. The soldier on the ground who had shot the bottle drew his pistol and fired. A bullet ripped through the baby's midriff, slicing it almost in half. Blood filled the air with a thin mist that showered the others with tiny droplets. They all laughed with enthusiasm, hands on their hips, heads back, mouths open.

Waves of nausea swept over me, but Tomer would not release me from my position against the wall. Thinking about it now, I suppose I could have closed my eyes, but the horror of what I'd seen was unbelievable and I kept watching, hoping that someone would intervene.

One of the men on the ground called out loudly and the man with the third baby appeared at the third-floor window. He leaned back to throw the baby but as he swung his arms forward, the baby slipped from his grip and dropped to the pavement below. The baby bounced once and lay there, silent and motionless. The soldiers stared at it a moment in silence, then one of them walked calmly over, drew his pistol, and shot the baby three times as it lay on the ground.

With those three shots, Tomer moved his hand from my back. I stumbled away from the corner, leaned over with my hands on my knees, and vomited.

"That is what Amos was talking about." Tomer slipped his arm around my waist. "That is the enemy we face. All of us." I slowly stood and leaned my weight against his arm. "We have to get out of here," he whispered. "Before they see us and make us one of their targets."

chapter 25

The next day, Yosef left the apartment to see what Tomer and the others were doing. I stayed behind with Yardina. After what I'd seen—soldiers shooting the women and babies—and what I'd learned about Amos and Tomer allowing Papa and the council to take the blame for Stephan, I really didn't want to see any of them right then. I just wanted time to think.

Yosef wasn't gone long when the door flew open and he rushed back inside. "The soldiers are here," he blurted. "In large numbers."

Yardina looked worried. "What are they doing?"

"I don't know, but I think you can see them from here." We followed him to the window in the front room. Yardina's apartment was on the fourth floor and afforded a view all the way to the building where Papa and Mama lived. As I watched I saw people coming from their building, being hurried along by soldiers. Trucks were parked in the street and I could see people climbing in back. I turned away from the window, rushed out to the hall, and hurried downstairs.

On the street, I pushed and shoved my way through a growing crowd of onlookers. Yardina ran after me, yelling for me to stop, but I ignored her and kept moving until I was across the street from the building where Papa and Mama lived. There I came to a stop. Yardina caught up with me and we stood together, watching. "I was afraid of this," she lamented.

"Of what?"

She gestured toward the people coming from the building. "They are all shopkeepers, artisans, and intellectuals."

"What does that have to do with anything?"

She shrugged. "To our captors they are nothing. Nonessentials. Incapable of contributing anything productive to society."

People continued to file from the building, their eyes fixed in a blank, emotionless stare, then Uncle Alois appeared. I worked my way toward him but as I came closer the soldiers pushed me back. He saw me, though, and called to me, "Be strong, Sarah. Be very strong." They shoved him toward one of the trucks where four men grabbed him, picked him up, and threw him in back. My eyes were still focused on him when Yardina nudged me and pointed back toward the building.

Through the doorway I saw two soldiers dragging Papa between them. With their arms hooked beneath his shoulders, his feet barely touched the ground. Mama was behind them, being shoved along by two more soldiers. I pressed forward once more and in the confusion that surrounded them, I reached past the soldiers for Papa's hand.

"I'm sorry," I cried. "I'm sorry." Tears rolled down my cheeks. "I didn't mean it." He squeezed my hand and I felt him press something against my palm. "It's yours now," he said, choking back tears.

As Mama passed me, she leaned over and kissed my cheek. Then one of the men grabbed her and pulled her away. I tried to follow them, but Yardina caught me by the arm. "Stay back," she warned. "You do not want them to take you, too."

Papa climbed into the back of the truck, then reached down to help Mama. Once they were in, someone shouted to the driver and the truck started forward. I watched until it turned the corner and disappeared from sight.

When they were gone, Yardina put her arm across my shoulder and turned me away from the building. We walked in silence a few paces up the street, then I stopped short, my eyes open wide. "Where's David?"

Yardina looked confused. "David?"

"My brother. I didn't see him with the people from the building."

"Perhaps he was already in the truck," she suggested. "Or maybe he is hiding." She nudged me forward and leaned near my ear. "We must keep moving," she warned in a low voice. "We do not want the soldiers to notice us. If David is still here, he will turn up."

Back at the apartment, I realized my fist was still balled tightly around the object Papa had pressed into my hand. I relaxed my fingers and opened my palm to find Grandma's necklace and locket. Tears filled my eyes at the sight of it. Papa told me it would one day be mine and he remembered. Then I thought of the jewelry box and my papers from Spain. *Papa didn't have the box with him when they came from the building,* I thought to myself. *It must still be in the space beneath the floor.* If the soldiers moved a new family into the apartment, I might never be able to retrieve the documents. Without a word, I wheeled around and started toward the door. Yosef was there and grabbed me. "What are you doing?"

"I have to go to the apartment."

"You can't go out on the street now. It's not safe."

"I have to," I insisted. "I have to get back to the apartment."

"We must stay right here." He blocked the door with his body. "You can't go now."

Suddenly gunshots rang out. We rushed to the window and looked out to see two bodies lying in the street below. A squad of German soldiers stood around them, laughing and pointing.

"That is what I mean," Yosef pointed. "They are just looking for a reason to shoot people. We must wait until things calm down." I knew he was right but I was determined to return to the apartment and find the jewelry box.

Late that night, when Yosef and Yardina were asleep, I rose from my place on the floor in the front room, slipped on my shoes, and quietly stepped into the hall. I tiptoed down the stairs to the front door. Moving carefully, I peeked around the doorframe and checked the street in both directions. There were no soldiers in sight, so I hurried across to the shadows on the opposite sidewalk and walked quickly down to the corner and over to the building where my parents had lived.

The front door was open and through it I saw the staircase with the hallway beside it, looking dark and ominous. I pushed my feelings aside and hurried inside. As I made my way upstairs I heard people moving around in the building. My heart sank at the thought that the Nazis had moved new families into the apartments already, but I kept going and in a few minutes reached the third floor.

To my relief, the door to the apartment stood open and I could see the rooms were empty. The furniture we'd collected was gone. I went inside and pushed the door closed behind me, then moved quietly to the bedroom. There I knelt on my knees and felt along the floorboards until I located the ones Papa had removed before. I slipped my fingernails into the space between the boards and gently pulled one of them loose. It came free without much effort and I lifted off the others to reveal the space between the floor and the ceiling of the apartment below. My heart skipped a beat when I saw the jewelry box. I removed the box from the space and put the boards back over the opening. Then, clutching the box to my chest, I walked back to the hall and started downstairs.

As I reached the first floor, two soldiers passed by on the street outside. I drew back into the shadows and waited to see if there were any more. Ten minutes later, a truck drove past and stopped a few meters up the street. Curious about what was happening I crawled to a window and raised myself up to see. Soldiers stood near the back of the truck, watching as a dozen men climbed from the back and entered a building across the street. In a few minutes, two of the men emerged carrying a chest of drawers. Moments later, two more came with a bed frame. "They're cleaning out the building," I whispered to myself.

With no hope of leaving through the front door, I turned away from the window and hurried down the first-floor hall to the basement stairs. I jerked open the door and walked quickly down the steps.

Dark even in daytime, the basement was now devoid of light and I felt my way along with my feet and hands. Slowly, my eyes adjusted to the darkness and I saw the outlines of the narrow windows near the coal chute. A fire still burned in the building's boiler and I could see the glow of it through a vent on the side. I moved in that direction. Moments later, I reached the front of the boiler and opened the door. In the glare of the flames from the firebox I lifted the lid on the jewelry box and looked inside.

My papers were still inside but on top of them I found a letter addressed to me. I took it out, propped the box against my side beneath my arm, and began to read. The letter was from Papa.

"Sarah, I know you did not understand why I could not tell you about Stephan, but it was for your own good. The Germans had information linking Stephan to a group planning a revolt in the ghetto. They also had information linking him to you. They knew Stephan was not the primary leader of the rebellious group, but they wanted to use you to make him reveal the real leader's name. When we were reluctant to do as they wanted, they demanded the Judenrat hand over one or the other of you, either Stephan or you. No one could decide what to do because we were all convinced that whomever we handed over, that person would be killed. To resolve the dilemma, we decided to cast lots—the way Torah says. No one had the correct stones so we used dice. Then no one wanted to choose who would die, so we chose who would live. We cast lots with the dice and the numbers fell to you. When Adolf Eichmann returned for our decision, we had Stephan in our custody and gave him to the SS. I know this was not the outcome you wanted and if the choice had been *yours you would have chosen differently, but we did the best we could in a difficult situation. Please forgive me. Papa."*

I heard heavy footsteps overhead as soldiers entered the building. Afraid now of what might ultimately happen to me I took the locket from my pocket and dropped it into the box. Then I closed the lid tightly and stepped behind the boiler. It was hot and I was worried I might get burned, but in the glow of the boiler fire I found a hole in the wall where pipes went through. It was just big enough for the jewelry box to fit and I slid the box as far into it as I could reach. At least it would no longer be trapped in the apartment and maybe, one day, I could find it again.

By then the sound of footsteps on the floor above was constant. Instead of trying to leave by the stairs, I turned toward the tunnel and made my way from the basement in that direction. As I felt my way through the darkness I stumbled over a chair and fell to the ground. I lay there motionless and quiet, waiting for some indication of whether I had been heard. When no one came to the basement, I stuck out my hands to push myself up. My hand pressed against something long and round and as I felt it I realized it was a candle. I groped my way back to the boiler and lit it, then used it to light the way back to the tunnel. A few meters inside, I saw the chair I had tripped over and realized this was the place where Papa and the Judenrat had met. A lump formed in my throat at the thought of him but there was no time to dawdle or reminisce. I continued on to the basement of a building up the block and climbed out to the street one block over. The building where Yardina lived was across the street. I hurried over to it and walked quickly up the steps to her apartment.

I arrived at the apartment to find Yardina waiting for me in the front room. "Where have you been?"

"I went back to the apartment."

"Of your parents?"

"Yes."

"Why did you do that?"

"I was looking for David." It was true; I had hoped to find him still there, but I did not think I could tell her the real reason.

"He is staying with Rabbi Gavriel."

"You know this for certain?"

"Yes. Yosef told me earlier."

"Why didn't he tell me?"

"He was worried you would try to go over there. I was going to tell you."

"When?"

"After the soldiers were gone and the streets were safe."

I wasn't sure she was telling me the truth, so I moved on to a different topic. "They are clearing the buildings."

"They will be here soon."

"Here?"

"Yes. Here, in our building. They will move us out soon."

"You are certain of this?"

"Amos Lurie has a friend who knows the SS well. He told us." She studied me a moment. "Do you have a skill?"

"I am a student."

"You must have a skill."

"Why?"

"The soldiers will return and take us. Maybe not tomorrow, but one day soon. They'll do another selection."

"A selection?"

"Between those who live and those who die. They might choose from the color of your shoes, or your hair, or your eyes, and," she pointed for emphasis, "it might just be by your trade."

"Was that really the reason why my parents were taken? Because he is a shopkeeper and she is a musician?"

Yosef rose from his sleeping mat. "No, they were taken because your father is on the council."

"But why did that cause them to take him?"

"Your friend Eichmann wanted them to conduct a census to learn everyone's trade. They are interested in only those with skills. Everyone else is useless to them. But your father and the council realized what was happening and refused to take the census. So the soldiers began moving us out anyway, using whatever means they saw fit to make their selections."

"I still don't understand the selection." I was bewildered by it all. "Why are some selected to die?"

"They select us for work. Those who can work are taken to the camps. And those who can't are killed."

A frown creased my forehead. "They would do that?"

"We hear reports."

"That is why you must have a skill," Yardina insisted.

"Like I said, I'm a student," I shrugged. "I want to be a historian."

"No. You're not a student. Students, they kill. Historians, they kill. Meek little girls who don't have an occupation, they kill. And after they kill you, they'll kill me for harboring you. So you are a cook and a seamstress."

"I can't do either."

"Fake it. They'll kill us all if you don't."

"But what about my papers? They show me as a student."

"I know someone who can help," Yosef offered. "He will get papers that can pass the scrutiny of any soldier."

chapter 26

A few days later, Yosef obtained Austrian papers for me that showed my occupation as a cook and seamstress. Not long after that, the soldiers returned to the ghetto and began moving people out of Yardina's building. All that day we waited in the apartment, listening as they emptied apartments on the floors below. I made sure the papers Yosef gave me were safely in my pocket and tried to remain calm as the soldiers worked their way up to our floor.

In a little while the soldiers reached our floor. I heard the thump of their boots on the staircase, then a fist banged on our door. Though I heard them coming and knew we were next, the sound of it made me jump. Before we could answer it, the door opened and a soldier appeared. "Out!" he shouted. "Leave everything and get out!"

"Not even a suitcase?" Yardina protested.

"Out!" the soldier repeated. He grabbed her by the hair and pulled her toward the door. "Get out now!"

I hurried after Yardina, squeezed past the soldier, and ran out the door. As I stumbled down the steps she glanced back at me over her shoulder. "Remember, you are a cook and a seamstress. Look them in the eye. Don't hesitate." It was cold that day and I wore only a thin cotton dress with a sweater bearing the yellow Star of David on the chest. I pulled it tightly around me but it did little to keep me warm.

Near the front door of the building, I caught sight of my brother David. In spite of all the confusion and uncertainty around us, my heart was glad at seeing him alive. He saw me too, and as I stepped out he came to my side and took my hand. "Yosef gave you the papers?"

"Where have you been?"

"I was hiding at first. Then Rabbi Gavriel gave me a place to stay. You have the papers?"

"Yes."

"Show them when they ask for papers. Do not hesitate. The papers will work."

Outside the building, soldiers separated the men from the women, with men on one side of the street and women on the other. As we stepped from the sidewalk, soldiers rushed toward me. One of them grabbed my arm. David leaned over and kissed my cheek, then they shoved him away and dragged us to opposite sides of the street.

Yardina was already with the others standing on the sidewalk with her back to the wall of the building. I made my way toward her and squeezed in beside her. I watched as wives were separated from husbands and babies from their mothers. Seeing the babies reminded me of what I had seen that day with Tomer. I felt sick at the memory of it and at the certainty of what would happen to those babies. For relief from the anguish directly in front of me, I looked away and scanned the men on the opposite side of the street, searching for David. I caught sight of him for a moment, then a truck backed in the way, obscuring him from sight. Moments later, he emerged from behind the truck and climbed in back. My heart sank at the thought of being separated from him and I wondered if I would ever see him again.

While the men were loaded into trucks, soldiers forced the remaining women into a line, single file. When we were in place, a man in a dark suit came down the line, checking our papers. I handed him the card Yosef gave me and waited, confident that if David said it would work, there would be no problem. The man glanced at it, shoved it toward me, and moved on to the next person. After a while, the line began to shuffle away. I turned in that direction and followed the others down the street. With soldiers guarding us, we walked back through the tenement buildings the same way we'd come when we first arrived from Linz.

Soon we came to the freight yard and found the tracks once again lined with cattle cars. The doors to the cars were already open and soldiers started herding us inside as soon as we arrived. Even so, getting into the cars was an awkward task and the area around the cars soon became jammed with women trying to get in and soldiers trying to force them in faster. By then Yardina and I were separated and she was nowhere to be seen.

Rather than delay the inevitable, I did my best to press forward, hoping to avoid rough treatment from the soldiers and wanting simply to get on with whatever was about to happen. As I moved toward a railcar and positioned myself to climb aboard, a soldier with a clipboard walked past. On the clipboard he had a list of names and he read them aloud, shouting at the top of his voice. When he called my name I turned toward him. A soldier stepped forward to prod me onto the car, but when I told him the man with the clipboard had called my name, he took me by the arm and dragged me in that direction.

Others from the list, about five or six in all, joined me next to the man with the clipboard and when they were gathered, he led us to a truck. We climbed in back on our own and as soon as we were inside, the truck started forward. Moments later, we passed through a gate that led to a bridge across the river. Once over it, we headed north through town. I stood for the ride and let the cold wind blow through my hair. It felt good to be away from the crowded ghetto and the stench of life there. The air was clear and fresh and I breathed it in, filling my lungs to capacity.

For a brief, fleeting moment I felt a sense of relief and was almost happy. I had no idea what lay before me and we were still at the mercy of the German soldiers, but for a moment life seemed suddenly lighter and almost hopeful. Then I looked back over my shoulder to see the train already far down the tracks and fading from sight. A sense of loneliness swept over me. Mama, Papa, and Uncle Alois already were gone. David, Yosef, and Yardina were on a train bound for some unknown destination and no one seemed to know where Stephan was or what had happened to him. As the truck rattled through the streets of Vienna, I realized everyone I'd ever known was gone and I had little hope we would ever see each other again.

* * *

Not long after we left the freight yard the truck came to a stop outside an office building on the north side of Vienna. Three soldiers appeared behind the truck and ordered us out. They were stern and demanding but, unlike the ones in the ghetto, did not abuse us or drag us by the arm. We climbed to the ground on our own and they lined us up along the wall of the building. Then the man with the clipboard appeared and began announcing work assignments. Some were sent to a warehouse across the street. Others were led off in a different direction. Finally, only I remained. The man with the clipboard checked his list once more, then gestured for me to follow him inside the building. He held the door open for me, then led the way upstairs. At the top of the staircase we came to a long hallway. A row of chairs sat against the wall to the right. He pointed to one and told me to sit and wait.

In a little while, a woman came from an office near where I was seated and motioned for me to follow. I walked with her up the hall to an open door and into an office. A desk sat opposite the door and behind it was Adolf Eichmann. He looked up as we entered and smiled. "Hello, Sarah." His tone was both smug and self-confident.

Looking back now, I should have known he was the reason I was called back from the trains. He was also the reason we had an apartment in the building near the front of the ghetto, several blocks from the worst conditions and safely removed from the places used by the soldiers who entertained themselves by killing the more helpless among us. I should have known I would see him that day, but when they brought me in the office and he was at the desk, I was surprised. I'm sure he was amused by the look on my face and satisfied that he'd been able to catch me by surprise. "Adolf," I said, acknowledging him with a nod of my head. "I thought you were at the hotel."

"I was, but that was only a temporary location." He gestured to the woman who was with me. She backed away and stepped out to the hall. I heard the door close behind her as she went out. When she was gone, Adolf continued. "This space is much better suited for our purposes than a hotel suite." He came from behind the desk and stood before me. His eyes met mine as he took hold of the sweater I was wearing and gently slid it off my shoulders. "You won't need this," he grinned. "We'll get you another one."

A shudder ran through my body. I was nervous and tense, expecting to feel his hands groping me and smell the foul odor of his mouth as he wallowed over my body. Instead, he tossed aside the sweater, took a seat on a chair beside me, and crossed his legs. I was still standing and he patted the chair next to his with his hand. "Have a seat." I did so, then he looked over at me and in the most casual voice said, "I was wondering if you would like to work for me."

I was taken aback, both by his manner and by the suggestion that a Jew could, or would, choose to work for him. "H...how could I?" I stammered. "I am a Jew."

He leaned closer and spoke in a hushed voice. "I can have anyone I want." He pointed with his index finger. "But I chose you."

A frown wrinkled my forehead. "You can have a Jew working for you?"

"I can have anyone," he nodded. "Anyone at all."

"Won't people notice? Won't that cause trouble for both of us?"

"That won't be an issue," he had a dismissive smirk. "No one will question me. And besides, you can pass." He flipped up the ends of my hair with his fingers. "Your skin tone, your eyes. They will all fit in perfectly. Others need never know." He took a second look. "Maybe you should cut your hair. But I think we will have no problems." He rose from the chair and moved behind the desk. "You will do it? You will work for me?"

I stared at him a moment, thinking of all that had happened and knowing that in the end, my fate was not in my own hands. Images of the ghetto filled my mind, the women and babies along the wall, and the Averbuch children lying in the street at Linz. Bringing me there to that office as if I were interviewing for a job, asking me if I wanted to work for him, was all a charade, and I finally realized, at a level deeper than I'd been willing to acknowledge before, that Jews in Austria, perhaps Jews in all of Europe, had no real choices anymore except the choice to persevere, to survive in spite of all they did to us—to live—because one day this would all come to an end. Nothing so evil and ludicrous as what we'd experienced could survive for long. I wanted to be present on that day when the world crumbled around our German captors, so I said, "I don't think I have much choice."

"No," he laughed. "You really don't. It's either work for me or go to the camps."

"Okay," I shrugged. "I will do it."

"Good," he grinned. "And I will help you." He opened the desk drawer and took out official Austrian papers. He glanced at them and tossed them on the desk in front of me. "Your name is now Ellen Krupp. You grew up in Linz, attended high school there, and lived just a few houses away from me when we were children."

"Most of that is true," I observed as I picked up the papers and scanned them. The identity card had a photograph of me affixed to it. I was surprised to see it and studied it a moment, trying to determine where he'd obtained it.

"You are correct," he continued, still standing behind the desk. "The best cover stories always play on the truth. That way, you have less to commit to memory. You will be working for me as my assistant. I want you to help me document the work we are doing here, create an archive of our accomplishments." He dropped onto a chair. "But we will go over all of that in the morning."

I looked over at him. "What about Stephan?"

The question caught him off guard. "Stephan?" he asked with a puzzled look.

"Stephan Rovina. I came to ask you about him when you were in the hotel. What happened to him?"

"Oh." Adolf's eyes darted away. "He is fine. The Security Office wanted custody of him but I persuaded them to give him to me." He had a tight, thin smile. "We sent him to the East. He will do well there."

"He is alive?"

"Yes," Adolf nodded reassuringly, but his eyes darted away once more. "He's very much alive."

"What about my parents?"

"They are fine, too." He rested his forearms on the desktop and laced his fingers together. "I saw them onto the train myself."

"You saw them?"

"Yes," he nodded. "I will check to make sure they are settled appropriately."

He reached across the desk to a tray filled with papers and took a document from it. "This gives you a room in our boardinghouse." He handed the paper to me. "It's located on the corner about two blocks from here. One of the men downstairs can tell you how to find it."

Now I was the one with a puzzled expression. "Boardinghouse?"

"You will have a room and two meals each day there. Lunch will be provided here."

Three meals and a room to myself. I felt guilty and glad at the same time. Still, it was too good to be true. "I can come and go?"

"You will live as one of us, but you must be very careful. If you are discovered, I will be forced to disown you as a traitor and have you shot on the spot."

"I'll do my best to avoid that," I said with a wry tone.

"I am sure you will. Now, you should get down there and show them that paper so they can put you up. Then return here in the morning for work." He paused a moment and let his eyes slowly roam over me from head to toe. "Do you have other clothes?"

"This is all I have. They told us to leave everything when they took us from the apartment."

"We have a warehouse across the street." He took a pad from the corner of the desk, scribbled a note, and handed it to me. "Take this to them. They will let you choose some clothes from their supply."

I was suspicious of his generosity but glad for the opportunity to have clothes to wear. I nodded and said, "Thank you."

When I didn't leave immediately, he gestured with a wave of his hand. "Go on. Return in the morning." I stood and started toward the door. Then he called after me. "And, Sarah, do not think of running away." His brow was heavy and his voice authoritative. "There is no other place for you to go. No one else to turn to for help. If you try to leave I will track you down. I found you once. I can find you again. And then things would not go well for you."

From the office, I walked downstairs to the front entrance. A guard at the door patted me down. I showed him the note Adolf had given me and asked where I should go. He glanced at the note, then opened the door and pointed to a building directly opposite where we stood. I crossed the street to it and went inside.

From the outside the building appeared to be a warehouse, but inside it opened to a long corridor with rooms on either side. A clerk met me in the hall and checked my note. Then he led me farther into the building to a room on the right.

"The coats are in here," he pointed to a huge pile of winter coats. All shapes and sizes, they were stacked higher than the door. "Dresses are in the next room. Shoes in the one after that. Find yourself a coat and I'll show you the rest of it." I stared at the pile a moment, unsure what I should do. He gestured again. "Go on. Find one that fits. We don't have all day."

I stepped to the pile and sorted through it a moment until I found a coat that looked nice. It was made of gray wool. A little too large, but it was as close as I could find in the brief time he gave me. "That will do," he said with a short tone. "Let's keep moving."

The next room held a pile of dresses as large as the coats. I picked out four or five. Turning, I spotted a pile of underwear and chose several pieces. I found a pair of shoes in the room next door and the clerk handed me a pair of women's boots. "You might need these if it starts to snow."

As we turned to leave, the clothes were draped over my arm and I held the shoes and boots in either hand. He seemed a little flustered by my appearance and led me farther down the hall to another room that was stacked to the ceiling with suitcases. He took one down, set it on the floor, and opened it. "Put your things in there," he pointed. I laid the clothes in the case, put the shoes on top, and closed the lid.

Suitcase in hand, I followed the clerk up the hall toward the front. As we made our way in that direction, we passed a room on the right. The door was ajar and through the opening I saw a man seated at a table. He had a jeweler's loupe over one eye, and before him was a small pile of stones that appeared to be diamonds. A soldier armed with a rifle stood in the far corner across from the door. While I watched, a man appeared with a small pouch. He opened it and poured the contents onto the table. Human teeth with gold fillings tumbled from the pouch. I gasped at the sight of it.

Then a man appeared at the door. He glanced out to the hall through the opening and gave me an angry look, then slammed the door shut. The clerk who was with me took me by the arm and hustled me to the front of the building. As he opened the door for me to leave he whispered, "Never let them see your emotions again. They will shoot you for being a sympathizer."

"But the teeth," I protested.

"Mind your own business," he slammed the door behind me.

Outside, the cool air helped me catch my breath and I filled my lungs with it over and over, as I had when we were riding in the truck. As it had then, the fresh, crisp air cleared my mind and I felt a sense of hope. But guilt quickly overwhelmed me. If what we'd heard was true, Mama, Papa, David, and everyone else faced a horrible life in the camps. And here I was, with fresh clothes to wear, a place to stay, and the promise of three meals each day.

Someone nudged me on the elbow and I turned to see a soldier standing beside me. "Are you lost?"

"No," I replied. Then I remembered the paper Adolf had given me for the boardinghouse. I took it from my pocket and showed it to him. "Can you tell me where this is located?"

He glanced at the document, reading it with disdain, hoping to find some reason to give me trouble. Then his eyes came upon Adolf's signature at the bottom. His body tensed, as if snapping to attention. He handed the document to me and pointed to the left. "Down the street. Two blocks on the right."

"Thank you." Gripping the suitcase in one hand, with the document in the other, I set off in the direction he'd pointed, wondering what would happen next.

chapter 27

The walk to the boardinghouse took only a few minutes. I arrived at the corner just before dark and checked the address on the paper. A soldier stood nearby with a rifle slung over his shoulder. I would later learn they manned all the corners in the city, at least during those early days after the Nazis occupied our country, but seeing him that evening with the rifle and all his gear left me unsettled. He looked in my direction and when I lingered longer than he expected, he started toward me. I was frightened at first, then I thought of the other soldier's reaction moments earlier when he'd seen Adolf's signature on the paper. No one would bother me. Not that night, anyway. Instead of cowering and waiting for the guard to accost me, I turned away from him, pushed open the door to the boardinghouse, and went inside.

The door opened to a short hallway with a coatrack. A staircase lay just ahead, and to the right a door led into the front room. I glanced inside and saw a sofa along the wall beneath a window that looked out on the street. End tables stood to either side with lamps on both. Chairs were arranged at right angles to the sofa. Paintings covered the walls. As I admired the furnishings, a woman appeared beside me. She wore a teal green suit with flat black shoes. Her gray hair was pulled up in a bun. She stared at me with cold gray eyes that seemed to bore right through me. Her name was Hilda Gedek and right from the start I did not like her.

"May I help you?" she asked in a tone that made the question sound like a threat.

"I was told you have a room for me." I handed her the document. "Adolf Eichmann sent me."

She seemed unfazed by the mention of his name and kept her eyes focused on the document, which she quickly scanned. "You have identification papers?" she asked without looking up.

"Yes." I handed her the identity card. She studied it a moment, then stepped aside.

A phone sat on a table at the end of the hallway by the stairs. She picked it up and clicked the button on the cradle several times. I heard her talking to someone but her back was to me, which prevented me from hearing what she said. The conversation lasted longer than I expected but after two or three minutes she hung up the phone and returned to me. "Very well," she handed me the identity card. "I will show you to your room."

She led the way upstairs to the second floor, then turned and brought me to a room in the corner on the backside of the house. The room was dusty but not as dirty as the apartment in the ghetto. Plaster on the walls was cracked, as was the ceiling. In the corner, a section near the window was broken away, exposing wooden lathing beneath. To the left was a single bed with a blanket folded neatly at one end. A chair sat beside it in the corner. A lone window overlooked a courtyard in back of the house. Next to the window, near the corner with the cracked plaster, was a chest with four drawers. A bare light bulb hung from the ceiling.

Hilda handed me a key. "You share a bathroom at the end of the hall. No smoking. No food in the room. And absolutely no visitors." She backed toward the door. "Breakfast is served each morning at six. Dinner at seven each evening. If you want to eat, you must be on time."

She glanced at the watch on her wrist. "Dinner will be served in two hours." Then without waiting for me to reply, she stepped into the hall and closed the door.

Alone in the room I found the silence overwhelming. Gone were the cries of hungry children and the wail of mourning mothers. No sound of footsteps in the hall or angry voices outside. I moved slowly from the door and stood near the foot of the bed, turning in a circle, my eyes scanning every detail. Between the bed and chair in the corner there was a closet I hadn't noticed before. I set the suitcase on the bed, walked around to the opposite side, and opened the closet door. A row of shelves stood to one side with a bar that extended from the shelves to the wall on the right. Several clothes hangers dangled there. I opened the suitcase, took out the coat, and hung it in the closet. Then I noticed a shelf above the bar and on it was a single large hatbox. I took it down and opened the top, hoping to find a long-lost treasure or at least a surprise. It was empty and I replaced it on the shelf.

With the coat put away, I walked to the chest on the opposite side of the room. When I opened the top drawer I found a copy of *Life* magazine dated in March of 1938. It was written in English and at the time I could only read a few words, but the cover was a picture of a German soldier with a bugle in his hand. My heart leaped at the sight of it. Months had passed since I had read anything. I took it out and laid it on the bed, then put my dresses in the drawer. As I placed them inside, I caught a glimpse of myself in the window and saw how dirty and disheveled I appeared. I felt ashamed and knew then why people on the street glared at me and why Hilda had been so suspicious. Then I thought of work the next day, and tears came to my eyes at the prospect of going there looking the way I did. I ran my fingers over my face, and tiny clumps of dirt appeared on my fingertips. "You are a mess," I told myself. "Sarah Batsheva. A dirty, stinking—" Suddenly I remembered the identity card. I glanced around for it and found it on the bed. Holding it in my hand I stared at the picture and whispered the name written beneath it. "Ellen Krupp. My name is Ellen Krupp. And I have papers to prove it."

Determined to take advantage of the opportunity I'd been given, I took a dress from the drawer and walked down the hall to the bathroom. I pushed open the door and found a large tub along the back wall. Next to it was a toilet and in the corner a sink with running water. I closed and locked the door, stripped off the dress I'd been wearing for months, and turned on the water in the tub. Steam rose in the air as hot water filled it. Then I stepped into it and let my body sink down, stretching all the way out. By the time I finished washing, the water was dingy with dirt but I was relaxed and refreshed. Afterward, I put on the new dress, washed out the old one, and returned to the bedroom.

The room was cold but I did not mind. For the first time in months I was clean. I hung the old dress on a hanger in the closet to let it dry. As I hung it in place on the bar, I brushed lint from the shoulders of the overcoat and held out each side, checking the fabric once more just to make sure there were no holes or tears. It had pockets on either side. I slid my hand into the one on the right and found it was empty. But in the one on the left, my fingers touched something that felt like paper. I pulled it out to see it was an empty envelope addressed to Ayelet Yavin in Pottenstein. I knew the village. It was located southwest of Vienna. As I stared at it a moment, wondering what happened to Ayelet, I heard voices from the first floor and the sound of footsteps in the hall. Then I remembered mealtime and turned away to go downstairs.

* * *

The next morning, I awoke at sunup and was downstairs in time for breakfast. I ate so much at dinner the night before that Hilda took notice. That morning I tried not to overdo it but I had been hungry for a long time. Now with food before me I found it difficult to resist.

After breakfast I put on the overcoat and started up the street toward the office. Several other women from the boardinghouse took the same route but I avoided them and kept to myself. The morning air was cold against my cheeks but the wool overcoat kept me warm inside, which made the walk rather pleasant.

When I arrived at the building, the guard at the door checked my identity card against a list on a clipboard. Then he handed me a pen and instructed me to sign beside my name. My eyes scanned down the list for *Sarah Batsheva*, but it wasn't there. My heart skipped a beat and for an instant I wondered if I was asleep and the day before had been a cruel dream, then I remembered my name was now Ellen Krupp. I found the name, scribbled a signature beside it, and went inside.

On the second floor I was met by a woman who introduced herself as Eva Fröbe. She was petite, a few years older than I, and very much German. She wore a plain wool suit with a swastika pin on each lapel and, like the woman I'd seen the day before and Hilda at the boarding-house, her hair was pulled in a bun that lay tightly against her scalp. I followed her down the hall past Adolf's office to a door on the right. Beyond it was a room with six desks arranged in rows, three on either side, each with a typewriter in the center, a tray for documents on the left, and a chair tucked neatly in place.

Eva led me to the center one on the left. "This is your desk," she pointed. "Colonel Eichmann expects you to keep it neat and orderly." She opened the top drawer. "Pens and pencils are in here, along with an extra bottle of ink." She shoved it closed and opened another drawer. "Paper is in here. The inkwell is kept in the drawer below when it's not in use." She turned to the right and gestured with her hand. "File cabinets are along the wall. Someone will show you the order as you work. Any questions?"

"What will I be doing?"

"Reports," she said tersely. "The new girls start with reports." She gave me a quick smile and turned away. "Speak up if you have any questions. No one expects you to know everything on the first day."

When she was gone I scooted the chair back from the desk and took a seat. I sat there with the coat wrapped around me, my head scrunched down against the collar, and let my eyes wander over the room. It was on the opposite side of Vienna from the ghetto, yet it was a lifetime away from the filth and squalor. Mama and Papa had not wanted me to associate with Adolf, yet I was here and they were…wherever they were because of my friendship with him. Friendship with Stephan put my life in jeopardy. My relationship to Mama and Papa put my future at risk. But my relationship with Adolf, which had been forbidden, rescued me from the peril they created. At the thought of it, the sense of guilt I'd felt before returned. *I shouldn't be so ungrateful. They were only doing what they thought best for me.* But it was true, Adolf was the reason I was sitting in that room and not in the camps Stephan talked so much about.

A few minutes later a woman entered the room and took a seat in front of me. She glanced in my direction and pointed past me. "Hang your coat back there." I glanced over my shoulder and saw a row of hooks along the wall by the door.

"Sorry," I said sheepishly. "I forgot I had it on." I walked to the back of the room, hung the coat on one of the hooks, and returned to my chair.

Ten minutes later, Eva entered the room with a handful of papers tucked under her arm. She dropped them on my desk, placed her hand on the back of my chair, and leaned over me. "Use the notes on these pages to prepare arrival reports for the locations indicated at the top." She tapped on the pages with her finger as she spoke and I could see information on the sheets had been written by hand. "Do you know how to use a typewriter?"

"Somewhat," I tried to sound confident. In reality, I had never typed a word on a machine like that or any other.

She opened a side drawer of the desk and took out several preprinted forms. "Use these." She laid the forms beside the stack of pages. "Prepare your reports in triplicate—three copies of each page. You should find some carbon paper in one of the drawers. Keep the pages square and even. Colonel Eichmann doesn't like sloppy work." She pointed to the empty desks in the room. "These were all occupied by women who did sloppy work. They aren't here now. You are. Make the most of it."

When she was gone, the woman who was seated at the desk in front of me turned around to face me. "I am Gerda Becker," she smiled. "You don't have a clue what she was talking about, do you?"

I gave her a wry smile. "Was it that obvious?"

"Don't worry. No one ever does at first." She rose from her chair and came behind me. "This is what you do." She opened a drawer on the right and took out carbon paper, then placed it between the blank forms. "Three forms, with a carbon between them." She held the forms between her fingers and gently bumped the bottom edge against the desktop. "Tap it like that to get the pages lined up, then feed it into the typewriter like this." She rolled it into place and tucked the top beneath a bar that held the paper against the roller. "You can press the knob on the end of the roller to get the lines in the correct position and then you're ready to type."

At the top of each handwritten page was the name *Mauthausen Camp*. I knew the town of Mauthausen. It was on the Danube River, not far east of Linz. Stephan told me about a camp there but I didn't believe it actually existed. Now I could see for myself that he'd been right. On the pages were lists of names with dates indicating the time when each person arrived at the camp. As I worked through them I saw many people whom I knew, some of them I had known all my life.

With Gerda's help I pecked away on the typewriter using both index fingers. Before long, my fingers learned the location of the keys and my typing speed increased. By midmorning I had completed the pages for Mauthausen and moved on to sheets for a camp located at Gusen, a town situated midway between Linz and Mauthausen. No one had mentioned a camp at that location and I wondered how many more camps there might be.

At midmorning, Eva brought a stack of completed reports from the previous day. She set them in the tray on my desk and told me to file them in the cabinet. Her tone was more abrupt than before and she didn't stay long to check on us. When she was gone, Gerda picked up the reports from my tray and gestured with a smile. "Come on. I'll show you what to do." I followed her to the file cabinets and watched as she pulled open a drawer.

"Completed reports are filed according to the location noted on the top of the form." She flipped through the files with her fingers. "The files we're looking at right here are for Mauthausen."

I gestured to the row of file cabinets that lined the wall. "We have this many camps?"

"Not everything in here relates to the camps. That's just where they start you out." She placed her hands on the cabinets in front of us. "These two cabinets are for the camps. The others you'll learn about as we go." She turned back to the open drawer. "Arrival censuses go in one folder. Transfers go in another. Deaths go in back. And there are separate files for correspondence, contracts, that sort of thing. You'll see that as you go."

A puzzled frown wrinkled my forehead. "We have death reports?"

"We get those about every other day." She said it in a matter-of-fact tone, as if deaths were a routine matter.

"How many?"

"How many what?"

"How many people die?"

"Ten or twelve pages."

The handwritten sheets I worked from that morning contained twenty-five or thirty names each. I quickly calculated the number in my head. "That many people die in two days?"

"I don't know," she shrugged. "I just fill out the forms."

Gerda checked the reports Eva put on my desk. "These forms she gave you just now are all from Gusen. That file is over here."

She moved to the left, but I remained with the open drawer, my eyes fixed on the death census file. I took it out and glanced through the pages. Names appeared on the left side of the form with the date and time of death in center and the cause of death on the far right. I scanned down the list, looking first at the names, then the dates, and finally the cause of death. It was all arranged so neat and orderly. The names in alphabetical order. The dates and times in chronological sequence. "This isn't right."

"What isn't right?"

I pointed to the form. "They're listed in alphabetical order."

"These were prepared according to the information on handwritten lists. Just like the census reports you've been working on. Someone checked them before they were filed. I'm sure they are correct."

"But they're in chronological sequence, too."

She looked at me and lowered her voice. "Just type what they give us. Don't ask questions about what you see."

"But this is impossible," I argued. "According to this report, these people all died in alphabetical order and in chronological sequence."

Gerda snatched the file from my hand, stuffed it back in place, and shoved the drawer closed. "Listen to me," her voice was barely a whisper. "If you want to keep your job, you'll do as you're told and only what you're told." She pointed to the empty desks behind us. "The others who were here weren't doing sloppy work. They were very efficient.

Much more efficient than you. But they noticed things, too, and asked questions. Too many questions. And now they aren't here anymore. So, unless you want to join them wherever they are, you'll keep your eyes on your work and your mouth closed."

"Why do they die?"

"You saw the reports. They all died of natural causes."

"In alphabetical order."

"What are you saying?"

"I'm saying, if the report was wrong about *when* they died, maybe it's wrong about *how* they died."

She leaned her shoulder against the cabinet and folded her arms across her chest. "From what I hear, most of them," she whispered, "are worked to death."

"Worked to death? How?"

"In the quarries. In the mines. The munitions plants. Wherever labor is needed."

"But how do they work them to death?"

"Work them too hard and feed them too little."

"Why would the Nazis do that?"

She gave me a startled look. "The Nazis? Are you not a German, too?"

"I am Austrian."

She shook her head. "You are German now." She turned to the next file cabinet, but I would not let the matter drop.

"Why are the workers treated that way?"

"They are Jews. They are animals. They have no soul. Why waste food on them when our own people are hungry?"

Her words stabbed me like a knife in the chest. I swallowed hard and struggled to maintain my composure. "I hear there are many old people in the ghetto."

She jerked her head to one side to look at me. "Have you seen the ghetto?"

"Only from a distance," I lied.

"Well, I have seen it."

"You've been there?" I asked with mock interest.

"Not inside it," she said with disdain. "I looked into it from the top of a nearby building and I can tell you, anyone who would live in those conditions deserves what they get."

Anger flared inside me. We didn't live like that of our own decision. We were forced there at gunpoint, and now she suggested we lived that way because of our own choices. I wanted to rip her hair out, but I stifled the impulse and forced myself to remain calm.

"But what about the old people and the babies?"

"What do you care?"

"Just curious."

"Curiosity is a bad thing in this job." She opened a file drawer for Gusen and pointed. "These reports go right here." She put them in the folder and closed the door, then turned to face me. "The ones who can work are put to work. The ones who can't are put away."

"Put away?"

"Eliminated."

"Killed?"

"That is what I am told."

"How?"

"I don't know." She turned away and started back to her desk. "We should get to work before someone notices. And stop asking all these questions," she complained. "You'll get us both in trouble."

I followed her across the room and took a seat at my desk. My fingers worked the keys of the typewriter, but for the remainder of the morning I thought only of what she said. *They are Jews. They have no soul.* And the more I thought of it, the angrier I became with myself for being duped by a comfortable bed and the promise of three meals. I sold out cheaply. Sold myself and the memory of everyone I knew. Traded them for a few bits of bread and a soft blanket at night. The Germans hated us. They loathed us. It was their official government policy and it was the way they thought as individuals. They meant to kill us all—some immediately as a drain on their precious Aryan society, and some they would use as animals until we were broken and exhausted.

A few minutes later, Gerda rose from her desk and disappeared from the room. She returned with a glass of water and set it on my desk. "Drink this," she ordered. "You look pale."

"Why concern yourself with me?"

"Colonel Eichmann gave you this job. I don't want you making him look bad." Over the rim of the glass I saw her eyes staring down at me. "You cannot let them see this kind of reaction from you," she insisted. "You must not show any emotion. This is simply the work they do. It's the work we do. They don't think about it this way. And you can't either. It's just a job." I nodded in response, but in my heart I knew it would never be just a job for me. Not any longer.

At noon we left our desks and walked down the hall to a room with a table and four chairs. An icebox stood in the corner and there was a counter with a sink next to it. A cabinet over the sink held plates and cups. Gerda took two down, and I found forks and knives in a drawer at the far end of the counter.

For lunch we had sausages, roasted potatoes, and sauerkraut, which we consumed with a small glass of wine. On any other occasion I would have enjoyed it immensely, but right then all I could think about was Papa and Mama. They were physically incapable of heavy labor, which made them no good for work in a mine or quarry. They were most surely dead by now. Put away, as Gerda said it. David and Stephan could survive for a while, but Papa and Mama could not. The thought of their demise, together with the sight of the food, made me sick.

While we ate, Eva joined us. I took a few bites as if finishing the food on my plate while they talked about the wine and food. Eva mentioned the warehouse across the street and the many bottles it contained. Then I remembered the room where the man sat counting diamonds and the pouch of teeth with gold fillings. Suddenly I knew those gold-filled teeth weren't the result of normal dental care. They were extracted from the bodies of dead inmates at the camps. Dead Jews. People I knew and loved. The thought of it roiled my stomach and I gagged. Eva gave me a worried look but I waved her off and took a sip of wine, saying, "I'm okay. Just a piece of sausage."

After lunch, Eva walked back to our office with us and reviewed my work. She was pleased with how much I'd done and after she checked the completed reports against the list, she took the reports with her. "Shall I file them for you?" I asked, hoping for another opportunity to search the files in the cabinet.

"Not now," she called.

That afternoon, I continued working through the pages on my desk until I came to Stephan's name. Tears filled my eyes as I read it over and over. "Stephan Rovina," I whispered.

Gerda glanced over her shoulder toward me. "Did you say something?"

"No," I quickly wiped my eyes with my fingers. "Just wanted to spell the name correctly."

"Some of the names are difficult to read."

"Yes," I tried to mask my despair. "The writing is not always clear."

According to information on the sheet, Stephan was sent to the camp at Gusen. Not to the East, as Adolf had said—although it *was* east of Linz. They had no plan to resettle us anywhere, only to work us until we died. We were their slaves. At least Stephan was alive when he left the ghetto, I consoled myself, and he lived long enough to be counted in the census at the camp, but there was no way to know what happened after that. He was young, healthy, and strong. Hopefully they would make good use of him in the quarry. It was an awful thought—praying that someone would be assigned to a life of agonizing misery—but at least he would be alive and now, more than ever, that seemed like the point of it all. Until that day, I had waxed and waned in my resolve to persevere, one minute determined to maintain my identity as a Jew and to survive, certain that the Nazis would come to a bitter end. Then the next, ready to give up and join them, to not merely "pass" as a German but to become one and forsake all I knew to be true, right, just, and holy. Now the duplicity was gone. Evaporated by the lies I heard from Adolf and read in the files, and by the hatred in Gerda's voice.

At the end of the day, no one was around to approve our work, so I followed Gerda's instruction and took the completed reports to Adolf's office and laid them on his desk. She said that was the way they should be handled. He was nowhere to be seen, but Eva came in while we were deciding what to do next. She took the reports from us. "I will look them over. You may go for the evening."

I returned to my desk and moved the stack of blank forms from the desktop to a drawer. Then I straightened up the typewriter and cleared away the pen and inkwell. A dozen handwritten sheets lay at the corner of my desk, the last ones I had completed that afternoon. Information from them was already entered on the forms we gave to Eva but the handwritten pages could not be destroyed until the completed forms were approved. So I opened a desk drawer to the left and placed the pages there until I returned the following day. As I laid them in place, my eyes scanned over the names once more. They were all fellow Jews from the ghetto. Once, they had homes and lives no one would ever know about and the notion struck me that the pages I prepared might be the last record of their existence. Files in the cabinets along the wall might be the only evidence of where and how they died. Documents like that, even the handwritten pages, weren't merely records. They were sacred relics of the lives they represented. I couldn't let them be destroyed. But what could I do? I thought about it a moment longer, then pushed the drawer closed and walked to the back of the room. There I took my coat from the hook and slipped it on. As I shoved my hands into the pockets I felt the envelope inside. Then a plan began to form in my mind. The pockets were deep. Perhaps I could simply put the pages in them and walk out.

Downstairs, a guard stopped me at the door. "Everyone must be searched before they leave the building," he said. Then he slipped his hands beneath my coat and patted me down, touching me from my waist up to my shoulders. When he finished with that, he ran his palms over the front of my coat at the pockets. *So much for simply walking out with the documents,* I thought. But he stopped there, having gone no lower than my hips. I waited with my hands in the air while he leaned around me and ran his hands over my backside, taking much too long for my comfort. When he was finally through, he stepped back and gestured toward the door. I walked out to the sidewalk and started toward the boardinghouse.

That night after dinner, I went to my room and continued to think about how to get the handwritten lists out of the office. I was determined to preserve them as a record of what happened to the people from the ghetto and from our neighborhood in Linz. As I thought about it, I replayed in my mind the guard's search when I left the building. He patted down the pockets of the coat on the outside, then slipped his hands beneath the coat and ran them over my sides, around my hips, and across my backside. If I could hide the documents inside the coat, below the pockets, he might never find them—especially if I only took one or two pages at a time.

I took the coat from the closet, laid it on the bed, and folded the front back to reveal the lining inside. It was well sewn along the hem at the bottom and around the edges. If I could slide the pages between the lining and the outer shell, they would be safe. They wouldn't fall out. Then I noticed the coat had an inside pocket that opened in a location closer to my arm. Using a nail from the broken place on the wall, I turned that pocket inside out and sliced open the bottom, giving access to the space between the lining and the shell. I put on the coat, stepped to the chest, and picked up the copy of *Life* magazine. I folded it lengthwise so it would fit through the pocket and shoved it inside. The magazine passed through the opening and slid to the bottom hem where it lay flat.

"That will work," I smiled.

The next day, I arrived at the office to find more handwritten lists on my desk. I spent the day typing the names into the spaces on the report forms. As I completed each list, I moved the handwritten sheets to the desk drawer, hoping no one would notice they weren't in the trash can. I suppose I should have thrown some of them away, to ensure the safety of the ones I kept, but in my mind that was not an option. Every name was precious and deserving of preservation.

That evening, as I prepared to leave, I left the inkwell on the desktop on purpose. Then I walked to the back for my coat. Wearing my coat, I returned to my desk to put the inkwell in the drawer. While doing that, I leaned forward and slid three of the handwritten pages into the pocket of my coat. When I stood, I felt them slide all the way to the bottom hem. As I hoped, the guard downstairs never checked farther than my hips.

When I reached the boardinghouse, I went to my room and laid the coat on the bed. With no real effort, I fished the papers back through the pocket and hid them in the hatbox on the shelf inside the closet. Then I went downstairs for dinner.

chapter 28

*A*ny doubt I might have harbored about what lay ahead for Jews in Austria vanished the following day. Adolf was in the office that morning when I arrived and he called me to his desk. "I want you to prepare a letter."

"What shall it say?"

"I am about to tell you." He tossed a notepad to my side of the desk and flipped a pencil after it. "Take down what I say."

I took a seat in a chair near the desk, rested the notepad on my knee, and gripped the pencil, waiting for him to begin. This was my first attempt at dictation and, in spite of how I felt toward the Germans in general, and Adolf in particular, I wanted to do a good job. I preferred working there to the alternative of disappearing into what I now knew was a complex web of interconnected prison camps.

Adolf leaned back in the chair, propped his elbows on the armrests, and laced his fingers together. His eyes were fixed straight ahead but from the look in them I could tell he was lost in thought. Then he began:

"General Reinhard Heydrich. In accordance with our discussions at Wannsee, I have now completed my review of facilities in the outlying territories. To date, more than 400,000 units have been

processed through these locations. The number yet to be transferred is at least twice that many, of which more than half will require the special treatment you outlined at our meeting. In an attempt to increase our processing rate, I have directed all facilities to pursue alternative means of effecting that treatment as rapidly as possible. However, ad hoc solutions to the situation will prove unworkable in the long term, as the skeletal waste produced from increased production will soon become unmanageable. Ash deposits and odor are also problematic in several locations and have generated complaints from nearby neighbors. I suggest we consider sending a team of architects and engineers to assess the facilities at Mauthausen with an eye toward developing a system that can be duplicated at other locations, which will achieve the desired daily capacity while reducing waste output to manageable quantities."

Eichmann paused there and stared silently into space. Finally he looked over at me, "Type that up for my signature. I need it delivered to Berlin by overnight courier."

At first I did not understand the point of what he was trying to say to Heydrich, but as I took notes, and later at my desk as I typed the letter, I realized he was talking about the disposal of humans who died at the camp. I was certain "special treatment" was an oblique reference to the execution of those found unfit for labor—what Gerda referred to as being "put away"—but the numbers to which he alluded seemed far beyond what one would expect from an operation designed to extract work from its victims and let them die of exhaustion. This sounded like the killing wasn't occasioned by the system but now had become the point. Not merely to dispose of bodies dead from natural causes, but to effect wholesale executions. I felt ill as I returned to my desk and twice while I was typing I had to swallow my own vomit. Still I was resolved to contain my emotions and to work in every capacity to see that as much of what they did was chronicled, not only in their own official files but in mine as well. One day the world would know what happened and when that day came, their own files would rise up as a witness against them, one way or the other.

Because this was my first letter, I asked Gerda for help. "Letters are prepared in duplicate," she told me. "One for delivery to the recipient and one for the file." I did as she instructed, but instead of preparing it in duplicate I prepared this letter in triplicate. When I finished it, I took the original to Adolf for his signature and filed a copy in the general correspondence cabinet. The third copy I tucked safely out of sight in my desk drawer.

Throughout the remainder of the morning, I continued working through the seemingly endless stack of prisoner census reports. Unlike previous lists, however, the ones on my desk that day contained only the names of women and children. At the top, in addition to the location, was the notation "people receiving special treatment." There was no doubt in my mind what that meant.

Those reports and the letter I prepared earlier that morning from Adolf to Heydrich were the most explicit documents I saw of the German plan for dealing with the Jews. Most of what Adolf and his fellow officers did was never committed to writing but entrusted to Adolf's memory. Since childhood he had shown a penchant for remembering minute details of seemingly innocuous events. Now, as a Nazi officer, he put that memory to use and, for their purposes, it served him well. Later, when their plans began to fail and their dream of a glorious Third Reich was all but lost, no one wanted to know him, but right then—when they seemed to be in control of everyone's destiny—he was the man with whom everyone wanted to be friends. He was their rising star.

* * *

In the months that followed, I collected the handwritten prisoner lists, made handwritten copies of documents that seemed important, and sometimes prepared an extra copy of the documents I typed. I also retained my notes and scooped up spoiled forms from the trash. All of these I hid in my desk and took them from the office in small batches using the pocket in my coat. At first I stashed them in the hatbox in the closet of my room, but one day as spring approached Hilda asked me why I was wearing a heavy coat on such a nice day. "It isn't that cold outside," she said, giving the lapel a tug. "Aren't you hot with that on?"

"Not really," I did my best to deflect her question.

Then, as I went upstairs, someone spoke to me from behind. "She should mind her own business," the voice said. I glanced over my shoulder to see a fair-skinned blonde following me up the steps. "I heard what she said to you just now. She was coming from my room when I arrived from work yesterday."

When we reached the second floor the woman smiled at me. "I am Claudia Dietrich," she said, introducing herself.

"I am Sa—" I caught myself. "I am Ellen Krupp."

"I meant to say something to you before," she continued. "But I wasn't sure how long you'd be staying."

"Almost a year now," I replied with a forced smile.

"Well, anyway," she pointed over her shoulder, "if you ever need anything, I'm just down the hall." I thanked her, then stepped inside my room and closed the door.

Now my mind reeled. First Hilda downstairs asking about my coat, and now a stranger from down the hall being friendly and chatty. Were they watching me? Did Hilda suspect something was wrong and set me up to meet Claudia? I didn't like Hilda at all but now, with questions about the coat and Claudia in the hallway suddenly being friendly, I was worried. I sat on the bed and slid the coat off my shoulders. "What should I do?" I mused to myself.

Hilda was right, the weather was warm outside, and wearing that woolen overcoat on a spring day made me stand out, which was the opposite of what I intended. And I didn't want to think about what would happen if they found those documents. But the issue was unavoidable and the more I thought about it, the more those documents became my biggest concern. When I first began taking them from the office, I had been consumed with preserving the names and records of people I knew. Then it became a task of keeping alive the memory of all who came through the German system. Now I was more concerned with preserving my own future than documenting their past.

Destroying the documents was out of the question. I knew of no place where I could burn them, and simply placing them in the trash offered no assurance that they would not be discovered. If they were found, the content on them would lead straight back to me. With the weather warming outside and wearing the coat no longer an option, I had no way to return the documents to the office, either. I was stuck with them but I needed a better place to hide them. Somewhere much better and more permanent than the hatbox in the closet. Hilda would find them there eventually.

From my seat on the edge of the bed, my eyes caught sight of the broken plaster in the corner of the room and the exposed lath behind it. Through the hole I could see the exterior wall and realized the gap between the two was at least three or four inches deep. Then the idea hit me. If I could hide the documents inside my coat, why not hide them in the wall? They wouldn't be readily accessible, but they would be safe and if I couldn't figure out a way to remove them later, perhaps someone would find them one day and understand what they meant. At least for now, they would be out of sight and safe from discovery.

Without hesitation, I went to the closet, took down the box, and set it on the bed. Then I removed the lid, picked up a handful of documents, and shoved them through the hole in the wall. The pages disappeared inside the wall and I heard them slide all the way to the bottom by the baseboard. Encouraged by the result, I shoved more papers into the hole and soon emptied the box. Then I returned it to the shelf in the closet and went downstairs for dinner feeling confident and secure in what I had accomplished.

chapter 29

The following morning, Gerda did not arrive at the office until mid-morning. A stack of reports from the previous day sat on my desk, awaiting filing. I put them in the appropriate files, then, alone in the office, I took the opportunity to peruse other files in the cabinet. At the far end of the wall I found cabinets that included records of people who had been processed for emigration, most of them to Palestine. The most recent of those files was two years old. Approval for emigration was now impossible. I knew that already from other documents I had prepared.

As I continued through the cabinets, opening the drawers and scanning the files inside, I thought of Papa and Mama and wondered what actually happened to them. They were removed from the ghetto after Stephan, but before I was. I had seen Stephan's name on a list, but not theirs.

Prisoner census reports were organized chronologically with the latest reports being added to the front of the file. When one file folder became too large, we created a new one. Gradually, files for most of the camps came to occupy a full drawer, then later they expanded to an entire cabinet.

That morning, I checked the cabinet for the Mauthausen files and located census records created about the time my parents were removed from the ghetto. I worked quickly, unsure when Gerda might arrive. At first I saw no one familiar to me. Then I found a page that included the names of people from the floor beneath our apartment. A few pages later, I found a sheet with Mama's name midway down the left side. She had been taken directly from the apartment building to Mauthausen.

I shoved the file back in place and knelt to open the bottom drawer where the death records were kept. If she was dead, I wanted to know it, but her name wasn't there. Finally I looked through the transfer records—lists of people who had been sent from Mauthausen to one of the other camps. I scanned the names quickly, turning from page to page until I found her name on a list of people transferred to Auschwitz. Tears welled up in my eyes. Auschwitz was located in Poland. Mama had been resettled in the East, as Adolf had said, but not to a place where she could live out her life in peace. Instead, she had been sent to one of the worst camps in the entire system.

Just then I felt someone standing beside me. I looked up to see one of the male clerks from the office next door peering down at me. They came in the office several times each day to use our files. I had seen him staring at me from across the room, not in a rude way but in the way a man looks at a woman when he is interested. He smiled at me. "Looking for something?"

"N...no." I quickly wiped my eyes with my fingers. "Just making sure the documents are in the correct files."

"You have been searching through that cabinet for quite some time."

At first I was intimidated by his presence, but the more he smiled, the angrier I became. "What does it matter to you how long I do anything?" I tucked the report back in the file and stood. "How long have you been standing there?"

"Not long enough." He was trying to be flirtatious but I ignored his attempts.

"Shouldn't you be at your desk?"

"Shouldn't you be at yours?" he countered. "I came in here to read a file from this cabinet, but I can't get to it until you move."

"You should have said something instead of sneaking up on me like that and lurking over me."

"I didn't want to startle you and cause a commotion."

"No," I retorted. "You just wanted to stand there and leer at me."

"Not leer," he replied gamely. "Watch."

He was cute, even if he was a German, which made it difficult not to smile while I pushed the drawer closed with my foot.

* * *

That evening, when I came from the office, he was standing outside waiting for me. As I came out, he moved beside me and walked next to me down the street. We walked half a block without saying a word. Finally I glanced over at him. "Did you get into trouble for taking too long at the file cabinet?"

"No," he smiled. "But I can take longer next time if you like."

I cut my eyes in his direction. "So you can leer a little longer?"

"Watch."

"Are you following me?"

"Just looking for an opportunity to say I'm sorry."

"For what?"

"I was brash this morning," he said with a serious tone.

"And this isn't brash?"

"No." He shook his head. "This is desperate."

"Desperate?" I frowned. "For what?"

"Desperate to know if you'll join me for a drink."

The thought that I could go anywhere other than the office and the boardinghouse never crossed my mind. "I do not think I am allowed."

"Certainly you are allowed," he insisted. "Are you not a citizen of the Reich?"

"Yes," I nodded, remembering Adolf's earlier word to me that I could pass. "I am a citizen."

"Well then," he grinned. "I suppose you can have a drink when and where you like."

"But I don't even know your name."

"Allow me to introduce myself," he said with mock formality. "I am Claus Dachsel."

"Pleased to meet you."

"Now, will you have a drink with me?"

"You still have one problem."

"What's that?"

"There is no one to introduce me to you."

"But there is no need for a formal introduction. I already know your name," he beamed. "You are Ellen. Ellen Krupp. From Linz. You lived near Colonel Eichmann. He talks about you often."

"And how do you hear Colonel Eichmann talking about *anything*?"

"He is good friends with my supervisor and comes by at lunch."

I stopped and faced him, no longer interested in the cat-and-mouse game we'd been playing. "Very well," I smiled. "I would love to join you."

He was startled by my abrupt response but recovered quickly and offered me his arm. I slipped my hand inside the crook of his elbow, and we continued down the street past the boardinghouse to a restaurant. After drinks, we ate dinner. It was the most delicious food I had tasted since leaving Spain.

All through our meal, Claus asked questions about my past and what it was like living near the Eichmanns as a child. I gave answers that were true, but lifted from their context gave the impression I was German and not at all Jewish. It really was much easier to answer in a natural way when I was giving information that, strictly speaking, was true. Suspending for the moment the fact that I was Jewish and

Claus was under oath to kill any Jew caught doing what I was doing, the evening was rather enjoyable.

Several hours later, he walked me back to the boardinghouse. Hilda was seated in the front room when I arrived. I said good night to Clause and went upstairs.

The following morning, Adolf came to our office shortly after I arrived. I could tell by the way his jaw was clenched that he was in a bad mood. He checked his watch but I was a few minutes early, which meant he couldn't complain. Still, he barked at me anyway. "Why aren't the reports finished?"

I glanced at the desk and saw a stack of handwritten documents in the basket. "The basket was empty when I left last evening."

Without hesitation, he slapped me across the face with the back of his hand. "Don't talk back to me!" he roared. "You were out late last night. I know all about your comings and goings, and don't think I don't. Now get busy." I took a seat at the desk and began typing the reports, doing my best to keep my head down and my eyes away from him.

A few minutes later, Claus entered the room. I lifted my head to change the form in the typewriter. Without making eye contact, I saw his countenance drop when he caught sight of the anguished look on my face and the red handprint on my cheek. Adolf appeared from the opposite side of the room. "You are late!" he shouted at Claus. "Did you not know that working here is a privilege?" His finger jabbed the air as he continued yelling. "Your fellow soldiers are out there fighting and dying while you are in here ogling the women."

Claus was startled by the sudden outburst but tried to defend himself. "I was only—"

"Don't talk back to me!" Adolf was giving a full display of the Eichmann temper. I had seen it before from his father, Karl. There was no stopping him now.

"Colonel Eichmann," Claus tried once more, "I wasn't—"

Adolf banged his fist down hard against a desktop. "Collect your belongings," he seethed. Then he reached over to my desk and snatched up a pen and pulled a clean sheet of paper from my typewriter. With a quick flourish, he scribbled a note and thrust it triumphantly in Claus' face. "You will report to General Von Küchler at once."

Claus' mouth dropped open. "Von Küchler?" he gasped. "He is on the Russian front."

"Yes," Adolf smiled with cruel glee. "Perhaps while you are there you will learn how to conduct yourself in a professional manner. Then perhaps you will know how to act should someone ever again reward you with a position of privilege."

I remained at my desk through Adolf's tirade, my eyes focused on the typewriter. But with my mind I sorted through events of the day before, trying to determine how he knew that I had been out with Claus. Very quickly I came to the conclusion that Hilda was the source of his information. I knew when I saw her seated in the front room that there would be trouble. I didn't know how or why or what might happen, but I knew it wasn't good that she was waiting for me when I returned. She was the only one who could have told Adolf where I had been and who had accompanied me.

chapter 30

Through the remainder of spring and summer, Gerda and I worked twelve hours each day, seven days a week, to keep up with the growing volume of records generated by the detention system. Adolf took delight in the number of people being forced through the network of camps in Austria and Poland, and with the accolades others heaped upon him for the results he produced. I was appalled at the death and misery each list represented and battled every day to keep from crying while I typed the names onto official forms. Most days I was too upset to take lunch and at night my sleep became fitful and restless.

In November, a new woman, Marianne Bernigau, appeared at our office and was assigned to one of the desks that sat to our right. She was slender, young, and had a pretty smile. Gerda and Eva showed her what to do. I was cordial to her, but she kept to herself most of the time and had very little to say.

Not long after Marianne arrived, Adolf invited me to join him for a trip. He refused to tell me where he was taking me, but from the schoolboy smile on his face I wasn't too worried. The next morning, he came to collect me at the boardinghouse with a car and driver. I wore my usual attire for work, one of the dresses from the warehouse and a light jacket. The weather was not yet cold enough for the overcoat. Seated beside him in back, we rode in silence through the streets of Vienna, arriving at the train station a few minutes later. There we alighted from the automobile and walked across the platform to a private railcar that was attached to the end of a passenger train.

We entered through a door at the front end of the coach and wound our way past a galley kitchen into the main space of the car. In the center was a dining table with upholstered chairs positioned around it. Along the windows on the far side were three seating areas with more chairs arranged around tables suitable for enjoying the passing scenery. On the near side was a desk with shelves and space for working. The rear of the car was occupied by a private bedroom. I caught a glimpse of it through an open door.

Adolph walked to the bedroom and deposited a briefcase there, then joined me at the dining table. "Please," he gestured to the chairs. "Have a seat." I took a seat at the table and he sat across from me. Before long the train started forward and not long after that stewards appeared with breakfast. We ate as the train rolled through the countryside, finishing with coffee, which we drank while seated in the chairs by the window.

When we finished the coffee, he stood and took me by the hand and led me across the car to the bedroom door. I didn't want to go in there, and certainly not with him, but I felt I had little option but to do as he suggested.

The door to the room opened to a short entryway about five feet long. Past that, a large bed dominated the center of the room. To the right was a sofa and near the end of it another door that led into a private bath that occupied the space between the bedroom and the main room of the car. A small table stood near the bed. On it was a wine bucket with a bottle already on ice.

As we entered the room, Adolf slipped off his jacket and tossed it on the bed. Then he placed his arm around my waist and drew me near, pressing his lips against my neck. "You always liked me," he whispered as he nibbled on the lobe of my ear. "Ever since you were a little girl you could not take your eyes off me."

"I am not a little girl anymore."

"How well I know," he grinned. "And I am no longer simply a boy. Now we can do something about our affections for each other."

"No," I pushed him away with my forearm. "It's not like that."

"You can't deny your feelings for me." He took my hand and pulled me back into his arms. "And I can no longer deny mine for you."

"That was a long time ago."

"And a long time to hold our emotions in check." His arm slid back around my waist and he tightened his grip. "Do you know where we are going on this trip?"

"No."

"I am taking you back to Linz." He nuzzled against my neck once more. "And can you guess why?"

"I can't imagine why anyone would want to go back there."

"I have a house there." He spoke in a low, husky voice. "Not far from where we used to live. You will stay there enjoying every luxury you could imagine. And when I arrive for a visit, you will serve my needs."

"I will not be your mistress," I pulled away from him once more.

"Well, you can't be my wife," he chuckled. "They would shoot us both for that."

"I won't be either." I was angry at the suggestion and wanted him to know it.

"Then you will be my whore!" His face was red with anger, the veins in his neck pulsing. He started toward me again but I slipped past him and darted out the door. As I rushed from the room, I collided with a man dressed in an army uniform. My forehead struck a medal pinned to his chest and I reached up to check for blood. My head slowly tipped back and my eyes ran up his chest to his face. Then I saw that the man was none other than General Reinhard Heydrich.

Adolf came after me, arriving in the doorway a few seconds behind, and was brought up short at the sight of him. "General," he smiled nervously, doing his best to act as if nothing was happening. "I did not know you were on this train."

"Obviously not," Heydrich said without amusement. "We have things to discuss."

"Very well." Adolf stepped back from the doorway and straightened his shirt. "Come in. We can talk back here."

They disappeared into the bedroom and I took a seat by the window in one of the chairs across from the dining table. A steward brought me a cup of tea, which I sipped slowly while the Austrian countryside moved past the window. The railcar rocked gently from side to side and the wheels clacked over the rails with a rhythm that soothed my mind and calmed my soul. *Perhaps Adolf is doing me a favor,* I thought. *Would it really be so bad to live in Linz at his expense and endure the pain of his occasional visits? Many are doing things to survive that they would never dream of doing otherwise. Is selling my body any worse than typing his reports and passing myself off as a German? Haven't I already sold out?*

As we continued down the tracks, my earlier resolve to rebuff Adolf's advances began to wane and I was to the point of agreeing to his arrangement when the train slowed. Out the window I saw the village of Geretzbach. Two boys were playing in the street, laughing and kicking a ball. They seemed to have not a care in the world, as it should be. And all at once I saw the Averbuch children, their eyes wide with fright, then the sound of the gun, and the next moment they were lying with their parents, blood oozing from their bodies onto the pavement. Then I remembered Papa and Mama. Adolf sent them to the camps, along with Stephan and David. How could I ever get into bed with a man who would do such a thing?

A steward appeared at my chair. "Did you need something?"

"No," I shook my head. "I'm fine now."

When we arrived at the station in Linz, Heydrich departed the bedroom by the exit at the end of the car. Moments later, Adolf emerged and gestured for me to follow. He appeared calm and not the least affected by what had previously transpired between us. I walked to the front, where he offered me his hand and helped me from the railcar to the station platform.

A black Mercedes automobile was parked near the station building with a driver standing near the front bumper. Adolf led the way and we walked toward it. The driver opened the rear door and held it while Adolf crawled onto the seat and slid over to the opposite side. I got in next to him and soon we were driving from the station.

We rode through the streets in silence, Adolf staring out the window, until we turned onto the street where we'd lived before. As we idled past our house, he glanced over his shoulder at me. "It still looks the same." I nodded without looking. He turned back to the window. "A little tired and run down, but much the same as when you left it."

"Nothing is the same as when we left it," I said softly.

He placed his hand on my thigh. "Life must go on, Sarah."

My heart jumped at the sound of that name. More than a year had passed since I had heard it. He turned to face me. "You should reconsider my offer," he whispered. "This is the opportunity of a lifetime for you. And it is the only way I can help. If you stay at the office, someone will eventually learn your real name and then they will know who you are. Hilda at the boardinghouse is already suspicious." My eyes opened wide at the mention of her name. "Yes," he nodded. "You know that she suspects something."

"Hilda should mind her own business."

"It is her business to keep an eye on everyone staying there."

"And Claudia?"

The mention of her name took him aback. "What about her?"

"Is she there to keep an eye on us, too?"

He leaned against the door. "You should not concern yourself with Claudia. What she does is none of your business."

"Is she one of your mistresses, too?"

Adolf grasped my wrist and squeezed it tightly. "Listen to me," he said through clenched teeth. "You are a Jew, living in a land controlled by the most powerful army in the world. And I am an officer of that army. You will never speak to me this way again." He released his grip and turned away.

Seeing the neighborhood where we once lived had the opposite effect from what Adolf intended. He hoped that by showing me the street and our old house I would be moved by nostalgia to agree to his arrangement. That seeing those familiar places would bring to mind memories of a glorious past, a past he would suggest I could reclaim by becoming his concubine. Instead, it only served to remind me of how I was very much alone in the world. Everyone I loved was gone and the houses where they once lived cried out to me, reminding me of all that happened to us when the Germans took over.

Just past his old house, Adolf began to talk again. "Do you remember the day you came to our house and I was sitting on the front steps?"

"Yes," I answered grudgingly.

"Your grandmother had just died."

I folded my arms across my chest. "And your father yelled at me."

"He yelled at everyone," Adolf chuckled. "You had a locket." He turned away from the window to look at me once more. "Whatever happened to it?"

"It was lost," I lied. "When your soldiers came for us it was lost."

He stared at me a moment before replying, "That must have been very traumatic for you."

I looked him in the eye. "Not as traumatic as what happened to my parents."

His face went cold. "What do you know about them?"

"I know my mother was sent to Auschwitz."

The muscles along his jaw flexed. "You have been in my files." His face turned red. "You could not know that any other way." He jabbed his finger in my face. "You have been looking through my files."

"I'm in your files every day," I said sarcastically. "It's my job to prepare reports and place them in your files."

He wagged his finger at me. "But you did not prepare a report for your parents."

"How do you know?"

"Because I know everything that happens in my camps and in my office." He slapped me in the face with the back of his hand. "I would never make you do such a thing. Requiring you to fill out a report about your own parents would be cruel."

"And killing them wasn't?"

"I am only doing my job," he snapped. "That is all. Just doing my job." Finally he admitted that they were no longer alive, but hearing it from him failed to give me the satisfaction I thought it would. Instead, I was outraged at his lack of remorse. He had no sense of shame or guilt. Worse still, he viewed the slaughter of my parents, people he knew and understood, as simply doing his job. Right there, in the back seat of the car, I wanted to kill him and I imagined myself doing it in the most grotesque manner. Surely *that* would give me the satisfaction and justice I craved.

The driver took a circuitous route along the river, back to the center of town. There we came to a stop at a building that stood ten or twelve stories tall. Adolf climbed from the car and handed the driver a note, then started toward the building entrance. I followed after him, unsure where we were going or what would happen next.

Inside the building, Adolf waited at the elevator for me to catch up. We stepped inside and he stood silently watching the dial above the door as the arrow moved past numbers for the floors. We rose higher and higher in the elevator, and my heart beat faster and faster. I had heard stories of women in Vienna who were accosted by soldiers, raped repeatedly, and then tossed out the window of an upper floor. I was worried that might happen to me but had little option other than to keep moving forward.

When we reached the top floor, the elevator attendant opened the door. We stepped out to a hall and Adolf led the way. At the end of the hall was a door and through it we entered an apartment. The main room had windows from floor to ceiling that looked out on the city and afforded a view of the Austrian countryside that lay to the east. It was decorated with richly appointed furniture and paintings on every wall.

"This would have been yours," he made a broad, sweeping gesture. "You could have spent your days enjoying the view and eating the best food available." He turned to look at me, expecting to see I was crushed with disappointment, but I was certain he had no intention of keeping me for long in such a place. He only wanted to indulge his lust with me, and when he grew tired of me I would be discarded like the workers in the camps and replaced by another. Still, the thought that I could have lived there in comfort gave me pause to wonder if I had made the right decision.

Adolf moved to the right and as my eyes followed him I saw a doorway leading to the kitchen. It was painted white and had cabinets on every wall. A counter beneath them ran around the room with a stove at one end and a sink at the other. He opened a cabinet, took out a bottle of beer, and flipped off the top with an opener from a drawer near the sink. Then he turned up the bottle and took a long drink.

Bottle in hand, he came from the kitchen and swaggered over to one of the windows. He unbuttoned his jacket and tipped his head back, taking another drink. Then he swallowed and pointed out the window, gesturing with the bottle. "You see that column of smoke rising in the distance?"

"Yes."

"That is smoke from the crematorium at Mauthausen." He paused for a sip from the bottle. "We control the quarry there. Do you remember it?"

"I remember hearing of it," I nodded.

He took one more sip from the bottle. "That is where they died." He said it in an offhanded way, as if telling me about the weather.

"Who?"

"Your father, and your brother, and that idiot Stephan."

A lump formed in my throat. I swallowed hard and struggled to maintain my composure. "And my mother? What happened to her?"

"She was a woman," he shrugged. "Nothing more worthless than a Jewish woman, except for a Jewish child. She was sent by train to Auschwitz and gassed upon arrival. Her bones were crushed and scattered in a field near there." He looked at me with disdain and contempt. "You're just like all the others," he snarled. "I thought you were different but you're not. You're just a Jewish whore using nothing but your Jewish tricks on me and everyone else. You think you can survive that way, but I promise you, you cannot."

"When have I ever tricked you?"

"First you embarrass me on the train in front of my superior and now I find you have been going behind my back, plundering through files that you had no permission to see."

"You gave me permission when you gave me the job."

With a flick of his free hand he slapped me in the face, this time harder than before. "Do not talk to me that way, you insolent little girl!" He leaned closer and looked at me with an accusing eye. "What else have you done?" When I didn't answer, he slapped me again. "Answer me when I'm talking to you! Have you been corresponding with that boy Claus? Is that it? Did you take him to your bed before he left for the front?"

"We had dinner once." As hard as I tried to prevent it, tears streamed down my face. "Just once."

"How am I to believe anything you say to me now?"

"It's the truth."

"You are a Jew. A weak, sniffling Jew. You know nothing of the truth. Only tricks and spells. That's all you know." His eyes opened wide. "And you almost fooled me."

I frowned. "What are you talking about?"

"You almost tricked me into getting in bed with you, just as you tricked Claus. Only I was more taken in than he. I was ready to set you up in a place of your own. Make you my mistress. Defy the Führer's orders and the laws of the Reich. You made it seem like my idea but it was all your doing."

"Are you crazy? Listen to yourself."

But he just kept going. "You thought that if I had sex with you I won't do to you what I've done to the others." He grabbed me and threw me onto a sofa that sat facing the windows. "We could do it right here, right now!" He reached for his belt to unbuckle it, then the door opened. He paused with his hand on his belt, took a breath, and lowered his voice. "I could have you right here, shoot you in the head before you got your clothes on, and never think of it again."

While he was speaking, three soldiers entered the room and stood near the kitchen doorway. Adolf straightened his jacket, squared his shoulders, and nodded over his shoulder to them. "This is what you came for," he said, pointing to me.

One of them grabbed me by the arm and pulled me from the sofa. I struggled to my feet, and another soldier grabbed me from the opposite side. Together they pushed me across the room. As we neared the door to the hallway, Adolf stepped in front, blocking the way, his face all but touching mine. "I rescued you from certain death," he whispered. "Gave you a place to live. Kept you safe. But you have chosen to repay my acts of kindness with insults and embarrassment. You are nothing to me now and there is no one who can save you." He nodded again to the soldiers and they led me out to the hall.

When we reached the first floor, they hustled me from the building. They lifted me off my feet and hurried across the sidewalk toward a car parked at the curb, with me dangling between them. Without a word between them, they threw me onto the back seat, slammed the door shut, and shouted to the driver. Moments later, the car started forward.

chapter 31

From Linz, the driver took me east, along the river, and I knew where we were going. Adolf was sending me to the same place he sent Mama, Papa, and all the others—Mauthausen. And if he had his way I would meet the same end. After all, I was nothing but a Jewish woman now.

When we reached the camp, the driver brought the car to a stop near the main building. A guard opened the car door and I was led inside. After a moment, a woman came with a clipboard and asked for my identity card. I handed her the card Adolf had prepared for me and she added my name to the handwritten daily census list. I had seen those lists many times before and knew that in a day or two, Claudia would transfer the information from it to an official report form. I wondered if she would even recognize my name as she typed it on the sheet.

The woman with the clipboard disappeared into an office and I could hear them discussing among themselves why a German citizen with the name Ellen Krupp was sent to the camp. Someone placed a phone call and I heard voices.

"Jewish sympathizer," someone said.

"Sympathizer? They send sympathizers here?"

"She was caught plundering the files of Colonel Eichmann," the first voice said sharply. "She will get what she deserves."

After that, the woman with the clipboard returned and led me out the back door. I followed her across the yard past the crematorium with its solid brick walls and tall smokestacks. Smoke rose from them and a foul odor hung in the air. Ash drifted down to the ground like snowflakes, but no one paid it any attention.

On the pavement outside the building, workers sorted through piles of clothing. Next to them, others were busy stacking empty suitcases on the bed of a truck. In the shadow of the building, corpses were piled high, awaiting the ovens, while men with dental tools searched their mouths for gold and silver fillings.

Because the crematorium was full when I arrived, I was not executed that day. Instead, I was assigned to the camp's only female barracks. Only slightly better than the housing for common prisoners, it held women who were part of the Sonderkommando—prisoners who worked the body-disposal detail at the crematorium—and female prisoners who were forced to work as prostitutes in the camp's brothel. Even though Jewish women were officially fit for nothing, it seemed the German soldiers had no problem using them for their physical pleasure.

The barracks overseer, a Jewish woman named Gila from Vienna, assigned me to a bed and I made my way toward it. One of the guards saw me and suggested I might make an attractive prostitute, but the overseer shook her head. "Special orders," she said dourly. Everyone seemed to know what that meant and from then on they had very little to do with me, though one or two tried to be friendly. I would find out later what they already understood.

The next morning I was awakened before dawn and rousted from the barracks with the Sonderkommandos. We ate breakfast in the lee of our building, a remarkably rich fare of sausages and potatoes. Prisoners who worked at the crematorium, it turned out, were afforded better meals and subjected to far fewer beatings than most inmates, an attempt by the Germans to buy their silence. They knew the details of the killing process and saw firsthand the soldiers who were involved, all of which the Nazi command wanted kept secret. Later I learned that, as an added security measure, most of the Sonderkommandos were murdered every four or five months and replaced with new ones selected at random from one of the arriving trains, but right then I was just glad for the extra calories.

At eight that morning, the first train arrived. We stood by while soldiers separated the women and children from the men. The men were marched off to a separate part of the camp. Women and children were led from the rail platform downstairs to an underground chamber just a few meters from the tracks. Once below ground, they were forced to strip naked under the pretense of taking a shower. They dutifully did as they were told and packed into the chamber shoulder to shoulder. When the room was filled to capacity, a guard locked the doors and donned a gas mask. Soldiers on the floor above dropped canisters of poisonous pellets down specially designed shafts into the chamber. Within thirty minutes they were all dead. Then we were sent in to remove the bodies and clean the room. It was an awful task and I threw up three times during the first session.

The routine repeated itself two more times before noon, then we took a short break while the German soldiers ate lunch. Women in the barracks were only provided breakfast and supper, but they were allowed to eat at noon from their own stores of food, most of it taken from the belongings of people killed in the chamber. They offered me a tin of fish, but I refused. The smell of food, with the odor from the ovens and images from the chamber, made me nauseated.

By the middle of the afternoon, bodies were piled in the sun outside the building, awaiting cremation. Still, the trains continued to arrive. I watched as more people were unloaded and wondered what the guards would do with them. After the men were taken away, the women and children were led in a steady procession down the road and into a patch of woods outside the fenced area of the main camp. I tried to ask where they were going, but no one would tell me.

Late that afternoon, as the sun neared the horizon and after the belongings had been sorted, soldiers came to where we were moving the bodies down to the crematorium ovens. They ordered us to stop our work and placed us in a line. Then one of them walked along choosing every second person. I was not chosen in that process but Gila, the overseer, redirected him to me and I was placed with those selected. The others were sent back to work while we were led off in the same direction as the group of women and children from the afternoon trains.

"Where are we going?" I asked.

"They have too many," someone replied.

"What does that mean?"

"The crematorium is full. They can't put us in the chamber."

"Us?"

"Yes," she nodded grimly. "Us."

"So, where are we going?"

One of the women pointed up ahead of us. I looked in that direction to see a line of women and children forming along the edge of a large open pit, easily a hundred meters in length. To the left, a bulldozer sat a few meters away, a driver perched on the seat. Flies were everywhere and the stench was awful. Then shots rang out in a hail of gunfire from automatic weapons. The bodies along the edge of the pit tumbled in order from left to right as bullets ripped through them. I turned away, but a soldier standing nearby grabbed me by the shoulder and pushed me back in line. When we moved nearer the hole, I saw it was half full of rotting corpses. The last rays of sunlight were fading but in the shadows below I saw a rat wriggle from the pit with flesh dangling from its mouth.

Someone whispered with wry frankness, "We'll be the last for this hole. It's almost full."

"And it's been open too long. They won't like the smell."

"Why don't we run?" I asked.

"Won't do any good," an older woman shrugged.

"And besides," another suggested, "they'll go to our group in the barracks and shoot them all."

Another pointed to the left. "They already have the tractor ready to fill the top."

Everyone seemed so calm, the soldiers relaxed as if merely doing a day's work, my fellow inmates resigned to the fate that awaited us. I was scared and my body trembled at the thought that death was just moments away. Still, the women continued to talk.

"If we run, they'll shoot us on sight and somebody will have to carry us back to the hole."

"Just more misery and work for everyone."

"I've seen that happen, too."

"I've carried the bodies," another added.

Behind us a line of women snaked down the dirt road, but I could see the end of it with soldiers guarding the way out. Like lemmings, we followed the person in front of us, moving nearer and nearer the hole. Periodically, shots rang out in a burst of gunfire that made me jump.

Finally it was our turn. Trembling and crying, I made my way close to the edge of the hole. Even though death awaited me, I was reticent to get too near the edge for fear of falling in. One of the guards stepped forward and shoved me forward until my toes were right at the edge.

On the opposite side, three trucks were backed into place. Canvas tarps covered the back, beneath which were mounted the machine guns we had heard while standing in line. With little fanfare, an officer to my left nodded and the shooting began. From the corner of my eye I saw bullets rip through the bodies to my right, sending a fine mist of blood and shattered bones into the air. Before they even reached me my skin was damp and sticky from the crimson spray. Then a bullet grazed me just above my right ear. Searing pain shot through my head and blood ran down my face. The world spun around and I tumbled forward into the pit. I landed face down on a pile of flesh and lay there, numb all over, unable to move. Seconds later, a body fell on top of me, pinning me in place. The odor was horrible and I felt millions of maggots working through the rotten flesh beneath me.

The guns fell silent and then I heard voices shouting down at us from the ledge above. Moments later, there was the *pop, pop, pop* of pistol fire. A shot pierced the body lying on top of me and I felt the lead sting my side.

After a moment the shooting stopped, and feeling returned to my arms and legs. I wanted to roll on my side to get my face off the body below me, but I was afraid someone would see me move so I lay there hoping the maggots didn't crawl inside my mouth.

From above came the sound of shuffled footsteps as more people appeared along the edge, and seconds later the machine guns began again. I heard the hollow plop of bodies as they landed in the pit. One of them fell beside me, then two more piled on top of me. The weight was almost more than I could bear, pressing my ribs against my lungs, making it difficult to breathe.

Finally the shooting stopped and once again I heard the sound of pistols being fired into the bodies of those recently fallen, just to make sure they were dead. Then the voices moved away from the ledge and in a few minutes I heard the sound of the tractor approaching. The ground shook as it rumbled closer and closer. Panic seized me at the thought of being buried alive, and in desperation I pushed the bodies aside and stood. If they wanted to shoot me, they could. I wasn't lying there waiting to be covered with dirt.

In the west, the sun had already set. Only the indirect light of dusk remained. I moved to the side of the hole where we had been standing and stumbled toward the end, finding a path away from the tractor. Dirt cascaded into the hole behind, sending a cloud of dust ahead of it, but I ignored it and kept moving. To my amazement, no one caught sight of me and when I reached the end, I climbed up to the edge.

Twenty meters away was a stand of trees and beyond it the woods. Instead of looking back to check for the guards, I kept my eyes fixed on the trees ahead of me and hurried to them. I crouched there in the dusky shadows and brushed the maggots from my arms and hair. Then, as darkness descended, I ran into the woods.

chapter 32

I had not gone far into the woods when darkness fell, enshrouding the trees and bushes in inky blackness, forcing me to feel my way forward. Still, I pushed on, threading through the undergrowth, doing my best to continue moving south. As I did so, I thought of where I might ultimately go that would be safe and how I could get away from Adolf and the Nazis once and for all. Linz was the closest city. I could get there rather quickly and it was a place I knew well, but there was nothing there for me now. Everyone I knew who once lived there was gone, and as that realization sank in I was all but overwhelmed by a sense that I was left to fend for myself. Loneliness threatened to drain me of all resolve, but I pushed it aside. *There has to be a way through this,* I thought. *I didn't come this far just to give up.*

As I wrestled with what to do next, an image of Grandma's locket came to mind. Then I remembered the jewelry box with the papers from Spain tucked inside. The box was in the basement of the apartment building in Vienna, assuming no one had found it. If I could get those papers, I might be able to leave Austria as a Spanish citizen. Vienna was far to the east, almost 200 kilometers away, but I resolved that night to make the trek. It seemed impossible to my mind that I could ever attain it, but the decision resonated with something deeper, a sense of purpose, a sense of hope that, as Papa and Mama told me more than once, in the end everything would work out all right.

With every step I took that night the hour grew later and later, and the temperature dropped lower and lower. I wore only the dress and light jacket I had on when I left the train with Adolf. Before long, I was chilled to the bone. Then, about midnight, hunger pangs became overwhelming. I hadn't eaten anything since breakfast. Papa used to tell stories about our ancestors surviving in the wilds of Europe eating nuts, roots, and berries. I knew nothing about which plants to eat and, even if I did, I couldn't see them in the darkness. My legs ached from exhaustion and I wanted to curl up at the base of a tree and go to sleep, but I knew if I did I would be found and by noon the next day I would be back at the edge of another pit facing a German machine gun or, worse, the gas chamber.

Sometime in the night, a full moon rose over the trees casting silvery shadows through the woods. It made for an eerie effect but at least I could see the trees before I ran into them and the logs on the ground before I tripped. Then the woods became less thick, and a few meters farther I came to the edge of a field. Off to the right, moonlight fell on a farmhouse with a barn next to it. I started in that direction, keeping near the edge of the woods, and soon came to a road. As I approached the house I thought about hiding in the barn to rest, but that would leave me trapped in the morning with no way out. So I kept going and continued down the road, still confident I was headed in a southerly direction.

Two hours later, as the sky turned gray with the approach of dawn, I crested a hill and saw the Danube River spread out below me like a broad silver ribbon, shimmering in the fading moonlight. A smile stretched across my face. I was right. I had been walking south and now I could follow the river east to Vienna. The road followed a gently-sloping route downhill toward the water. I picked up my step with renewed energy and a sense that, in spite of the great distance yet to be covered, I really was on my way.

Less than half a kilometer from the riverbank, the road came to an end at an intersection with another road that paralleled the river. "This is Mauthausen Strasse," I said quietly, the road that led from Linz, just a few kilometers to the west, through Mauthausen just to my east.

Having figured out my location, I turned left, heading east, and in less than an hour came to the village of Mauthausen, the community from which the camp took its name. Houses stood to my left, along the uphill side of the road, and around a turn in the road I saw an alley that led behind them. I made my way to it and crept along, searching for a place to hide.

Three houses later I came to a tool shed. It was in poor condition with several boards missing on the sides and tin missing from the roof, but sunrise was only minutes away and I needed to get out of sight. I crouched low, ducked around the corner, and tried the door. It was unlocked so I slipped inside.

A workbench stood along the wall to the right with boxes stacked all around it. To the left, broken window frames leaned against the wall and on them sat more boxes, newspapers, and an assortment of rusted hand tools. I picked my way across the room to the workbench and crawled beneath it, then pulled some of the boxes closer to hide me from view. A draft rushed through a hole in the wall, but as the sun rose in the sky the building began to warm. I lay there a moment with my knees tucked against my chest, my head resting on my arm, and looked out between the boxes at the junk that filled the room. For a moment I thought of where it might have come from and who might have put it there, but before long my eyes grew heavy and I fell asleep.

Midmorning, I was awakened by a sound at the door. I looked up to see an elderly man with a saw in his hand standing two meters from the bench. He took a board from the corner of the room, laid it on the bench, and cut it with the saw. Dust drifted past my nose and I felt the urge to sneeze. I pinched my nostrils closed and held my breath, hoping and praying he wouldn't find me. When he finished cutting the board, he tossed the waste end aside, turned away, and left, pulling the door shut behind him. I rubbed my nose and listened for sounds of his return, but before long my eyes once again grew heavy and I fell asleep.

When I awakened, the sun was setting in the west. I felt rested but I was even more hungry than before. I waited in the toolshed until dark, then watched through a crack in the door as lights went out inside the house. A little while later, I slipped from the shed and started back toward the alley. Near the corner of the yard I saw a trash barrel. I leaned over to see inside and spotted unburned garbage inside, a chicken bone and a piece of molded bread. I fished them out of the barrel, pinched off the worst of the mold, and consumed it with one bite. Then I chewed off the end of the bone and sucked the marrow from it while I walked. Almost two days had passed without any food to eat. I was desperate.

For most of the night I walked in solitude, headed east from Mauthausen. The road followed the river part of the way, then veered north. Once or twice I hid in the bushes to avoid an oncoming car or truck, but otherwise there were no serious incidents. I reached Baumgarten, a tiny farming community, as the first light of dawn appeared.

Not much of a village, Baumgarten consisted of five or six farmhouses with barns and outbuildings clustered around a store and a mill that was used to grind grain. The first place I came to had a barn that stood near the road. In spite of my sense that sleeping in a barn was risky, I took that chance and made my way to the one nearest the road. *It isn't that much of a risk,* I told myself, *and perhaps there is something edible inside.*

Beyond the barn door was an open area that held an electric milk churn and a vat like the ones used for making cheese. Four stalls stood along the back wall with a feeding trough in each. A ladder was affixed to the wall and led through an opening to the floor above. I took a deep breath and smelled the rich blend of hay, grain, sour milk, and feed. The smell of it made my mouth water.

From behind me I heard a noise and turned to see a woman coming from the farmhouse fifteen meters away. I hurried to the ladder and climbed into the loft. Loose hay was piled there with several sacks of feed, a broken chair, and two small tables. I made my way to the far side of the hay and burrowed beneath it.

Moments later I heard the sound of a creaking board. I lay motionless, listening as footsteps came toward me, paused, then retreated back to the ladder. In a little while I heard the plodding sound of a cow as it entered the barn, followed by the rattle of a bucket. When it seemed safe to move, I turned on my side and looked down to see the woman from the house milking a cow in the stall below me. She sat on a stool working the cow's teats, squeezing streams of white liquid into a pail. When she finished with the cow, she moved on to the next stall and I saw they each held an animal.

After a while, I turned away and closed my eyes, somehow convinced that sleeping was the safest way to pass the time. A few minutes later, I heard the sound of footsteps below, this time walking with purpose. My heart began to race at the thought that I had been discovered and betrayed. Surely soldiers were on the way to find me. But when I looked down again at the floor below, all I saw was a milking stool set near the ladder. On it was a small loaf of bread and next to it was a pail about half full of milk. Such a feast could not have been left there by mistake, it was intended for someone, but no one was around. Still, if I ate it they would know I was in the barn and then they would look for me in earnest. Wisdom told me to leave it alone but the hunger in my stomach compelled me to act. Throwing caution to the wind, I stole from my hiding place, climbed down the ladder, and snatched up the bread. Even now, when I'm hungry and take the first bite of a meal, I often think of that loaf of bread and the pail of warm, fresh milk. Nothing ever tasted so good.

In a while I heard voices from outside and looked up to see the woman standing near the house, talking to a man. From the way they talked I was sure he was her husband. I moved closer to the door and peeked out for another look. He was standing beside a truck with his back to the barn. She stood a few meters beyond him, and when she glanced over his shoulder I was certain she made eye contact with me. After a moment, he opened the door of the cab and climbed inside. She moved closer and pushed the door closed behind him. They continued talking through the window of the truck. While she talked to him, she gestured with her hand toward the back of the truck. When I didn't respond, she glanced in my direction with a knowing look and gestured again.

Trusting anyone was a risk that often meant the difference between life and death, especially now that the Nazis controlled our lives. But not everyone in Austria agreed with them. There were still those who looked upon us with compassion. The bread and milk had not been left by mistake. They were offered as an act of kindness from a stranger. I wanted to trust her. I needed to trust her. Walking for two days took me closer to my destination but I knew from that experience that unless I found a faster way to travel, I might never reach Vienna. So when the woman gestured once more, I took the hint. I hurried from the barn, climbed into the back of the truck, and curled up in the corner behind the cab.

The ride from Baumgarten took me to Grein, a town on the river not quite halfway to Vienna. There we turned from the road onto an unpaved lot beside a store. We idled around to the back and came to a stop alongside a larger truck parked a few meters behind the building. The cab door opened and the man slid from behind the steering wheel. As he did, his hand came through the slats on the side of the truck and he dropped a five Reichsmark note beside where I was lying. I looked at it a moment, thinking what a huge sum of money it represented and how he must have dropped it by mistake. Then I snatched it up and shoved it into my pocket.

A few minutes later I heard footsteps approaching and then the door to the truck beside us opened. When the engine started, I climbed from the truck I was in and crawled into the back of the one beside us. Thankfully, I guessed right. It was headed west and took me all the way to Stockerau.

I found out later that the farmer and his wife were part of a network that rescued people who escaped from the camp. When the Germans came through the area searching for escapees, they and their friends searched, too. Those whom they found, they gave overnight shelter and did their best to shuttle them as far away from Mauthausen as possible. I never knew their names, or the name of the second driver who took me to Stockerau, but they are to me some of the Righteous Among the Nations, without whom many thousands more of us would have perished during those dark years of German occupation.

From Stockerau, Vienna was only a day's walk away. That walk, however, took almost a week to complete. For one thing, German military patrols were much heavier around Vienna, which meant I always had to be on guard, and I found no one offering assistance. Once when I stopped to buy a bit of something to eat, I was certain a woman recognized me and went out to find the soldiers. I left before they arrived, but the added scrutiny meant that inside the city I had to slip from building to building and limit my exposure on the street to only those times when it was absolutely necessary. Making my way to the ghetto was all the more difficult, as I had no means of reckoning its location except by our trek into it from the railway depot when we first arrived, by my short excursion beyond the wall with Tomer, and by what I saw while riding in the truck when we were selected to work for Adolf.

After five days of searching, I succeeded in locating the bridge across the canal on the south side of the ghetto. I was rather certain I could get across without being seen, but getting inside the wall was a problem. To do that, I would have to enter through the sewer pipe and climb up the ladder to the manhole cover. After days of walking and little to eat, I wasn't sure I could push the cover aside—and there was the problem of the rats. I hate rats.

The Cathedral of St. Stephan stood nearby and I retreated to it to consider my options. Hiding in the lee of an alcove of the basilica, I realized my choices were few. I could continue to live on the streets of Vienna, eating scraps from garbage cans and sleeping in basements at night, or I could get myself across the river, through the sewer pipe and into the building where the jewelry box was hidden. Either way was risky. The only difference was, if I obtained the papers from the box, I had the possibility of a future. Without them, I had none.

Late that afternoon, I returned to the canal. A park lay along the southern bank with trees and bushes. Using them as cover, I made my way beneath the bridge and climbed up into the steel structure. Then I walked carefully along a beam to the opposite side. From there I found the entrance to the sewer and went inside. To my amazement, it had not been blocked or sealed, but as I feared, the rats were still there.

Using my memory as a guide I felt along the left wall of the pipe until I reached the ladder that led up into the service shaft. Rats ran over my feet, but this time, instead of squealing, I kicked them aside, took hold of the ladder, and started up. Gripping the rungs carefully, I pushed myself up with my feet and moved my hands from rung to rung. The access shaft grew darker with every step, but I kept going until I banged my head against the cover at the top. I paused there a moment, trying to listen for the sound of anyone on the ground above, but my arms were weak and I couldn't hang there long. Finally, I moved my feet up one more rung, reached up with one hand, and pushed with my legs as hard as I could. Thankfully, the cover lifted up and I moved it out of the way. As quickly as possible, I scrambled out of the hole, replaced the cover, and walked away as if nothing were out of the ordinary.

Twenty minutes later, I turned a corner on the north side of the ghetto, not far from where we had lived, and ran headlong into a group of refugees only just then arriving for placement. The soldiers were busy forming them into ranks, as they had with us months before, and when they saw me they shoved me in line with the others. I wanted to protest that I wasn't with them, but what would I say? Instead, I kept quiet and tried to think of how this might work out right.

In a little while a soldier appeared with a clipboard and began calling out names from a list. *They're assigning apartments,* I thought. *They will find me for sure.* Panic seized me as I realized I had no assignment, but they called the family standing next to me. The soldier checked his list and from the look in his eyes I knew he saw that there were four names on the sheet, but only three people responded—a father, mother, and a little girl. I saw him counting and while his head was down, checking his papers one more time, I positioned myself shoulder to shoulder with the mother. When the soldier looked up, there I was and he had his four people. He was satisfied and they seemed not to realize what was happening. Then he motioned with his arm for us to follow, and we walked behind him to a building up the street.

Once we were alone inside their apartment, the father turned to me. "Who are you?" he asked.

"It does not matter who I am. You must remember to tell no one you saw me."

"They will kill us all if we do not report you," the mother objected.

"I have lived here before," I countered. "No one will ever notice. Only, you must do one thing more."

The father had a questioning look. "What is it?"

"You must not let them take you."

"What do you mean?"

"A month from now. Two months from now. They will come again with trucks and load you onto them. If you go, you will be taken to one of the camps, where you will die a horrible death."

The mother wrung her hands. "They told us we would be resettled."

"You will be exterminated," I explained. "They are gassing women and children as soon as they come from the trains. I saw this myself. With my own eyes. Men who can work are worked until they die. Everyone else, they are killing." I turned toward the door. "Whatever you have to do, when they come, don't go."

The father looked grim. "They will shoot us if we refuse."

"It will be better than what awaits you in the camps. Tell everyone. Don't go."

Before they could say anything further, I slipped out to the stairs and made my way to the basement. In the darkness below, I found a tunnel and followed it to the building next door. There I looked out on the street through the narrow windows and got my bearings.

As best I could determine, I needed to move four blocks over, but doing that would not be easy. No tunnels ran in that direction. To get there, I would have to cross to the opposite side of the street in the open. With people still being settled by the soldiers, no one was out on the sidewalks. If I went out there now, I would be found and questioned by the soldiers.

Instead of waiting, I continued through the tunnels up the street two more buildings away. I was moving laterally to the direction I needed to go, but I thought it was safer than staying in one location and waiting. Then I caught a break.

The last building I came to stood on the corner. Not the corner where Stephan and Tomer gathered with their friends, but a corner just the same. From the sounds above me, I was certain the building was already filled to capacity. When I checked the cross street from the basement windows, I saw no soldiers. One or two men came from the next building over, and a young girl leaned out from the second floor. With the resettlement taking place farther down the street, perhaps the soldiers weren't patrolling this section. I decided to take a chance.

I crept from the basement to the first floor and stepped out to the sidewalk. With a quick glance to my left and right I saw I was in the clear. I scooted across the side street and walked back to the corner, in the direction I needed to go. Just when I was making real progress, two soldiers appeared at the next corner and came toward me. I ignored them, kept my head down, and walked to the left, once again making my way deeper into the ghetto and farther from the place I needed to be.

Three buildings farther, I found an alley and made my way to the next street. Now I was only two blocks from the street where my parents had lived, but still many buildings to the left. To get there, all I had to do was cross the street, get into the basement of the first building I came to, and work my way back through the tunnels to the right.

An hour later, I peered out a basement window at the entrance to the building I'd been searching for. Images of our arrival that first night flashed through my mind. Papa and Mama ahead of us. David walking beside me. Soldiers on either side. That night I was worried we would never return to Linz, but as they led us up to the apartment, I wasn't at all afraid of the soldiers. Away from the group, on their own, they seemed to be merely doing their job, evil though it was. As I later saw, that first assessment was quite naïve. Now everyone was gone. Our entire neighborhood wiped out. Not a person on our street from home remained alive.

As I watched through the window two soldiers passed by, but no other people appeared on the street and not a sound came from the building where I hid. From all I could see, no one lived in this part of the ghetto. That made it less likely that I would be found, but it also meant that if I crossed the street now anyone who was looking would know immediately that I wasn't supposed to be there. With the last light of day fading away, I decided to sit and wait. The basement was dark and musty but not an unpleasant place to hide, and if I waited for nighttime I could dart across the street with the least risk of getting caught. Resigned to that, I found a spot below the windows and sat down with my back against the wall. In a few minutes, I was asleep.

An hour later I awakened to find I was sitting in total darkness. Even from the windows above I could see only the faintest gray of reflected light from the guard towers in the distance. Fear crouched close at hand but I ignored it and crawled across the floor on my hands and knees. Moving carefully, I felt my way to the wall on the opposite side and then over to the left until I found the stairs. There I stood, placed my foot on the bottom step, and moved upstairs without a problem.

At the top of the stairs I came to a door that opened onto the main hall of the first floor. I eased it open a few centimeters and looked out to see if anyone was there, then stepped out and crept toward the front, working my way alongside the staircase. Soft light filtered down from the open stairs above and through windows on either side of the front door, which made it easy to find my way. I paused at the entrance to check for soldiers, my eyes searching to the left and right. Seeing none, I gently opened the door and stepped outside to the sidewalk. Then I walked quickly to the building across the street and went inside.

As I moved down the hall toward the basement stairs I caught a whiff of the smell inside, and once again images from the past flooded my mind. Mama and Papa, crushed by the loss of our home yet putting on a brave face in the hope that we would still find a future of hope and promise. David, playing the gallant older brother and doing it well. Stephan, the daring young man who won my heart long before we came to the ghetto. Seeing them in my mind filled my heart with sadness and my eyes with tears. They were gone and I would never see them again, never get to tell Papa how much I admired his bravery, or Mama how much her smile meant to me. I was the only one left. The only one to remember their story. By the time I reached the basement door my cheeks were wet. I wiped them with the backs of my hands, opened the door, and started down into the darkness once more.

When I reached the basement I paused a moment, hoping my eyes would find even the faintest sliver of light. At first it seemed there was only thick blackness everywhere, but then from the far side of the building, a silvery glow filtered through the basement windows. As my eyes became accustomed to it, I saw the barest outline of the wall to the left with the furnace and the opening for the tunnel where Papa and the council had met. I crept toward the furnace, scooting my feet forward one at a time until finally I reached the handle on the firebox door. It felt cold against my fingers. The box hadn't held a fire in a long time.

With an outstretched hand I moved down the side and around to the pipes in back. They were smooth and round and I followed them to the place where they entered the wall, a rough and jagged opening in the bricks that formed the building foundation. *Probably rats in there,* I thought. *Fewer people living here. And maybe they aren't as desperate as we were, or as hungry.*

The thought of what might be in there made me shiver, but that box held the key to my future. I took a deep breath and slid my hand slowly through the opening. At first my fingers touched only the pipe, but as I went deeper I heard something and then felt the soft, furry skin of a rat. It hissed at me and I jerked back my hand. My heart raced at the horror of a bite from a rabid rodent, but I had to get that box.

In frustration, I rapped my knuckles on the pipe. It made an awful noise that reverberated through the building, but as it did I heard the rat scurry farther into the hole. With it out of the way, I stretched out my arm again and felt with my hand deeper inside, this time almost to my armpit. And then I touched it.

Back upstairs I knelt with the box on the floor and lifted the lid. In the soft light from the street I saw my papers from Spain were right where I put them in the top tray. Beneath them, the locket and chain were tucked into a corner. Other pieces that lay in the tray—earrings with a pewter setting, a ring made of oyster shell, and two bracelets of gold-colored metal—were the last bits of our life in Linz. Nothing else remained. Sadness swept over me at the thought of leaving it behind but I could not carry the box with me. It was a bitter choice but I had no option. With tears in my eyes, I put the papers in the pocket of my jacket, dropped the locket and chain into the pocket of my dress, and left the box right there on the floor, then I turned away and started for the door.

For the remainder of the night I picked my way back through the streets, trying to return to the far side of the ghetto near the manhole that led to the sewer and the canal. My plan was to go back through the pipe to the canal at sunup and get over to the streets of Vienna early in the day. From there I could search for a way out of the country. German soldiers occupied Austria and the Sudetenland, an area previously part of Czechoslovakia, and they were charging across Poland. My only hope was to travel in the opposite direction—west toward the Swiss border— but to do that, I had to first get out.

As the sky turned gray with the approaching dawn I finally located the manhole. It was early, and I was certain the pipe would be too dark to see my way through, but I didn't want to wait any longer. I slid the cover out of the way, lowered myself into the access shaft, and started down the ladder.

Two hours later, I was on the streets of southern Vienna. My face and hands were dirty. My clothes were filthy, but I didn't care. Finding the jewelry box with the papers and locket inside filled me with a sense of accomplishment and optimism. I was on my way.

chapter 33

For the next two days I wandered the streets of Vienna, hiding in basements and eating from garbage cans. I had no idea where I was or what I needed to do next. I just wanted to stay alive, get out of the city, and travel west. I kept walking in that direction as nearly as I could, but it was difficult to avoid German military patrols at the same time.

Finally, late on the third day, I came to a railroad track. It seemed to lead west so I followed it until I came to a tannery. The smell was awful, but when I realized they were tanning animal hides I thought I might find something edible—a bone or a scrap of skin. Since the time I arrived again at the ghetto I had eaten almost nothing.

Three sidetracks led from the main line to a loading area with platforms in between the tracks. Freight cars stood there in rows and as I approached, men were loading them with bales of tanned skins. Beyond the loading docks were a dozen large vats filled with putrid liquid.

Sunset wasn't far off. Only a few workers remained near the vats, and I wandered among them, searching for scraps of anything that looked good enough to put in my mouth. But when two men noticed me, I darted into the bushes and rested while nighttime slowly descended.

When it was fully dark I emerged from my hiding place and walked among the freight cars. The doors were closed on the ones in the first line and I had no strength to open them. There was nothing there to eat and with every passing minute the temperature dropped lower and lower. I needed a place for the night that was safe enough to allow me to sleep and warm enough to keep from freezing.

Then I heard approaching footsteps on the loading dock and people talking. I ducked around the corner of a car and watched as two men opened a boxcar and climbed inside. Moments later they emerged with one of them holding an animal hide. As they walked back among the vats, I heard them talking about the quality of the skin, the price they could get for each, and how many more they could sell.

Once they were gone, I came back around the end of the car and climbed onto the loading platform. The men had left the door to the railcar open, so I climbed inside and saw that it was only half full with bales of hides stacked on one end. It smelled awful in there, but I was dirty anyway so I wedged my way between the bales and found a spot where I could sit. Then I pulled the corner of a hide free from the bail strap and poked it in my mouth. It wasn't much but it was better than nothing. The pain of hunger was agonizing and my weight was down to less than a hundred pounds. Gradually the hide became wet and I tasted a hint of salt from the curing process. I chewed on it awhile but that only made me thirsty, so I stopped and rested my head against the bale behind me. Surrounded by the hides, I began to warm and soon my eyelids were heavy. Before long I was fast asleep.

Sometime in the night, I was awakened by a thud against the freight car. I peered out from my hiding place to see workmen inside the car, loading it with more bales of freshly cured hides. They filled the opposite end of the car, then stacked more on top of where I sat. By the time they were finished, I was trapped with just enough room to turn on my side and barely enough space to breathe.

Not long after that, the sound of a locomotive filled the air and the rumble of it shook the ground. Workmen shouted to each other and then there was a jolt and a rattle. "Oh no," I gasped. They were connecting the cars to a train. I was worried about where the train might take me but trapped as I was between the bales of hides, there was nothing I could do.

Then the train began to move slowly down the track out of the loading area and onto the main line. The car rocked gently from side to side. On most occasions it would have rocked me back to sleep, but mixed with the smell the motion made me nauseous. There was nothing in my stomach to vomit and no place to do it, so I closed my eyes and forced myself to remain calm as the train picked up speed.

Somewhere along the way I fell asleep again, but after sunrise I was awakened by the sense that the air outside had grown even colder. I turned my head to the right and found that I could see along a gap in the stacks to the wall of the car. Through a crack in the wall I saw a white blur rushing past the train. "If that is snow," I said to myself, "then we are in the mountains." That meant we were still in Austria. From the look of the light, we were traveling toward the sun, which meant we were headed toward one of three places—Italy, Switzerland, or Germany. But I had no idea which.

A few hours later, the train slowed and eased onto a siding. From outside I heard the bark of dogs and voices as men moved along the train cars. *German soldiers,* I thought. *Inspecting the train.* I sat motionless and waited while the door to the car opened. Almost immediately, someone gagged. Then I heard a dog whimpering. "Not even the dogs can get a scent in this," someone groused. The door banged closed and there was the sound of shuffling feet as the men moved on. An hour later, the train started forward again, rolled out to the main line, and continued down the track.

My back ached from sitting all day and my feet tingled from lack of circulation. The odor was overwhelming and the tight fit made me want to scream. When I could take it no more I drew my feet up beneath my thighs and pushed against my back, forcing myself to stand. My head rose up, squeezing between the bales.

The gap where I'd been sitting ran down the center of the car. It was just wide enough for me to stand but not wide enough to walk. So I turned sideways and shuffled along. Moving my legs made them feel better, and the tingling in my feet soon stopped.

Near the middle of the car I felt a bale above me move. I lifted my hands over my head and pushed against it. After two or three tries it rolled from the stack. I looked up to see the top of the car and realized it wasn't packed completely full.

With my back braced against a bale on one side of the gap, and my feet against a bale on the other side, I pushed my way up from the gap where I was standing and sat atop the bales near the center of the car, a few meters from the sliding doors on either side. It felt good to be free of the narrow space where I'd been traveling but now the cold air surrounded me. I reached over to the bale beside me and tugged at one of the hides. It didn't come free but I moved the bale to my right, positioning it to block the air from that direction. I tried another bale, then another, and eventually found one that was loose enough to pull a hide free. I used it as a wrap and covered myself from shoulders to ankles. After a while, I lay back on the bales, still wrapped in the hide, and dozed off.

A few hours later, the train came to a stop. I peeked out through a crack in the wall and saw we were in a freight yard. Workmen uncoupled cars from the train, and a locomotive shuttled them onto adjacent tracks. I waited until the car I was in came to a stop, then climbed over to the door and found the lever. Using my legs, I was able to lift up the handle and slid open the door. Then I jumped to the ground and scurried away.

Across the yard I came to a railway station. A sign on the building identified it as St. Galen. My eyes grew moist and my heart beat faster. A smile spread across my face. I really was in Switzerland, a country whose neutrality Germany recognized. Now all I had to do was get to Zurich and find the Spanish Consulate. I wiped my eyes and continued past the station to the street out front, where I waited for an approaching truck. Instead of continuing past me, as I expected, it slowed to a stop at the curb in front of me and the driver leaned out the window. "Just come in on the train?"

"Yes," I nodded suspiciously, unsure why he was asking.

"Where you going?"

"Zurich."

"Zurich?" he frowned. "Why didn't you stay on the train? Take you right to it."

"No money."

"Oh," he smiled. "Well, get in and I'll give you a ride as far as Winterthur." I was a little unsettled by his friendliness, but nothing could have been stranger than the life I had led to that point, so I walked around to the passenger side and got in. As we started forward, he glanced over at me and his eyes opened wider as he saw my condition. "You don't look like you came on the train."

"Not the passenger train."

His jaw dropped. "You rode the freight?"

"Yes," I nodded.

"And nothing happened to you?"

"Not at all."

"You could get hurt doing that."

"Not much choice," I shrugged.

"Well, it's no wonder I smell you," he chuckled.

"Sorry," I replied sheepishly.

"Don't worry about it." He made a dismissive gesture with his hand. "Had anything to eat?"

"Not much."

A lunch box sat on the seat and he opened it. "Have a piece of cheese," he handed me a small package. "Left over from my lunch. The wife always packs me too much." I opened it and took a bite. It was the first real food I'd eaten in a long time.

After a moment he sniffed the air and wrinkled his nose. "What's that smell, anyway? Smells like…dead animals."

"Animal hides," I said in a matter-of-fact tone.

He gestured with his right hand. "Lean a little that way, would you? The smell is really strong." Then he looked at me and laughed. "You're a real sight, you know."

The truck driver never told me his name, but I learned as we talked that he made that drive in his truck every day. He found it boring work but the pay was steady, so he didn't want to quit. To make the drive more bearable, he picked up passengers along the way to keep him company. I was his rider that afternoon. He never asked who I was or what had happened. Instead, we talked about nothing of substance the entire drive and kept each other entertained. Many survivors from the camps have gone through hours of therapy in an attempt to recover. In my darkest days I longed not for the therapist's couch or the rabbi's office, but just for one more ride with that man in the cab of his truck through the Swiss Alps.

When we reached Winterthur, he stopped at a café and went inside. His route took him north, toward Kemmental, but he wanted to help me so he went inside to ask around. In a little while he returned with a driver going to Zurich. I rode with that second driver to a warehouse on the north side of the city. It was dark by the time we arrived there, and with nowhere else to go I found a church and went inside. The building was warmer than sleeping on the street and much safer. I used a hymnal for a pillow and stretched out on a pew. I slept unbothered until morning when the priest found me. He gave me breakfast of pastries and coffee. I ate lightly, knowing that with the sparse diet I'd had, sweets would easily make me sick. After we ate, he paid for a taxi to drive me to the embassy and sent me out with a blessing.

* * *

The embassy of Spain was located on Riedtlistrasse. A guard at the door didn't like my appearance, but when I showed him my papers he stepped aside and let me pass. Not far inside I located a restroom and there I washed my hands, face, and feet for the first time in weeks. Then, with my hair straightened and a pleasant look on my face, I walked to the desk. A woman looked up at me as I approached.

"May I help you?"

"I am Sarah Batsheva. A citizen of Spain. And I need help getting to Cordova."

She peered at me over the rim of her glasses. "You have papers?"

"Yes," I handed her the documents.

She glanced at them and pointed to a row of chairs. "Have a seat," she said dryly. "Someone will be with you shortly."

Thirty minutes later I was escorted to the office of a man named Victor Aranoa. He was a little older than I, but not that much. Slender, with dark hair and dark eyes. He stood when I entered the room and nervously straightened his jacket. I liked the kindness in his eyes.

After once more checking my papers, he listened to my story and nodded attentively while I told him all that had happened to us, from the time we lived in Linz until then. When I was finished, he smiled and said, "Now that you are here, what do you wish to do?"

"I would like to travel to Cordova."

"You have the means to do that?"

"No," I shook my head. "I have nothing."

"Well," he shrugged, "that might be a problem. But if you reached Cordova, where would you stay?"

"My cousin lives there. I could stay with him."

"And what is this cousin's name?"

"Oscar Murillo." I said the name without thought. He was my cousin. I was simply answering the question. But when I said it, I saw something flicker in Victor's eyes. He sat up in the chair and scooted closer to the desk. His eyes darted over the papers on his desk, then he glanced up at me. "You will excuse me. I have to speak with someone."

In a little while Victor returned, accompanied by Joaquin Valdivia, an older man who was tall with broad shoulders and graying hair. He wore a tan suit that fit perfectly across the shoulders, and his brown shoes were polished to a brilliant shine. Standing straight and walking at a brisk gait, he carried himself as a man accustomed to having his orders obeyed. He crossed the room to the desk, greeted me with a pleasant smile, and got straight to the point. "They tell me you are related to Oscar Murillo from Cordova."

"Yes." I was concerned that Oscar's political involvement had finally gotten him into trouble. "Is something wrong?"

"No," he replied softly. "Not at all. I just need a little more information."

"What would you like to know?"

Valdivia folded his arms across his chest and leaned against the desk. "Tell me, how are you related to Oscar?"

"Like I said, he is my cousin. His mother, Haya, was my aunt."

He arched an eyebrow. "Haya Murillo is your aunt?"

"Yes. She's deceased now, but she and my mother were sisters."

"And you knew Haya's husband?"

"Uncle Carlos. Yes. He was my uncle." My concern turned to curiosity. "Do you know of them?"

"I was an assistant at the Interior Ministry when Carlos was the minister."

"Oh." I nodded politely, but this was the first I had heard of Uncle Carlos being Minister of Interior. "He was a wonderful man," I added.

"Yes. And a good friend." Valdivia placed his hands at his side. "Your family, did they escape with you?"

"No," I replied with sadness. "So far as I know, they are all gone. They tell me Mama was transported to a camp at Auschwitz, in Poland, where she was killed. My father and brother were sent to a camp near Mauthausen, Austria."

"Surely you have other family members."

"Mama and Haya had a brother, Alois. But I do not think he lived. Everyone we knew in Linz, where we lived in Austria, was sent to the ghetto in Vienna, then on to one of the camps."

Valdivia had a troubled look. "You are certain Alois is dead?"

"Not certain, but I think so." I noticed the frown on his forehead, so I pressed the point. "Did you know Uncle Alois? Alois Raveh?"

"Yes," he nodded. "I knew him well. Alois was my friend and the most honorable man I've ever known." He stood up straight, said something to Victor, then glanced back at me. "It will take a few days to arrange things. Victor will take care of you." He clasped his hands together and bowed. "I am sorry for your loss, but I am glad that you are alive." Then he turned away and walked from the room.

That afternoon, Victor drove me to a hotel not far from the embassy. I waited while he checked me in at the lobby desk, then we rode together in the elevator up to the room and he helped me get settled. There wasn't much to do. All I had was the dress and jacket that I wore.

"I'll bring you some more clothes. My sister is about your size. She lives here. I'm sure she won't mind giving you a few things."

"I hate to trouble you," I replied politely, but I needed something different to wear.

"It's no trouble at all." Then he looked at me, and his countenance clouded. "But there is one slight problem."

As a Jew living in Europe, I had grown up expecting there to always be "one more thing." What Americans call "the catch"—when a thing is too good to be true and just when you believe this time it really is true, they hit you with something they want in return that ruins the whole thing. I had been waiting for this moment, hoping it would never arrive. Now, it seemed, it was here. I did my best to give no hint of displeasure. "What is that?" I asked calmly.

"Our arrangement with the hotel provides breakfast and dinner. Lunch is not on the plan."

Inside I wanted to laugh. I had survived by eating rats in the ghetto and from garbage cans on the street. Having only two hot meals each day might have been a problem for some, but for me it was heaven. "That will be fine," I smiled.

"I can come get you tomorrow," he offered quickly, "and we could eat together."

"That's not necessary," I said, flattered by his eagerness to care for me. "I don't need much to eat right now and you have been more than generous."

"Okay," he sighed. "But if you are hungry later, call me and I will come over to help."

"Okay," I nodded. "I'll remember that."

"And one more thing," he added. "The Swiss government is officially neutral, which means they will not assist anyone contravening German policy. The people here are very kind, but the government has proved quite intransigent in its position. So you should probably stay in the hotel unless you are with one of us."

"Right," I nodded. It was yet one more reminder of the second-class status of Jews, but in light of where I had been it was an indignity I could endure for the moment.

"We have made your case a priority and are working diligently to return you to Cordova."

"I appreciate that."

"Okay," he said again as he backed toward the door, "if you don't need anything else, I will leave and let you relax."

"I appreciate your help."

He reached back to open the door. "I think there's a robe in the bathroom that you can use. And housekeeping will launder your clothes if you like."

"Thank you."

He pulled open the door to leave, then stopped and turned to face me. His shoulders relaxed and he said calmly, "Would you mind if I joined you for dinner?"

Romance was the last thing I wanted, but his attention made me feel alive once more and I was glad to see his interest. I smiled at him coyly. "I would like that very much."

"Good," he grinned. "Seven?"

"That will be good."

Then he stepped out to the hall and was gone.

chapter 34

After Victor left the room, I drew a tub of warm water and spent an hour soaking. Then I washed my hair and put on the robe that was hanging on a rack near the sink. As I ran my fingers through my hair I looked at myself in the mirror. My eyes were sunken, with dark circles beneath them. Cheekbones protruded beneath them. When I moved my jaw from side to side, I could see the bone pressed tightly against my skin, producing the faint outline of my lower teeth. I stretched out my arm and pulled back the sleeve of the robe to see the bones of my wrist were like knots and the bones of my fingers were visible beneath the skin. I had lost far more weight than I first imagined. "It was brutal," I whispered. "More brutal than I have allowed myself to acknowledge."

After a moment before the mirror, I returned to the bedroom, threw back the covers from the bed, and lay down. The mattress was soft, the sheets clean and fresh. I pulled the cover over me, rested my head on the pillow, and went to sleep. While I slept I returned to our street in Linz. I saw myself walking up the sidewalk past the house where the Eichmanns lived. Weeds grew around the foundation and litter covered the lawn. The windows were missing and the door hung by a single hinge. As I moved past, a man appeared in the doorway. He was tall and fat and he wore an army uniform that was tattered and dirty. His eyes bore in on me and I looked away, but as I continued up the street I could feel them following me. Three houses later I came to the walkway that led to our front steps. I looked up expecting to see the porch but there was nothing, only an empty lot swept clean and bare. Then I heard the roar of laughter from behind me and a voice shouting, "You stupid Jew!"

I awakened with a start and glanced around, for a moment unsure where I was or how I came to be there. Then I remembered the train ride in the freight car, the truck driver, and meeting Victor at the embassy. The room was darker than before and from the bed I glanced toward the window. Outside the sun was setting. Soon it would be dark. My stomach rumbled and I felt again the pangs of hunger.

Victor returned that evening with four dresses and a coat from his sister's closet. They hung loosely from my shoulders but I wore one of them anyway, and we went to the dining room for dinner. I enjoyed the time, but it was very surreal to be eating in a restaurant in Zurich when only a few days before I was crawling through a sewer in Vienna. When they brought our food I wanted to dive headfirst into my plate, but I disciplined myself not to eat too much. In spite of how I appeared in the mirror, I could feel myself getting stronger, just from the small amounts of food I received from the truck driver and the priest, but I did not want to rush and make myself ill.

* * *

For the following two weeks I lived in the hotel. Each morning, I rose for breakfast and returned to my room for a nap. In midafternoon I walked through the hotel and sat in the lobby, just to get out and relax. Most evenings, Victor joined me for dinner. Afterward, we strolled around the hotel and twice we went for a ride to see the city. It was a simple life, which I enjoyed physically, gaining weight and energy with each day, but it proved mentally and emotionally taxing.

During the day, everything I saw brought back images of the horrors I had endured. At night when I slept I relived each episode again and again in my dreams and often awakened feeling frightened and upset. As time wore on, I struggled with depression. Seeing Victor helped draw me out of the darkness in my mind, but it only lasted as long as he was around, and being with him brought its own problems. From the way he looked at me and from his doting acts of kindness, I was certain Victor wanted more between us than mere friendship. I had nothing more to give right then. Aside from being emotionally drained, I could not remain in Zurich and I was already seeing a vision of my life that took me far beyond my stated destination of Cordova.

In those first days after escaping from Mauthausen, I had concentrated solely on getting to Vienna, finding the documents, and traveling to Spain. As that journey unfolded, my thoughts turned to Palestine. Mama had wanted to go there, thinking we would be safe, but she didn't have the courage for it when we could have done so and by the time she was ready to act, the opportunity had passed. Now, knowing only what I learned from reading while at Aunt Haya's house, Palestine seemed the best option for my future. Life in the Middle East would be difficult, but at least I would be free to live openly as a Jew, without fear of Germans lurking in the shadows waiting to shoot me on sight. The journey from Zurich to Palestine seemed as impossible as the one I'd just completed. Having completed one arduous trek, however, gave me confidence that I could achieve the next as well, and that became my goal. Palestine.

On my fourteenth day in Zurich, Victor arrived at my room to collect me for dinner carrying a small leather suitcase. It was tanned a beautifully deep mahogany color and was smooth as silk to the touch, but the sight of it brought to my mind images of the hides stacked inside the railcar. The odor flared in my nostrils and my heart rate quickened. For a moment I was there again, sitting on the bales with the cold air rushing around me. In that same instant, I pushed the images aside and forced myself to focus on the moment at hand. Thankfully, Victor seemed not to notice my distress.

"A report arrived yesterday from the Interior office in Cordova," he began. By the look on his face I could tell he was not happy with the news. "They confirmed the details of your story."

"That upsets you?"

"I have enjoyed spending time with you," he sighed. "I don't want to see you go."

I took his hand and gave him a friendly smile. "But you know I can't stay here. Right?"

"I know." He let go of my hand and hugged me close. "I know you have to go. I just don't like seeing you leave."

Under any other circumstance I would have kissed him, but that would only offer him something I could not give, so I leaned away and pointed to the suitcase. "What is in there?"

He set the case beside the bed. "I brought it for you. We have a plane leaving in the morning for Madrid. I reserved a seat for you. You'll need a suitcase to pack your things."

I wanted to shout and laugh, but the sadness on his face was too much. Instead, I gestured with my hand toward the closet. "Everything I have belongs to your sister. I have nothing to take."

"She gave them to you. They belong to you now." He reached inside his jacket and took out an envelope. "This is for you, too." I opened the envelope and found it contained currency—Swiss francs and Spanish pesetas. "You'll need it for expenses along the way," Victor explained, "and to purchase a train ticket to Cordova, once you arrive in Madrid."

Tears came to my eyes. All my life I had been helped by others. Just when it seemed the worst would happen to me, friends stepped in to rescue me. Here was another. I only met Victor because he worked at the embassy. He wasn't a family member or an acquaintance from back home. Yet he was sending me on my way with a blessing. Not the blessing the priest gave me, and not the blessing a rabbi might give me at the synagogue, but a blessing just the same. I wrapped my arms around him, rested my head on his chest, and pressed my face against his neck.

The following morning Victor returned to the hotel and drove me to the airport. The airplane was waiting, just as he said. We said goodbye and I boarded with a group of diplomats. I glanced back at him as I entered the plane. He was standing on the tarmac a few meters beyond the wing of the plane. At my seat I glanced out the window and he was still there, hands in the pocket of his coat, his hair blowing in the wind from the plane's propellers. I have never seen a sadder face than his.

The plane landed once in Lyon, France, to refuel. Soldiers guarded the airport and I was worried something might happen, but we left without incident and continued toward Spain. No one said a word to me the entire flight.

It was late in the afternoon when we landed in Madrid. The weather was balmy and humid. I rested my coat on my arm and walked from the plane, carrying the suitcase in my hand. As I crossed the tarmac with others from the plane, an official from the Interior Ministry met me. He escorted me inside the terminal building and smoothed the way through customs. Then he drove me to the train station and waited while I purchased a ticket. The train didn't leave for a couple of hours so we ate dinner in a café across from the station. I don't remember his name and I'm not sure he ever gave it. He was much older than I and interested only in getting me aboard the train and getting on with his evening. After we ate, he walked with me to the platform and sat on a bench until the train arrived.

Six hours later I arrived in Cordova. It was four in the morning by the clock in the station, much too early to find Oscar. To pass the time, I sat on a bench in the lobby and dozed. An hour later, a café across the street opened and I went there for breakfast, using some of the money Victor gave me. Afterward, I hailed a taxi and gave him directions to

Aunt Haya's house. The last time I was there, government workers were removing her belongings. Oscar told me that he sold the house to them, but I never really believed him. I was sure they seized it for reasons I would never know. That morning as I rode in the taxi toward the river, I was certain he never stopped searching for a way to get the house back.

Across the river we turned right, passed several shops. In the distance I saw the house, three stories tall sitting at the crest of a low hill. When we were abreast of it, the driver turned into a short driveway and brought the car to a stop at the base of the front steps. I paid the fare, climbed from the back seat, and started toward the porch of the house.

Before I reached the top step, the front door opened and two small children appeared—a boy and a girl. Behind them was Oscar, looking older and more tired than before, but Oscar just the same. He placed his hands on the children's shoulders to restrain them and stared at me a moment, then a smile spread across his face. "Sarah," he said slowly. "You came back."

Behind him I saw a woman standing in the hallway near the staircase. She had auburn hair that fell to her shoulders and eyes that seemed to look right through me. In spite of the excitement created by my arrival, she remained by the stairs, watching and alert.

"Oscar," I nodded when I reached the porch. "It's been a while."

He came from the house and we embraced, then he led me past the children and inside to the front parlor. The woman I'd seen by the staircase was Inés, Oscar's wife. She stepped forward to greet me as I passed by. "I have heard a lot about you. Oscar tells us stories from your visit almost every day." She had a distant smile, polite but not at all engaging.

"I am sure he has a vivid memory."

Oscar gestured to the sofa and I took a seat. He sat in the chair by the fireplace, the one Aunt Haya enjoyed. Inés excused herself and retreated from the room. When she was gone, I looked over at Oscar. "Already your wife doesn't like me?"

"It's not you," he countered. "She doesn't care for visitors, even if they're family."

"Oh." I leaned back on the sofa. "Well, it wasn't my intention to intrude."

"Think nothing of it," he said with frown. "Tell me about everyone. After the Germans invaded Austria, we lost all our contacts. The network fell apart. We have been unable to get news about any of you in more than two years."

"It has not been an easy time." I was unsure where to begin or how much to tell him.

"So, how are Aunt Orna and Uncle Moshe?"

"As best I can determine, they are no longer alive."

"Both of them?" The news did not seem to faze him one way or the other.

"Mama was sent to a camp at Auschwitz."

He looked puzzled. "Auschwitz?"

"In Poland. Papa and David were sent to a camp near Linz. From what I have learned, Mama was killed immediately. Papa and David were worked to death."

"We have heard of these things," he nodded thoughtfully. "And Uncle Alois?"

"Dead also, but I do not know any of the details."

He had a serious look but still did not appear upset. "How did such a thing happen?"

Carefully and with measured words, I gave him the account of how we'd been moved from Linz to Vienna and all the things that happened to us in the process. I kept it as brief as possible, not wishing to aggrandize myself in telling about the awful things that happened to others, and because I did not want to frighten the children whom I was certain were listening. After half an hour, his attention began to wane and I could see that whatever his involvement had been in the rescue effort before, he was no longer interested in it now. I glanced around at the room. "You got the house back."

"Yes," he nodded, suddenly attentive. "Isn't it an odd twist?"

"How so?"

"We were hoping the Monarchists would win, but they were the ones who seized the house. They lost the war and we got the house back from the Nationalists." He chuckled at the irony and glanced at me, expecting that I would find it amusing, too.

While he was still smiling, I looked him in the eye. "Oscar, I need your help."

His face turned sober. "You can stay here a few days, but that's all I can do."

"I want to go to Palestine."

He looked away. "I'm not doing that anymore."

"But you still know people."

"I'm not sure they're even around now."

"Will you make some calls?"

"Look, I don't—" He interrupted himself and stood, then nodded for me to follow as he started toward the door. I rose from the sofa and walked with him to the porch and down the front steps. When we were away from the house he turned to me. "Inés does not like for me to talk about my involvement with Mama and Uncle Alois. If she knew I was talking about contacting anyone from those days, she would be very upset."

"Doesn't she realize you are Jewish?"

"Half Jew."

So this is what it had come to with him. Better to deny your identity than confront it. "You can divide yourself?" My voice was louder than normal but I could barely control my anger.

"She knows who I am and that is not the problem."

"Then what is?" I insisted.

"It's complicated."

"How complicated can it be?" I implored. "Is she a Nazi?"

"No," he scowled in disgust, "she's not a Nazi. She's a member of the royal family."

"And that is a problem?"

"It is now. Or at least, it could be. After you left, the conflict between the Monarchy and the Nationalists got really bad. Civil war broke out all over the country. I knew it was coming. That's why I wanted you to go. The Nationalists won and then there were reprisals against many of the key leaders from the previous government. Royals in almost every city were the subject of executions and beatings. Entire families were murdered."

"That sounds like what they did to us."

"Yes," he agreed. "It was much the same."

"Was Inés subjected to such treatment?"

"No," he shook his head. "She and her parents escaped into the mountains. To the cabin where I wanted to send you and Mama. They remained there until things calmed down, but she is still worried that it is not over. And now," he sighed, "with the children. Javier and Angelina are her world."

"As it should be."

"I suppose." He was silent for a moment, then turned to me once more. "Look, Sarah. I will make some calls. See what I can find out. I still know a few people who might help. But you can't talk to Ines about this. If she asks, you must tell her you are just visiting for a few days on your way to Malaga."

That bothered me. "You want me to lie?"

"It's not really a lie," he argued. "If I can't find a way to help you get to Palestine, I'll send you to my sister in Malaga. She knows as many people as I do, and if I can't take care of it, she will."

"Good," I nodded. "And thank you for your help."

"Come on." He took me by the elbow. "I'll show you to your room."

"The same room as before?" I asked expectantly.

"No. That is Angelina's room. You will have Mama's old room."

We had lunch together in the kitchen and I napped most of the afternoon. That evening, we ate dinner in the dining room. Oscar made small talk, the children were polite. Inés was both aloof and gracious, as only those who've enjoyed money and position can be, especially when addressing one they perceive to be of a lower station in life. Afterward, I retreated to my room and lay on the bed thinking of Aunt Haya and all that had happened in our lives since I was last at the house.

Oscar was gone from the house most of the following day. He returned that afternoon with news of a ship leaving for Haifa. "It sails from Barcelona in two days, but you will need immigration papers from the British. They still control access to the region."

"Can you get them?"

"Yes, but they cost money, as does passage on the ship. And you will need a ticket for the train to Barcelona."

I handed him the envelope with the money from Victor. "This is all the money I have."

He glanced at it and shook his head. "This won't be enough."

"How much more do we need?"

"I'm not sure. Do you have anything else?"

The way he said it, standing there in that three-story house with his wife of royalty, after all I'd been through, pierced my heart. He had always treated me this way, but I thought that perhaps, after all we'd both been through, he might realize the gravity of my situation and come to my aid and defense. But no, here he was the same Oscar to the very end, even if it meant taking the last thing I owned. But I couldn't stay there and I needed to complete the journey.

"Yes," I sighed. "I have one more thing. Wait right here." Then I ran upstairs to the bedroom, opened the suitcase, and took out the locket.

Tears filled my eyes as I looped the chain on my finger and watched it spin back and forth in the air. I remembered the day Grandma died and her last words to me: "The locket belongs to you." Seemingly from out of nowhere, a sense of grief overwhelmed me and I began to sob. Grandma was dead. Papa and Mama were gone. I would never see David and Stephan again. The sense of their loss had been with me always but I kept those emotions at bay, consoling myself at least subconsciously that my struggle to survive united us and that we were, in some small measure, bound together by the locket, the last remaining artifact from our past. The thought that it, too, would be taken from me brought to the surface all the grief I'd been holding inside. I collapsed on the bed and wept.

In a little while, there was a knock on the door behind me and I heard Oscar's voice. "Sarah, are you okay?"

I wiped my eyes with my hands and sat up. "Yes. I'm fine." I wiped my eyes again. "You may come in."

The door opened and he entered the room. I picked up the locket by the chain and turned to him. "This is gold. It belonged to my Grandmother Batsheva. It must be worth something. It's the only other thing I have."

Oscar slipped his finger in the loop of the chain and gently lifted it from my finger. "You have kept it all this time?"

"Yes."

"How did you do that? After all you've been through."

"I hid it when we were in the ghetto." I wiped my eyes once more. "Will that and the money be enough?"

He had a tight-lipped smile. "I'll see if I can make it do."

About midmorning the following day, Oscar came to my room with an envelope. "This is your ticket to Barcelona, passage on the ship, and entry documents for Palestine."

"When do I leave?"

"We should leave for the train within the hour."

chapter 35

F our days after leaving Cordova, I stepped from the ship onto the
dock at Haifa. I was prepared for a long and tedious interrogation
by British officials, questioning my right to enter the country. Instead,
all I encountered was a cursory review of my papers, which the officer
dutifully stamped, and then he waved me through the checkpoint. And
there I was, in Palestine, immersed in a world of sights and smells like
nothing I had experienced before. Even the sound was different, with
everyone around me speaking Yiddish, Hebrew, and Arabic—but not a
word of German.

With no money and nothing of value in my possession, I needed
a job quickly. I began by inquiring at cafés and stores, in search of any
work that paid a wage. After a day of that proved unsuccessful, someone
suggested I might have more success in Jerusalem. So I caught a ride in
a delivery truck and headed in that direction.

Once there, I made the rounds of all the usual places, asking for
work at stores, cafés, and later at one or two factories, but they all turned
me away. I wandered the city, moving from business to business until
the sun began to set. With darkness approaching, I found myself once
again living on the street and hungry. Behind a restaurant near the city
wall I found a trash can with scraps from the tables inside. It was fresh,

having been tossed out that evening, and when I pushed aside the paper and bones, I discovered the contents of a plate that had gone all but untouched. I dug it out with my fingers and ate, glad for a meal that filled my stomach.

By then nighttime had settled and the streets were dark. I sat on a bench at the corner opposite the King David Hotel and wondered what I should do next. A group of young Arabs sauntered by, laughing and snickering among themselves. I watched them all the way to the corner. When they turned around and started back in my direction, I decided it was time to move. Four or five blocks later I came to an alley. It was narrow and dark, which made it a good place to hide. I walked as far as the third doorway, set the suitcase near the threshold for a pillow, and lay down. Soon I was fast asleep.

The next morning, I was awakened by a man standing over me. "Who are you and what are you doing here?" he demanded.

Groggy and disoriented, I replied in German, "Ich bin Sarah Batsheva." Then I saw the frown on his forehead and quickly said in Hebrew, "I am Sarah Batsheva. Who are you?"

"My name is Yohai Cohen." He gestured over his shoulder. "This is my shop, and I don't allow anyone to sleep in my doorway."

"I had no place else to go." I stood and dusted off my dress.

His eyes widened. "Your accent," he pointed a finger at me. "It is from...central Europe. Right?"

"Yes," I nodded.

"And that language...you are from Germany."

"Austria."

"Why do you have no place to go?"

"I only arrived two days ago. From Spain."

He arched an eyebrow in a suspicious gaze. "I thought you said you were from Austria."

"I am from Austria. I escaped."

"Escaped? From the Nazis?"

Before I could answer, a woman appeared behind him and elbowed her way past. "Yohai Cohen," she fussed. "What are you doing? You can't leave her out here like this." She took me by the arm. "Come inside. Come inside."

The woman's name, I later learned, was Chana. She was Yohai's wife. Together they operated Café Vienna, a popular coffee shop located on Zion Square in the center of the city.

Chana ushered me through the doorway and into a hall that divided the back portion of the shop into two sections. To the left was a sink with counters on either side, stacked with dirty dishes. Along the wall were racks filled with clean ones. To the right of the hall was the food-preparation area, with ovens and stoves. A man about my age stood there, his back to us. Chana hit him on the shoulder as she pushed me toward a table in the corner. "Fix her something to eat," she ordered. The man glanced at me over his shoulder. At first he had a look of contempt at being inconvenienced by the interruption, but when his eyes met mine I saw the same look I'd seen many times from Stephan. Seeing it made my heart skip a beat.

I sat at the table with Chana and she took hold of my hands. "Look at this," she shook her head. "So dirty and rough. You should have the hands of a princess to match your beautiful face." Then she let go of me and pointed over her shoulder. "Go wash your hands. You can't eat with hands like that. Go wash them in the sink." As I stood and started in that direction, she called over her shoulder, "Eli, show her the sinks."

"I'm cooking," he protested.

Chana's tone was even more forceful. "Don't argue with your mama. Show her the sinks."

Eli smiled at me as he reached over my shoulder and turned on the water. "She means well," he muttered. Then he handed me the soap and laid a towel across my shoulder.

When I returned to the table, Chana looked at my hands again. "That is much better, but they need lotion. We will take care of that." She reached up to my forehead and brushed back the hair from my face. "You were out there all night?"

"Yes," I nodded.

"You should have banged on the door."

"I didn't know."

"Well, it's okay now. I will look after you." Eli appeared with a plate of food and set it on the table before me. He turned to leave but Chana took him by the arm. "This is Eli. My son." She nodded to me. "Tell him your name."

"Sarah Batsheva," I answered politely.

"Sarah Batsheva," Chana repeated. "That's a good name." She swatted Eli on the bottom. "Now get back to work and let us talk in peace." Eli's eyes met mine and we both began to giggle. "What?" Chana exclaimed. "Did I say something funny?"

"It was nothing, Mama," Eli replied.

Eli drifted away from the table, but not very far. As I ate, Chana probed me with questions about my past. In between bites, I told her some of what had happened. Eli lingered close enough to hear and in a few minutes Yohai joined him. I told them about our life in Linz and how treatment of the Jews became increasingly hostile, the movement of Jews from the countryside into the city and how we were forced to give them space in our home, and I told about being uprooted and moved to the ghetto in Vienna. I talked slowly, making sure to finish the meal before I told them everything. They seemed to hang on every word.

When I finished eating, Eli took my plate and refilled my glass with water. While he did that, Chana rose from the table and walked with Yohai into the café dining room. I watched through the doorway as the two of them talked. They were such a study in contrasts. Chana, loud and animated. Yohai, stern but compassionate. She poked him in the chest to emphasize her point, then pressed her palm flat against him in a tender gesture. He shook his head in an expression of solemn resolution, then placed his hands on her shoulders as if to hug her. Such frankness, such honesty, such love I had not seen since…our family was together in Linz.

In a moment, Chana returned with a reluctant Yohai in tow. They came to the table where I sat, and Chana gave him a nudge. He cleared his throat and began. "Chana says you need a job."

"Yes," I nodded, "I do. A job, not a gift."

"We need you," Chana interjected, pointing to the sink across the hall and over her shoulder to the dining room. "Look at all those dishes. Look at all those customers. We need you."

Yohai clasped his hands together and held them at his waist. "You work for me and I will give you a room upstairs and three meals each day."

Eli moved behind him and held up two fingers, mouthing something I could not understand. At the same time, Chana held up three fingers. I was bewildered by what they meant but glad to have the offer of a job. "I'll take—"

"She'll take it," Chana blurted out. "Plus one pound Palestinian per week," she added triumphantly. "In cash."

"A pound?" Yohai growled. "Are you out of your mind?"

"You cannot work her all week and leave her with nothing," Chana argued. "She must have a little money in her pocket."

"Okay," Yohai sighed. "One pound Palestinian per week." He turned to walk away. "Eli will show you what to do."

"Thank you," I beamed. "I accept. When can I begin?"

"You can begin right now," Yohai called over his shoulder. "Eli, get those orders ready."

"She will begin tomorrow," Chana said, talking over him. "Today she will take a bath, and I will find her some clean clothes." She took me by the arm and tugged on it for me to follow. "Come," she insisted. "Come with me." I glanced at Eli for advice, but he only shrugged in response, so I rose from the table and followed Chana upstairs.

* * *

Late that afternoon, I came to the kitchen. Eli was standing at the stove, right where he was that morning. I came up behind him and touched him on the elbow. He jumped with surprise, but the startled look turned to a smile when he saw me. "You startled me," he chuckled.

"Sorry. Your mother said I should ask you what to do and you would show me."

He turned from the stove and glanced at me, then his eyes darted away. "You...ah—"

"You like the dress?" I interrupted in an effort to break the tension.

"Yes," he nodded with a nervous smile. "It looks great on you." He set aside the pan he was working with and wiped his hands. "I thought you weren't supposed to start until tomorrow."

"Chana told me I better start now. So your father won't be angry."

"Ah," he nodded. "Feeling a little guilty about the way she talked to him earlier?"

"Maybe." I didn't want to talk about her. "So, show me the kitchen."

"Well," he began, gesturing to the room around us. "This is it. Cooking on this side. Cleanup over there. You will wait on tables eventually. When you do, you write the order on a ticket and clip it right there so I can see it." To the left of the stove was a pass-through window. A string ran from one side of it to the other with small clips to hold the order tickets. "When the order's ready, I'll shout. You pick it up and take it to the table. When they're finished, you bring the dishes over there," he pointed, "to the counter by the sink."

I looked in that direction to see the counter was stacked with dirty dishes, just as it had been earlier that morning. "Who washes them?" I asked.

"We all take turns,"

"When?"

"Well," he smiled, "your turn begins now." He led me across the hall to the sink.

"I thought you said I would wait tables."

"Eventually," he replied. "But first you must begin here at the sink." He reached up to a hook on the wall and took down an apron. With his help, I wrapped it around my waist and tied it in place. Then he patted me on the back and said, "Get busy. You're already half a day behind."

"But I thought you said we *all* would wash dishes."

"I'll help you when I'm finished over here."

That evening, after the dinner rush, Eli and I stood together by the sink, washing and drying dishes. He was easy to talk to and before long I was telling him many of my secrets. Not the darkest ones, but more than I told anyone else since we were taken from our home in Linz.

That began a routine with us. We worked all day in the café and at night we sat on the steps out back at the door to the alley and talked. I gave him more details of the events I'd already described, and he told me about his life in Jerusalem, the city where he was born and had lived all his life. Gradually, our friendship deepened and over the next few months I told him more and more of my story—the ghetto and the women and babies who were shot by the Germans for sport, the food we ate and the food we didn't, Eichmann, the work in his office, the death of my family, and my escape from execution at the mass grave. More than an emotional journey for me, revealing those stories was a journey of trust, hoping upon hope that he would listen without judging or condemning me as I wrestled with the guilt of having survived the fate that befell everyone I knew.

One cool autumn evening, we went for a walk up the street. As we strolled along I told him again about the time the German soldiers came for us, to move us from the house in Linz. Much of it was a repeat of things I'd told him before, but rather than reminding me of that he kept quiet and listened while I talked. Eventually, I came to the story of Ehud Averbuch and how he was shot with his wife on the street in front of our house. Tears filled my eyes, and my voice broke. Eli reached down to take my hand. "You saw this?" he asked quietly.

"Yes," I nodded. We'd been through this before. He knew about Ehud being shot with his wife. The fact that he still was willing to listen touched me even deeper. "But there was more," I said, wiping my eyes with my free hand.

"What happened?"

"They shot them," I blurted, and began to cry.

"Ehud and his wife?"

"No," I said, shaking my head. "The children." I was sobbing. "They shot the children. For no reason at all the soldiers plopped them down right next to the bodies of their mother and father, and they shot them."

My body shook as tears streamed down my face. We'd stopped walking by then, and I draped my arms over Eli's shoulders. He slid his arm gently around my waist. "It must have been horrible to see," he whispered.

"Why would someone do such a thing? Why would they do that?" Eli didn't answer, he just held me.

After a moment I looked up at his face and I was sure he was going to kiss me. I wanted him to kiss me, to feel his lips against mine and know that after all I'd been through I still was desirable to him. His head moved forward, then he hesitated and I drew back, feeling confused about what just happened.

* * *

309

Not long after that, a handsome young man came to the café. His name, I soon learned, was Tobin Halutz and he sat at a table with two friends. All through their meal he flirted with me, making comments about my eyes and hair. I smiled politely but did my best to ignore him. Each time I returned to the kitchen, I noticed Eli was standing in the hallway, watching.

When they finished eating, the friends got up to leave but Tobin lingered behind, and when I came out to collect the dishes he asked if I would join him for dinner the following evening. They had arrived at the café in a car that Tobin drove. It was parked out front and several customers stopped to admire it. Most people still walked or rode one of the few buses, and sometimes they used a donkey or burro. No one his age had a car. He was handsome, with broad shoulders, a nice smile, and curly hair. Anyone looking for a date could have easily done worse, but he looked at me the same way Victor did, as one who wanted to rescue me, and smother me, not someone who wanted to set me free to be myself. I turned him down without remorse.

After he was gone, one of the regular customers shook his head. "You should have said yes."

"Why?"

"His family is one of the leading families of the entire Palestinian region. They've been here for many generations."

Yohai was standing nearby and overheard our conversation, but kept quiet. Someone at another table spoke up. "I hear he's getting married but he doesn't really want to. The family arranged it."

"Might still be time for you."

I shook my head. "I would be just another of his ornaments."

When I turned from the table, I saw Eli in the hallway. He'd been listening too, and I could tell from the look on his face that he did not like what he heard.

Later that evening, Tobin returned and called me out to the street. When I went out, he asked me once more to join him the following evening. "Men like you are only interested in the things they can't have. Once they get them, they move on to something else."

"I am not one of those men."

"Oh? I hear you are already engaged."

"Where did you hear that?"

"What kind of man asks a woman out when he is engaged to someone else?"

"Suit yourself," he sighed.

When he was gone, I walked into the café. Yohai met me near the door. "Tobin seems upset."

"He'll get over it."

"This isn't good." He had a look of concern.

"Why not?"

"We get our coffee from their company."

"And you think if I don't go out with him they will refuse to sell it to you?"

"The thought crossed my mind."

"Yohai, this is the most popular café in Jerusalem. I don't think they would risk offending all of our customers over the refusal of a waitress."

Late that evening, after our work was finished, Eli did not come immediately to the steps out back, as had been our custom. I found him still in the kitchen, needlessly rubbing the stove top with a cloth. He seemed tense and when I tried to talk to him he avoided making eye contact with me. I kept trying and finally coaxed him into taking me for a walk. When we were away from the restaurant I looked over at him. "What is the matter?"

"Nothing," he sighed.

I hooked my arm in his. "We've spent too many nights talking about too many things to keep secrets now. Tell me what's on your mind."

"I saw you with Tobin Halutz tonight."

"Yes," I nodded.

"Twice."

"Your father spoke to you?"

"Not really, but I know how he thinks," Eli sighed. "He's always worried about offending someone."

"I thought he would be someone who didn't care what others thought."

"He doesn't care if he's addressing someone he perceives to be beneath his station in life. But Tobin isn't one of those people."

"He's someone who can affect your father's life."

"All our lives."

"You think I should have gone out with him?"

"No." Eli shook his head. "But I suppose it must have been difficult to refuse him."

"Not really," I smiled.

"Did he invite you to one of his family's vacation retreats?"

"He invited me to dinner."

"And apparently you refused."

"I am here, aren't I?" I tugged on his arm. "Let's talk about something else."

"Good." He stopped and turned to face me. "I wasn't really thinking about him anyway."

"Then what were you thinking about?"

"You. And me. And us." Then he leaned forward and pressed his lips against mine, and I kissed him back.

After a moment we paused, and he looked me in the eye. "I am not as handsome as Tobin Halutz and certainly not as wealthy."

"If I wanted Tobin Halutz, I would be walking with him this evening." I wrapped my arms around his neck and kissed him, then moved my lips to his earlobe and whispered, "Do my kisses make you feel handsome now?"

"No," he replied with a giggle. "Your kisses make me feel like I've never felt before."

"Good," I smiled. "Let's keep it that way." And we kissed once more.

chapter 36

A few months later, we married and moved into an apartment several blocks from the café. We worked together, trying to expand the business without destroying its appeal. While war raged across Europe and Asia, Palestine, by comparison, went largely untouched. There was fighting in the region but none that affected us. On the surface, everything looked great, but inside my life took on a dual nature.

In many ways it was more rewarding than it had ever been—I had a husband who loved me without condition and a family that accepted and respected me. But still I was troubled by memories of the past, the loss of my parents, as well as David and Stephan, and with the guilt that I had lived and they had not. During the day I did well, most of the time, but at night while I slept the horror came to life in my dreams and I often awakened terrified by what I saw.

On the best days, I was filled with a sense of optimism and confidence, but on the worst, darkness hung over me like a gloomy fog, and I struggled with doubt and depression. Eli paid attention to me and learned to recognize those days as they approached. He became very adept at diverting my attention to something else and many times helped me avoid the temptation to recede into myself. Yohai noticed the mood swings, too, and sent Chana to talk to me. We talked several times but I particularly remember when we sat together one afternoon at a table in their apartment upstairs from the café.

"Some things in life cannot be explained."

"Their actions were intentional," I argued. "They may have had their excuses, but these were conscious acts."

"But the why of it," she countered. "That is what I'm talking about. The 'why.' Sometimes we cannot know the why, and those things we cannot understand we must simply accept."

"Perhaps I could do that if it was something that was only directed at me. But this was against all of us, solely because of who we were. I cannot merely *accept* what I saw them doing."

"I am not suggesting that what happened was okay or right," she continued patiently. "I am only saying that it cannot be explained. That you cannot find the answers you are looking for. There is no accounting for evil in the hearts of men."

That phrase—*no accounting for evil in the hearts of men*—stuck with me and I thought about it often. Not because it was an answer; it wasn't. Instead, it was a succinct articulation of the issues that plagued my mind. An accounting for the evil in the hearts of men. I wanted an accounting. Someone was accountable. Many someones. And all I wanted was for them to pay for it. That conversation, more than most, helped me to see there was some logic to the things going on inside my head, and I began to sort my way out of the confusion that troubled me.

With Eli's help, and with Chana and Yohai lending support, my days began to even out. Business at the café improved and life settled into an otherwise happy routine of work followed by time alone with Eli, which I enjoyed immensely. Two years later, I gave birth to our son. We named him David—Stephan David—and the past receded a little more.

* * *

In the spring of 1945, news reached Jerusalem that the war in Europe was over. Some took to the streets in celebration. They rode past the café in trucks, blowing the horn and shouting. A few carried rifles, which they fired into the air. Eli stood with David and watched from the sidewalk. I sat at a table in the café and sipped a cup of tea. For so many of our people, that day had come too late.

The Japanese surrendered in August of that same year, but by then everyone in Jerusalem was focused on what the news of peace meant for Palestine. Japan was far away. The Arabs lived right next door. How we settled our differences would affect us all.

Several Jewish factions argued for the creation of a Jewish state—the reconstitution of Palestine as a homeland for the Jewish people. They spent much time and effort convincing the United Nations to back their plans. Most Arabs in the region were opposed to it, claiming just as adamantly that we were interlopers and refugees who should return home to Europe now that the war was over. The British government, which administered the area under a commission sanctioned by the United Nations, wanted only to see its involvement brought to a logical conclusion that would allow their withdrawal. Yohai and Eli spent many hours talking about it with anyone who would listen. My attention was drawn in a different direction.

In the final days of the war, newsreels brought the world a glimpse of the camps where we'd been forced to live and where millions of Jews, Poles, Gypsies, and others were systematically murdered. Faced with clear and convincing evidence of the horrors foisted on us by the Germans, the Allied powers established a war crimes department to prosecute those who were responsible. Not long after Wilhelm Keitel signed the instrument of surrender, he and many other German officers were put on trial at Nuremberg. I followed news of the trials in the newspapers and magazines, eager to see whether the truth would come out and how many of the Germans actually stood trial. I was most interested in whether Adolf Eichmann was charged and how much of his involvement they disclosed.

Each day, *The Palestine Post* carried articles that included stories of witnesses detailing all that they had encountered. Customers in the café were interested too, and when they learned something about my story they brought me newspapers and magazines from other places with articles on the trials. At night I sat at the kitchen table and studied each of them, making notes and pinpointing locations on a map for the places mentioned. For a year or more I sorted through articles and notes, comparing what I read to the facts I knew from experience.

By the end of 1946, twenty-four senior German leaders had been tried. Most had been convicted. Only five escaped sentencing. Then the news stopped. I searched the papers for word of what would happen next but found nothing. As my anxiety mounted, Yohai became concerned that my past would overwhelm me again. He was friends with Haim Rotschild, an aide to David Ben-Gurion at the World Zionist Organization, and asked him to talk to me in hopes of easing my mind. Not long after that, Haim appeared at the café for lunch. We sat at a table in the kitchen and talked.

"Yohai tells me you have been following the trials at Nuremberg."

"I was, but now the newspapers stopped covering it and I don't know why."

"They stopped covering the trials because the trials have ended."

"Ended?" I was startled. "Why did they end?"

"Most of the senior leaders have been dealt with," he shrugged. "Most of the ones who remain are either dead already or their whereabouts are unknown."

"What of Adolf Eichmann? I read all the newspaper articles and yet I saw nothing of him."

Haim arched an eyebrow. "Eichmann has not been found."

Anger rose inside me. "Where are they looking?"

"Officially, no one is looking."

"What does that mean?" I blurted out. "They don't care anymore? This was just a show for them and now they've moved on?"

"In some ways," he nodded, "yes, they have moved on. What they discovered was more horrible than they imagined. To continue to delve into it would bring up more unpleasantness than they wish to bear."

"It *was* horrible," I slapped the table for emphasis. "It *is* hard to bear. But the world has to know."

"Yes. That is true," Haim agreed. "And the ones they tried are only the surface of a very putrid, vile cesspool. But no one knows how deep it goes and no one wants to find out what's at the bottom."

"Why not?"

"Because when they get to the bottom of it, the question will arise, why didn't they do something sooner?"

"That's a good question," I nodded. "Why didn't they?"

"But then," he continued calmly, "we would face the dilemma of determining where complicity with the enemy stops and survival of the victims begins. And that would cast a cloud over many of our own people."

"Collaborators," I said flatly.

"Collaborator versus survivor." He gave me a knowing look. "Many who survived that horrible ordeal did so by engaging in otherwise unseemly acts. Women who found prostitution preferable to the gas chamber. Men who chose the job of extracting gold-filled teeth from the corpses of their fellow Jews over hauling five-ton blocks of marble from a quarry. One survived, thousands did not. Or men of distinction serving on community councils who decided, in some instances, those who lived and those who died."

"But they had no real choice. They could choose or the soldiers would choose for them."

"And many of them chose to bear the pain of death themselves in order to give others an opportunity for survival and life. But you see my point. The world can only do so much. The rest we must do for ourselves."

"I witnessed a soldier shoot a husband and wife because they did not possess the proper documents. While their bodies lay bleeding on the pavement, their two small children were brought to their side. Then the soldier who shot the parents, shot those two innocent children in the head. Their last name was Averbuch. They died right in front of me. Blood from their heads splattered on me. Every night when I sleep I am awakened by the sound of that gun." Tears rolled down my cheeks and my voice quivered. "Who is going to find those soldiers and make them pay for what they did?"

"Officially," he replied, seemingly unmoved by my response, "no one."

"Officially?"

"Yes," he nodded. "Officially, no one will make them pay. The time for paying has passed, officially."

"But unofficially?"

He cleared his throat and lowered his voice. "People are working on it. In an individual effort. Following leads, searching for clues of the location of many second-tier leaders. But it is not an easy task, and it will not be accomplished by the Allied governments. They have moved on to war in Korea and the struggle against the Soviet Union at the effort to rebuild Europe. Even here in Palestine those who could lead the effort to find the Nazis and bring them to justice are distracted by the work of establishing a Jewish state." He paused and leaned over the table and in a whisper he said with righteous anger, "But when that work is done, we shall find them all."

That evening at home I packed away my notes with all the articles I had clipped and the map I made. I had spent more than a year of my life consumed with details of the trial. My son was growing older. He needed my full attention. It was time to be done.

But that night when I went to sleep, the nightmares returned. Over and over I saw the soldier's face standing near the curb in front of our house. One minute smiling, the next contorted in a hideous snarl. The Averbuch children with big, sad eyes, watching as their parents died, and in the next instant they lay at the soldier's feet. Over and over the images flashed through my dreams and always they ended with the loud report of a gunshot, jarring me awake, bolting me upright in bed.

Eli tried to talk me back and most nights he kept me from drifting over the edge, but some mornings I struggled to get out of bed. I just wanted to curl up and go to sleep and never dream again. Finally, when it seemed we were getting nowhere, Eli suggested I talk to Abraham Meir, the rabbi at the Great Synagogue just up the street from the café. We met in the sanctuary one afternoon. I wasted little time on small talk and got right to the point.

"I understand that evil exists, but God knows everything. He sees everything. Where was He when the soldiers sent us to the camps?"

"You have a profound sense of justice," he observed. "I have seen that in you since you first started attending services here."

"Yes," I nodded. "I want justice."

"Have you considered the possibility that these dreams you are having are not a problem?"

"No," I shook my head. "I dread the night." I was barely able to contain my sense of indignation. "I never want to get in the bed. Of course they're a problem."

"Do you take naps?"

"Sometimes," I nodded. "When I get a chance. Our son naps in the afternoon. When I'm with him I take a nap."

"And when you nap, do you have these dreams?"

"No," I replied, suddenly realizing it for the first time.

"I'm certainly no psychologist, but I think that's an important point. You only have these dreams at night. Not when you nap."

"But I have no idea what that means."

Rabbi Meir stroked his chin. "I think it might mean the dreams aren't a sign of a problem. They're a sign of something more."

I was intrigued but still a little irked that he wasn't identifying with my pain. "And that *more* would be what?"

"I don't know," he shook his head. "But I would not be surprised if it had something to do with your desire for justice. Maybe a way to remind you, because deep down inside you're afraid you'll forget what happened and you don't really want to do that. Maybe you think that if you continue to relive those things you will become so distressed that you might do something about the things you actually saw." Then he smiled. "Or maybe it's God."

"God?" I frowned.

"Many times God communicated to the prophets of old through dreams. Maybe He's communicating with you. Maybe He doesn't want you to forget because there's something you must do."

"Justice?"

"Do justice, love mercy, walk humbly with your God. Justice isn't merely an idea. Justice can't only be a thought. It must be done."

"Micah," I whispered.

"Yes," he nodded. "The prophet Micah, from Moresheth."

As I talked to Rabbi Meir, I sensed the truth of what he was saying, and a great weight rolled off my back. I didn't want to forget. Someone had to remember, and I was that person. I didn't know all that happened to every Jew caught in the *Shoah*, what the world called the Holocaust, but I knew what happened to me and to those around me. I would seek justice. I would do justice. I would remember their stories and write them down.

On the way back to the café, I stopped at a shop and purchased a notebook. That evening, after everyone else was asleep I sat at the kitchen table and began to write. The first thing I thought of was Grandma, lying in bed on the day she died. And that's where I began. I wrote in the notebook until two in the morning and when I finally went to bed, I slept the remainder of the night without the slightest interruption.

chapter 37

While I was absorbed with the war crimes trials, David Ben-Gurion had pressed forward with his efforts to establish a Jewish state. He succeeded in uniting the Zionist factions behind a single effort and formed the *Moetzet HaAm*, the People's Council, to prepare the way for creation of a new government. They met in a building across the street from the café. We served them lunch almost every day.

In 1948, after heated debate and a series of complicated diplomatic maneuvers, Ben-Gurion won approval of a United Nations resolution calling for the creation of the state of Israel as a homeland for Jews. On the day before the British commission for Palestine expired, Ben-Gurion and Moetzet HaAm announced our independence in a ceremony at the Tel Aviv Museum.

Almost immediately, war broke out with the surrounding Arab nations attacking from every direction. Eli was called up for service in the army. Not long after that, Yohai was called up, too. With the men gone, Chana and I worked the café alone.

Within weeks, Jerusalem, already the scene of civil strife the year before, became the focus of both armies. Arabs seized much of the city to our east and later moved into the old quarter near the temple ruins, not far from the café. Through the café window I watched the troops march past. One day they were Israeli soldiers headed in one direction, and the next day Arabs going in the opposite. Day and night, artillery shells exploded all over the city. Commerce all but stopped and food quickly was in short supply. We cooked what we had and fed most of it to the soldiers for free. It was the least we could do and it would have spoiled anyway.

In addition to soldiers, bands of Arab and Jewish thugs roamed the streets taking what they wanted. During the first few weeks, when business was still possible, Chana and I took turns sleeping at the café each night. It wasn't safe but we didn't want to leave the business unguarded. As fighting intensified, I brought David, our son, to the café and we lived there with Chana. He liked playing in the water so we placed a stool by the sink in the kitchen, tied an apron under his arms, and put him to work washing dishes.

A few months later, forces from Jordan fought their way into our neighborhood and came up the alley behind the store. Chana snatched David from his place at the sink and ran with him upstairs to the apartment. When she returned, she held a pistol in her hand.

My mouth fell open. "What are you doing with that?"

"I will not let them take us without a fight." Her voice was calm and she had a determined look. "This is our café. We live *our* lives. No one decides how I shall die except for me."

Moments later I heard the sound of footsteps and then the back door flew open. Chana stood in the hallway between the stoves and the sink with the pistol firmly in her grip. The soldier, wearing an Arab headdress, grinned at her. "You are mine, old woman," he taunted. "After I rape you, I will kill you with that pistol."

Chana squeezed the trigger and the gun fired, instantly ripping a hole in the soldier's chest. He clutched at the wound, eyes opened wide in a look of disbelief. Then he dropped to his knees and fell face down on the floor. When the man behind him raised his rifle, Chana squeezed off a second shot, striking him in the neck. He clutched at the hole, gasping for breath, and staggered backward, colliding with two men who stood in the alley. Startled by the commotion, they ducked to the side to get out of the way.

Suddenly the front door of the café flew open and Tobin Halutz appeared with a small band of Israeli soldiers. They rushed past us into the alley while we ran upstairs. I scooped up David and we all hid in the bathroom while fighting raged in the alley.

Thirty minutes later, Tobin came to find us. We followed him downstairs and peeked out the back door. Six Arabs lay dead in the alley and a dozen more were held prisoner by Tobin's men.

"You should leave," he suggested. "My men will escort you out of the neighborhood and you can get a ride to Haifa or Tel Aviv. It's much safer there."

"No," Chana replied. "I will not leave. This is my store. My business."

"The fighting is only going to get worse. You could be killed." He glanced down at David. "All of you."

"And we could lose the store," Chana countered.

"Better it than your lives."

Chana shook her head. "Without it, we have no life."

"Suit yourself." Tobin's eyes met mine. "You sure about this?"

I squared my shoulders. "Whatever Chana says, that's what we will do."

Chana walked to the back for a broom and while she was gone, Tobin took my hand. "You should think about your son. We can stay here tonight. Just to make sure things are quiet."

"No." I drew back my hand from him. "If you stay tonight, they will surely return."

Tobin glanced again at David, who stood beside him, arms wrapped around my leg. "You can't stay here with him."

"He is my son. Where am I supposed to send him?"

"Away," Tobin said with a wave of his hand. "Send him away."

"His father is fighting in the army. His grandfather, too. Am I supposed to say to my son that while others stand and fight, he must turn and run?"

"He is a child."

"And I am his mother."

"Well," Tobin sighed, "I can't protect you."

"Protecting me is not your job. Your job is to win the war."

"Maybe so, but I'll send someone around to check on you just the same." Tobin was a man who let his emotions guide him to places he should not go, and I saw again the look in his eye I had seen before. I wanted him to know, and to remind myself, that I was Eli's wife and loyal to none other. It was a loyalty that would soon meet a much more serious test.

Over the next few weeks, our soldiers fought valiantly and retook major portions of the city. Chana and I swept out the café, and although electrical service was sporadic we did our best to be ready should anyone come by. Business was all but nonexistent in Jerusalem. Most people were doing all they could simply to survive. Being ready for our customers was our way of surviving.

Gradually, as calm was restored to our neighborhood, a few people ventured out on the streets and before long word spread that we were still there. A trickle of customers wandered in to marvel at our chutzpah and to sip from their cups of coffee. Then a soldier from Tobin's squad arrived to tell us that Yohai was injured and being held in a field hospital on the road to Ramallah, north of the city. The location was near the heaviest fighting, but Chana insisted on getting him out and bringing him home.

Relatives came to take care of the café while a friend, Miriam Ohrenstein, drove us toward the front in her car. Troops were fighting all around us, and artillery shells exploded near the car, but we kept going and eventually came to a group of large white tents with red crosses on top. Soldiers guarding the road tried to prevent us from entering but we paid them no attention, and when they saw the car held only three women and a small child, they stepped aside to let us pass.

After a hurried search of the tents, we located Yohai languishing on a cot beneath a tent that covered a dozen others in similar condition. He'd been injured by shrapnel in his stomach. From the smell of it, I was sure his wounds were infected. Chana took one look at him and insisted on taking him home. When attendants and doctors objected, she turned on them.

"Why should I leave him here?"

"He is a soldier in the army," a nurse explained. "We must treat him."

"You?" Chana roared. "You think you can save him? You can do nothing but watch him die!" She lowered her voice and pointed a finger at herself. "He is my husband. I know how to make him well."

An orderly stepped forward to intervene, but as he reached out for her, Chana stopped him with a glare. "You would touch me?"

"Let her go," someone said from across the way. We all turned to see a doctor just entering the tent. "She is right. There is nothing more we can do for him." His voice had a hint of sadness, and I could see that though he wanted to help them all, he had very little medicine or supplies with which to work.

Two orderlies helped us lift Yohai from the cot and together we carried him to the car. When we arrived back at the café, we lugged him upstairs to the apartment over the café and put him in his own bed. Chana and I took turns looking after him, bathing his wounds and dressing them, wiping his forehead, and coaxing him to eat. He remained near death for several weeks but then began to recover. Two months after we brought him home, he was strong enough to sit in the café. As word of his recovery spread, friends and customers dropped by to see him.

Chana watched from the kitchen as he sat with them, drinking coffee. "See," she beamed, "I know what to do for him. God hears me when I cry to Him on Yohai's behalf."

Business continued to pick up and before long we put Yohai to work out front while I operated the stoves. Being in back kept me busy, which took my mind off Eli, and it allowed me to care for David.

Late one afternoon, Yohai appeared in the hallway near the pass-through window. I could see from the look in his eye that something was wrong. As I came from the stove I saw an army officer standing with him.

"I am sorry to tell you this," the officer began, "but I have bad news about your husband."

My heart seemed to stop. Tears filled my eyes and I put my hand to my face.

"It's not that," Yohai interrupted. He put his arm around me and drew me close. "He's alive."

"Then what is it?"

"I'm afraid he's been captured."

"Captured?"

"Information we've received indicates he's being held as a prisoner by the Egyptians."

"Where?"

"In Egypt."

Chana heard him talking and came to my side. She put her hand on my shoulder. "Let us pray he is dead, rather than tortured at the hands of the Egyptians."

I jerked away from her and shouted, "He is not dead! He is alive and one day you will see him right here in this very spot."

Chana tried to comfort me, but I turned away and ran out the door to the alley. From behind me I heard David crying but all I could think of was Eli as a prisoner in an Egyptian camp. Images from the past flooded my mind and I saw again the squalid conditions of Mauthausen and the bodies in the mass grave, only now Eli was one of the prisoners.

* * *

As weeks turned into months and still we heard nothing more about Eli, people began to whisper that he was dead and had been so all along, only the army didn't want to tell us. Yohai and Chana tried to be hopeful, but Yohai had seen the misery of war and the brutal way men fought. Inside I was certain he feared his son would never return.

Then Tobin Halutz appeared at the café. Dressed in his army uniform he looked sharp, trim, and handsome. He had seen documents confirming that Eli was captured but knew nothing more. For the next several weeks he returned each day at noon to eat lunch. Apparently, Eli had been captured by the Egyptians near Beersheba and taken to a camp in Egypt, where he was interrogated under British supervision.

Yohai was livid. "The British," he fumed. "I knew someone was assisting the Egyptians. They never could have fought so well against us without outside help."

I kept to my work in the kitchen and heard none of what Tobin said firsthand. Yohai and Chana brought me reports of their conversations with him. This kept up, with Tobin coming for lunch and Chana reporting on what he said, until one day she came to the kitchen and drew me from the stove to the hallway. Standing there, in plain sight, she pointed to Tobin who was seated at a table near the window. "Look at him," she began. "Isn't he handsome?"

"Yes," I agreed. "He makes a fine appearance in a uniform."

"He is an officer now," she added with enthusiasm.

"I know," I gestured over my shoulder. "There's a pot on the stove. I need to see about it."

"Forget about the stove," Chana snapped. "Listen to me. Tobin is a good man. He's an officer in the army now. A respected man. His wife died last year when an artillery shell hit their house. He was interested in you once, and I think he's still interested in you now."

I was astounded by what I heard but I knew she meant well. "I'm married," I said with a dour voice.

"He comes here almost every day," she continued. "You should talk to him."

"You think Eli is dead?"

Her eyes were full. "It has been many months," she said softly, "and we have heard nothing new about him."

"We knew nothing of Yohai for months, either. Did you give up on him?"

"It was different with him. I knew in my heart he was alive."

"Do you not have that same assurance about Eli?"

Chana looked away. "I know things." She was on the verge of tears. "I can see. You need a husband. And your son needs a father. Perhaps it is time for you to move on."

"You talk to Tobin Halutz if you wish," I groused. "And comfort him in the loss of his wife. I am married. My husband will return soon." Then I stepped back to the stove and continued to work.

* * *

A week or two later, I was busy in the kitchen when someone tapped me on the shoulder from behind. I glanced back, expecting to see Yohai or Chana. Instead, I saw Eli. He was much thinner than before and he had a scar on his forehead, but when he smiled at me I felt like crying. He put his arms around me and pulled me close. "Did you miss me?"

"Everyone thought you were dead," I sobbed.

"Did you?"

"No. I told them you would come back."

I wiped my eyes on his shirt and kissed him until smoke from the pan on the stove filled the air.

chapter 38

In the spring of 1949, Ben-Gurion and the Israeli government reached peace agreements with our neighbors. That same year, I turned thirty-nine years old. I still wrote every day, continuing to preserve now in multiple notebooks all the things I remembered about events from my past, but doing justice somehow seemed to require more. None of the missing Nazis had been caught and there was still nothing new about Adolf Eichmann or the location where he might be hiding.

That spring, a customer at the café had a brochure announcing the establishment of a law school at Hebrew University. When the customer finished eating, he left the brochure behind. I read it and remembered Uncle Alois, the difference he made in the lives of so many people, and the things Rabbi Meir said to me about the quest for justice being my primary motivation, perhaps even a motivation from God.

During a lull in work that afternoon I found Eli at a table in the kitchen reading a book. When I asked about it, he closed it and showed me the front cover. "Just a book by a rabbi," he explained. "Doing some reading to pass the time."

I took a seat at the table and laid the brochure in front of him. "I found this out front."

He glanced at the brochure, then looked over at me. "I heard about it. That would be a good thing. New country needs its own lawyers."

"You think so?"

"Yes," he said enthusiastically. "Of course. We need good lawyers to help us build a society that stands on the law."

I caught his eye and pointed to the brochure. "I want to do it."

A frown wrinkled his forehead. "You want to attend law school?"

"Yes," I nodded.

Before we could say much more, Yohai appeared. "What's this talk about lawyers?"

"Just talking."

He glanced down at the brochure, snatched it from the table, and quickly scanned through it. Then he tossed it on the table and looked down at Eli. "Don't you have to finish college first?"

Eli shook his head. "It's not for me."

"Oh." Yohai looked puzzled. "Then who's it for?"

"Sarah."

Yohai looked over at me. "Law is a profession for men. It's not a job for women."

"Learning isn't just for men anymore," I argued.

"Women should study things that are useful in the home," he countered. "In my day, you would have not even been permitted the education you already have. You should be glad."

"Those days have passed."

"Not in my house," he stated emphatically.

"Show me where it says in Torah that I can't learn."

"You have a family to care for," Yohai's voice was getting louder and louder. "And you have a job. Right here." He jabbed the table with his finger for emphasis.

"But I—"

"I forbid it," he snapped. Then he turned aside and walked away. Eli said nothing in my defense, so I rose from the table and stalked out of the kitchen. For the remainder of the day I did not speak to either of them.

Later that night, I approached Eli. He was seated at the kitchen table, reading the same book he had earlier at the café. I entered the room and scooted a chair close to him, then leaned my head on his shoulder. "Do you share your father's opinion of my interest in law school?"

"You really want to be a lawyer?"

"Yes," I nodded. "I really do."

"Well, okay," he grinned. "Find out how to enroll."

I sat up straight. "What about your father?"

"I will take care of things with him."

"What if he throws us out of the business?"

"It won't come to that."

"But what if it does?"

He put aside the book and took my hand in his. "Then I will find work elsewhere."

"You're sure?"

"You apply to school. I'll handle Papa."

The following day I called the school and then paid it a visit. While I was there, I applied for admission. That summer, shortly after my thirty-ninth birthday, I learned I had been accepted for the first term in the fall. I was the only woman in the class, but not the oldest.

Attending class meant I was not at the café, and studying each day kept me busy. I was soon immersed in study, and other than taking time out for Eli and David, I lived in my own world. About three weeks after classes began I came to the café with David late in the afternoon. As I stepped through the door, Yohai called to me from across the room, "Where have you been? I've been waiting tables for weeks by myself with only Chana to help." Then I realized Eli had not talked to him. I felt like I'd been hit in the pit of my stomach and for an instant wondered why Eli had let me down.

Yohai came toward me and from the look in his eye I knew he wanted an answer. My mind reeled as I tried to think of what to say. Then Eli appeared from the kitchen.

"She's in school, Papa," he said calmly.

"School?" Yohai was confused. "What school?"

"Law school." Eli looked him in the eye and said it without flinching.

Yohai was beside himself. "I forbid it!" he shouted, right there in front of the customers. "I told you already. This is my house and I forbid you to go to that school!"

"Papa," Eli used the same even tone as before, "she is my wife. My family."

"Your family?"

"Sarah and David are my family."

"And you think that gives you—"

"Papa," Eli interrupted, "she and Mama kept this business alive while we were fighting the war. They didn't run and hide. They stayed right here. When you were dying in that field hospital, Sarah came with Mama to get you." By then he was face-to-face with Yohai and he lowered his voice even more. "And when everyone thought I was dead, she never gave up hope."

"But I—"

Eli cut him off again. "She had faith in me, Papa. And I have faith in her. Don't you think she can do this?"

"That's not the question. Of course she could do it. She can do anything she sets her mind to."

"Then what is the problem?"

"I ... I don't know," he stammered.

"Okay, then." Eli put his hand on Yohai's shoulder. "You're going to show a little faith in her, too. I don't know where this is leading us, but Sarah needs this and I'm going to help her do it."

Yohai picked up the dirty dishes from a table and walked to the back. I watched as he disappeared into the kitchen. When he was out of sight, Chana appeared in the doorway and smiled.

I asked Eli later why he hadn't told his father earlier that I had enrolled in school. He said, "If I told him earlier, he might have called someone and tried to prevent it." I'm glad he handled it that way and I was proud to see him stand up for me.

* * *

For the next two years I worked harder at school than I ever worked at anything in my life. I wanted to do well, to prove that Eli's faith in me was well placed, to take the next step forward in my life, wherever it led, and to learn what it meant to "do justice." Perhaps because of that and because I came to law school for a purpose greater than simply entering a profession, my test scores ranked me at the top of the class.

As I entered my third and final year of school, several law firms expressed an interest in hiring me. They had much to offer, including a salary that would have dramatically altered our lifestyle, but I wasn't sure I wanted that kind of professional life. I wanted to help people, to make a difference, as Uncle Alois had done. And, as impossible as it seemed, I wanted to find the people who shot the Averbuch children and hold them accountable.

* * *

Late that year, Youssef Kastner, one of my professors, took me aside after class. "You are doing well," he said with pride. "Many did not think it was possible for a woman to do this, much less reach the top of her class."

"It didn't come easy."

"No. I'm sure it didn't. You worked hard and your grades show it. Now you have opportunities opening before you."

"But they seem to offer me only a professional career."

"You had more in mind?"

"Much more."

"Perhaps I can help," he suggested. "If you want to make a difference, there's someone I think you should meet."

"Who is it?"

"I would rather introduce him to you than give you his name. Could you meet tomorrow afternoon?"

"I have a break from two to three."

"Good. I'll set it up."

The next day Kastner sent a note telling me to meet him at the coffee shop across the street from the campus. When I arrived, he was seated at a table in back. Sitting beside him was a man of medium build. Not quite six feet tall, he had a balding head and intense eyes that were alert and bright, as if seeing everything at once. He was dressed in a dark gray suit and when I saw him I was certain I had seen him before. They both stood as I approached, then Kastner introduced his companion as Reuven Shiloah, and I knew then why he looked familiar.

When we were seated, Shiloah looked across at me. "You know who I am?"

"I've seen your picture in the newspaper."

"I am the director of the Institute for Intelligence and Special Operations."

"Mossad."

"Yes," he nodded. "Mossad. Your father-in-law is Yohai Cohen?"

"Yes." I was puzzled that he knew Yohai. "How do you know him?"

"We are acquainted from the war. I have been in his coffee shop many times." He glanced around, then back at me. "It's much better than this one, frankly. But we could not risk meeting there. Too many prying eyes."

"I have a class in about an hour," I checked my watch. "What did you want to talk about?"

"We are putting together a team of young lawyers. We think you would make a good addition to that team when you graduate."

"At Mossad?"

"Yes."

"What kind of team?"

"As you are aware, after the war in Europe came to an end, the Allies captured and put on trial several key Nazi leaders. They got the big names, but finding the second-tier leaders—the ones who actually put into effect their final solution—has proved a tedious task. Allied interests have been diverted to other issues. No one is pursuing the people we would all like to see brought to justice."

I looked at him a moment. "Do you know where he is?"

"Who?"

"Adolf Eichmann," I said in a low voice. "Do you know where he is?"

Kastner looked at Shiloah. "I told you she was a good choice."

Shiloah smiled at me. "He is one of the reasons we want you to come work with us. I know from your file—"

"I have a file?"

"Yes. We have been following developments in your life for some time now. Particularly since you enrolled in law school."

"Why would you want to know about me?"

"Mossad was formed to know things."

"Well, I don't like it," I leaned back in my chair.

"Would you like to see Eichmann brought to justice?"

"Yes, but not at Nuremberg."

"Not there." He tapped the table with his finger. "Here. In Jerusalem. We would bring him to justice in Jerusalem. Try him. Convict him, hopefully. And execute him."

"And what makes you think I could be of help to you in that effort?"

"As I was saying, we know from your file you have been acquainted with him since childhood." He gave me a knowing look. "Some think perhaps it was more than friendship."

Anger flared inside me. "Never," I snapped. "It was never more than friendship and that only of a little girl infatuated with her teen-aged neighbor."

"You are interested?"

"Yes. I am interested."

"Good." Shiloah stood. "We will be in touch."

That night I told Eli about the offer. He was excited, but concerned. "You realize if this works out, it will bring you face-to-face with all those things that used to bother you at night."

"I know."

"Are you ready for that?"

"I think this is something I must do, ready or not."

chapter 39

Early in the summer, I graduated from law school and went to work for Mossad as part of a group meeting in offices near the King David Hotel. Known officially as Bureau 06, the team was comprised of people from Mossad, investigators from *Shin Bet*, Israel's internal security agency, and prosecutors from the Attorney General's office. Our sole mission was to locate Nazis who were involved in the persecution of Jews and build a credible criminal case against them. The team was supervised by Nathan Metzger.

Metzger was born in Buczacz, a town that is now in western Ukraine, and came to Israel with his family long before the war. He had a distinguished career in the army during our fight for independence and went on to work as a prosecutor for the military court. He was diligent and relentless in his job and had a thoroughness about him that astounded me. We all prepared reports for him on each of our issues and cases, which gave us mastery of the details about those specific cases, but Metzger knew the details about every witness, every issue, every case.

Not long after I took the job, Reuven Shiloah's term as Mossad director came to an end. Isser Harel, former director of Shin Bet, replaced him. I was concerned about the change, but Metzger reassured me this was actually good for us. "Shiloah was committed to finding the Nazis, but he had many other issues on his mind. Harel has moved our work to the top of the list. He is particularly interested in Eichmann and is very glad you are assisting us."

"He knows of me?"

"Yes," Metzger nodded.

I was skeptical. "How could he possibly know anything about me?"

"He read your file, of course."

Then I saw the twinkle in Metzger's eye. "You mean, he read all our files."

"Well," Metzger grinned, "he was impressed by your story."

My first assignment was to track down credible leads on Eichmann's last known location and sift through the details, separating valid reports from those found to be inaccurate. I quickly learned we had very little information with which to work. Files in our office on Eichmann consisted of one folder with background information compiled from magazine articles and one or two personal accounts. Another folder had reports of his location immediately following the war, the most recent of which was a report passed to us by the French government several years after the war, indicating Eichmann had been seen in Italy and was perhaps living there permanently. I read through them in a matter of minutes and spent my first week on the job scouring newspapers and interviewing embassy contacts in an effort to update our files, but no one had any more recent information about him.

Then Yaakov Rothenberg, one of the interns in our office, suggested Yad Vashem, a then fledgling organization working to collect and preserve the names and testimonies of Shoah victims, might have some useful information. Although at that time it was in the early stages of its work, they already had collected files and dossiers on hundreds of thousands of survivors, victims, and perpetrators.

That afternoon, I walked up the street to their offices. An archivist showed me their file on Eichmann. "Unfortunately, we do not have much," she said.

The file contained a few notes about his life, pictures of his childhood home, newspaper clippings from the 1930s, and two reports from the US Army—one about his capture by Allied forces after the war, and a second on his escape from an Allied POW camp. I studied the pictures of his childhood home and in one of them I saw the edge of the roof of our house in Linz.

"Where did you get these photographs?"

She checked the back of the picture, but it was blank. "I'm not sure. Many of our earliest files came from a documentation center in Vienna that was operated by Tuviah Friedman."

"Do you have an address for them? Perhaps they can help."

"The center no longer exists. That's how we came to have their files. Mr. Friedman sent most of what he'd collected to us."

I arched an eyebrow. "Most?"

"He kept some things for himself on one or two matters that particularly interested him."

"Any chance one of those he kept was the file on Eichmann?"

"Perhaps. Finding Eichmann was the central focus of his work."

"Where is he now?"

"Eichmann?"

"No," I said, frustrated. "Tuviah Friedman."

"He lives in Haifa."

The following day I rode to Haifa and located Friedman at a nondescript office building on Chen Boulevard. A brass plaque on the office door read *Institute for the Documentation of Nazi War Crimes*. From the name on the door I expected to find a neat and orderly office. Something like what one might expect from a police station. Institutional. Instead, I opened the door to a cramped outer office with boxes stacked three high around two large steel desks. A man sat at one, a woman at the other. To the right, a young girl was sorting through an open box, taking documents from it and placing them on the desks. When I asked to see Friedman, she escorted me across the room to his office.

Friedman's office was much like what I had just seen. A wooden desk sat in front of two windows that looked out on the street below. On it were stacks of documents and files that covered every available space. Seated behind the desk was a short man, almost bald, with a prominent nose and ears that stood out at an angle. He was dressed in a light gray suit, white shirt, and dark blue tie. As I entered, he was bent over a file that lay open before him, forehead with a slight wrinkle, eyes focused and intense. He glanced up at me and I explained why I was there, just beginning on the trail of Adolf Eichmann. I expected him to be excited that someone connected with the government had been assigned the specific task of locating Eichmann. Instead, he seemed skeptical and suspicious.

"You work for Metzger?"

"Yes," I replied.

"What do you know about Eichmann?"

"I read the file on him at Yad Vashem." Knowing little about him, I wasn't prepared to divulge any secrets.

"Huh," he chortled. "Not much to that, from what I hear."

"No," I agreed. "There isn't, but they said many of their other files came from you and that you might be able to help."

"Perhaps." He leaned back in his chair. "What is your interest in all of this?"

"Mine?"

"Yes." He pointed with his index finger. "You. Personally. You seem like a smart young woman. Why would you be interested in tracking down former Nazis? Is it just a job?"

His tone was brusque and I was rather put off by it, but I reminded myself that he'd been working at this a long time, probably with great frustration. I was new to the effort and needed his help. Without providing much in the way of detail, I told him briefly about my experiences in the Vienna ghetto, Mauthausen, and my escape. "What about you?" I asked when I was through. "What's your interest?"

He avoided discussion of his own death camp experiences and talked instead about the Documentation Center he operated in Vienna and how he closed it due to lack of interest or support from the Allies and the Jewish community. He came to Israel to pursue other interests, but in Haifa he found renewed motivation for the cause in the stories he heard from others, and so he started again. His voice had an edge, not quite bitter but intense and unrelenting. As if he'd spent his entire life trying to get people to listen, and then was forced to watch as the conversation he tried to start about the misery each had endured turned into an argument among victims over who among them had the right to speak.

After a while, his attention began to wane. He pushed back from the desk and stood. "Come with me. I'll show you our files."

I followed him to a door along the wall to the right. He opened it, and I stepped into a room filled with file cabinets and boxes. I looked around and sighed, "This is a lot."

"The files in this room," his voice had a hint of reverence, "contain the souls of all of us. The living and the dead. The soul of everyone who endured the Shoah is right here in this room." He pulled open a file drawer and took out a folder. Holding it with one hand, he gently flipped to a document that was browned with age. "You see this?" He pointed to it, and I leaned closer to see that the document was stained and dirty. "This is the memory of a man who died at Auschwitz." He pointed to a line scrawled across the top of the first page and read aloud, "'A list of the people I knew who were deported from Beuthen'—that's a city in southern Poland. The person who wrote this document hid it in a tin can and buried it near the apartment where he lived, hoping someone would one day find it."

"And they did."

"Yes. It was unearthed as they were razing a site in Beuthen after the war, preparing it for construction." He carefully replaced the document in the file and closed the drawer. Then with a broad, sweeping gesture he continued, "This room is filled with similar stories. Someone made a list, wrote out an account, kept a diary. Many of them include not just names and locations but dates, physical descriptions, notes from events that happened, as if they were trying to capture an image of their lives for us to see." He paused and smiled at me politely. "The files on Eichmann are over here." He stepped across the room to three cardboard boxes filled with documents that sat on the floor near a worktable. He lifted the boxes from the floor and set them on the table. "You may study them as long as you like. If you need anything else, just ask." Then he retreated from the room, leaving me alone with all those memories.

For the next two days I sorted through pictures of Eichmann, records from his job as a traveling salesman for Vacuum Oil Company, documents from his early years in the Nazi Party, and records from his enlistment in the German Army. There were copies of several identification cards showing him a German citizen and reports from the POW camps where he was held after the war. In the third box were two files with written accounts of people who claimed to have seen him in various locations after the war. I made an inventory of the contents from each box and took extensive notes from the statements that gave information about his location after the war.

Late the third day I stepped into Friedman's office. "You have more here than I can digest in just a few days, but I think I gleaned enough of it to get me started."

"Feel free to come back and review them anytime. I'll tell the others to let you in the file room whenever you like."

"I appreciate the help. We're interested in finding his present location, and I think information from the past will help with clues about that. People don't change that much."

"We've had several reports of sighting him after the war. Many of them proved to be cases of mistaken identity. I'm sure you noticed that from the files. I think it's rather well established that he disappeared from Italy. Many did that."

"But how?"

"Priests and other officials with the Catholic Church were heavily involved in refugee resettlement work. All of Europe was in disarray. Many people were stranded far from home with no documents and no way to return. Catholic officials issued thousands of refugee passports through the Red Cross. It was a good work and benefited many, but the volume of people seeking help was overwhelming and some who worked in that field were less discrete in their effort. Many Nazis traveled abroad on passports obtained through the church—a church, by the way, which Hitler fully intended to destroy."

While we talked, I remembered the day Grandma died, when I was talking to Eichmann on the steps of his house. He was reading a pamphlet about Argentina.

"Do you think he went to South America?"

"I suspect so," Friedman nodded. "Many Nazis have been sighted there. So far as I know, there are no facts to substantiate that idea, but many of us think he did. Something you saw in the files made you think that?"

"Not really." I pulled a chair up to his desk and sat down. "I knew Adolf Eichmann when I was a child."

"You knew him? Personally?"

"When he was a teenager, we lived three houses up the street from him, in Linz."

"Then you should talk to Simon Wiesenthal. He lives in Linz. Not far from the Eichmanns."

"The Eichmanns are still there?"

"His mother is still alive. And he has many relatives in that area."

"I saw from your files that he married."

"Yes. Married and had children. A few years ago, his wife tried to have him declared legally dead."

"To get his pension."

"That's what most people thought," Friedman nodded.

"But you think otherwise?"

"Eichmann was crafty and paid close attention to details. If he was officially dead, not many people would continue to look for him. Certainly not the Americans or the British."

"But the courts refused."

"Thankfully. They saw through the whole thing. But after that, she and the children disappeared. No one knows what happened to them. Wiesenthal could tell you all about it. You should go talk to him."

chapter 40

The following morning I returned to the office in Jerusalem and told Metzger about seeing Friedman. "He thinks Eichmann is in South America."

"And why?"

"Just a hunch. A number of former Nazis are known to be living there. It was a popular location with Germans even before the war. Strong German culture there. They would provide him a ready-made place to fit in."

"Interesting idea. You've read more about Eichmann now than anyone here. What do you think?"

"I think Friedman's right." Then I told him about the incident from my childhood, seeing Eichmann with a brochure on South America.

"Maybe so," Metzger smiled, "but we can't send someone to South America based on a memory from your childhood. We have to connect the points on the line from where he was to where he is now."

"Friedman suggested I should talk to Simon Wiesenthal. Do you know him?"

"I know of him. Never met him."

"Think I should see him?"

"Yes. By all means. Last I heard of him, he was living in Linz, Austria."

"It would take several days to go there, see him, and get back."

"You'll have to fly," Metzger added. "We will make the arrangements."

"We have the money for a trip like that?"

"We have the money for the things we need." Then he looked at me thoughtfully. "Have you been back there since the war?"

"No," I answered. "Not since I escaped."

"Think you're ready to see it?"

"Yes," I nodded confidently. "I think I am."

"I do, too."

That night, after David was in bed, Eli was sitting in the living room, reading a book and making notes. I didn't bother asking why he was doing that, I just pushed the book aside and sat in his lap. He smiled at me. "What's on your mind?"

I knew what he wanted me to say but instead I replied, "I need to go to Linz."

"Austria?"

"Yes."

"When?"

"Soon. Later this week, probably."

"Want me to come with you?"

"Yes."

"Great," he beamed. "I would love to see all the places you talk about."

"But you can't."

His countenance dropped. "Why not?"

"I need to go alone."

He had a questioning look. "Have you really told me all that happened to you back there?"

"As much as I remember."

"Is this job helping you remember more?"

"No. But it's keeping me from forgetting what I knew."

"That's good." He looked into my eyes. "But I still think you need me with you."

"Yes, I do," I agreed.

"Then I will go."

"Not this time."

He looked puzzled. "I don't understand."

"Having you with me would be much easier than going alone, but if you are with me I will let you shield me from the past." I rested my head on his chest. "You have always been my protector, and you did it by letting me be myself. I need you to keep doing that. I won't be gone long."

He wrapped his arms around me. "Okay," he whispered. Then he picked me up and carried me to bed.

* * *

Four days later, I boarded a plane and flew to Linz. From the airport, I took a taxi to a hotel near the center of the city and deposited my luggage in the room. Then, briefcase in hand, I walked toward the street where we once lived. It wasn't far and I had a few minutes to spare before I was to meet Wiesenthal. Seeing the sites again on foot, with the sounds and the smells around me, brought back many memories, not all of them unpleasant.

As I crossed the corner and stepped onto our block, my heart sank. The house where we once lived was gone and in its place was an apartment building. I lingered out front, imagining the way things used to be and remembering many of the things that happened there. While I stood there, a woman walked past, then came back and asked if I was all right.

"I'm fine," I replied. "There used to be a house here years ago."

"Yes. It was ruined by all the Jews who lived here," she said with a hint of disgust. "After the war they tore it down to build these apartments."

"Any idea what happened to the people who used to live in the house?"

"Which ones? There were so many we couldn't keep track."

"Before then. Before the Germans arrived."

"Oh." She paused as if in thought. "I don't know. I think they're all gone."

"Gone?"

"Dead."

"Did you know them?"

"No. I don't think so. Our neighbors did, though."

"Who were your neighbors?"

"Rovina. Yardina Rovina." A smile came to her face. "It rhymed, which made it easy to remember. Her son used to be friends with a girl who lived here."

"What happened to them?"

"Yardina?"

"Yes."

"She and her son died at Mauthausen. I think his name was Stephan. But that was a long time ago." She touched my arm. "Sure you don't need some help?"

"I'm fine." She turned to leave, but I called after her. "What about the Eichmanns?"

She glanced back at me. "What about them?"

"They used to live down there," I said, pointing. "Three houses down."

"The mother and father are dead. He died a few years ago. She passed away only recently. One of their sons lives there now. Otto."

I walked in that direction and stared at the house, thinking about the day Karl yelled at me while I was talking to Adolf on the porch. For an instant, I considered knocking on the door to say hello and let them know that in spite of their hatred of me I was still alive. Then I thought better of it and walked back to the corner, where I hailed a taxi.

A few minutes later I arrived outside an apartment building not far from the hotel where I was staying. On the third floor I came to a door with a plaque on the wall next to it that read *Jewish Historical Documentation Center*. I pushed open the door and went inside.

Like Friedman's office in Haifa, Wiesenthal's office in Linz was crammed with file cabinets and boxes. An assistant turned from an open file drawer to face me as I came inside. "May I help you?"

"I'm here to see Simon Wiesenthal."

Before she could answer, a man appeared in the doorway behind her. He looked to be about fifty years old with thinning hair and a thick mustache. Dressed in a rumpled gray suit he seemed more like a college professor than an investigator. He spoke gruffly, "I am Simon Wiesenthal. And you are?"

"Sarah Cohen. Nathan Metzger sent me."

"Yes," Wiesenthal nodded. "We were expecting you earlier."

"I apologize. I grew up here as a child and stopped by our street to see the house. It took longer than I expected."

"Those trips often do." The look on his face changed to a pleasant smile. "Was the house still there?"

"No. It was torn down and replaced with an apartment building."

"That must have been sad."

"Somewhat, but not as sad as I would have expected."

"Tuviah Friedman called me." Wiesenthal gestured with a wave of his hand for me to follow. I crossed the room toward him as he continued to talk. "He told me you would probably be coming my way. I've tried to get people interested in finding Eichmann, but no one cares anymore." By then he had reached a desk in his private office. He moved behind it and took a seat. I sat in a chair across from him, put the briefcase on the floor beside me, and listened as Wiesenthal expounded on his frustration. "I'm not sure if they ever understood what we were trying to do. But now they are oblivious. No one in America can be bothered. Jews in Germany have moved on. Not even in Israel." He looked over at me. "So what brings you here?"

"We're interested now."

"I see," he replied with a hint of sarcasm. "Someone in Jerusalem with a sense of the historic?"

"Reuven Shiloah and Isser Harel have created a special unit within Mossad to track down those who are responsible for the murder of our people during the war."

"You are after Eichmann." He spoke with a flat, unaffected tone that made the words sound like an indictment.

"Not just Eichmann," I offered, trying to anticipate what he might be thinking, "but others as well."

"You think they will do it?"

"Find Eichmann?"

"No. Continue looking for others after they find him."

"That is the goal. I certainly hope they do. I should like to continue this work for the rest of my career."

"Career?" he scoffed.

"I am a lawyer. This is what I want to do."

"I see," he nodded thoughtfully. "Metzger is in charge?"

"Yes."

"He's a good man. Used to be in charge of Shin Bet. Internal security, and all that." Wiesenthal sat up straight in his chair. "How can I help?"

"I'm trying to pick up the trail on Eichmann. There have been numerous reports of people seeing him in various locations, some of which seem like they might be helpful but many of which are mutually exclusive. Rather than chasing after all of them, I would like to go back to his last known location and build from there. I know that after the war he was confirmed to be in at least one prisoner-of-war camp and I know that he used the name of Adolf Barth and then Adolf Eckmann when he was being held by the Allies."

"That was the name he was using when he was captured at Ulm. Then he was transferred to several POW camps and escaped. When they recaptured him, he gave the name of Eckmann. Worked around Germany under several names. Otto Henninger was one you did not mention. That was the last name he used in Germany for which we have hard evidence."

"Hard evidence?"

"We have copies of identity papers using that name and his photograph."

I took a notepad from my briefcase and scribbled down the name. "From what I've read so far, about the time he escaped from the Allies, the trail gets thin, and then it goes cold."

"I like you," he smiled. "And I like your methodology of beginning. Grasp the key points and keep moving forward, pressing into what you don't know. There are many details in between, but you have gleaned the high points." Wiesenthal cleared his throat. "The last known confirmed location for Adolf Eichmann is in Rome, Italy, shortly after he left Germany. From there, the trail goes cold because that is when he left Europe."

"You know this for a fact?"

"I have a sworn statement from Vincent Tradini, now an official at the Vatican. At the end of the war he was an assistant to a Catholic bishop named Hudal. Under the auspices of Bishop Hudal, Tradini issued official church documents that were forwarded to the International Red Cross and used by that organization to issue a passport to Eichmann. He said the passport was issued under a different name but he was certain they were one and the same person."

"What name did he use for the passport?"

"He would not say."

"Why not?"

"I think he felt bad about his participation but was concerned that he might lose his appointment to the Vatican if his involvement became public. And I think he was worried that this would reflect poorly on the Holy See."

"I heard a version of this from Friedman, but he had no evidence to support it and didn't think anyone did."

"Good," Wiesenthal grinned. "I wanted to keep it from him."

"You don't trust him?"

"Not with everything."

"So Eichmann was helped by a priest?"

"The church was instrumental in helping to resettle many refugees after the war. Genuine refugees who had nowhere to go. But some of their priests also helped many Nazis. Hudal was a supporter and defender of Hitler."

"What else do you have that might help?"

Wiesenthal rose from his seat behind the desk and moved across the room to a file cabinet. I turned to watch as he stood with his hand on the handle of a drawer. "This is my Eichmann file."

"That entire file drawer?"

"No. The entire cabinet. Four drawers full of information I have collected about him over the years. In here are hundreds of statements, eyewitness accounts given by survivors, all of them about Adolf Eichmann. Does Nathan Metzger intend to put Eichmann on trial?"

"Yes. That is our intention, though Mr. Metzger won't be the prosecutor. I assume the Attorney General will do that."

"Yes."

"Good." He laid his hand atop the file cabinet. "The witness statements in these files will be invaluable in proving his case."

"I'll need a lifetime to sort through all of that."

"Yes," Wiesenthal agreed, "but that is not necessary."

"Why not?"

"Because you have me. I will supply the lifetime of information. You supply the operatives to capture him."

"Okay. To do that, we have to build a case from Italy forward. Where do we begin?"

He returned to his desk, opened the top drawer, and took out a letter still in its envelope. "This is where we begin." He dropped the letter on the desktop in front of me. "Notice the return address and the postmark on the front—Buenos Aires, Argentina."

"Right."

"The letter is from a friend of mine who lives there."

I slipped the letter from the envelope, glanced over it, and was astounded to read a report of someone sighting Eichmann in Buenos Aires. I rechecked the postmark and looked over at Wiesenthal. "This was sent to you last year. Why didn't you tell someone?"

"I tried, but no one was interested."

"I thought you said you had no documents to prove where he was."

"This is anecdotal." Wiesenthal collapsed onto the chair behind the desk. "It proves that my friend was in Argentina. It doesn't prove Eichmann was there."

"Still, you should have told someone. We could have sent agents to find him."

"I gave this information to the World Jewish Congress and they said, 'Give us the complete address.' I said, 'I don't have the complete address. I'm asking you to send someone to verify that it is really him.' They said, 'Without the complete address we cannot verify your information.'" Wiesenthal leaned back in his chair and shook his head. "Sometimes even smart people are stupid."

"I believe he's in South America, too. And I've told them that myself. That's why they sent me to see you."

"I have a sworn statement, a letter, and an educated guess that tells me he's there. What information do you have?"

"Only a memory."

"A memory? Of what?"

"I remember one day when I was a little girl, sitting on the steps outside Eichmann's house, talking to him. He was reading a pamphlet about opportunities in South America. He was particularly interested in pictures of young cowboys in Argentina."

"See!" Wiesenthal shouted. "That's what I'm talking about. That's what I've been searching for all these years. Someone from Israel who understands the nature of the man we are dealing with. Someone who is paying attention."

"But what do we do next?"

"The first thing is, you need one of these." He opened a desk drawer and took out a photograph, which he handed to me. "This is Eichmann. You can't find him if you don't know what he looks like. This one was taken in Italy. After the war. It's the most recent one available to anyone."

"I can take this?"

"You may keep it. I have other copies."

"Is there some way to confirm he is actually there in Buenos Aires?"

"Send someone to see if it's really him." He pointed to the photograph. "Give them that photograph. Tell them to use it to confirm it's him."

"Others have suggested that very thing, but Metzger says we need more than just a hunch."

"I will give you a copy of the letter and a copy of the statement from my contact at the Vatican."

"A little more would help."

"More? We could convict him in court on less."

"But I'm not dealing with a judge. I'm dealing with a government agency."

"Bureaucracy," he grumbled. "Always feeding the bureaucracy."

"Well, that's where we are and that's why I'm here. Metzger thinks we'll get only one chance at catching him and this is our best shot. He wants to have enough information to make it work on a single try. Otherwise, he's afraid if we get down there and just ramble around, we'll end up scaring Eichmann away and then we'll never find him." I took a deep breath. "So, someone from the neighborhood says his brother Otto lives in the family home. Any of his other relatives still live around here?"

"Otto, who lives in the house, has children living here. Some cousins. They operate the store."

"Store?"

"After the war, the father opened an electrical appliance store. Electric Eichmann. It's just a few blocks away. Want to see it?"

"Not really. Have you had any success getting information from any of them?"

"Nah." He gave a dismissive wave of his hand. "They all stand up for him. I questioned them but they refused to cooperate. I still go around there from time to time, just to let them know I haven't forgotten about Adolf. They know me by sight and from the way they react, I'm sure none of them likes me. But he has several mistresses who live near here, and his wife's family lives in Waldegg, just at the edge of town. They might be helpful, but I haven't found a way to approach them."

"Who did he marry?"

"Veronika Liebl."

"I don't know the name. Did they have children?"

"Three boys. But they are all gone now. Veronika, the children, they all moved away. Disappeared. I think they have gone to join Eichmann. But come on," Wiesenthal said with a mischievous smile. "I'll show you where her mother lives." He stood and straightened his jacket. "You can at least see that much."

chapter 41

With Wiesenthal behind the steering wheel, we rode to Waldegg, a neighborhood that lay near the river, south of the city center. There we turned onto a residential street and rode quietly past well-kept houses. A few blocks later the scene began to change and we passed into an area that looked tired and rundown. At one house, I saw an elderly woman standing on the front steps. Paint peeled from the eaves and the roof was patched and worn. A rug lay over the banister of the porch and the woman beat it with a broom.

"That's her," Wiesenthal pointed at the woman. "That's Eichmann's mother-in-law. Maria Liebl."

"You're positive?"

"Yes."

"And you've never found a way to talk to her?"

"I tried the direct approach with his siblings but it didn't work very well. I didn't want to burn her as a source by using the same approach."

"Think she would talk to me?"

"What would you say?"

"I could ask about Adolf, I suppose. Or the children."

He shook his head. "Not a good idea. If you ask about Eichmann, I'm afraid they will mention it to someone and word will get back to him that someone is looking for him. He has stayed alive because of his wits. If he hears that someone is asking about him, it will spook him and he will run again. We'll lose him and have to start all over." He continued to shake his head. "Not a good idea."

"What about her?"

"Maria? The mother?" His voice had a hint of frustration. "That's what I'm talking about."

"No," I corrected. "Veronika. Eichmann's wife. What if I asked the mother about Veronika? Say I'm an old friend."

"I don't know," Wiesenthal shrugged. "Might work. Maybe it's worth a try. We are running out of options."

Wiesenthal dropped me at the corner and I started back toward the house on foot. When I reached the walkway to the porch, I looked up at Maria and gave a friendly greeting. "Mrs. Liebl," I smiled, "so good to see you. I was just passing through town and wondered if Veronika was still around."

She responded while continuing to swat the rug with the broom, "And who are you?"

"I'm Ellen. Veronika and I were acquainted through a mutual friend."

"Vera don't live here no more."

"Oh," I said with mock disappointment. "That's too bad. I was just passing through and thought I'd catch up with her. Where is she? What's she doing now?"

"She ran off to South America."

"South America?"

"Yeah."

"Wow. That's quite a change. What brought that on?"

"Love." She put down the broom and looked at me. "She did it for love."

I wrinkled my forehead in a frown. "She found someone from South America?"

"Yes. Ricardo Klement." She said the name as if making fun of the whole ordeal. "Can you believe it? I don't understand it." She lifted the broom in the air and gave the rug a whack. "First she takes up with that Eichmann. And now a South American." Then she stopped in mid-swing and looked over at me again. "Who did you say you were?"

"Ellen Krupp."

"I don't recall her mentioning any Ellen."

"Some people called me Sarah."

"Oh," she mused. "Sounds familiar, maybe."

"Well, sorry to bother you."

I turned away and started toward the street. As I reached the sidewalk, she called after me, "I'll tell her you were asking about her."

"No need to mention it. I hope she has a lovely time in South America."

I wanted to run and shout and scream, but I forced myself to walk calmly to the corner. As I reached the curb, Wiesenthal came by with car and I got in the front seat. "Veronika ran off to South America," I said triumphantly. "She married a man who lives there named Ricardo Klement."

Wiesenthal looked at me in disbelief. "She told you that?"

"Yes."

"How? How did you get her to do it?"

"I asked."

"You asked?" He had a look of surprise. "That's it?"

"I asked, she told me."

A sly smile came to his face. "You think it's true?"

"I think it is."

"Hah! We've got him." He beat his hands against the steering wheel with excitement. "You must return to Jerusalem and tell Metzger at once. He should be able to confirm that information rather easily."

"Yes," I said with a suddenly downcast voice. "You're right. I should return at once and tell him."

"What's wrong? Are you not excited?"

"Yes," I nodded. "I'm excited. But I had hoped to go to Vienna before leaving."

"What's in Vienna?"

"Nothing really." I was thinking of the boardinghouse, all those documents in the wall, and wondering if they still were there. "Just more of the past," I sighed.

"It would take all day to get there by train. I know you want to go, but you should get this information to Metzger right away and I don't think you should trust it to the telephone."

"No," I said reluctantly. "You're right. I shall go on the first flight tomorrow."

* * *

I returned to Jerusalem the following day and went straight to the office. Metzger was standing in the hallway when I arrived. He looked up as I entered. "Good news?"

"Yes," I grinned. "Come into my office." He followed me up the hall, and when we were alone I closed the door and turned to him. "Eichmann is living in Buenos Aires under the name of Ricardo Klement."

"You're sure?"

"Positive." I set the briefcase on my desk and took out the documents I received from Wiesenthal. "This is a statement from an official at the Vatican. During the war he was an assistant to one of their bishops." I handed the document to Metzger. "He says that after the war, Eichmann appeared in Rome and asked for their help. He and the bishop gave Eichmann documents that were then used by the Red Cross to issue a passport. It was issued under a name other than Eichmann, but he says the two are one and the same."

"This helps, but it isn't enough by itself."

I handed him the second document. "This is a letter from Wiesenthal's friend who lives in Argentina. In it he says he spotted someone he's certain is Eichmann, living in Buenos Aires."

"I know this man," Metzger pointed to the name on the letter. "Why didn't we get this sooner?"

"Wiesenthal sent it to the World Jewish Congress, but they gave him the runaround. I'm not sure who else got a copy."

"Okay," he sighed. "This is all very good, but it doesn't give us the name. How did you find that out?"

"Wiesenthal wanted to show me where Eichmann's mother-in-law lived, so we went out for a drive. As we rode past the house, she was on the porch."

"The wife?"

"No. The wife's mother. I convinced Wiesenthal to let me talk to her. Posed as an old friend of Veronika."

"The wife."

"Right," I nodded. "Got her to talk and she told me Veronika had run off to South America with Ricardo Klement."

That brought a grin to Metzger's face. "We need to get someone in Argentina to confirm his identity."

"How would we do that without raising his suspicions?"

"If they went there intending to one day return rather than become citizens of Argentina, they might have registered with the embassy." He leaned against the wall in a thoughtful pose. "The question is, which one?"

"Austrian, I suppose. That's where they lived."

"They were living in Austria, but no doubt they thought of themselves as Germans."

"Many Austrians did and still do. The national boundaries are more arbitrary than a true demarcation of Germanic people."

"Eichmann was a German citizen. When he became a soldier he claimed German citizenship. Friedman has a copy of his identification card at the center in Haifa. They showed you those things?"

"Yes. But which Germany? East or West?"

"Good point," he nodded.

"Can't we ask of both?"

"I suppose." Metzger stood up straight. "I will make inquiries." He opened the door and glanced back at me. "Good work. Now go home and see your family. I'm sure they've missed you."

* * *

A few days later, Metzger came to my office. He stepped inside and closed the door behind him. "We have a report from the East German Embassy in Argentina," he was barely able to suppress the smile on his face. "All three of the Eichmann children are registered there under their own names. Registered by their mother, with an address in Buenos Aires."

"It's him."

"Yes. It would appear we've located him."

"What now?"

"Operations is taking over."

"Operations?"

"Yes. We're part of Mossad, remember."

"Right."

"They'll locate the house and put him under observation. Find a way to confirm his identity. Once they have done that, they'll move forward with rendition."

"Bringing him here?"

"Yes. As I told you before, once we have him in our custody we will put him on trial in Jerusalem."

"So, until then, we wait?"

"We wait. And while we wait, you get to work on documenting everything you've learned. We need original documents if we can get them, especially for official documents. Certified copies will work if we can't find the originals. And we need to start lining up witnesses."

"People who knew him?"

"People who knew him at the death camps. Survivors. We need survivors. I don't want this to be merely a document-intensive trial. We'll have to use plenty of documents. Hopefully it will turn out to be an official, substantiated, unquestionable record of what the Nazis did to us. Not exhaustive, but complete. But I don't want to use documents alone. I want the details to come from the mouths of those who survived, people who can speak for themselves and for all those whose remains are scattered across the European countryside. I want the world and our own people to hear what really happened. So begin working on a list of people who could testify."

"What topics do you want them to address?"

"Just begin at the beginning and work your way forward, telling the story through the stories of people who were there. You've studied this extensively. And you've lived it. Arrange them as you see fit to make the story as complete as possible. We'll review your work later."

chapter 42

ith Metzger's instructions to guide me, and his confidence to motivate me, I returned to the center in Haifa and asked Tuviah Friedman for help sorting through the many survivor statements in his files. I did this under the guise of searching for people who might have information about Eichmann and avoided telling him what we already knew. He and his assistants helped me prepare lists of people who either mentioned Eichmann by name, or who might have seen him or had interactions with him.

While preparing those lists, I immersed myself in the accounts of people who were interred at the camps, made photo-static copies of their statements, and descended into the emotional gloom that plagued my earlier life. Because of the emotional toll, I made the added effort of returning home each evening to David, Eli, and the serenity of our life together in Jerusalem. The two-hour drive was long, but the joy of being with my family with their love and support put my mind at ease and cleansed my soul of the evil that seemed to be conjured up by images from those files.

As I read the accounts I learned that, like the ghetto in Vienna where we lived, most other ghettos had their own Council of Elders—the

Judenrat. German officials required it of every location. Many of the written accounts talked of decisions made by the council, which, in effect, decided who among them lived and who died. I knew that councils were used at most locations, but seeing their activity from the perspective of others put the issue in a different light than I had considered before and brought me once again face-to-face with the question of Jewish collaboration, an issue raised by Haim Rotschild when we talked years earlier. Each ghetto had a Judenrat. There was no way to avoid it. However, some were more diligent than others in fulfilling the duties assigned by the Nazis. As I considered what that meant and the effect it had, I thought of Papa and Uncle Alois, and I wondered how faithfully they discharged their duties. Were they faithful to the Nazis, or to us?

Late one afternoon I found Friedman at his desk and posed the question to him. He leaned back in his chair and ran his hand over his forehead. "The Nazis," he began slowly, "put all of us in an untenable position."

"But is that just an excuse we make to appease our conscience?"

"For some perhaps, but not for men like your father and uncle. Good men can withstand honest scrutiny."

"I wonder what I would find if I really looked."

"Think of what they faced," he suggested. "No doubt they knew that if they refused, the Nazis would find others who would serve in their place. Perhaps far less scrupulous men. Not serving meant closing their eyes to all that happened around them. Serving forced them to walk the line between good and evil. It was a tough position, but merely serving on the council was not wrong."

"But were there any who did not use their position to their own advantage?"

"Not to defend those who did, it depends on where you draw the line."

"That sounds like we're mincing words."

"Not exactly. I suspect that your family received some benefit from your father's service, without you being aware of it. Perhaps without him being aware of it, either."

I felt my forehead wrinkle in a frown. "How so?"

"You were in the Vienna ghetto?"

"Yes."

"Which part were you in? Where was your apartment? On the river side, or the canal side?"

"We were by the river. One block over from the fence that ran along the riverbank."

Friedman nodded. "That was the best location they had to offer." He rested his hands in his lap. "Third floor?"

"Yes. Why?"

"On the inside, or on a corner?"

"In the middle. We had a window that looked out on the street, but we were in the center of the building."

"Window looking out the front?"

"Yes."

"This was one of the best apartments in the building."

I scowled in disbelief. "It was filthy and we had no furniture."

"But you were on the third floor, which meant the floors below you insulated you from most of the noise, and in winter they insulated you from the cold. Heat rises, so whatever heat was generated on the two floors below you rose up to help keep you warm. The floor above you meant you weren't exposed to the winter cold from any direction except the one wall along the front. And you were on the inside, rather than a corner, which meant there was no draft."

The frown on my brow turned to a questioning look. "You think someone did that intentionally?"

"Absolutely," he nodded. "Absolutely."

"Papa did not request it," I countered. "We were assigned to the apartment before they asked him to serve."

"You were assigned that apartment because they knew your father *would* serve."

"They didn't know that. What could have possibly made them so sure?"

He had a satisfied smile. "They sent your Uncle Alois and the rabbi to ask him."

I was struck by the realization that what he said was true, and by the awareness that I had never thought of that as a possibility. Now I wondered what other things I'd missed.

"The bad ones," he continued. "The ones I find reprehensible were the ones who went over to the evil side and tried to take advantage of the situation for their own benefit. Choosing only their family members for work permits, only their families for travel documents, only their family members for extra food rations. And if anyone else wanted those privileges, they charged double." His eyes brightened. "What did your father do with his extra ration? I know he received one. That was standard procedure. What did he do with it?"

"He gave it to a woman who had small children. It was a condition of his acceptance, that he could give it to anyone he chose."

Friedman's eyes grew moist and full. "He was a man of God. A true Jew, in whom no one could find fault." He paused a moment and we sat there in silence. Then he cleared his throat and continued quietly, "Those people who used their position only for themselves were no longer Jewish at heart. They became Nazis themselves and should be tried as criminals." His eyes had a far-off look, and the way he said it sounded more like a prayer than simply a statement.

"Will they?"

He looked up at me. "Will they what?"

"Will they be tried as war criminals?"

"I do not think so." He shook his head slowly. "Not now." Then he sat up straight. "Your Uncle Alois…what was his full name?"

"Alois Kuffner."

"Wait here. I will be right back."

Friedman came from behind his desk and disappeared out the door. He returned a few minutes later with a file. "Here he is." He began reading as he entered the office. "Died at Mauthausen in 1943. They listed him as dying of natural causes, but someone who knew him says he was shot for not giving up the name of a prisoner who took an extra slice of bread from the meal rations." He tipped the file so I could see a handwritten statement, then he moved to the chair behind the desk and began reading. "He was on the prison council. One of the many groups that were formed to run the camp." He paused to look up at me and explained, "They also had a barracks manager in each building. Most of them were crooks and should be shot on sight. The councils tried to do a better job, mostly." Then he glanced down at the file and began again. "The officer in charge of the kitchen, which could hardly be called a kitchen, reported that a slice of bread was missing. The guards called everyone out to formation and demanded to know who took it. No one would answer. After an hour or two they grabbed Alois Kuffner and demanded that he give them the name or they would shoot him instead. Alois stood silent, so they shot him and the two men on either side of him. He was a member of the council, but he was an honorable man." Tears welled up in my eyes. Friedman leaned back in his chair. "Mere participation does not count as collaboration. There has to be more, otherwise we were all collaborators. We carried the stone from their quarries. We washed their clothes. Those were terrible times. There are no simple answers. But men like your father and Alois Kuffner were an example to us all." I turned away to wipe my eyes. Friedman put aside the file and changed the subject. "How are you coming with the lists?"

"Making progress," I caught my breath as I spoke.

"What is all this about anyway? Why the sudden interest in names and statements?"

"It is part of our investigation." I didn't want to say more.

His eyes narrowed. "You're getting close to Eichmann?"

"We are making progress."

"And Mengele?" He arched an eyebrow. "Making any progress on him?"

"We have researchers working on all the names that have been unaccounted for. I am focused right now on Eichmann. Retracing every step, looking at every detail, waiting for a break." It was true, I was waiting, and if the information we'd compiled proved accurate, it would produce a huge break.

*   *   *

After a week at the center in Haifa, I returned to work at the office in Jerusalem and began sorting through the lists and notes I had amassed from the statements in Friedman's files. Once again, Metzger's instructions guided me as I arranged the statements into groups based on the subject matter of each witness's experiences. Then I began the tedious task of locating addresses and telephone numbers for the ones who lived in Israel. I started with them because they seemed readily accessible. The more people we could use who lived nearby, the less expense we would incur in interviewing them and preparing them for trial.

Two days later, I went for my first appointment, a meeting with Nadia Yogev, a woman of fifty who was born in Poland. Her family was relocated from the countryside to the ghetto in Warsaw. She came to Israel during our fight for freedom. I met her at her home and we sat together in the living room.

"At first," she began, "it wasn't so bad. The buildings were filthy and the stone that paved the streets had been removed, so when it rained the streets were rivers of mud. But it was manageable, except for the food. We were always hungry. Then they came for the children." Her eyes filled with tears. "I held on to my younger brother to keep them from taking him, but a Nazi soldier snatched him from my arms, swung him by his legs, and smashed his head against the wall," she sobbed. "His little skull exploded and his brains spattered my dress."

We paused a moment while she collected herself, then I showed her an array of photographs. "Did you see any of these men in the ghetto? Either during that selection or at some other time."

She glanced at them and tapped a picture of Eichmann with her finger. "Him."

"He was there?"

"Yes."

"You are certain of it?"

"Positive. He was there when we arrived and at each of the selections."

"Do you know his name?"

"Eichmann," she nodded with resolve. "Adolf Eichmann."

"So, you were in the ghetto and they came for the children. What happened after that?"

"Not long after they took the children—maybe two or three weeks— the soldiers returned for the women. They forced them into the back of the trucks and hauled them away."

"Any idea when this was? What year?"

"Not really. It was before the uprising."

"What happened to the women? Do you know?"

"All of them were killed."

"You saw it?"

"I saw them when they were selected, but I was not at the camp."

"How did you avoid being sent to the camp?"

"My father shaved my head and dressed me in boy's clothes." She tugged at the sleeves of her top. "I was very slender then. I passed myself off as a boy."

"Did you live out the war in the ghetto?"

"No. They sent me to a manufacturing plant. We made bombs." Tears began to flow once more. "The bombs we made were used to keep the Nazis in power. We sabotaged as many as possible, but when we didn't meet our quota they would grab fifteen or twenty of us at random and shoot them. So we tried to only make sure we kept just within the margin of allowed error."

"And your family?"

"My younger brother was killed when they came for the children. My father and older brother died in the Warsaw uprising."

"They participated?"

"Yes. Very much so. Before the children were removed, everyone thought that if they cooperated everything would be all right. And many people continued to think that way after they took the children, but then they came back for the women and a few days later we learned what really happened to them."

"To the women?"

"Yes. We received news of what really happened to them and that changed everything."

"What happened to them?"

"They were killed at Auschwitz the day they arrived, as were the children earlier. One of the women escaped. She was eventually found and shot on sight by an SS trooper, but before they found her she told someone what she'd witnessed. After that, no one wanted to cooperate any longer with the Nazis."

"And your father was part of the resistance."

"He helped organize the revolt."

"Was he killed in the fighting?"

"Not directly. There were battles and skirmishes. Unlike what some have said, we didn't just go blindly to the camps and gas chambers. We fought back, but the Germans had so many more resources. Eventually they overwhelmed us and when that happened they came through the ghetto and killed all the participants they could find and many more besides. Then they made the few people who survived pick up the bodies."

"You were there? You saw this?"

"Yes. I was one of those who cleaned up the bodies. I found my father on the street corner, two blocks from our apartment." She started crying again. "Two women helped me throw his body onto a truck." She looked at me with desperation in her eyes. "I threw my own father's body on that truck with my own hands."

"And your brother?"

"He was not located for several days, then someone found his body in the basement of one of the buildings. He had small round burns all over his body where he had been poked with something hot. His eyes were gouged out and his hands and feet were cut off. They covered his body before they disclosed the discovery and would only let me see his head. One of the men in our group was a doctor. He told me that my brother bled to death."

"They tortured him."

"Yes," she nodded. "My brother knew the names of almost everyone involved in the revolt. The location of their weapons and supplies. He had a good memory and kept the details in his head. The Nazis were trying to make him give them that information. But I do not think he talked."

chapter 43

By the time I finished with Nadia, I was an emotional wreck. She talked until well after dinnertime, and it was late when I returned home. David was already in bed, and Eli was once again seated in the living room, reading a book. We sat together at the kitchen table while I ate supper. We continued to talk while I showered and dressed for bed. It seemed like a normal night and I was looking forward to a few hours of rest. But while I slept, things began to happen in my dreams.

As if transported back in time, I was standing in the hallway outside the door to our apartment in the Vienna ghetto. Around me people were plodding toward the stairs, all in a straight line, each one following the one in front. I fell in line with them.

When we reached the first floor, we shuffled through the doorway and stepped outside to the street. Then, from out of nowhere, German soldiers appeared and began shoving people along, shouting and yelling for us to hurry, only no one paid them any attention. The line continued to move at the same pace. I wanted to hurry, but an elderly man ahead of me wouldn't get out of the way, and my feet seemed incapable of moving any faster.

A soldier appeared and pushed his way past us. He carried a rifle with a bayonet attached. Without a word, he rammed the bayonet through the old man's back. Blood squirted out as he crumpled and fell. The soldier looked back at me and laughed.

I screamed and shouted at him and flailed the air with my hands, trying to hit him, but he was always just out of reach. Others around me were oblivious and continued past as if nothing happened, heads down, eyes focused on the pavement beneath their feet.

The soldier stared at me in disbelief. "You would shout at me?" He pointed to the insignia on his uniform. "I am an officer of the SS." He lunged toward me, and suddenly I bolted upright in bed, wide awake, my gown wet with sweat.

Eli awakened beside me. "What's the matter?" I was panting, trying to catch my breath and calm my racing heart. "The dreams?" he asked.

"Yes," I nodded as I threw back the covers and climbed from the bed. I walked to the bathroom and splashed water on my face. Eli followed me and stood in the doorway. He just stood there, not saying anything, and finally I looked over at him. "It's those people," I sighed.

"What people?"

"The survivors. Their stories. Every day I read their statements and it all comes back. Today, listening to Nadia, it was finally just too much. It's like I'm back in the ghetto, back in the camp, and I can't turn it off. It played over and over in my mind all the way home."

"And when you finally got to sleep…"

"I saw them in my dreams."

"Is this the first time? Recently?"

"It started last night," I admitted reluctantly.

Eli took me by the arm and led me into the kitchen. "Come on." He put on the kettle and we sat at the kitchen table, not saying much of anything until the tea was ready. Then, as we sipped from our cups, he looked at me and asked, "So, what was the dream about?"

"I was in the ghetto and the soldiers were moving us out of the apartments. An old man was walking in front of me, only he was slow and the guards got frustrated and one of them stabbed him in the back with a bayonet."

"What made you wake up?"

"I yelled at him. The soldier got mad and lunged toward me."

Eli took a sip of tea and slowly swallowed. "Back when we went through this before," he said finally, "and you went to see the rabbi and things started to get better—did you tell me everything that happened to you?"

My eyes darted away. "I don't know," I sighed.

"Don't put me off."

"I'm not putting you off. I don't know if I told you everything because I don't know if I remember it all. I told you everything I remembered. But I don't know anymore…"

"Don't know what?"

"These last few weeks, reading statements from other survivors. We all shared common experiences, but they remember horrible things I—"

Just then a scene flashed through my mind of a baby suspended in midair, then the sound of a gunshot and I jumped. Eli laid his hand on my shoulder. "Are you okay?"

"Yeah," I whispered. "I think so." But my mind was filled with images and I struggled to make sense of them.

Eli stared at me. "What did you see?"

"I…I saw a baby," I said softly. "And then there was a gunshot and the baby's body exploded."

"What was it?"

Tears ran down my cheeks as I remembered. "Tomer, one of Stephan's friends."

"The guy who showed you the sewer."

"One day after Stephan was missing and I moved in with Yardina, I was with a group on the street corner and I kept going on about how awful it was that my father served on the council and how he was selling us out. Amos Lurie, one of the resistance leaders, actually took up for Papa and told Tomer to show me what happened at the other side of the ghetto. He took me to the back wall."

"Where they shot the women."

"But after they shot the women, something else happened."

"What?"

"There were babies lying on the ground at their feet. I didn't see them before. I guess some of the women were their mothers. After they shot the women, the soldiers took the babies upstairs and threw them out of the building. Another soldier on the ground shot them while they were sailing through the air. The bullets ripped their little bodies in half." I looked over at him. "The soldiers just laughed."

"They were—"

"And now I remember something else," I interrupted him. "When I arrived at Mauthausen, after Adolf had me taken away, they were shooting little babies the same way." I looked at Eli as if in a dream, my mind so preoccupied with the horror of the memory. "What kind of person would do such a thing?"

"Evil lives in the world," he said calmly.

"I know that, but it does not answer my question. God lives in the world, too. He knows everything."

"He sees everything," Eli offered.

"Yes," I agreed at once. "So how could He let them do that to us? To me? How? I did nothing to deserve that misery. This misery that I bear even today. They did nothing to deserve it. He had the power to stop it and He did not."

Eli took my hand. "Life is filled with choices."

"I don't—"

"Listen to me. I don't know if this will help, but this is what I know. We were created *b'Tzelem Elohim*—in the image of God. Part of that image means we have the ability to choose. And not just Jews have that but everyone. What we do with those choices is, mostly, our responsibility. Evil choices are human acts, not the acts of God. Human acts don't diminish the character and nature of God. They only call into question the morality of the men who make those choices and do those acts."

"But God could have set it right," I argued.

"Yes, but that is not the world He created. If He stepped in every time someone did something wrong, He would violate His image that He instilled in us. He could have kept our ancestors from being enslaved in Egypt. He could have kept them from being taken captive by the Babylonians. But He did not. Instead, He gave us a history and a present that is as alive as man himself. He isn't totally outside history, or totally inside it, either. It's this movement of a relationship back and forth between God and man. We act, He acts. He acts, we act. We are all like Him in that respect. We get to act. We get to participate. The Germans you encountered chose to do wrong. You and many others paid the price for it. And in the end, the Germans paid a price for it, too."

I was astounded at what I heard coming from his lips, and profoundly moved by it. He was right. They made bad choices, and those choices had consequences that ultimately came back to them, just as it came to us. I knew that would be their end when I first went to work for Adolf at his office and realized how contradictory their culture of hate really was. Now, on the other side of that Shoah, I was beginning to see things come back together again, and while Eli spoke to me, the weight of the past few weeks rolled away, just as it had when I talked to Rabbi Meir.

I looked across the table at Eli and smiled. "How did you get so smart?"

"I have a smart wife," he quipped. "I have to work hard to keep up with her."

"Is this what's in all those books I see you reading at night?"

He leaned over and kissed me. "I knew this was the real question for you. I wanted to help you find the answer." He took my hand. "Come on. Let's go back to bed."

* * *

At the office, I continued the process of locating and interviewing witnesses on an informal basis, usually at their homes. While doing that, I also began to take witness depositions at the office, formal statements from the first people I vetted. These were given under oath and recorded by an official court reporter. Bureau 06 was moving forward with trial preparation, even though we still did not know for certain whether Ricardo Klement was Adolf Eichmann.

A few weeks into the deposition process, Metzger came to me at my desk. He held a plain white envelope. We talked about the witness interviews and touched again on the order we might use at trial. Then he closed the office door and gestured with the envelope. "I have some pictures I want to show you. Tell me if you recognize any of the people in these photographs."

He took out six photographs from the envelope and spread them on my desk. I looked at each one for a moment and then pointed to the third one from the left. "That is Adolf Eichmann. He's older. And he has less hair. But that is Eichmann."

Metzger turned over the photograph to reveal the name Ricardo Klement written on the back. My heart skipped a beat. He smiled. "One of our agents took this photograph three days ago. Eichmann is living in a suburb of Buenos Aires, just as you and Simon Wiesenthal suggested. He is using the name Ricardo Klement."

"We found him?" I grinned.

"We have found him," Metzger nodded. "Now the only question is how to get him out."

It seemed almost surreal, like my first meal in the hotel in Zurich after I escaped. One minute Eichmann was an unknown, and the next he was within our grasp. Still, there was much to be done and I forced myself to think like a lawyer. "Will Argentina extradite him to us?"

"I don't know, but even asking them is a big risk. I'm not sure they would take him into custody on the evidence we have. And I'm even less sure I want to show it to them. The German community is very influential in Argentina. Rather large investments have been made there by German individuals and corporations. I'm afraid if they pick him up, he would simply disappear again."

"You were thinking of simply taking him?"

"It is one of the options being discussed," Metzger admitted. "But you must not breathe a word of it to anyone."

"Certainly. But wouldn't that set a bad precedent?"

"What do you mean?"

"We have many enemies," I argued. "They take hostages from time to time and we condemn them for it. Wouldn't we be engaging in the same conduct?"

"Perhaps you can find a solid legal argument that distinguishes the two." He collected the photographs from the desktop and returned them to the envelope. "I'll tell Operations that you have confirmed their identification of him. Let me have your thoughts on the ramifications of taking him without resorting to legal process."

"Executive extradition."

"I like that," he smiled. "Executive extradition. But we still have to get him home."

"We can't simply fly a plane to Argentina and bring him back?"

"We have no regular air service directly to that country. Sending our own plane without a bona fide reason would raise too many questions. They would get suspicious very quickly."

"Then we need an official delegation," I offered.

Metzger looked puzzled. "For what?"

"For an excuse to send a plane. Set up a conference with someone. Create a reason to send officials to something. There must be something they can attend or discuss."

Metzger was intrigued by the suggestion. "Diplomats are good at meetings."

"They could meet about agricultural issues. We have plenty of farms here that would welcome the opportunity to enter a new market. Cooperate on new farming techniques."

"A group of our agricultural officials come to check out some kind of development in farming. I'll see what I can do with it." He turned to leave and I called after him. He stepped back to my doorway.

"Eichmann will be prosecuted in our courts, won't he?" I asked.

"Most certainly."

"Will you lead the prosecution?"

"Yes."

"Any possibility I could participate? As part of your in-court staff, I mean." It was a lot to ask. I was fresh out of law school. Many on our staff had worked as lawyers for years. But this was a once-in-a-lifetime opportunity. I had to ask.

"We'll see," Metzger replied. "Get to work on that executive extradition memo."

chapter 44

Three weeks later, I took the extradition memo to Metzger in his office. He glanced at it and laid it aside. "Tell me what it says."

"The crimes for which Eichmann could stand trial—murder, execution, enslavement, plundering of private property—are all defined as war crimes by the Nuremberg Principles, established to guide trials before the International Military Tribunal."

"We don't want to suggest that we are actually an extension of that tribunal," Metzger cautioned. "We want to try him under Israeli law."

"I understand. My point is, no one doubts that Eichmann should stand trial for his participation in the German treatment of Jews. He's included on the 'wanted list' of the UN War Crimes Commission and almost every law enforcement agency in the world. The only question is the legality of our acquiring him through nontraditional means, and that is a political problem, not a legal one."

"You're sure about that?"

"Yes."

"The manner in which we bring him here won't affect our right to try him?"

"Not legally. Once we have him on Israeli soil, the manner of how he came to be here is irrelevant to the Israeli court."

"Interesting point."

"I suggest we ask him to waive his right to trial in any other jurisdiction and agree to stand trial here."

"I doubt he'd go for it."

"It's a long shot but if he agrees, we have an answer to the jurisdiction argument."

"We'll consider it," Metzger offered.

"Anyway, if we get him here by whatever means necessary, we can smooth out the political problems later. Israeli courts will not order him sent to any other venue."

"We just have to be ready for the backlash from other nations."

"Right," I conceded. "If the world wants to discuss the manner in which we have done this," I added, "they will have to discuss the manner in which they have done nothing. I don't think they want that discussion, even if most of them still hate us."

"Good." He put the memo in a folder and tossed it into the basket at the corner of his desk. Then he looked up with a curious smile. "Your timing is remarkable."

"How so?"

"I just received this." He reached across the desk and gave me a note. On it was a simple handwritten statement that said, "Cleared air space." I looked over at him, and he smiled. "They just left Argentina."

My mouth dropped open. "We have him?"

"Yes," he nodded. "We have him."

An excited grin spread across my face. "How did we do it?"

"Took him off the street near his home."

"But how did we get him out of the country?"

"An official delegation."

"You're kidding," I laughed. "Really? A delegation to what?"

"Not long after you and I discussed it, the prime minister's office received an invitation to attend a ceremony commemorating Argentina's independence. They flew down, attended the ceremonies, and returned with a few extra people."

"God was on our side."

"God," Metzger added, "has always been on our side."

* * *

Two days later, David Ben-Gurion announced Eichmann's capture. I listened to the announcement on the radio at the coffee shop with Eli, Yohai, Chana, and a café full of customers. We were all very proud of the work Mossad and other agencies did to make Eichmann's capture a success. When the telecast ended, Yohai came to me and put his arm on my shoulder. "You did it."

"We did it," I said, making sure not to take all the credit.

Then he leaned closer to my ear. "I was wrong."

"About what?"

"About you. About law school. About many things. You are as capable as anyone, more so, and I am glad for the success that is coming your way." I hugged him, knowing how difficult it was for him to say that.

* * *

In the days following Eichmann's arrest, we redoubled our effort to prepare for trial. Everyone expected the case would take about a year to move through the court system, but we didn't want to waste the time we'd been given. Unforeseen issues were bound to arise and if we prepared early, we would be able to address them without undue difficulty. No one wanted to give the appearance that we were rushing Eichmann to the gallows, either, though I think everyone knew from the start that was where he was headed.

Over the next several days after his arrest, I continued to think about Eichmann and how he'd come to be where he was, locked in a jail cell at a secure facility in Israel. I wondered what he thought of the way his life turned out and whether he would ever know that I had a small part in determining his fate. I was sure he had not thought of me since the day in Linz when he ordered the soldiers to take me away. But if he did think of me, I know he never would have considered that I might have contributed to his final undoing. As time passed, I felt the growing need to see him for myself, to know for certain that it really was Adolf Eichmann sitting in that cell, to see the kind of man he'd turned out to be, and to reconcile in my mind the person I knew as a young girl with the man I feared as an adult.

After several days of debating with myself, I approached Metzger and asked if I could have a look at him. The request caught Metzger totally off guard. He stared at me a moment with the strangest look before asking, "What do you mean?"

"I don't want to talk to him," I explained. "And I don't want him to see me or even know that I am there. I just want to have a look at him."

Metzger was silent for a moment and as I watched, the look on his face softened from that of a reluctant trial attorney to an understanding mentor. "Well, maybe that's not such a bad idea. I'll see what I can do."

The following day, Metzger came to me in my office and without any preparation said, "Are you ready to go?"

I was working through the testimony of a survivor witness, and his appearance at my door was rather distracting. "Go where?" I asked without looking up.

"I thought you wanted to see Eichmann."

I had assumed my request would take weeks for approval, if at all, and that ultimately I would be turned down. The offer to see him now, less than twenty-four hours later, found me totally unprepared, but I knew this was probably my only chance to see Eichmann before he appeared in court. "Yes," I said courageously, and I followed him downstairs to the building lobby.

From there we rode across town to a detention center. After clearing several security checkpoints, we were escorted into a room. A large steel door stood along the opposite wall. Metzger pointed to it and spoke in a low voice. "He is just through that door." A peephole was located in the center of the door and he gestured to it with his hand. "You may slide back the cover from the hole and have a look."

"Can he see me?"

"No."

"Will he know someone is watching?"

"Perhaps. But if you are quiet you may go undetected."

I crossed the room, slid aside the cover from the peephole, and leaned forward, pressing my eyebrow against the opening. Although the hole was small, with my eye close against it I could view the entire room. Eichmann was seated at a table with his back to the door. I watched him a few minutes, taking in the whole of him without intending to focus on any single aspect, but as I watched, my attention was drawn to the smallest gestures—the way he held the pen in his hand, the tilt of his head while he read, one shoulder slightly lower than the other, and a hand always propped on his thigh. Like archaeological remains, they were traces from the past, remnants of the teenaged Adolf I knew when we lived in Linz.

Then he pushed back from the table and stood. He turned in my direction, providing a full view of his face. The sight of him made me gasp and I was afraid he heard me, but he made no sound and gave no response. I watched a moment longer, then backed away from the door, suddenly lightheaded and faint. Metzger replaced the covering over the peephole.

"Well?" he asked.

"It's him," I answered as I leaned against the wall and struggled to regain my composure.

"No doubt?"

"No doubt."

"Good." Metzger opened the door to the hallway and glanced back at me with a look of concern. "Are you all right?"

"Yes. I'm fine." I walked with my head down, trying to shut out images from the past that crowded my mind. We were still deep inside the facility when someone called to me. I looked up to see the voice was that of Tobin Halutz.

Metzger was surprised. "You two know each other?"

"Yes," I nodded. "Tobin used to come to my father-in-law's coffee shop." I looked over at Tobin with a curious frown. "Why are you here?"

The question seemed to catch him by surprise and he appeared awkward, an uncharacteristic reaction for him. Metzger spoke up. "Tobin was on the team that brought Eichmann from Argentina."

"Oh," I said with surprise. "That must have been harrowing."

"Not too much, until right at the end. One of the Buenos Aires detectives became suspicious, and we had a little trouble getting our flight plan approved. Things got a little touchy. But we worked it out. What brings you out here?"

"I work with Mr. Metzger."

"Oh?"

"Sarah is an attorney with our office," Metzger explained.

Halutz's face brightened. "You went to law school?"

"Yes. You seem surprised."

"I thought you'd be working in that coffee shop the rest of your life. Are you still…"

"Yes," I nodded. "I'm very much married to Eli. He's the reason I'm here."

"Oh." Halutz's countenance dropped. "I see."

We reached the security checkpoint and Tobin went on his way. Metzger and I left the building and walked to the car. "Tobin is a good man," he offered as we reached the car.

"Yes," I agreed. "He is. Fought valiantly in the war for independence."

"I'm surprised he let you get away."

"Just now?"

"No," he chuckled. "When he first met you."

"He tried," I grinned, "but Eli is the love of my life."

chapter 45

Several months after Eichmann's arrest, I received a package in the mail from Simon Wiesenthal. In it was an advance copy of *Life* magazine with an article written by Willem Sassen. The article contained excerpts of an interview with Eichmann. Apparently, Sassen conducted the interview over a rather lengthy period of time and intended to use it as the basis for a book. The *Life* article was meant to attract publishers to the project. I read it and was fascinated by the way Eichmann reinterpreted and, in many ways, reconstructed events of the past to portray himself not only in an appealing light but as a man tolerant of Jews and sympathetic with our situation in Europe during the Nazi era. When I finished reading it, I made a copy of the article for myself and took the magazine to Metzger. He scanned it quickly and asked the question we would hear from many others. "Is it really an interview with him?"

"I think so."

"You read it?"

"Yes."

"And what did you think?"

"I think it's him. It sounds like him."

"Just the same," Metzger insisted, "we'll have someone authenticate it." He laid it aside and looked up at me. "What did you think of it?"

"I think that article is the outline of his defense. He is going to claim he never ordered the death of anyone. Only that he arranged their transportation. Did his best to get as many out of the country as possible, never mind that he stole everything they had in the process. And never mind the fact that only a few people were ever issued the promised travel documents."

"You got that from the article?"

"Yes. Why?"

"Because that is precisely what he is saying to our interrogators."

"But it's not true."

"I know it's not true, and you know it's not true, but I think he has convinced himself that it is."

"Incredible!"

"It's infuriating," Metzger added, "but I've learned over the years that defendants always have a story, a version of events that shows how they couldn't possibly be guilty of a crime everyone knows they committed. You're much better off letting them have their say and getting them committed to a version of the facts, no matter how outlandish that version may be. Once you've done that, it's rather easy to pick their story apart with the facts. But we have to have the facts, the details, to pin him down with."

"We have hundreds of witnesses who can place him at the camps. Some who can put him there during gruesome executions and later at the gas chambers."

"But," Metzger pointed out, "we have no one who can say he actually gave the order for even a single execution. What we need is someone who can show the other side. The inside."

I felt my heart rate quicken. "We have one witness like that," I suggested.

"Who?" he asked in disbelief. "You know this person?"

"Yes, I do. And you do, too."

"Who do we have?" Metzger picked up a witness list from his desk and tossed it toward me. "Who on that list can tell us about what happened on the inside?"

I didn't bother to look at the list, I just looked at him and said, "I am that witness."

"You?" He looked at me like I was crazy.

"Yes," I answered, unmoved by his reaction. "Me."

"You can do that? You can tell us what Adolf Eichmann did during the war."

"Yes."

"How?"

"I was there. I've known him my entire life. When I was a little girl, our families lived three houses apart in Linz."

"I understand you knew him as a child." Metzger waved me off with a dismissive gesture. "But that is not what we need."

"I knew him as an adult, too."

"As an adult?" He had a mocking sneer. "Look, I know you want to participate and I'll see if I can get you on the trial team for a couple of days. This is going to be a long trial and we'll need to swap people out so no one gets overloaded. But not as a witness." He sat up straight. "I think maybe we should both forget we had this conversation."

"They came to the ghetto and moved us to the freight yard to load us on a train and sent us to the camp. We were all there in line and they were shoving everyone into the railcars. Then, at the last minute, someone shouted my name. I was on a list. They took me out and drove me to Eichmann's office. There were several of us from the ghetto who were taken in the same way, but they put the others in the warehouse sorting through clothes and belongings taken from the prisoners. Eichmann put me to work in his office. He asked for me personally."

Metzger seemed to take me more seriously. "So you saw what happened in the office?"

"In the Vienna office. I typed the reports."

"What kind of reports?"

"Population censuses from the camp. Reports on the living and the dead. Inventories of property taken from people who were brought there. And I typed letters."

"What kind of letters?"

"All kinds. Glad-to-see-you letters. Letters about trouble with the rail schedule. The need for better facilities."

"Better facilities?"

"Most of the documents I saw dealt with the camp at Mauthausen. There were letters and memos about the need for a new crematorium. Expansion of the facilities. They had trouble disposing of the bodies. They could kill them faster than they could get rid of the remains."

Metzger sat quietly, a stricken look on his face. Finally he asked softly, "Any idea what happened to those documents?"

"I don't know what happened to the official version, but many of the reports were prepared from handwritten information, lists, notes and things like that. For some of the ones I typed I made extra carbon copies. I might be able to get them for you."

A puzzled frown wrinkled his forehead. "What are you saying? You have those documents?"

"Eichmann thought I could pass for a German. My hair was shorter then and I was much younger. From the way things ended between us, I'm sure he had a romantic interest in me. He gave me papers under the name of Ellen Krupp, and I lived in a boardinghouse a few blocks from the office. While I worked there I took as many documents as I could to my room and hid them in the wall."

"The wall?"

"It was already damaged. There was a hole near the ceiling. I dropped the papers through it to hide them."

"Think they're still there?"

"I don't know. Can you get me to Vienna?"

"Yes. But you'll need to move fast. The trial will begin soon and we still have a lot to do."

"I can go at once. Do we need to locate the—"

He cut me off with a wave of his hand. "I don't want to hear the details. I'll send someone with you. Someone from our office who knows how to handle situations like this."

"From Mossad or the Attorney General's office?"

"Mossad." He paused a moment and glanced at me. "I would send Tobin Halutz, but is that going to cause a problem?"

"Not if Eli can come with me."

"I don't know," Metzger grimaced. "He's a good guy but…he's a civilian. There might be a problem."

"I need him. And if I travel with only Tobin, it will look suspicious— a married woman with an unmarried man. If Eli goes with me, we are a couple in the company of an old friend."

"Very well," he conceded. "I'll arrange it. Pack your bags."

* * *

That night, when I told Eli about the trip to Vienna, he was less than enthusiastic. "You want to go back there?" he asked with an unusually skeptical tone.

"I have to retrieve something I left behind."

"Nothing you can find there will bring you peace," he cautioned.

"I know. But this is different. This is for the trial. The outcome of our case against Eichmann may depend on it."

"I don't like it. I love you, I support you, but I just don't think it's good for you to keep going over and over these same incidents."

"You're worried the nightmares will return?"

"Yes. I am."

"Well, I'm not." I smiled at him playfully. "And one reason I'm not worried is you."

"What does that mean?"

"You brought me out of the darkness, and I know if it returns, you can get me out again." I leaned over and kissed him. "But I have to do this."

"Okay," he said resolutely. "But if you have to go, I have to go with you."

"Good," I grinned. "I was going to ask you to come with me."

"They'll let me?"

"It's already approved. Mr. Metzger said it was okay. There is just one other thing."

"What's that?"

"Tobin Halutz works for Mossad now. Mr. Metzger is sending him with us."

"Okay," Eli nodded.

"You're all right with that?"

"Sure. Tobin is a good man. I haven't seen him for a while. Used to come in the shop all the time. I wonder why he stopped coming around."

And that's when I realized no one ever told him about Chana and what she'd said to me during the war when Eli was missing. If he didn't know, I certainly wasn't going to bring it up. I just nuzzled my head against his chest and sighed, "I'm sure he had a reason."

* * *

Two days later, we left David with Chana and Yohai early in the morning and drove to the airport. Tobin was waiting for us when we arrived. We boarded the plane and traveled together to Vienna, arriving there in the afternoon. After wandering around in a taxi for half an hour, we retreated to the river and located the bridge that led to the site where the ghetto once stood.

"We crossed the river there," I said. "And then we drove up the street." The taxi driver turned in the direction I pointed and we started north. "We crossed a second bridge." I closed my eyes as I imagined the route—the wind in my hair, the sound of the truck as it rattled along. "And then we turned right, I think. Onto a wide thoroughfare."

"I know the street," the driver offered.

In a few minutes we reached a major intersection and turned right, traveling east. I glanced around searching for landmarks, but the area had changed since the war. "What if it's not here," I worried.

"Relax." Eli patted my leg. "We'll find it."

"If this is correct, there should be a convent on the right."

In a moment, the driver slowed the car and pointed out the window toward a building. "This was a convent before the war. It's been converted to apartments now, but I think the church still owns it. Is this the place you were looking for?"

"No. Turn right at the corner."

We turned right and idled past the building to a residential neighborhood. And then I saw the boardinghouse on the corner. It was three stories tall and had a green lawn now, but there it was. The driver brought the car to a stop at the curb. I pointed out the front windshield. "The office was down there."

"You're sure?"

"Yes. I'm sure. This is it."

We climbed from the car and Tobin paid the driver to wait. Then we walked together to the front door and knocked. A flood of memories threatened to distract me but I pushed them aside and concentrated. A moment later, the door opened and a woman appeared. I explained to her that I had lived there when it was a boardinghouse during the war and asked if we could come inside and have a look around. It all seemed suddenly awkward, the three of us appearing unannounced and her standing there in the doorway of her home, but it was too late to back down now. The woman was reluctant to let us inside and stepped back from the door to call for her husband. While she was distracted, Eli prodded me forward and we entered the house.

The door opened to an entryway, and the stairs were straight ahead. I made my way toward them and moved up to the second floor. Behind me I heard the woman talking to her husband in an excited voice, trying to explain why we were there.

At the top of the stairs I turned left and at the end of the hall came to the bedroom where I once lived. It was now a child's room, decorated in pink and green. The walls were repaired with a smooth finish that was painted and fresh. I glanced back at Eli. "I can't find the spot. There was a hole in the wall and I shoved the papers inside. But I can't find it."

"Picture it in your mind." He pointed toward the window, which stood along the wall near the door. "Was this here?"

"Yes." I looked out to the yard below and saw children's toys strewn across the grass. After a moment I turned away and pointed to the left. "The chest was here." I moved to the side and stood where it would have been, then I turned to the left and pointed. "The hole in the wall was over there in the corner near the top. I had to reach up to drop the papers through the hole and then they fell to the bottom."

"You're sure?" Eli asked.

"Yes," I nodded. "I think I am." I looked up at the ceiling for a reference point, then tapped with my finger on the wall until it sounded hollow. "Here. It should be right here." I looked over at Eli. "But what if I'm wrong?"

He touched my arm. "Stand back. We're about to find out."

Suddenly the woman's husband stormed into the room with an angry look on his face. "What are you doing?"

"Wait a minute," Tobin cut him off before he reached us. "It's okay."

"No, it's not okay," he roared. "This is my house and I want to know who you are and what you're doing here."

"There's an item hidden in that wall. We need to get it out."

"An item. What item?"

"Documents."

"Papers?"

"Yes."

"And that gives you the right to come into my house like this?"

I leaned near Eli. "What do we do now?"

"Just stand back," he muttered. I turned away and he kicked the wall with the toe of his shoe.

The husband started shouting in an Upper Austrian dialect, which I don't think either Eli or Tobin understood. Eli ignored him and kept kicking the wall until finally his foot went through. Then he stooped down and tore the hole larger with his hands. "Here it is," he announced.

The husband squeezed past Tobin. "Here *what* is?"

"This." Eli stood, holding a document in his hand.

"What is it?"

"Part of a prisoner list," I answered. "From people who were held at Mauthausen camp during the war."

"Oh." The intensity suddenly drained from his voice. "Well, who's going to fix my wall?"

"I'll see that it gets fixed," Tobin offered. "Right after we get the documents out."

"There's more?"

"One way to find out." Tobin moved around him and joined Eli in kicking the hole much larger.

"This is crazy," the man complained. "I'm calling the police." He was almost to the door when documents began sliding from the hole.

Tobin looked over at him. "I don't think you want the police here."

"Why not?"

I started crying, but Eli was laughing as he gathered the papers into a neat stack. He looked up at me. "This is what you were looking for?"

"Yes," I sobbed. "That is exactly what I was looking for."

"How do I know you'll fix my wall?" the man insisted. "I really should call the police and get them involved."

Once again he turned to leave and once again Tobin stopped him. "I'll stay right here until we get this settled." He glanced back at me. "Get the papers and go."

"But those are my papers," the husband protested.

Tobin glared at him. "These are documents from Nazi concentration camps listing people who were executed as a result of mass murder. Do you really want to be a part of that?"

"No," the man replied timidly. "I suppose not."

"I didn't think so. We'll take the documents out of here and you will never have to deal with them again. I will get your wall fixed and pay you for the inconvenience, and it will all be done."

"Okay," the man sighed.

Eli checked to make certain we had all the papers from the wall cavity, then we bundled them in our arms, hurried down the steps to the first floor, and out to the waiting taxi. As I climbed in back, I caught the driver's eye in the rearview mirror. "Airport," I said. "Quickly."

Eli glanced over at me. "We still have Tobin's stuff in the trunk."

"He knows how to live without it."

chapter 46

We arrived back in Jerusalem on the last flight of the night. I called Metzger from the airport to find out what we should do with the documents. He met us at the office with three members from his staff and we began sorting through them right then. At three in the morning we finally locked the pages away and went home to sleep.

For the next two weeks I worked to organize the documents and assemble them for trial. Then I spent another week explaining them to Gideon Hausner, the newly appointed Attorney General and the man who would be leading the prosecution in court. Finally we brought in a court-certified translator who translated them into English and Hebrew. Hausner insisted that the trial record be both thorough and accessible to as many people as possible. He wanted the trial to be not just a legal proceeding but an exhibit to the world of what happened to us at the hands of the Nazis.

As the opening day of trial approached, Metzger handed me the final witness list. We broke it down into a schedule based on the amount of time we anticipated each witness would need to tell their story and for what we expected could be grueling cross-examination by Eichmann's attorney. I was in charge of getting the witnesses to court at the required time. If things went as we expected, I would testify with the documents during the second week of trial, probably on Wednesday. At trial, however, Eichmann's attorney chose to ask very few questions of our witnesses. That meant the trial proceeded much more quickly than we had expected. My testimony was moved up to Monday.

The Sunday before I was to appear in court, I worked at the office all day going over my testimony with Hausner. About five that evening, he looked at me with a kind smile. "I think you're ready."

"Yes," I nodded. "I believe I am."

"You do realize whether Eichmann's attorney asks any questions or not, your testimony means reliving much of what happened to you in the past."

"I know."

"If you don't want to do this, I can find a way to work around it."

"No you can't." I knew he was only trying to be kind.

"No," he said wryly. "I suppose I can't."

"I'll be fine."

I arrived home that night exhausted. Eli was seated on the sofa, waiting for me. I set my briefcase on the floor and flopped down beside him. "You look tired," he said.

"I *am* tired."

Tears filled my eyes and he pulled me close. "What's the matter?"

"I'm scared."

"Eichmann won't get to you."

"I'm not scared about that. He'll be in the defendant's box with glass all around him." I looked up at Eli. "What if I can't remember?"

"You'll remember. Didn't you spend the day going over everything?"

"Yes. But that was in the office. What if I get nervous and I can't remember what to say?"

"You've spent your entire adult life remembering. You have notebooks full of memories. You'll remember."

"How do you know?"

"Do you remember your friend Stephan?"

"Yes."

"When was the last time you saw him?"

"On the street corner in Vienna."

"Tell me about it."

"Why?"

"Just tell me about it," he insisted.

"It was almost dark," I began. "He told me to be careful what I said and to pay attention when they came for me. To watch how they divided the groups. I asked him what he meant, but he said never mind and for me not to worry about it. That everything had worked out right for me and he was sure it would continue to be that way. Then he kissed me and I went inside."

"Where was that?"

"The ghetto in Vienna. Just down the block from where we lived."

"What month was it?"

"I don't know the exact month. It was fall. The weather was pleasant outside during the day but the nights were rather cold."

Eli smiled at me. "I think your memory will serve you just fine."

"Maybe you are right," I sighed. "I hope so."

"If your mind starts to wander, think of Stephan and David and all the others. And if their image fades from your mind, remember their names and you will hear their voices. It will be okay. You will do well."

I rested my head on his chest. "I am so blessed to have found you."

"No," he whispered. "I am blessed that you found me." Then he kissed me lightly on the lips and gestured with a nod. "We should get to sleep. Tomorrow will be a long day."

"About that." I sat up straight on the sofa.

Eli had a puzzled look. "What about it?"

"I think I need to do this alone."

"What do you mean? It's all arranged. We put David on the bus for school in the morning. Mama will meet him after school and take him to the shop."

"I know, but the trial will be tedious and I'll need to focus. I think it would be best if you stayed away. Go to work at the shop. This is going to take several days and you can't be gone from work all week."

He leaned back and stared up at the ceiling. "Are you worried I might get in the way?"

"No. You are never in the way. I'm just worried I might focus more on you and less on what I need to do. And I need to face him. Alone. Just me."

"Is that all of it?"

"He killed my mother and father and brother."

Eli put his arm around me. "And he killed Stephan."

"The man was responsible for six million deaths." I started to cry and I could barely speak. "I don't want anything to happen to you."

"Nothing's going to happen to me." He squeezed me tight against him. "Everything will work out right."

* * *

The following morning we awakened early and put David on the bus to school, then Eli rode with me in a taxi down to the courthouse. We got out and walked in silence to the building's rear entrance. I gave him a brave smile as we neared the door. "Wish me luck?"

He took my hand. "Sarah Cohen, I shall do no such thing. I'll give you my blessing and peace, but there won't be any luck about it. God's purposes are at work in your life." He kissed me one last time and stepped away. "Come by the shop if you get finished in time today," he called. "Otherwise, I'll see you at home for dinner."

Inside the building, I made my way to an elevator reserved for court personnel. It took me upstairs to a hallway that led to a reception area near the judges' chambers. An assistant escorted me to a holding room just behind the courtroom. I sat there alone, waiting to be called to the witness stand.

My body seemed to tingle with nervous energy and my palms were clammy. I tried to focus on the task at hand but over and over my mind returned to my first day on the job, typing reports for Adolf at the office in Vienna. As I thought of that day I remembered Eva Fröbe. I didn't want to think of her. I wanted to think of Mama and Papa, of David and Stephan, but my mind kept coming back to Eva, so after a while I gave in and went where my thoughts wanted to go. She was seated at her desk in front of me when she turned to introduce herself. From all that appeared, she was a German woman with a job. Then I remembered the day she saw me looking through the files. She tried to warn me that others had worked in my position and tried the same thing. They were no longer there because of it. Now, all these many years later, I heard again the pitch of her voice and saw the look in her eye. Only now she didn't seem quite as German as before, and I thought for the first time perhaps she was like me, one of Eichmann's Jewish girls. For the next twenty minutes I searched my memory for other hints and clues that might provide an insight into the person she really was. Then I remembered another day, when we were working through an unusually large stack of handwritten sheets and she—

The door opened behind me, interrupting my thoughts. One of the lawyers from Hausner's office appeared. "We're just about ready for you." I nodded in response, rose from my chair, and followed him from the room.

At the door to the courtroom we paused, waiting for the bailiff to announce my name. Through a window in the top half of the door I saw Eichmann seated in the defendant's dock, looking smug and confident.

While I watched, doors at the far end of the courtroom opened and a clerk from Hausner's office entered, pushing a dolly that held two large cardboard cartons. Eichmann seemed to pay them no attention as the clerk set the boxes on the prosecutor's table.

When he was gone, Hausner stood and addressed the presiding judge. "Your Honor, the prosecution calls Sarah Cohen."

As I pushed open the door to enter the courtroom, I saw Eichmann glance in my direction with a puzzled expression on his face. I felt his eyes follow me as I made my way to the witness stand and took a seat. He was seated directly across the courtroom from me and for the first time in years we were face-to-face. When I was settled, Hausner turned to me and said, "State your full name for the record, please."

With my eyes focused on Eichmann, I responded confidently, "Sarah Batsheva Cohen." At the mention of my name, Eichmann's mouth dropped open and all the color drained from his face.

Without missing a beat, Hausner turned to one of the cardboard cartons and opened the top. The cartons were packed with the documents I purloined from Eichmann's office and hid in the wall at the boardinghouse. He took one out, marked it as an exhibit, and showed it to me. "Do you recognize this document?"

I glanced at it and nodded. "Yes. I know what it is."

"What is it?"

"It's a prisoner census list." I pointed to the heading at the top of the page. "This one is a list of new arrivals at the Mauthausen camp."

"And how is it that you are familiar with this document?"

"I typed it when I worked for Adolf Eichmann at his office in Vienna." A gasp rippled across the courtroom. Eichmann slumped to one side in his chair.

For the remainder of the week I told my story and the stories of as many people as the judge would permit—how we were forced from our homes and crowded into the ghetto, about Stephan who went missing and how I later learned he'd been killed, my rescue from the camp by Eichmann and the duties assigned to me in his office. Slowly, meticulously we went through each document, one page at a time, and in between documents I filled in the details about how the office worked, the decisions that were made there, and Eichmann's responsibility for it all.

After almost two full days of testimony, I was drained, but there was still the defense's opportunity to cross-question me. It was a little after one on Friday afternoon when Hausner concluded his examination, and I braced for what might happen next. The presiding judge looked over at Eichmann's attorney, Robert Servatius, a lawyer from Cologne, and said, "You may begin your cross-examination."

Servatius shook his head. "We have no questions," he said dryly.

The judge dismissed me and I walked out of the courtroom through the same door I entered the first morning, earlier in the week. Though my part in it was finished, the trial itself was far from over, and all of the witnesses I interviewed were set to appear. Their files were stacked on my office desk awaiting my attention. But they could wait. I walked out to the street, hailed a taxi, and rode to the coffee shop.

Instead of entering through the front I came in through the alley and slipped up behind Eli as he stood at the stove. I touched him on the elbow and he turned around, startled at the interruption. I grinned at him, "Remember me?" Without a word, he kissed me deeply and wrapped his arms around my shoulders.

After a moment, he leaned away. "It's over?"

"It's over for me, and I think it's over for him."

"You want something to eat? Something to drink?"

"I was hoping we could sit on the steps out back."

Eli took my hand and led me through the kitchen to the back door. We walked outside to the alley and sat on the steps. I snuggled next to him. He put his arm around me and drew me close. "I was praying for you all week," he said softly.

"I know. I could feel it."

"You never said much about what happened. Did you have any trouble?"

"No."

"What kind of questions did his lawyer ask?"

"He didn't ask a single one."

"None?"

"Not a single one."

"He hasn't asked *any* of the victims any questions."

"So they concede that he did what everyone says he did."

"They concede that it happened. But they're arguing that he was only acting under orders."

"And you put that notion to rest."

"I hope so." I looked up at him. "Thank you."

"For what?"

"For being you. For being here for me. For making all this possible."

"I'm just a guy who works at a coffee shop."

I kissed him full on the mouth. "You are a faithful man of God. And the love of my life."

chapter 47

$\mathcal{A}$fter four months of trial, Adolf Eichmann was convicted for his involvement in the atrocities of the Shoah. The court sentenced him to death by hanging. It had taken a year from the time of his arrest to reach that result. It would take another year of appeals and legal maneuvers before the sentence would be carried out. Many from our office attended his hanging. I was not one of them.

At the time of his execution, just before midnight on May 31, 1962, when Eichmann was executed, I was seated alone on a pew in the darkened sanctuary at the Grand Synagogue, just up the street from the coffee shop. I was there praying for the souls of all our friends and loved ones who had died by his hand.

Over the years, my response to him had run the gauntlet, from infatuated adolescent girl to a woman obsessed with finding justice for myself and for all on whom he imposed such misery. That later reaction involved much of my adult life. Having seen justice applied, my heart turned to forgiveness. He was but an instrument of Evil, the real culprit behind all that happened. The law gave him no reprieve.

I continued to work at Mossad, tracking down Nazis who were wanted on war crimes charges. That effort kept me busy from early in the morning until late in the afternoon. Occasionally, however, I left the office early, usually on Fridays when I came to the coffee shop to collect Eli before the evening service, which marked the beginning of the Shabbat.

On one of those Friday afternoons, not too long after Eichmann was hanged, I arrived at the shop and entered through the front door. After I testified in court, many of the customers at the shop wanted to talk about what I had done. They often took me aside and told me of their own experiences during the war. Articles about me appeared in the *Jerusalem Post*. Yohai had some of them framed and hung them on the café wall.

That day, as I came through the dining room, a woman stopped me and began telling me about her experiences at Bergen-Belsen, a camp where thousands of Jews died, many of them from typhus. She jotted down the name of a prison guard she remembered and asked if I would look into his present location. Our office routinely received numerous requests just like hers and I told her I would check into it.

As I rose to leave her table, Eli appeared in the doorway from the kitchen. He caught my eye and gestured for me to come to him. I excused myself and walked in that direction. When I reached him, he nodded to the right and with a smile said, "That man over there is waiting to see you."

I glanced in that direction and saw an older man with gray hair, olive complexion, and deep-set eyes seated at a table in the corner. "Who is it?" I asked.

"Ask him," Eli replied with a sly grin. "I think you'll be surprised."

As I approached the table, I studied the man's face, searching for a sign, a hint, something to jog my memory and remind me who he was. Then he looked up at me with a smile and I recognized him at once. He was Oscar Murillo, my cousin from Spain.

He stood and I offered him my hand, which he shook politely. Then he pulled a chair from the table for me. "Please," he insisted. "Have a seat."

"You are a long way from Cordova," I said, unsure where to begin with him.

"Not so far that we haven't heard about your testimony at the Eichmann trial." He took a sip of coffee. "That must have been difficult."

"Twenty years ago it would have been very difficult. But now, after all that has happened, it was mostly just very tiring."

"I never imagined you as a lawyer, but it suits you perfectly."

"Uncle Alois had something to do with that."

"He was a good man."

"Yes. He was. And that reminds me. There's something I've wondered about. Perhaps you can tell me."

"I will, if I know."

"When I was in Zurich, at the Spanish Embassy after I escaped, they asked me numerous questions about who I was and where I came from. They were cordial but very much like government bureaucrats until someone noticed Aunt Haya's name on my papers. When I told them Carlos Murillo was my uncle, they got very interested in my well-being. Victor, the man who was questioning me, sent for his supervisor, a man named Joaquin Valdivia. I thought I was in trouble but it turns out Valdivia was friends with your father. They put me up in a hotel for two weeks, flew me to Madrid, and bought a train ticket for the trip down to Cordova." I paused to catch his eyes. "I never knew Uncle Carlos was once minister of the interior."

"Yes," Oscar nodded. "He was. And Joaquin Valdivia was his best friend."

"From the way they acted, it seemed as if there was more to the situation than that. The way they looked after me. When I arrived in Madrid, someone was waiting for me and took me to the train station. He stayed with me until it was time for me to leave."

Oscar had a knowing smile. "Valdivia wasn't merely someone's supervisor. He was Spain's ambassador to Switzerland—an appointment he received on the recommendation of my father." My mouth dropped open. Oscar grinned. "Uncle Alois introduced Valdivia to the woman who became his wife."

I slumped against the back of my chair. "I had no idea they were that influential."

"Things are very different now," Oscar sighed. "Valdivia has retired and lives in London. Victor lives in Madrid. The monarchy is gone. My father's generation has passed from the scene. Others are in charge now." He took another sip of coffee. "But that is not why I came to see you." He reached into his pocket. "I came to bring you a gift."

"A gift?"

"Hold out your hand and close your eyes." I did as he said and felt something touch my palm. When I opened my eyes I saw Grandma's locket and chain resting on my hand. "I should have never taken it from you," he said.

Tears filled my eyes. "I was glad for you to have it."

"And I am glad for you to have it back." His eyes were full. He blinked back a tear. "Can you ever forgive me?"

"There is no offense to forgive." I wiped my eyes with my free hand. "But yes, I forgive you."

We both sat there in silence for a moment, staring at the locket. Then I glanced over at him. "Did you look inside it?"

"No," he shrugged. "For some reason, the thought never crossed my mind."

"I used to ask Grandma about it often, but she would never say what was in it, and even after she was gone somehow I didn't feel free to look inside."

Oscar smiled at me. "I don't think she would mind now."

"No," I agreed. "I suppose not." But still, I couldn't bring myself to flip it open.

He took a sip of coffee and gestured with his cup. "Go ahead," he urged. "Let's have a look."

I slid the edge of my thumbnail into the groove between the two halves of the locket. With the slightest nudge, the top came free and I gently lifted it open on its hinge. A smile came to my face as I stared down at the hollow space in the center.

Oscar set his cup on the saucer. "What is it?" He leaned forward to see, and with the locket resting on my palm, I turned my hand to show him its contents.

A Note About Adolf Eichmann

Adolf Eichmann was born in Solingen, Germany, in 1906. When he was eight years old, his mother died and the family moved to Linz, Austria. Eichmann attended school there, but his performance was less than stellar. Eventually, his father removed him from class and sent him to work in the family mining business. His stepmother intervened and persuaded a relative to help him obtain a job with the Vacuum Oil Company, then a subsidiary of Standard Oil. While working there, Eichmann joined the Nazi Party. When the Nazis came to power in Germany in 1933, he applied for acceptance in the active-duty SS. He was admitted and assigned to the staff of Dachau concentration camp. Later he obtained a transfer to the SS security service and worked in the Jewish Section.

When the German Army invaded Austria in 1938, Eichmann was assigned the task of removing all Jews from the newly annexed region. He initially attempted to persuade Austrian Jews simply to leave and created a streamlined emigration process that facilitated their removal but stripped them of their property. The efficiency of that effort landed Eichmann a new job as head of the Jewish Emigration Office, where it was hoped he could duplicate his success in removing Jews from other regions. But as the war expanded, and countries closed their borders to

Jewish refugees, removing Jews from German territory grew problematic, and the Nazis turned to the Final Solution.

Although Eichmann is often called the Architect of the Holocaust, the idea of exterminating the Jews actually came from his boss, Reinhard Heydrich, in a plan announced at the Wannsee Conference in 1942. To implement that plan, Eichmann was given responsibility for transporting Jews from the occupied lands to a network of death camps, where they were murdered. By the end of the war, he had risen from the rank of lowly enlisted recruit to lieutenant colonel and had sent six million Jews on a train ride to death.

As Germany's defeat became obvious, many Nazi officers sought to distance themselves from Eichmann in a desperate attempt to minimize their association with the death camps. Eichmann followed that same tactic, assuming various aliases and identities in an attempt to elude Allied authorities and evade responsibility for his wartime activities. Twice captured by the US Army, first as Adolf Barth and later as Otto Eckmann, he managed to escape and lived in northern Germany under the name Otto Heninger before finally slipping away in 1950 to Italy. There, with the assistance of the Catholic Church, he obtained a refugee passport, which allowed him to travel to Argentina under the name of Ricardo Klement.

In Argentina, Eichmann found a thriving German community that gave him a warm reception. With their help, he settled into an obscure life and a year or two later his wife and children quietly joined him.

As time passed, the world seemed eager to forget the atrocities foisted on millions by the Nazis, but in Israel, no one forgot. Accounts of how Eichmann was located vary depending on the source. Some, who lived in Israel at the time and were closely associated with events involving the Israeli government, provide one account. Others, who lived in Europe and spent their lives tracking down Nazis both great and small, give a different account of events leading up to the Israeli government's direct involvement. However, once the Israeli government chose to act, the story is rather clear.

In 1960, following tips from several sources, a Mossad team was dispatched to Argentina to confirm Eichmann's identity and location. Once that was ascertained, plans were laid for his capture and return to Israel. The details of how Eichmann was captured can be found in *The House On Garibaldi Street* by Isser Harel, who was instrumental in the planning and execution of that mission.

Eichmann was returned to Israel, where he stood trial in Jerusalem on charges of crimes against humanity, war crimes, crimes against the Jewish people, and membership in an outlawed organization. He was convicted in 1961, and, after all appeals were exhausted, he was hanged. An authoritative account of the trial and execution can be found in *Justice in Jerusalem*, written by Gideon Hausner, the Israeli Attorney General who prosecuted the case.

The Locket is loosely based on a compilation of events from Eichmann's life and information drawn from varying accounts about how he was located. These events have been portrayed as realistically as possible but with an eye toward creating an entertaining and engaging story. Characters, events, and locations in *The Locket* are the work of fiction and have been arranged and compiled with the story of Sarah, our fictional character, to give a poignant glimpse of the devastating effect Nazi injustice and racial hatred had on so many. Our hope is that in seeing events through Sarah's life, you will be inspired to read further on the subject of the Holocaust, the need for justice in the world today, and the healing that can only come through forgiveness.

BOOKS BY MIKE EVANS

Israel: America's Key to Survival

Save Jerusalem

The Return

Jerusalem D.C.

Purity and Peace of Mind

Who Cries for the Hurting?

Living Fear Free

I Shall Not Want

Let My People Go

Jerusalem Betrayed

Seven Years of Shaking: A Vision

The Nuclear Bomb of Islam

Jerusalem Prophecies

Pray For Peace of Jerusalem

America's War: The Beginning of the End

The Jerusalem Scroll

The Prayer of David

The Unanswered Prayers of Jesus

God Wrestling

Why Christians Should Support Israel

The American Prophecies

Beyond Iraq: The Next Move

The Final Move beyond Iraq

Showdown with Nuclear Iran

Jimmy Carter: The Liberal Left and World Chaos

Atomic Iran

Cursed

Betrayed

The Light

Corrie's Reflections and Meditations (Booklet)

GAMECHANGER SERIES:
   GameChanger
   Samson Option

THE PROTOCOLS SERIES:
   The Protocols
   The Candidate

The Revolution

The Final Generation

Seven Days

The Locket

COMING SOON:

The History of Christian Zionism

Living in the F.O.G.